CARROLL-KELLY

'Has usions of adequacy'
Mr tree, History

v personal standards and consistently fails to meet them'
English

' is depriving a village somewhere of an idiot'
Mr Lar kin, Biology

'I've never set eyes on the boy'
Mr Allen, Maths

'Reached rock bottom in fifth year and has continued to dig'
Miss Cuny, h

'The next Ollie Campbell'
Fr Fehily, Principal

This special combined edition first published 2008 by The O'Brien Press Ltd,
12 Terenure Road East, Rathgar, Dublin 6, Ireland.
Tel: +353 1 4923333; Fax: +353 1 4922777
E-mail: books@obrien.ie
Website: www.obrien.ie

The Miseducation Years first published by The O'Brien Press 2004
Originally published in 2000 (without new material and revisions) as
The Miseducation of Ross O'Carroll-Kelly by the *Sunday Tribune*.

The Teenage Dirtbag Years first published by The O'Brien Press 2003
Originally published in 2001 (without new material) as
Roysh Here, Roysh Now, The Teenage Dirtbag Years
by the *Sunday Tribune*.

ISBN: 978-1-84717-136-8

British Library Cataloguing-in-Publication Data
A catalogue record for this title is available from the British Library

1 2 3 4 5
08 09 10 11

Typesetting, editing, layout and design: The O'Brien Press Ltd
Illustrations: Alan Clarke
Author photograph, p.4: Emma Byrne
Printing: CPI Cox & Wyman, Reading, RG1 8EX

The Temple of Academe

2 BOOK SPECIAL

Book 1
The Miseducation Years

'For once I agree with Fionn about the, like, **education possibilities**. I mean, where else can you learn about "Judge Judy", fake IDs and how to order a Ken and snog a chick at the same time?'

PAUL HOWARD hasn't done anything remotely athletic since running for and missing the 8.08am Dart from Greystones to Pearse Street on 12 February 2001. The last time he went to a rugby match he broke out in hives. The points he earned in the Leaving Cert barely reached double figures, but his record score on Larry Gogan's Sixty Second Quiz is 10. He's not much to look at and yet he does alright, thank you very much.

The Mis-Educa-tion years

Ross O'Carroll-Kelly

[As told to Paul Howard]

Illustrations by Alan Clarke

THE O'BRIEN PRESS
DUBLIN

Dedication

To Laura and David Howard, for a life filled with love and laughter.
You made everything worthwhile. There aren't enough words.
Mum, we miss you every day x

Acknowledgements

Thanks to my mother and father for it all. Thanks to Mark, Vin and Rich for the interest you've taken in your adopted brother. Thanks to Matt Cooper, Paddy Murray and Jim Farrelly for taking a chance on an obnoxious little south Dublin shit, and thanks especially to Ger Siggins, who was there for the conception, the difficult birth and did most of the initial breast-feeding. For a whole myriad of other reasons too numerous to mention, thanks to Lady Dowager Genevieve; Wally; Ro and Johnny; Mick and Lorna who saved me from leeches; Mousey; Walshy; Paddy; Róisín; Dave; both Barrys; Fi and John and the lad Liam; Neil with the second name that goes on till Christmas and Liz; Karen with an e; Jenny Lowe and Claire Even Lower; Enda Mac; Lise with a totally unnecessary e; Fleur (!); Jimmy who's real name isn't Jimmy at all; Malachy; One F; at least two Michelles; Maureen, Deirdre and her south Dublin princess daughter Anne; Lisa and the Nordie Bogball Down Under Tour Party; and Dion and John from the cabal. Thanks to Ryle and Gerry for your restraint in never sending me a solicitor's letter. Thanks to Michael, Íde, Mary, Ivan, Lynn and everyone at OBP for accepting Ross into the OBP family. Caitríona, I miss you. And lastly – stay awake, these are the biggies – thanks to Emma for making these books look edible, to Alan for capturing our hero with the genius of your pen, and most of all to Rachel (Dublin 24), a brilliant editor who knows Ross better than I do. The funny bits are hers.

Contents

What's my name? I don't even bother answering him, just reef open the glove compartment and hand him my licence through the window, roysh, and he gives it the once-over and he goes, 'This is a provisional licence,' making no effort at all to hide the fact that he's a bogger. It's like he's actually proud of it. I go, 'Your point is?' and the way he looks at me, roysh, I can tell he just wants to snap those bracelets on me and haul my orse off to Donnybrook. He's like, 'Provisional licences are issued subject to certain restrictions. One is that you have a fully qualified driver accompanying you at all times.'

I turn around to the bird beside me and I go, 'Have you passed your test?' and she's like, 'Oh my God, ages ago,' and she storts rooting through her Louis V for her licence, which she eventually finds and I hand it to focking Blackie Connors through the window. He throws the eyes over it, roysh, then he hands it back to me and I'm thinking of taking a sneaky look at it myself, maybe find out this bird's name, because she's a total randomer and at some point between her telling me her name in Annabel's and us doing the bould thing out in her gaff in Clonskeagh, I've managed to forget what she calls herself. In the end I don't. The goy goes, 'Where are your L-plates?' and I have to admit, roysh, that he has me there, although he knows he can't lift me for it, which is what he'd really like to do. I go, 'Don't own a set. Never did. To me they're a total passion-killer,' and I smile at the bird beside me. Martinique rings a bell. The goy goes, 'Did you know that it's an offence for a driver operating a vehicle on a provisional licence not to display Learner plates?' but I don't answer because it's not, like, a real question, and he looks at my licence again – like it's a forgery or something – and he tells me to, like, stay where I am and then he walks back to his cor, roysh, and in the rear-view I can see him getting on the radio. The bird's there giving it, 'OH! MY! GOD! Why are you giving him such attitude? I am SO not being arrested, Ross. HELLO? I've got cello in, like, half an hour,' and I tell her to drink the Kool-Aid, the goy's only trying to put the shits up us.

I'm always getting pulled over by the Feds, especially here, just after you go under the bridge at, like, UCD. I'm too smart to get caught doing more than forty, but what happens is they see the baseball cap, they see the Barbie doll next to me and they hear 'Smells Like Teen Spirit' blasting out through the windows at, like, a million decibels. Boggers or not, they're not thick, these goys, and because it's a focking Micra, they know straight away that it's a young dude driving his old dear's cor and – probably out of total jealousy – they end up pulling me over. I'm still looking at the goy in the mirror. He's finished talking on the radio and now he's just trying to make me sweat, which I'm SO not.

People always ask me, roysh, how did I get this cool? Not being big-headed or anything, but they genuinely want to know how it is that I pretty much have it all – Dead Eye Dick with a rugby ball and the stor of the school team, good-looking, amazing body, big-time chormer, great with the ladies and absolutely loaded.

But to be honest with you, roysh, I wasn't always shit-hot. Between me and you, when I was in, like, transition year I was actually as big a loser as Fionn. I used to basically get bullied. I remember the day I found out that we didn't always live in Foxrock. Two or three fifth years were in the process of, like, stuffing my head down the toilet one lunchtime when one of them happened to go, 'Go back to the focking Noggin.' So that night, roysh, I went to the old man, who's a complete and utter dickhead by the way, and I go, 'Did we live in Sallynoggin?' – straight out with it, just like that – and he looks at me, roysh, and he knows there's no point in lying, so he goes, 'It was more Glenageary than Sallynoggin, Ross,' and he tells me it was a long time ago, before the business took off.

But that whole Noggin thing followed me around for years. If they weren't stuffing my head down the pan and flushing it, they were giving me wedgies, or setting fire to my schoolbag, ha focking ha. Then one day, roysh, I'm walking down the corridor, minding my own business and these two fifth years grab me in a headlock and drag me into, like, one of the locker rooms. They stort giving me the usual crack, roysh – 'Are you getting a spice burger from the Noggin Grill later?' and 'Are you going up to the Noggin Inn for a few jors?' – when all of a sudden, roysh, I hear a voice behind them go, 'To get at him, goys, you're going to have to come through me first,' and I look up and it's, like, Christian. So all hell breaks loose and the two of us end up decking the two fifth years and afterwards he tells me that Obi Wan has taught me well and I tell him he's the best friend I've ever had, which he is, roysh, even if it sounds a bit gay.

Of course the word went around, roysh, that we'd basically decked two goys who, it turned out, were on the S, and nobody laid a finger on me after that. Then the next year there was, shall we say, an incident that helped me complete the change from geek to chic – basically I got my Nat King Cole before anyone else in our whole year. AND it was with an older woman.

To cut a long story short, roysh, our school arranged this thing called The Urban Plunge, which was basically an exchange programme between us and a school from, like, Pram Springs. It was typical of the Brothers in our place. They knew we were loaded, roysh, and most of us would never have to work for a thing in our lives, but it was their 'Christian responsibility' to show us how people less fortunate than ourselves – meaning skobies – lived, as if we wanted to know.

The way it worked, roysh, was that you got paired off with some Anto or other – in fact, I think my one was actually called Anto. Anyway, he ended up half-inching everything in our gaff that wasn't nailed down. I remember the old man and the old dear, the silly wagon, walking around the house making a list of all the stuff that had disappeared, the old dear going, 'Your Callaway driver, darling,' and the old man shaking his head and writing it down. Of course Castlerock agreed to pay for everything on condition that they didn't involve the Feds.

But while this was all going on, roysh, I was getting my own back by scoring his older sister, we're talking Wham, Bam, that's for the old dear's Waterford Crystal limited edition votive, Ma'am. Tina was her name, roysh, a total howiya, but she was, like, twenty and I was, like, sixteen and by the time I got back from my two-week tour of duty in Beirut – every meal came with curry sauce, roysh, and they never answered the door in case it was the rent man or a loan shork – I was a legend in the school. The head-lice were gone after a couple of weeks and I settled well into my new existence as a complete focking stud.

'What speed were you doing?'

Glenroe's finest is back at the window. I was miles away there. I'm like, 'I think you'll find I was just under forty,' which he knows well from his speed camera. He's just trying to put the shits up me. He hands me back my licence and he goes, 'I'll let you go … this time,' and I have to stop myself from going, 'Oh, I'm SO grateful, orsehole,' and he goes, 'Get a set of Learner plates when you're in town, Rod.'

I'm there, 'Rod? *Rod?* It's Ross! Ross O'Carroll-Kelly! You might not know the name now, but by the seventeenth of March you will.' He goes, 'Why? What's happening on that day?' The smell of turnip and spuds off him. I go, 'What's happening on that day? That's the day I become

Ross O'Carroll-Kelly, living focking legend.'

CHAPTER ONE
'Comes to class unprepared'

'Mister O'Carroll-Kelly, will you pay attention please.' That's what Lambkin says. He goes, 'Entertaining the troops as usual,' but I'm not, roysh, I'm actually about to spew my ring all over the desk, and we're talking totally here. If I'd known we were going to be looking at an actual focking cow's eye this morning, roysh, I think it's pretty safe to say I wouldn't have been out on the batter last night. And Oisinn's not helping. He was more hammered than I was, but he's got a stomach like a focking goat. He's got it in his hand, roysh, and he's, like, squelching it and you can hear all the, I don't know, guts inside. The goy actually wants to see me spitting chunks.

The teacher's going, 'How do we see? Well, the eye processes the light through photoreceptors located in the eye, which send signals to the brain and tell us what we are seeing. There are two types of photoreceptor and these are called rods and cones,' and then he walks around handing us each a scalpel, and I'm thinking he couldn't seriously be suggesting we ... He goes, 'These photoreceptors are sensitive to light. Rods are the most sensitive to light and therefore provide grey vision at night. Now there are a number of differences between the human eye and the cow's eye, which I will discuss as we proceed with the dissection.'

I'm just, like, staring straight ahead, trying not to think about what we're about to do, when all of a sudden Oisinn taps me on the shoulder and – HOLY FOCK! – he's somehow managed to stick the focking eyeball onto his forehead, roysh, and he goes, 'Look at me, Ross, I'm from Newtownmountkennedy,' and I laugh and heave at the same time and old focking Lamb Chop throws me a filthy, basically telling me that I'm pushing my luck here.

He's going, 'Cones are, in the main, active in bright light and enable you to see colour. There are one hundred million rods located in your retina compared to just three million cones.'

I just need to get through this class, then I'll hit the canteen and get a Yop or something to settle my stomach. But Oisinn knows how close I am to hurling here and it's become, like, a challenge now. He turns around to Fionn and goes, 'Gimme your glasses,' and Fionn's like, 'Why?' and Oisinn just grabs them off him. Then – this is focking horrific – he puts the eye basically onto his own eye and then he puts on Fionn's glasses, which sort of, like, hold it in place. Then he turns around to the rest of the class and goes, 'ESMERELDA!' and the whole class cracks up, roysh, and Lamb Chop, who's been writing some shite or other on the blackboard, turns around and goes, 'O'CARROLL-KELLY!' and he looks at me in a way that basically says Last Chance Saloon, and of course I can't tell him that I'm doing fock-all, roysh, because I can taste the vom at the top of my throat and if I open my mouth it's coming out. Oisinn throws Fionn back his goggles and Fionn's, like, majorly pissed off, trying to clean them on his shirt, but of course they're covered in, like, blood and shite and all sorts, but I'm trying not to, like, think about it.

'If you walk inside from the sun,' – this is Lambkin again – 'you can't initially see anything. This is due to the activity of the cones and the lack of activity of the rods. Similarly, when you leave a cinema during the day, it's the rods that are mainly activated and the cones have to adjust to the sunlight.'

I'm thinking, I better actually listen to some of this shit because it might, like, come up in the Leaving. Then I hear Oisinn going, 'Ross! Ross! I know you can hear me!' and I'm trying my best to, like, ignore him. Rods and cones, I get it now. He just, like, grabs me by the back of the neck, roysh, and spins me around so that I'm, like, facing him and then – Oh! My! FOCKING! God! – he pops the eyeball into his mouth like it's a focking Bon Bon and then – get this – he actually bites into the focking thing and all this, like, blood and yellow goo and everything just, like, squirts out of the side of his mouth and, like, dribbles down his face and I just go, *Weeeuuuggghhh!* and basically explode.

There's vom everywhere, all over my Dubes, the desk, my biology book, the floor. I'm like a focking volcano. It just keeps coming and coming. Goes on for about ten minutes and everyone's just, like, staring at me, and when I've finished I've got, like, my face on the desk and the table feels nice and cold against my cheek, and I'm slowly getting my breath back and Lamb Chop's basically speechless and I'm thinking, I don't even remember having a kebab.

XXX

Castlerock boarders are Total Knackers it says in, like, black morker on the bus shelter opposite Stillorgan Shopping Centre, roysh, put there by some tool who doesn't realise that (a) writing graffiti actually makes *him* a knacker and (b) so does getting the focking bus. Nothing against public transport myself, but the old pair are basically rolling in it enough for me and the old 46A to lead parallel lives. The old dear, who's a total focking weapon, pulls up in her Micra – total shamer – and I hop in, and she's all smug and delighted with herself because she's just been to the printers to collect the posters for this anti-halting site group she's involved in, Foxrock Against Total Skangers or whatever the fock they're called, and she says that Lucy and Angela are going to be SO pleased with how they turned out, basically not giving a fock how long she left me sitting around waiting.

I go, 'I am SO late,' but she makes a big deal of ignoring me, roysh, humming some stupid Celine Dion song to herself, and I pretty much know what this is all about. Last week, roysh, the old man found out I've been, like, skipping my grinds. It's already January, roysh, and I basically haven't gone to one. The old Crimbo report comes and I ended up failing, like, six of my seven exams, and of course the old man's going, 'Don't be too down in the mouth, Kicker. I'll phone that Institute tomorrow and see if I can't get to the bottom of it.' I'm like, 'What are you banging on about, you dickhead?' and he goes, 'Well, you're not stupid, we know that. My brains and your mother's, that's a formidable combination, with a capital F. No, they're obviously not teaching you the right things. No, wait a second, maybe it is the school after all. Yes. Clearly they've either miscalculated your marks, given you the wrong report, or simply didn't understand what it was you were trying to say.' The tosser actually thinks I'm the next Stephen what's-his-face with the focking voicebox. *My eyesight is very important to me.*

So thinking of the old man, roysh, trying to help him not make a *complete* tit of himself, I end up telling him that I haven't been doing the grinds. He has an eppo, of course, reminding me how much they cost him – we're talking two thousand bills, the scabby focker – and then he asks me, roysh, what I've been doing every Friday night and Saturday morning, and I tell him I've been, like, hanging around town and shit, not mentioning, of course, the fact that I've been going on the batter with the goys. So the old pair have a major freak out, and we're talking major here – they basically don't understand the pressure of being on the S. All this results in the Mister Freeze treatment, which suits me because I hate having to talk to them. Anyway, the schools cup storts in two weeks and they'll be all focking over me then, you mork my words. Still can't believe I failed six of my seven exams. Actually, it was news to me that I even took English.

The goys are already sitting in Eddie Rockets when I arrive. Oisinn's wearing the old beige Dockers chinos, brown dubes, light blue Ralph and a red, white and blue sailing jacket by Henri Lloyd. He high-fives me, then he hugs me – nearly breaks my back, the fat bastard – and he goes, 'YOU THE MAN, ROSS,' seven or eight times in my ear. JP high-fives me and tells me he's glad I took the idea of having a nosebag offline. JP's also wearing beige Dockers chinos, brown dubes, light blue Ralph and a red, white and blue sailing jacket by Henri Lloyd. Aoife leans across the table and, like, air-kisses me on both cheeks, totally flirting her orse off with me, while Sorcha gives me daggers and goes, 'We've already ordered,' and I look her in the eye and I know she basically still wants me.

Oisinn goes, 'Question for you, Ross. If anyone can answer this, you can,' and I'm there, 'Shoot, my man.' He goes, 'Is it proper to wear Dubes with, like, formalwear?' and of course I'm there, 'How formal is formal?' and he goes, 'We're talking black trousers, we're talking white shirt, we're talking black blazer.' I rub my chin and think about it. The food arrives. JP is having the Classic without dill pickle, bacon and cheese fries and a large Coke. Oisinn is having the Moby Dick, southern chicken tenders, chilli fries, a side order of nachos with guacamole, cheese sauce, salsa and hot jalapenos and a chocolate malt, the focking Michelin man that he is. Sorcha is having a Caesar salad with extra croutons and Romanie lettuce. Aoife is having a bag of popcorn which she has hidden inside her baby-blue sleeveless bubble jacket. She's looking over her shoulder every few seconds, roysh, going, 'I have to be careful. Me, Sophie, Amy and clarinet Deirdre got focked out of the one in Donnybrook last week for ordering, like, a Diet Coke between us.' and Sorcha says that is, like, SO *Duhhh!* And Aoife's there, 'Totally. It's like, OH my God! HELLO?' and Sorcha goes, 'No, it's more like, OH MY GOD!' and Aoife's there, 'Oh my God! *Totally.*'

The waitress, roysh, is a total babe, we're talking Kelly out of 90210's identical twin here, and when she drops the last of the food over she turns around to me and she goes, 'Do you want to order something?' and I go, 'Well, what I want and what I get are probably two different things,' and I'm hoping it didn't sound too sleazy, roysh, but she just goes red and out of the corner of my eye I can see Sorcha giving me filthies, and we're talking *total* filthies. I go – cue sexy voice, roysh – I'm like, 'Could I get a, em, dolphin-friendly tuna melt, maybe a chilli cheese dog and a portion of, like, buffalo wings,' and she writes it down and then, like, smiles at me and when she focks off Sorcha goes, 'That girl is SUCH a knob.' I'm there, 'You don't even know her,' and she goes, 'HELLO? Her name HAPPENS to be Sian Kennedy and she's doing, like, morkeshing in ATIM.' Aoife goes, 'She is like, *Aaaggghhh!*' and Sorcha goes, 'Totally.'

Oisinn's there, 'Ross, you never answered my question, dude,' and I'm there, 'I don't know why you have to rely on me for this stuff,' secretly delighted of course, and then I'm like, 'Dubes are traditionally a casual shoe.' I look at Sorcha, who stirs Oisinn's chocolate malt and then takes a sip from it. I go, 'But to be passed off along with formalwear, the Dubes must – and I repeat *must* – be black.' Oisinn whistles. JP goes, 'They can't be brown?' in a real, like, suspicious voice. I go, 'Too casual for black trousers. Beige definitely. Black's a complete no-no.'

Sorcha's mobile rings, roysh, and it's, like, Jayne with a y, who used to be her best friend until she caught me wearing the face off her in Fionn's kitchen on New Year's Eve, which was basically one of the reasons Sorcha, like, finished with me. Anyway, roysh, they're obviously back talking again and they're blabbing on about some, like, dinner porty they're organising, but then all of a sudden Sorcha turns around to her and goes, 'Is Fionn there with you?' and of course immediately the old antennae pop up, and I'm wondering what that four-eyed focker's doing sniffing around – looks like Anna Friel this bird, I'm telling you – and JP must cop the look on my face because he goes, 'Message to the stockmorket – friendly merger going down between Fionn and Jayne with a y.' I'm there, 'And for those of us who don't speak morkeshing?' and he goes, 'They're going out together, Ross,' which is news to me, roysh, because I've been seeing her on the old QT for the past three or four weeks and she asked me to, like, keep it quiet, the complete bitch.

Sorcha must cop my reaction, roysh, because she's suddenly going, 'Ross, I'm talking to Jayne with a y. Fionn's sitting beside her. Do you want a word with him?' and I go, 'Tell him I'll pick him up for rugby training in the morning,' playing it Kool Plus Support Band. I run my hand through my hair, which needs a serious cut. Might get a blade one all over this time instead of, like, just the sides, seeing as the Cup's about

21

to stort and everything.

Sorcha hangs up and of course she can't let it go. She goes, 'Oh my God, they make SUCH a cute couple, don't they?' and Aoife's there, 'Yeah, it's like, Rachel and Ross cute,' and Sorcha goes, 'No, it's more like, Joey and Dawson cute,' then she turns to me and she's like, 'You've gone very quiet, Ross. Not jealous, are you?' Where's my focking food? I'm there, 'Not at all. Been there, done that ... worn the best friend,' and she's bulling, and we're talking bigtime.

The waitress comes over and I decide to up the old ante. She's putting my food on the table, roysh, and I'm giving it, 'You're Sian Kennedy, aren't you?' and she goes, 'Yeah,' and I'm there, 'First year morkeshing in ATIM?' and she goes, 'Yeah, I know your face. You go to Annabel's, don't you?' and I'm seriously giving it, 'Sure do. Maybe I'll see you there tomorrow night?' and she goes totally red, roysh, and she's there, 'Em ... yeah,' and I go, 'Cool,' and she's like, 'Bye,' and I'm giving it, 'Later.'

Oisinn and JP both high-five me and Aoife goes, 'Oh my *God*, you don't ACTUALLY fancy her, do you?' and I go, 'She looks like Kelly off 90210,' and Aoife goes, 'But she's a sap, Ross. A total sap,' and out of the corner of my eye I can see Sorcha's face is all red, the way it gets when she's pissed off. I'm on match-point now. She turns around to Aoife and she goes, 'So, do you think I should go?' and Aoife's there, 'What?' and Sorcha's like, 'Do you think I should go?' Aoife's there, 'Oh my God, you SO should. I'm telling you, you SO should go,' obviously wanting me to ask, roysh, but I'm in the game too long to fall for that one. But JP – the loser – he goes, 'Go where?' and Aoife's like, 'She's been invited to the Gonzaga pre-debs,' and JP's there, 'By who?' and Sorcha goes, 'Jamie O'Connell-Keavney,' all delighted with herself and she's looking at me for a reaction, roysh, because she knows damn well we have Gonzaga in the first round of the Cup.

The goys look at me for a reaction too, roysh, but there's no way I'm, like, taking the bait. JP goes, 'That is SO not cool, Sorcha. That is SUCH an uncool thing to do,' and Sorcha's like, 'Why?' and JP goes, 'Because Gonzaga are our TOTAL enemies,' and Oisinn nods and goes, 'Tossers.' Sorcha goes, 'Jamie's not like that. He's SUCH a cool goy,' and Aoife's there, 'What do *you* think she should do, Ross?' As subtle as a kick in the old town halls. I pop the last piece of tuna into my mouth and I go, 'If she wants to go, that's cool. I think she should do what makes her happy,' and JP's going, 'Yeah, but not with someone from Gonzaga ... Oh my God, we are SO going to kick their orses now,' and him and Oisinn high-five each other.

Aoife gets up to go to the toilet and Oisinn goes, 'That's three times she's been in there since we arrived. What kind of load could she possibly be dropping off? It's not as if she ever eats anything.' Then he says he can definitely taste dill pickle on his Classic and he takes the top off the bun to investigate. Sorcha takes off her scrunchy and slips it onto her wrist, shakes her head, smoothes her hair back into a low ponytail, puts it back in the scrunchy and then pulls five or six strands of hair loose. It looks exactly the same as it did before she did it.

Aoife comes back, wiping her mouth, calls one of the other waitresses over and asks can she have a glass of, like, water. The waitress asks us if we want dessert and Oisinn and JP both order the Kit Kat Dream and Sorcha orders the New York toffee cheesecake with ice cream and cream. Aoife goes, 'OH MY GOD! Do you KNOW how many points are in that? Have you, like, TOTALLY lost your mind?' and Sorcha goes, 'I'm not counting my points anymore,' but before it arrives the guilt gets to her, roysh, and she takes one mouthful, then pushes the rest across the table to me. I just pick at it, roysh, then I get up to go. JP goes, 'You heading home?' and I'm there, 'Yeah. Big training session tomorrow. Got to, like, keep my focus.'

I walk up to the counter, cool as a fish's fart, tell Sian what I had and she tots it up. I hand her twenty bills and tell her to, like, keep the change. Then I tell her I might see her tomorrow night, which is, like, Saturday, and she says that would be cool. Behind me I can hear Oisinn saying he's sure he can taste dill pickle on his burger and he is SO not paying for it. Aoife goes, 'See you tomorrow night, Ross. Annabel's,' but I totally blank her and go outside. I stand in the cor pork and try to ring the old dear, but the phone's engaged and so's her mobile. Her and that focking campaign of hers. I try Dick Features, but then I remember he's out at the K Club tonight with Hennessy, his orsehole solicitor.

I stand out on the road for ten minutes looking for a taxi, roysh, but there's fock-all about. I don't focking believe this, but there's nothing else for it, I'm going to have to get the focking bus. Mortification City, Wisconsin. I cross over to the bus stop. There's two birds there. Skobies. One is telling the other that Sharon – no, Shadden – is a dorty-lookin' dort-bord. The bus comes and I let them get on first. I hand the driver two pound coins, roysh, and he tells me to put the money in the slot, which I do. I pull the ticket and wait for my change but the tosspot storts driving off. I go, 'What do you think that is, a tip or something?' and he goes, 'Sorry, bud, we don't give out change. You have to take your receipt into O'Connell Street to get yisser change.' I go, 'Are you trying to be funny?' and he's there, 'Sorry, bud?' I'm like, 'O'Connell Street?' and he goes, 'Yeah, you know where Dublin Bus is?' and I'm there, 'No. I don't *do* the northside,' and I sit down. He probably had one of his mates lined up to focking mug me.

I sit downstairs. There's a funny smell off buses. Actually it's probably the people. I take out my mobile and, like, listen to my messages. Some bird called Alison phoned and said OH MY GOD! she hoped I remembered her from last Saturday night and she couldn't remember whether I was supposed to phone her or she was supposed to phone me, but she decided to call me anyway and if it's after midnight when I get this message I should phone her tomorrow, but not in the morning because OH MY GOD! she's just remembered she's at the orthodontist and she gives me the number again.

XXX

It's Saturday morning, roysh, and I'm hanging, but try telling that to the old man. He comes into the sitting-room where I'm trying to watch MTV, roysh, and of course straight away I grab the remote and higher up the volume. The Prodigy SO rock. The dickhead doesn't even take this as a hint, roysh, just marches straight in and storts giving it loads, like we're long-lost friends or something. He's there, 'I expect you heard me getting up in the middle of the night,' and I know he's basically dying for me to ask why, but I'm not going to give him the satisfaction. He goes, 'Difficulty sleeping, Kicker. Got up and had a glass of milk, which can sometimes help. Hope I didn't wake you.' I just look at him, roysh – give him this total filthy – and I go, 'Well, given that I fell in that door at half-six this morning, I don't think so. I was probably still in Reynords.'

He goes, 'The reason I couldn't sleep, in case you're wondering, is all this halting site nonsense. It's not that we're anti these types of people. That little one who sings off Grafton Street? Tremendous fun. Your mother will tell you, I wouldn't pass him without putting a few pence in his tin and whatnot. But a halting site in Foxrock? It's just not appropriate. I'm thinking about them as much as anyone else. They wouldn't be happy here. Good lord, Ross, who is that chap?' I don't answer him, roysh, and he goes, 'Who is he, Ross?' and I'm there, 'Are you focking deaf? I said his name's Keith Flint.' He's there, 'Very peculiar-looking individual, isn't he? I suppose they can do all sorts with make-up.'

I just, like, shake my head but he still doesn't take the hint. He goes, 'Travelling people. *Travelling*. It's like when that client of Hennessy's woke up one morning to find three caravans on that little patch of grass opposite his house. In *Dalkey* of all places. Year of our Lord nineteen hundred and ninety-seven. Six months they stayed. As he said – you'll have to get Hennessy to do the voice for you – he said, "I don't know why they call them travelling folk, hell, they never bloody move." Because he's a terrible snob, old Wilmot Ruddy. A great old character, even if he is a bit much at times.'

Shania Twain comes on. I would, before you ask. The old man's still blabbing away. 'You do understand, don't you, that I've nothing against these people? I'm all for them. I just happen to think they'd struggle to fit in, inverted commas. Can't say that to these councillors, of course. Racism, that silly woman accused me of. There were times, of course, when all you had to do was pop a few hundred pounds in an envelope and hey presto you had the council on your side. These are changed times, thank you very much indeed Mister G Kerrigan of Middle Abbey Street, Dublin 1.'

I look at him and I go, 'Are you still here?' He winks at me, roysh – actually focking winks – and he goes, 'I've got my Mont Blanc pen out, Ross. Which can mean only one thing. Yes, I'm going to write one of my world-famous letters to *The Irish Times*. Oh, I love the letters page of

The Irish Times. The cut and thrust of the debates on all the important issues of the day. The cheeky humour. Throw in a witticism or two at the
start and you've got a winner on your hands. Winner with a capital W.
Let me read you what I've put down thus far,' and he whips out this
sheet of paper, roysh. He's there, 'Have a listen to this: I need only say
the words 'Hiace van' and 'Family Allowance Day' to evoke the image
of–' and straight away, roysh, I'm there, 'If you're not out of this room
in five focking seconds, I'm leaving home.'

XXX

I place the ball on the ground, stand up and raise my head slowly.
Christian's behind me going, 'One of the great taboos of the twentieth
century and no one's prepared to talk about it.' I look down, take five
steps backwards and look up again, tracing the line of the posts
upwards. Christian's still in my ear, giving it, 'It's, what, twenty years on
and there's never been any discussion on the subject.' I take three steps
to the side, look down at the ball, lick my fingers, run my right hand
through my hair, do my usual dance on the spot, then I run at the ball.
Just as I'm about to kick it, roysh, Christian goes, 'I mean, far be it from
me to tell George Lucas his business ...' and of course I end up skying
the focking thing to the right of the posts and there's this, like, chorus
of OH MY GODs from the Mounties on the sideline.

I'm just there, 'Fock's sake, Christian, you're supposed to be helping
me practice,' basically ripping the dude out of it, and he looks at me,
roysh, like I've just dropped a load in one of his Dubes. Of course I
stort feeling bad then, roysh, basic softie that I am, and I go, 'Look, I'm
sorry. It's just this Gonzaga match. Storting to feel, like, the pressure,
you know. What were you saying?' He goes, 'I was talking about the in-
cestuous undertone running through the first half of the original

trilogy. Have you not been listening to me? I'm talking about the sexual frisson between Luke Skywalker and Princess Leia.' I just go, 'Oh, roysh,' and try to look interested, he *is* my best friend, the focking weirdo.

He goes, 'Okay, you might think it was a harmless, hand-holding, carry-your-books-home-from-high-school kind of attraction. When Leia kissed Luke in the central core shaft ...' I'm there, 'Kissed him *where?*' and he goes, 'The central core shaft? Of the Death Stor? Before they swung across the gorge? Okay it was just a peck on the cheek, like the one she gave him in the main hangar deck on Alderaan. But there's no doubt they were the main love interest in *A New Hope*. Then in *Return of the Jedi* we found out they were brother and sister all along. We're talking *twins* here!' I'm there, 'Your point is?' and he goes, 'My point is, if George Lucas knew that these were Anakin Skywalker's kids, why the fock were they playing tonsil hockey in the medical centre on Hoth at the stort of *Empire?*'

I'm just, like, staring at the dude. He's totally lost me. The goy's focking Baghdad. He walked up to two Virgins on the Rocks at the Trinity Open Day last week and he went, 'What planet is this? What year is this? Where is your water source?' But like I say, roysh, we've been best friends since we were, like, kids, so I just go, 'That's a good point,' and he tells me not to worry about Gonzaga, he heard they're running on empty this year, and he tells me to let go of my conscious self and trust my instinct.

XXX

'I'm thinking of sleeping with you.' That's what Erika says to me when I meet her for lunch. We're talking Erika as in Sorcha's friend Erika. We're talking Erika who's the image of Denise Richards Erika. We're talking Erika as in total bitch Erika who never sleeps with anyone who's never been on 'Lifestyles of the Rich and Famous'. And she doesn't even look up from the menu, roysh, she just goes, 'Don't have the split pea soup, the croutons are always stale. I'm thinking of sleeping with you,' and I sort of, like, resent the fact that she thinks she could basically have me any time she wants me, even though she could. She looks up and she cops the delighted look on my face, roysh, and she goes, 'Not for pleasure, Ross. It's just that I know you're on the rugby team this year. And you're the goy all the girls will want to be with.'

The waitress comes over, roysh – bit of a hound, truth be told – and I order a roast beef sandwich, a portion of fries and, like, a Coke. Erika asks for just a latte, roysh, and the waitress points to a sign on the wall, something about a five quid minimum charge between twelve and two o'clock. The waitress is like, 'Can you read?' which is a big mistake, roysh, because quick as a flash Erika goes, 'Yes I can. You're the one earning three pounds an hour for collecting dirty dishes, remember.'

The waitress – she's actually a bit of a howiya – she goes, 'Between twelve and two the tables are reserved for *lunch* customers,' and Erika just, like, looks her up and down, roysh, and she goes, 'Just bring me a latte and you can charge me five pounds for it,' and the bird doesn't know what to say, roysh, obviously no one's ever said that before. Erika goes, 'Five pounds is hordly expensive for a cup of coffee anyway. Have you ever been to Paris, dear?'

She's, like, fascinating to watch when she's in this kind of form. The waitress, roysh, she mutters something about having to ask the manager and as she's walking away, Erika goes, 'On second thoughts,' and the bird turns around and Erika's like, 'I will have something to eat. I'll have the spaghetti bolognaise,' and she closes the menu and hands it to her. She goes, 'And that latte. *Thank you*,' real, like, sarcastic. Then she turns to me and goes, 'Where was I?'

I'm there, 'The thing is, Erika, I'm very flattered to think that you'd want to be with me, even for the reason you said. But maybe *I* don't want to be with *you*.' She looks at me, roysh, through sort of, like, slanty eyes, and she goes, 'Listen to yourself, will you? Do you think I'm blind or something? Do you think I haven't seen you looking at me and practically salivating? You can't help yourself around me. You want me, Ross. You always have,' and like an idiot, I go, 'That's true. But what about Sorcha? She's your friend. And she still has, like, feelings for me? And I wouldn't do anything to—' Erika just goes, 'Don't give me that, Ross. More than any other goy I know, you think with that,' and she points at my ... well, let's just say she points down.

The food arrives. Erika gives the waitress a filthy, roysh, and the waitress puts the plates on the table and throws her eyes up to heaven. Erika pushes her spaghetti bolognaise away from her, like it's infected or something. She goes, 'Don't kid yourself, Ross. Two squirts of *Issey Miyake* and that black Karen Millen top I have that you're always trying to look down and you'd be mine.' I go, 'And you'd do that? Even if it hurt Sorcha?' and she's there, 'Ross, have I got the words 'social worker' tattooed on my forehead? Do you think you're talking to someone who actually *gives* a shit about other people? Do you think I actually *enjoy* listening to Sorcha going on about how she is SO over you, then telling me she's going to lose a stone before the summer and "OH! MY! GOD! Wait until Ross sees me then." She's a sad case.'

She still hasn't touched her food. She goes, 'Face it, Ross. I'm the object of your desire. I'm the object of many men's desires. Whether I sleep with you or not is entirely up to me.' The next thing, roysh, her phone rings and she answers it and goes, 'Well, talk of the devil,' and of course I'm on the other side of the table, doing the actions to tell her not to tell Sorcha I'm here. 'Where am I?' she goes. 'I'm in town, having lunch with the love of your life ... yes, Ross. He's just been admiring my black top, the Karen Millen one?' The next thing, roysh, she puts the phone down on the table and goes, 'She hung up, the silly girl.'

I cannot focking Adam and Eve this, roysh, but twenty minutes later or whatever, we're both getting up to go and Erika gets the plate of spaghetti, which she hasn't eaten a single mouthful of, and she just, like, tips the whole thing onto the floor. It's one of those, like, wooden floors and she's made a total mess of it, and she just goes, 'Oops,' as in I've just done that accidentally on purpose. Then she walks straight up to the waitress, roysh, and she goes, 'Oh dear, I am SUCH a klutz. I seem to have spilled that food you made me order all over your clean floor. I really don't envy you the job of cleaning it up,' and before the waitress has a chance to say anything back, she goes, 'You obviously think you're made for something better than taking orders in a restaurant. But until Aaron Spelling discovers you, this is it for you, dear.'

She's incredible. She's right. She could have me like *that*.

XXX

I'm in the kitchen, roysh, lorrying the chicken and pasta into me, loading up on the old, I don't know, carbohydrates I suppose, what with this match coming up, when all of a sudden Knobhead comes into the kitchen with the portable, like, clutched to his ear, roysh, and he's going, 'What do you mean you won't be publishing my letter?' and at a guess I'd say it's someone from *The Irish Times*. He's going, 'Elements of it could be construed as being racist? What a lot of nonsense, pardon the French ... Weddings? Yes, that was just a bit of good-natured fun, to stop it getting too heavy and political. In fact, I think I may have actually spelt the word machete with two Ts instead of one. But look, I'd be willing to take it out if it meant ... Well, many of them *don't* tax or insure their cars, that's a fact ... Carpets? How can a reference to them selling poor quality carpets be construed as ... Hello? Hello? I think she might have bloody hung up on me.'

Tosser.

xxx

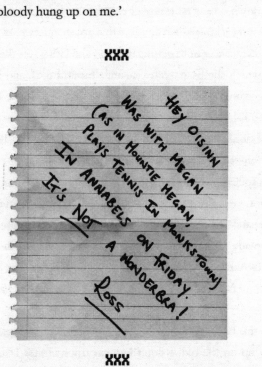

xxx

'Fucus is a multicellular alga consisting of an unbranched filament in which all of the cells are cylindrical and haploid and each has a cell wall surrounded by mucilage.' This is what passes for basically conversation among the birds. Sophie's going, 'Each has a chloroplast which is wound spirally inside the cell wall and the nucleus is suspended in the cell vacuole by threads of cytoplasm and—' Sorcha's, like, shaking her head. She goes, 'Sophie, HELLO? That's not fucus. That's, like, spirogyra,' and Sophie's giving it, 'Couldn't be,' and Sorcha's like, 'HELLO? I got an A in this at Christmas, remember?' Sophie sort of, like, squints her eyes, roysh, like she wants to rip Sorcha's face off and goes, 'They're practically the same focking thing anyway,' and Sorcha, being a total bitch, goes, 'No they're not. Spirogyra is a simple-structured, filamentous alga commonly found in ponds and ditches. Fucus is a multicellular marine-living brown alga commonly found on the seashore. They are SO different. We're talking habitat, structure, the way they reproduce. Ross, grab a seat. Is anyone else coming to the Ladies'?'

No one moves, roysh, so she focks off on her own. The second I sit down, Sophie goes, 'How the FOCK did you go out with that girl?' and I probably should defend her, roysh, but I just, like, shrug my shoulders instead and Sophie gives it, 'She is SUCH a bitch. Oh, and Ross, she still wants you.' Chloë goes, 'Sophie, oh my God, don't be a bitch yourself,' and Sophie's there, 'Fock HER. Ross, she talks about you all the time. I told her she's making a fool of herself. I was like, "Sorcha, you're one of my best friends, I don't want to see you get hurt," but she's like, "He's the love of my life." Oh and you know that song, 'I've Finally Found Someone'? It's, like, Bryan Adams and Barbra Streisand? Well, that's *your* song. She even bought the CD. She is SUCH a sap. *Ssshhh*, here she is back.'

I ask Sorcha if she wants a drink, roysh, and she asks me to get her a vodka and Diet 7-Up and as I'm getting up to go to the bor, roysh, I tell her in front of the rest of the birds that she looks really pretty tonight, and she looks at me sort of, like, suspiciously, then she asks me if I need money and I'm there, 'It's a compliment, Sorcha. I like your top. And your hair really suits you like that. You look really well,' and she looks like she's about to die of focking happiness and it really pisses off the others.

The goys arrive while I'm up at the bor, we're talking Oisinn, JP and Fionn. I come back with the drinks, roysh, and Oisinn tells me he wants a word, sort of, like, pulling me to one side kind of thing. I'm there, 'What's on your mind, dude?' He goes, 'Ross, you know Sooty's asked me to captain the S this year?' and I'm there, 'I know that,' and he's like, 'I just wanted to make sure there were no, I don't know, hord feelings, as *you* were the logical alternative.' I'm there, 'It's cool, Oisinn, you're an amazing rugby player and a natural leader. I'd bleed for you. You *know* that.' He's like, 'Hey, not on my Dockers,' and I just, like, laugh and admire his new chinos. He goes, 'Anyway, look, I've got something to ask you. Ross, I'd like you to be my vice-captain.'

I am, like, so, I don't know, filled with pride at that moment, roysh, that I nearly, like, burst into tears. I try to speak, roysh, but the words don't come out. He just goes, 'I know, buddy. I know,' and we just, like, hug each other – we're talking a goy's hug, though – and then, like, high-five each other, then go back over to the goys. Fionn's on the Cokes, roysh, because we've all got, like, grinds tonight, as in History, and the fact that Einstein there is getting History grinds himself proves that it's not me who's thick, it's that Crabtree's basically a crap teacher. JP's also supposed to be going, but he has a pint in front of him and he's drunk, like, half of it already and maybe I'm taking the whole vice-captaincy thing a bit too seriously, roysh, but I get this serious urge to tell him he's going to have to lay off the sauce when the serious stuff begins, though that would make me a bit of a hypocrite, roysh, given that I've got a pint of Ken in front of me myself. It's still a couple of weeks before we play Gonzaga, I suppose. There's probably going to be quite a few blow-outs between now and then.

Sorcha is telling Sophie that fucus vesiculosus is dioecious and you can see Sophie getting, like, frustrated, roysh. She shrugs her shoulders and asks what THAT means and Sorcha goes, 'HELLO? You don't have to KNOW what it means. You just have to remember it and write it down in the exam,' but when Fionn thinks no one is listening I hear him telling Sophie that dioecious means there are, like, separate male and female plants, the four-eyed basic knob-end.

My phone rings and it's, like, Dick Features, trying to get all *in* with me again, probably been telling all his dickhead mates that I'm playing outhalf on the S this year. He's like, 'Hey, Kicker,' and of course I don't say anything back to him. He goes, 'Hello? Hello, can you hear me?' and I'm there, 'Yes I can hear you. Unfortunately. What do you want?' He goes, 'Oh, just thought I'd, em, give you a call. See did you hear the team Warren Gatland's picked for the England match.' I just go, 'Pathetic,' and hang up. No one in the group seems to notice except, like, Sorcha, who gives me this smile, like she understands what I'm basically going through.

Chloë says that – OH! MY! GOD! – she has been eating SO many sweets since she storted work on her special study topic for honours History and Sophie says – OH! MY! GOD! – she's become addicted to Smorties and Skittles and is getting SUCH a study orse it's not funny. She goes, 'HELLO?' JP says he doesn't give two focks about the Leaving, roysh, because no matter how bad he does, he's going to end up working for his old man, who's, like, an estate agent, as in Hook, Lyon and Sinker?

I knock back the rest of my pint and get up to go. Oisinn goes, 'Shit the bed, Ross, you're John B,' and I'm there, 'I'm only going in because the old pair have guilted me into it.' And as me and the goys are leaving, roysh, Fionn sort of, like, sidles up to me and goes, 'Did you read that stuff he gave us last week about Sinn Féin and the 1918 election?' and I stop and look at him as if to say, you know, what the fock do you think? He just, like, nods, like he gets the message. Stupid focking question.

XXX

I'm already, like, half-awake when the old dear comes into my room. She goes, 'Ross, it's half-past eight,' and I totally blank her. She goes, 'Ross, it's half-eight,' and I'm like, 'I FOCKING SAID I ALREADY KNOW,' and of course she storts going, 'Don't use that kind of language to me. I'm just saying, you're going to be late for school.' I'm there, 'No shit, Sherlock,' and she takes the hint and focks off downstairs, the stupid cow.

Oh my God, I need a serious shower this morning, roysh. My hair and my face are all, like, sticky and they smell of orange. I reach down and feel around the floor, roysh, and find my dark blue 501s and my blue Chaps jumper with the stors and stripes on it and they're, like, sticky as well. Sorcha basically threw a Bacordi Breezer over me in Annabel's last night, roysh, had a total knicker fit when she saw me giving it loads in front of Sian, and we're talking total here. Wasn't even going to go out, roysh, but the goys talk me into going for a few scoops in Kiely's and – surprise, surprise – we ended up in Annabel's.

The second I walk in, roysh, I spot Sian up at the bor with a few of her mates, trying to play it Kool and the Gang but failing miserably by looking over every twenty seconds. I'm playing it cool like Fonzarella. Get the Britneys in – Ken for Christian and Oisinn, Probably for JP and, I don't know, a focking wine spritzer for Fionn. Half an hour later

Sian's so gagging for me that I'm storting to, like, feel sorry for her, so I mosey on over and I'm like, 'Hey,' and she goes, 'Hihoworya?' and I'm there, 'All the better for seeing you. You look so ... different. Without your Eddie Rockets uniform, I mean,' and she goes, 'OHMYGOD OHMYGOD OHMYGOD, SO embarrassing!'

Has to be said, she's looking pretty hot. Kelly from 90210, eat your focking heart out. She's wearing a black strapless mini dress which I, like, compliment her on and she mentions it's from, like, Morgan and also that her pony mules are Karen Millen, roysh, and apparently her leather jacket is a real Lawrence Streele, or that's what I overhear one of her friends saying to someone else. I introduce myself to her crew. Get in with the friends and it's green lights all the way. Melissa is a complete babe. Olwen is a total dog. In case you're interested – which I'm not – Melissa is wearing a white mini dress by Fenn Wright and Manson and sandles by Gucci. Olwen is wearing a black gypsy top by Prada, black trousers by Prada and black boots, also by Prada. I'm thinking, it's a pity Prada don't do paper bags. There's, like, ten or fifteen minutes of this crap, roysh, everyone dropping the names of labels, it's like sitting through an episode of 'Off the Rails' and I have to pretend I'm actually, like, interested and at one point, roysh, I just go, 'Clothes are SO impor-tant,' and I don't know what Melissa thinks I said, but I see her mouth something to Sian and I'm pretty sure it's, 'He is SO nice.'

I stort flirting my orse off with her then, we're talking Melissa. Does no harm to make a bird, like, jealous. I'm there, 'You used to go to school in Killiney, didn't you?' and she goes, 'Oh my God, how did you know that?' and I'm there, 'Because you did *West Side Story* with the sixth years in our school last year.' She's like, 'OH! MY! GOD! I am SO embarrassed. HELLO? Total shamer,' and I'm there giving it, 'No, it was cool,' and she's there, 'Oh my God, Oh my God.' Then she goes, 'You're in Castlerock, aren't you?' and I'm there, 'Sure am, baby,' playing like SO focking cool. She goes, 'Oh my God, do you know Jamie McIvor?' and I'm like, 'He's in my Art class, I think. I've only been once.' She goes, 'Oh my God! I'm taking him to my debs,' and I'm there, 'He's a good guy,' even though he's a focking asswipe, and she shakes her head and goes, 'I can't believe you know Jamie McIvor,' and when she thinks I'm not listening, roysh, she turns around to Sian and goes, 'OH my God! He is SO gorgeous.'

Olwen, roysh – not being a bastard or anything but the girl's a focking hound – she tries to get in on the act then, asking me who else I know in Killiney and I name a few birds I've been with, we're talking Elinor Snow, Amie Gough, Bryana Quigley. Their ears all suddenly prick up. Sian's there, 'How do you know Bryana Quigley?' really sort of, like, accusingly, if that's a word, and I go, 'I was with her twice during the summer. Met her in Irish college,' and Melissa and the focking moonpig just, like, turn their heads away and I ask Sian what the problem with Bryana Quigley is and she goes, 'Don't go there, Ross. Do NOT even go there.'

Melissa turns around to me and she goes, 'Hey, you're on the senior rugby team, aren't you?' and I'm there, 'Guilty as charged,' trying not to be too big-headed. She goes, 'We were thinking of going along one night to watch you practice your kicking, weren't we, Sian?' and I'm there, 'Hey, the more the merrier,' but Sian's not happy, roysh, she's giving Melissa a filthy, probably unhappy with the vibes going back and forth between me and her, and Melissa takes the hint and focks off to the jacks, bringing the Token Ugly Mate with her.

Sian goes, 'That girl is SUCH a sly bitch. Wouldn't trust her as far as I could throw her.' I'm like, 'How long have you been friends?' and she goes, 'Since we were three. She always does that, storts, like, flirting her orse off with goys I like.' There's my in. I go, 'So you like me, yeah?' and she goes red and sort of, like, looks away. I move in for the kill. I'm there, 'Don't be embarrassed. I've liked you for ages,' which is horse-shite, roysh, but birds love hearing that stuff. She goes, 'Oh my God!' and, well, to cut a long story short, roysh, I end up being with her.

The next thing, roysh, I open my eyes and who's standing over us only Sorcha. I think it's the smell that I get first – she's wearing the *Allure* by Chanel that I bought her for her birthday and a face like a well-slapped orse. She goes, 'Didn't take you long, did it, Ross?' Sian's still, like, wearing the neck off me at this stage. I'm there, 'Hey, Sorcha. How's things?' She doesn't say anything, just, like, stares at me. Sian's copped her now. They're both looking each other up and down. I go, 'Sorcha, you were the one who finished it,' and she looks at me and goes, 'HELLO? Because you were with one of my friends,' and I'm there, 'That wasn't my fault. I told you before, *she* came on to *me*.' 'Oh roysh, and now you've moved on to someone like *her*,' and she basically gives Sian daggers.

Of course Sian's not having that. She's there, 'OH my God, sorry, WHO the fock do you think you are?' It's actually a bit of an ego boost having two birds fighting over you like this. A lesser man than me would basically get a big head over it. 'I'm Sorcha Lalor,' Sorcha goes, 'and I know who you are and where you're from. Collars Up, Knickers Down.'

She can be very funny at times, Sorcha. I'd actually just taken a mouthful of Ken and nearly spat it all over the focking place. I go, 'Oh yeah, the Whores on the Shore!' sort of, like, laughing to myself, maybe try to defuse the situation. Sian looks at me like it's, I don't know, some sort of, like, betrayal. Then she looks at Sorcha and goes, 'It's better than Mount Anything,' then she turns around to me and gives me this, like, total filthy, pretty much to tell me to get rid of Sorcha. Now. And if I'm going to get beyond base camp tonight, I know I'll have to.

I go, 'Look, Sorcha, you ended it and as far as I'm concerned you basically did me a favour. We're both free agents. Just get over it,' and with that she ends up throwing pretty much a full Bacordi Breezer over me. Aoife and Sophie and all those arrive over and take her away, telling her that I'm SUCH an orsehole and that I'm, Oh my God! SO not worth it, roysh, and there's also that bird Nikki, who's, like, repeating in the Institute and as they're heading off I notice for the first time what a great orse she has.

Sian goes, 'I SO can't believe you went out with that knob,' and even though I probably should defend the girl, I end up going, 'I don't want to talk about the past. I only want to talk about the future. And that future is us,' and I throw the lips on her again, because if I'm honest I actually couldn't be orsed talking to her anymore. Didn't get any further than that. Turns out she's one of these birds who wants to go out on, like, dates before she'll let you pick her lock. End of the night she gave me her number, roysh, but I've no intention of ringing her.

Anyway, the upshot of all this is that I'm feeling pretty shabby this morning, roysh, and I'm not sure if I'm going to be able to get my head together for this, like, talk we're supposed to be getting from Sooty – Mr Sutton – who's, like, the coach of the S. He says the game against Gonzaga is, like, the toughest first-round draw Castlerock has ever got in the competition, although I heard he says that every year, just to make sure all the goys are, like, totally focused, put their heads down and work.

I finally get my act together and get out of the sack. Probably had three or four scoops too many actually. I have a shower and lash on my beige chinos, my All Blacks jersey and my brown Dubes, then head down to the kitchen. I grab a carton of, like, milk and stort, like, knocking it back. Didn't know the old dear was standing behind me. She goes, 'Ross, I've told you before to use a glass. Honestly, sometimes I wonder whether you were brought up in Foxrock or one of those frightful council estates.' I go, 'I'm eighteen. I'm not a focking kid,' and she goes, 'That's why I can't understand why you act like one,' playing the whole Responsible Parent act. I go, 'Shut the fock up and gimme your cor keys.' She goes, 'I need the car today, Ross. Friday is lunch with the girls in Avoca Handweavers. You know that,' and I just shake my head and go, 'What did I do to deserve someone like you for a mother? I need a focking lift.' So she drops me off at the school, the stupid wagon, and as I'm getting out of the cor she goes, 'What time will you be home?' and I just, like, totally blank her. We're talking totally as well.

Sooty – he's a good goy, roysh – he puts us all sitting in, like, a circle, roysh, and he goes, 'Heavy night on the sauce last night, lads?' and everyone's, like, breaking their shites laughing because, like, Sooty knows most of us usually head out for a few on a Thursday, but he basically doesn't give a fock. He's pacing back and forth, going, 'No, lads, in all seriousness. I want to say to you what I was saying to Father Fehily just this morning. We can't underestimate these fellas we're playing next Friday. They are serious players. Gone are the days when Gonzaga were considered the poor relation of the Leinster Schools Senior Cup. They have a great team this year. If you win this game, I guarantee you won't have a more difficult match until the final. So what I'm saying is that I want you to get your heads down for the next few days, lads. Lay off the sauce, lay off the late nights.'

He goes, 'I've spoken to your various teachers and they've agreed to excuse you all from homework for the weekend. It's like I said to you before, the Leaving Cert doesn't matter a damn. You can sit it again next year. I want to make sure you have time and space to concentrate on the job in hand. Do your gym work. Focus on your own game. Now, I want to do an exercise with you, if I may.'

He stops pacing backwards and forwards. He goes, 'It's an exercise aimed at building trust and morale. I want to go around you all individually and ask you what your goals are.' Which is what he does, roysh. JP goes, 'I guess to make everyone in the school proud of me.' Fionn's there, 'Well, Castlerock has a long and storied history and its victories in the Leinster Schools Cup are an integral part of that tradition. I guess I'd like to become part of it,' the steamer. Oisinn goes, 'I want to win the Cup because the old man said he'd buy me a Golf,' and we all totally crack up.

Sooty's like, 'No, lads, it doesn't matter what your own personal motivation is, as long as you are focused on the matter in hand, ie, winning the match. What about you, Ross?' I rub my face. I should have actually shaved. He goes, 'Well, Ross. What are your expectations?' I look up, roysh, we're talking really slowly here, shrug my shoulders and I just go, 'My expectations? Only one ... Kick ass!' And with that, roysh, the whole place goes totally ballistic, everyone's suddenly, like, standing up on the tables and screaming and cheering and giving it, 'YOU THE MAN, ROSS! YOU THE MAN!' And I look over at Sooty and he's, like, standing on the desk at the top of the room and he's, like, punching the air, going, 'KILL! KILL! KILL!'

XXX

JP grabs my orm, roysh, and shakes me and he's like, 'Ross, are with you us?' I snap out of it and I'm there, 'Sorry?' He goes, 'I asked you can you hear them?' and I'm like, 'Who?' and he's there, 'Our supporters.' I'm basically too focused to hear anything, but then I listen, roysh, and I can hear them, outside the dressing room, going, 'WE WILL, WE WILL ROCK YOU – FOCK YOU, ANY WAY YOU WANT TO,' which Sooty is supposed to have banned, though it won't even get mentioned at, like, assembly tomorrow if we kick orse today.

Yesterday, me and Oisinn were asked to give a speech at, like, choir practice, roysh, just to let the rest of the school know how much their support means to all the goys and, like, how we have to totally frighten the fock out of the Gonzaga crowd today. And they're doing us proud alroysh, judging by the noise they're making.

At this moment in time, I think it's pretty fair to say we're all, like, fairly tense and worked up. One of the goys, Simon – we're talking second row, he's, like, crying, roysh, and Oisinn's, like, hugging him and telling him to focus. Christian high-fives me, as does Fionn, while JP and one of the other goys, Eunan, are standing with their foreheads pressed together and giving it, 'GONZAGA, YOU ARE TOTALLED! YOU ARE TOTALLY FOCKING TOTALLED!' going completely apeshit basically. Even Oisinn storts losing it, punching one of the lockers, going, 'WE'RE CASTLEROCK. CASTLE-FOCKING-ROCK!'

Has to be said, roysh, the speech Father Fehily gave us this morning has, like, totally fired us up. He was like, 'I think I'm on the record as saying, quite a long time ago now, that I believe schools rugby is a gift from the Lord Himself. Yes, indeed. In fact, I like to believe that had

Our Lord had a little bit more time to compose His Sermon on the Mount, he would have given a little mention to the Leinster Senior Schools Cup, maybe leaving out the bit about the meek inheriting the Earth if he was under some class of time constraint. *For verily, I say unto thee that schools rugby is truly blessed. Tend it, guard it and nourish it, for it is written.'*

It was pretty emotional stuff, I have to say. He was like, 'We here at Castlerock have decided to declare this year ... the Year of the Eagle. Yes. Yes, indeed. The eagle is the most magnificent of all of the manifold species of bird that God has given us. Strong and clever, the eagle rules the skies with a majesty that simply takes the breath away. And I draw an analogy between the eagle and the students here at Castlerock. Like the eagle, you are the very best of your species. The élite. You are better than everyone else in the whole world and the success of the school's rugby team – oh blesséd thing – is an expression of your superiority over people from other schools.'

I had, like, tears in my eyes at that stage. He was there, 'To add, if I might, a serious note – the perpetuation of the purity of our race depends on you. One day, difficult as it is to imagine, you will all leave this institution of education and social advancement. It is my earnest hope that you will take with you the moral principles and Christian lessons we have inculcated in you, when you go off to work for investment banks that destroy the Third World, or management consultancies that close down factories and throw poor people onto the dole. But ... oh but, oh but ... Verily, I say unto thee that what's more important than any of that is the good name of this school. And that is why it is *vital* that this Year of the Eagle proves he really is ... KING OF THE SKIES!'

The whole place went ballistic, roysh. I looked around and, like, everyone – we're talking me, Fionn, Simon, even Oisinn – was, like, bawling their eyes out. Then all of the goys on the S had to, like, stand up and walk up onto the stage and everyone in the whole crowd was, like, cheering and screaming, roysh, and then everyone sang the Castlerock anthem, 'Castlerock Above All Others', which has been the school song since, I don't know, the Thirties or something. It was actually Fehily's old man who wrote it. It's like:

> *Castlerock boys are we,*
> *There is nothing that we fear,*
> *Bold and courageous we morch,*
> *Danger will never faze us.*
> *We will sully the school's name never,*
> *You know we belong together,*
> *You and I forever and ever,*
> *Onwards and upwards we morch.*
> *We'll shy from battle never,*
> *We need our Lebensraum,*
> *We'll take the Rhineland,*
> *And the Sudetenland,*
> *Ein Volk, Ein Reich, Ein Rock.*
> *Castlerock above all others,*
> *Castlerock above all others.*

I'm telling you, roysh, if we'd played the game there and then, we'd have put, like, two hundred points past those tossers. Even, like, two hours later, every time I think about it the hairs on the back of my neck just, like, stand on end.

Oisinn stands up and tells us it's time to kick ass and a couple of the goys, obviously realising how much is riding on my kicking today, grab me by the shoulders and stort giving it, 'YOU THE MAN, ROSS! YOU THE MAN!'

We walk out of the dressing-room and the noise is, like, deafening. You'd basically swear there was only one team playing if you heard it. The Gonzaga crowd are being totally drowned out. It's all, like, 'WE ARE ROCK, WE ARE ROCK, WE ARE ROCK ...' The nerves just, like, disappear when I hear it. It's like Fehily said, it really does feel as though God wants us to win. I know I have to focus, though, so I kick a few balls from, like, different angles and I just know in my hort of horts that I'm not going to miss anything today. And the crowd are going, 'WE'VE GOT ROSS O'CARROLL-KELLY ON OUR TEAM, WE'VE GOT ROSS O'CARROLL-KELLY ON OUR TEAM ...'

I'm so focused on my own game during the warm-up, roysh, that I don't even look at the opposition. When I do, I have to say I'm not impressed. A few of them look like they should be on the old Slim Fast plan. Then I see that tosser who asked Sorcha to the pre-debs, we're talking Jamie O'Connell-Keavney, and I notice he's, like, captain, which shows you how hord up they must be. I just walk straight over to him and I go, 'You're history, dude.' He just, like, looks me up and down, roysh, and he goes, 'Yeah, Sorcha said you were a spa,' and I'm there, 'That is *it*. That is SO it. You are totalled. You are totally focking totalled,' and it takes the two biggest goys on our team – we're talking Oisinn and Simon – to drag me away. Oisinn's going, 'Save it for the game, Ross,' which I know is good advice.

And it's basically what I do. I settle whatever, like, butterflies are left by kicking a penalty after, like, two minutes. Christian – delighted for the goy – he scores an amazing try pretty much straight afterwards, which I convert, and Gonzaga are in total disarray. There's, like, twenty minutes gone and we're already 22-0 ahead and, not being, like, crude or anything, but we're pissing all over them. And I can't take all of the credit for it either. It's just one of those games when basically every cog in the machine works. Our pack destroyed them. Oisinn and Simon must have won nine or ten of their lineouts. Eunan, our scrumhalf, gave me so much good ball, JP didn't put a foot wrong at the back and even Fionn had a stormer outside me, though I'd never tell him that. The man of the match, for me and pretty much everyone, was Christian, who ended up scoring, like, three tries, and as we were walking off I was like, 'The Force was with you today,' and he goes, 'It was with all of us, young Skywalker,' which is fair enough. All the crowd are giving it, 'WE'RE RICH AND WE KNOW WE ARE, WE'RE RICH AND WE KNOW WE ARE ...' and the buzz is totally cool. Of course I ended up kicking five penalties and five conversions – we won, like, 60-6 – and you should have seen that tosser's face, Jamie whatever-the-fock-he's-called, about halfway through the second half when he kicked his first penalty and I went up to him and storted giving it, 'Happy birthday to you ...' He just, like, pushes me, roysh, and I push him back and I go, 'Do you want to finish this now?' and I swear to God I'm about to, like, deck the focker when Oisinn comes over and reminds me that I've already shown the retord who's boss.

And I SO did.

CHAPTER TWO
'Has minimal attention span'

I call out to Fionn's gaff and his old pair open the door. Not his old man, roysh, not his old dear, but the two of them. And they both hug me and tell me it's absolutely wonderful to see me, which is, like, slightly over the top given that I met them in the Frascati Centre on Thursday night, which they also thought was wonderful, and then they tell me to come into the kitchen because they're having quiche and it's got, like, artichokes and hickory bacon in it and it's wonderful. They walk me towards the kitchen, basically holding one orm each, and they sit me down at the table and they tell me it's wonderful that Fionn has made the school team, roysh, and they tell me that Fionn's grandfather also played centre on the great Castlerock team of the Thirties. Oh and that was also wonderful as well.

They completely freak me out, these two. My old dear's got these two sort of, like, porcelain apples with big smiley faces hanging up in the kitchen, roysh, and that's what Fionn's old pair remind me of, two focking apples with big mad shiny faces, red cheeks, the lot. They even colour-coordinate the way they dress, for fock's sake. She's got on a pair of beige slacks and a charcoal grey cardigan, roysh, and he's wearing beige cords. And they're all over each other, roysh, all this putting their orms around each other and giving each other, like, compliments.

I don't know how Fionn sticks it basically. If I go to watch telly and my old pair are even sitting next to each other, roysh, I go into the next room to borf.

Fionn's old man asks me how the studies are going and I tell him I haven't been to a single class since before Christmas, when you can basically get away with murder. He goes, 'Wonderful. Old Maximus Barry still doing the rounds, is he?' and I'm there, 'Yeah, I have him for French this year. Or is it Maths?' and he goes, 'He was there in my day, you know. Wonderful. And old Halitosis Henderson is still the first year dean, I believe. I shouldn't be unkind, of course.'

Fionn's sister Eleanor comes in. We're talking Carolyn Lilipaly here and I've been there twice and that wrecks Fionn's head. She goes, 'Hi, Ross,' and she air-kisses and hugs me, roysh, then says she heard we were doing *Wuthering Heights* as our novel – which is focking news to me, of course – and if I want any notes on it she can give them to me. I'm there, 'That'd be a huge help because I'm finding the book quite challenging. Hey, give me your mobile number and I'll ring you during the week,' and she gives it to me. Putty in the hand. She's got on the old boots and jodhpurs, roysh, and she announces that she's going riding, and I am SO tempted to comment it's not funny, but I manage to, like, bite my lip. It's hugs and air-kisses for everyone in the audience and then she focks off.

The old dear finishes setting the table, then she asks if Lorcan, Fionn's wanker of a little brother, is in and the old man says no, he's out with his pals on their skateboards, roysh, and suddenly she's like, 'Ewan, ask Ross now, before Fionn comes downstairs.' The old man goes, 'Rather delicate though, darling. Can't just blurt it out, can you?' and the old dear goes, 'But it's important that we know.' He's like,

'Ross, being young is a, what's the word, a wonderful time in anyone's life. But it's a difficult time, a time of confusion, of inner conflict, of bodily changes, of feelings we don't understand ...' The old dear goes, 'Oh for heaven's sake, Ewan. Ross, we think that Fionn might be gay.'

I go, '*Gay?*' There's, like, silence in the kitchen. They're looking for an answer. I look down at the table and I go, 'Oh, I get it now. The quiche.' The old dear goes, 'Well, we heard there's all sorts of things they eat, didn't we, Ewan?' He goes, 'I'll tell him about the sun-dried tomatoes. Ross, we bought a jar of sun-dried tomatoes, I suppose as a test more than anything. Popped them in the cupboard. Two days later the jar was empty. Now Eleanor didn't eat them. She has her allergies. And Lorcan wouldn't have touched them. It had to have been Fionn.' The old dear jumps up from her seat, yanks open the cupboard and goes, 'He's made a big hole in that crumbled feta cheese as well.' She closes the cupboard, sits down again and goes, 'These are just little bits of clues we've been putting together. But it's not just the food. I mean, I've suspected for years. Probably since that day I caught him cutting pictures out of that *Freemans* catalogue that came through the door. I think a mother knows, deep down. Ross, you need to tell us.'

I look away, roysh, doing my best not to crack my hole laughing. I go, 'He begged me not to say anything. I just feel I'm letting him down telling you this.' The old man goes, 'But he's our son, Ross. It's important that we know what he's going through.' I just, like, pause for about ten seconds, roysh, just for, like, dramatic effect, then I go, 'Okay. You're right. He's gay,' and the old dear jumps backwards, roysh, and claps her hands and sort of, like, squeals and goes, 'My son is gay! That's wonderful. I have to ring Alannah and Stephen. And Helen. Oh and the girls from golf.' The old man goes, 'Whoah, Andrea. Slow down there.

It would be unfair to let any of this out until Fionn tells us himself. And he'll tell us in his own time.' The old dear's, like, staring off into space and she's like, 'We could arrange a dinner party to announce it ... Oh, Ewan, we've been so fortunate. Three wonderful children. One of each.'

I'm seriously about to explode here, trying not to laugh. The old man goes, 'Wonderful. And Ross, bit delicate this as well, but you and Fionn aren't—' and I go, 'FOCK OFF! ... I mean, no. No, I'm, em, I'm actually normal.' He goes, 'Thought that, Andrea. Hasn't even looked at the quiche. Well, each to his own. And this young lady who's been coming to the house. This Jayne. Lovely girl. Her father's with Grabbit and Leggit Solicitors, and I go, 'She's actually mine. As in *my* girlfriend. Fionn is sort of, like, using her as a cover.' I'm actually shocked at how easily this stuff is coming to me. The old dear puts the quiche back in the fridge, roysh, and she goes, 'Because they spend hours up in that room and, without wishing to sound smutty, there's never a sound out of them.' Maybe he is a steamer. I'm like, 'I think they just talk about fashion and make-up and 'Ally McBeal'. They get on great as friends. It's often the way,' and the old man's there, 'We know. We got all the information off the Internet.' The old dear goes, 'We thought we should know everything. Autoerotic asphyxiation and what have you.'

Of course the next thing, roysh, Fionn walks into the kitchen with a book in his hand and I'm wondering has he heard any of what was said because he gives me this look, roysh, basically a filthy, but then he just goes, 'Hey, Ross. Sorry. Running a bit behind schedule. Bit wrecked actually. Was out with Jayne last night. You know Jayne with a y, don't you?' and I go, 'Yeah, the girl you're, em, going out with. What were you doing up so late? Looking at the new *Family Album* catalogue?' but he doesn't get it. I nod at the book and I go, 'What are you reading?' and he's like, 'It's a play,' and out of the corner of my eye I see his old man nodding his head at the old dear and she smiles back. Fionn goes, 'It's *Shadow of a Gunman*,' and I'm there, 'What? Hang on, how many books are on this course?' He's like, 'It's not *on* the course. *The Plough and the Stors* is. I'm actually reading *around* the course at the moment. I think they're going to hit us with a question about O'Casey's penchant for humanising political drama this year.' I go, 'Yeah, wake me when it's my stop. Come on, are we going?'

Fionn's old pair are looking at him, roysh, and they can't stop smiling, to the point where he actually has to ask them if everything's alroysh. They say that everything's wonderful and his old dear tells him she's so proud of him and I have to leave the room because I'm about to crack up in their faces.

XXX

The doorbell's been ringing for the last focking twenty minutes, roysh, and I've been screaming for someone to answer it, but it looks like I'm going to have to. The old pair must have gone into town. I look at my phone and it's, like, eleven o'clock and I'm wondering who in their right mind could be calling to the door at this time on a Saturday morning. I throw on my grey Russell Athletic T-shirt, roysh, and go down to answer the door, and who is it only Sorcha. She's obviously heard about the result of the Gonzaga match and is trying to, like, work her way back in. Before I get a chance to ask her what the fock she wants, roysh, she hands me a bottle of *cK One* and she goes, 'A peace offering.'

I'm freezing my towns off standing there in my boxer shorts, roysh, so I end up having to ask her in. I had it in my mind to be a total, like, dickhead to her, but it's only when we get into the kitchen, roysh, that I notice how well she looks, and we're talking totally here. She's obviously dressed for my benefit, roysh, because she's wearing that charcoal grey cashmere polo neck, the Calvin Klein one that I admired when I met her two weeks ago in The Bailey, and the Donna Karan boot-cut trousers she shelled out two hundred bills for and, unless I'm very much mistaken, the Dolce & Gabbana boots her old pair bought her for Christmas. She's basically dressed to kill and I actually want to be with her.

I give her a hug, roysh, and say she must be cold. She's not wearing a jacket, even though it's, like, freezing outside, but she is wearing a pink scorf and pink gloves and also her Chloe aviator sunglasses, though as a hair-band. She goes, 'Yeah. It's, like, SO cold out there.' I'm going, 'You're up early,' and she's like, 'I'm heading into town. The sale's storting in BT2 today. Dad gave me some money. Wondered did you fancy coming in with me?' I'm there, 'Don't know. I'm pretty sore after the game. Bumps and bruises,' and she goes, 'Please, Ross. You know what they say. It's just no fun, shopping for one.' I'm there, 'Yeah, fine. Want some coffee first?' and she goes, 'I'll make it while you get dressed.'

I open the cupboard to try to find where the old dear keeps the gourmet shit she buys. I'm, like, throwing boxes and jors and stuff around, roysh, trying to lay my hands on it and Sorcha comes over to help me and OH! MY! GOD! the smell of that *Issey Miyake*, roysh, I'm going to end up basically hopping the girl in a minute. She finds the coffee and she goes, 'I saw what Tony Ward wrote about you,' and I go, 'Haven't seen the paper yet.' She's like, 'He described your kicking as peerless,' and I'm there, 'Well, he's always had it in for me. Pure jealousy because he never achieved the heights in the game that I did.' She gives me a funny look and goes, 'No, Ross. It's actually good what he said. Peerless is good.' I whip out a packet of Jaffa Cakes and I'm there, 'Oh, roysh. That's cool, but we've still got a long way to go to the final.'

I tell her I'm going upstairs to get changed and she asks me, roysh, what I'm going to wear and before I get a chance to, like, answer she asks me to wear the French Connection shirt she bought me for our six-month anniversary, the light blue one, and my DKNY jeans and I don't know why, roysh, maybe it's just that, like, old habits die hord, but I end up doing what she says. As I'm walking out of the room, I grab my glacier blue lambswool V-neck, which I tie around my waist, to make it look like she hasn't totally dressed me, and also my Ralph Lauren baseball cap. A splash of *Carolina Herrera* and I'm ready.

'Is that *Carolina Herrera*?' she goes and I nod, and she's there, 'Oisinn?' and I'm like, 'Yeah,' and she goes, 'So he's still working in the airport? In duty free?' and I'm there, 'Just on Saturdays. The amount of birds he ends up chatting up at that perfume counter ...' Sorcha's standing next to the sink. She still has her gloves on and she's, like, holding her mug with both hands. She blows into her coffee before she takes, like, a tiny sip. I'm there, 'So what did you say you're buying today?' and she doesn't answer, roysh, just keeps sort of, like, smiling at me, which freaks me out, and then eventually she goes, 'Who's Alyson?'

Fock.

I'm there, 'Who?' and she's like, 'Alyson? With a y?' So I'm there pretending to be wracking my brains, going, 'Alyson with a y ... doesn't ring any bells ...' and she's like, 'Your mum left you a note on the table, saying she phoned last night. Apparently you left one of your CDs in her car.' Snoop Dog, yeah. I'm there, 'Oh, that Alyson with a y. Look, Sorcha, she's only, like, a friend,' and she just, like, bursts out laughing and goes, 'I'm not jealous, Ross,' and I'm there, 'No skin off my nose if you are. We're both–' and she goes, 'Free agents, I know. Look, Ross. I came here today, well, portly to clear the air. I've been doing SUCH a lot of thinking and – OH! MY! GOD! – I was SO out of order that night in Annabel's, throwing drink over you. I guess when I saw you with that Sian what's-her-name I just totally flipped. I thought at first it was because she thinks she's all that on the hockey pitch when in fact she's a TOTAL knob. Then I realised it was because I still have strong feelings for you ...'

Fock the shopping. I put my orms around her, roysh, and get ready to throw the lips on her when all of a sudden she goes, 'Ross, what the hell do you think you're doing? I have feelings for you, but not in that way,' and I just, like, pull away. She goes, 'Like I said, I've been doing SUCH a lot of thinking and I won't deny there's still something there. But I accept that it's over between us. Me and you as, like, girl-friend-boyfriend, it's not healthy. But I still want us to do stuff together. I value your friendship too much to ever want to lose you.' I've made a total tit of myself here, which was her plan all along, and I end up going, 'That's what I want too. Come on, let's hit the shops.'

Sorcha's driving the RAV4 her old man bought her for her eight-eenth. She's got the new Robbie Williams album on and she totally loses it when 'Angels' comes on, going, 'OHMYGOD OHMYGOD OHMYGOD, that is my favourite song of, like, ALL time,' and when it's over she asks me to, like, hit the button and play it again and we listen to it for the second time and then she turns around, roysh, and she tells me that it SO reminds her of Josh, and when I don't ask her who Josh is she tells me he's this amazing goy she met in Reynords a few weeks ago, he's in UCD, has an amazing body and plays Gaelic football. I go, 'Is he a bogger?' and she's like, 'He's *actually* from Dalkey,' and I say basically fock-all after that, which must make her day. I thought she'd be all over me like a rash after the Gonzaga result, not playing hord to get.

I spend the rest of the drive in, flipping through a magazine that was, like, on my seat when I got in and there's an article in it about shedding those unwanted pounds after Christmas and the headline is, like, WHAT YOU EAT TODAY, YOU WEAR TOMORROW.

We pork in the Stephen's Green Shopping Centre and Sorcha links my orm as we walk down Grafton Street and steers me into BT2. The place – I can't believe it, roysh – it's full of skobies. It's the sales that attract them, JP always says, like flies to a rotting dog. We're talking major skobefest here and these two birds – REAL howiyas – they stort giving Sorcha filthies. So I'm just there, 'Sorry, do you two have a problem, aport from the obvious?' and one of them gives it, 'Fookin poshie bastard,' and I go, 'Fock off back to your own side of the city,' and I turn around to Sorcha and I'm there, 'Pram Springs on tour.' She's like, 'What do you expect? They're offering, like, seventy percent off some of these clothes. It's bound to attract those sorts of people,' and I'm there, 'I know. It's like TK Maxx. Every focking skanger in Dublin is wearing Ralphs since they opened.'

Sorcha ends up buying a blue fitted jacket by Dolce & Gabbana, black knee-high boots by, as far as I remember, Alberta Ferretti, a black hooded evening dress by Elle Active and two white sleeveless T-shirts from, like, French Connection. Then we go and look at, like, the men's clothes. I notice that the black and white Ralph sweater I bought before Christmas is reduced from a hundred and ten bills to, like, fifty-five and the blue and white striped Polo Sport rugby shirt the old pair got me for Crimbo is reduced from, like, a hundred and fifteen bills to, like, eighty.

I turn to Sorcha and I'm there, 'This is totally unfair. I've a good mind to ask for the manager.' She goes, 'Cheer up, I bought you this,' and she hands me this bag, roysh, and she goes, 'Open it,' and I do and it's, like, a blue Armani Jeans baseball cap with a white AJ insignia on the front, and I take off the cap I already have on and put on the new one and Sorcha says it SO suits me. She's like, 'You don't already have it in blue, do you?' and I'm there, 'No,' and she's like, 'Thank God for that. Because I, like, bought it and then I got this, like, horrible feeling that I saw you wearing one in the Red Box a couple of weeks ago,' and quick as a flash, roysh, I'm there, 'Maybe you're thinking of Josh,' and the second I bring up his name, roysh, I regret it because I know I really shouldn't give her the pleasure. She just, like, smiles at that, roysh, and goes, 'I just bought you that to say thanks for coming into town with me,' and then she goes, 'Come on, I'll shout you a cappuccino.'

We're about to hit Café Java, roysh, when all of a sudden who do we bump into only Hennessy, the old man's penis of a solicitor. I crack on not to see him at first, roysh, trying to, like, distract Sorcha's attention into the window of some shop, which turns out to be the focking Scholl sandle shop, *duuuhhh!* But she cops him in the reflection of the window, roysh, and she goes, 'OH! MY! GOD! Ross, isn't that your dad's solicitor? Hennessy?' and she turns around – the dope – and she calls him and of course he's straight over.

He's like, 'Hello, Ross. Hello there, young Sorcha. Ross, I have to agree with every word Tony Ward said. Peerless is right. The trusty right foot. Gonzaga simply had no answer to it. It's like your father said, first round of the Leinster Schools Senior Cup or not, Warren Gatland will have taken note of that performance,' and he says all of this to me, roysh, without taking his eyes off Sorcha, and of course she hasn't copped him practically drooling over her. She goes, 'Are you doing some shopping?'

He goes, 'Getting a few last-minute things, darling. Flying out to-night,' and she's like, 'Oh my *God*, where?' and he's there, 'Bangkok. These tribunals are a licence to print money. I can't spend the bloody stuff fast enough. So it's Bangkok. You wouldn't believe the things that are still legal over there.' Of course this comment passes completely over Sorcha's head, as does the sly little look he has at her top tens.

She goes, 'Mrs Coghlan-O'Hara must be SO looking forward to it,' and he laughs and he goes, 'You don't bring coal to Newcastle, darling,' and he looks at me for the first time and winks. When he's focked off, roysh, Sorcha says that OH! MY! GOD! he is SUCH a nice man and it, like, frightens me how easily she's taken in by people.

We hit Café Java and end up getting a table near the window. She takes off her gloves and her scorf, roysh, and she, like, lays them down on the table and then storts looking through the menu. She orders a feta cheese salad, roysh, with tomato bread and no olives and a Diet Coke, and I order a club sandwich, which comes with, like, a side order of Pringles, and also a Coke, but I'm still Hank afterwards so I order, like, a ciabatta filler and then a Chocolate Concorde.

Sorcha says she's been eating SO much shit lately, trying to get her head around her special topic for history, which is the war poets, and she is SO not having dessert, although she ends up eating half of mine when it arrives. I order a coffee and she has, like, an espresso mallow-chino, which she plays with for, like, ten minutes with her spoon, mak-ing different shapes out of the marshmallow as it melts on the surface. I can tell there's something on her mind. Eventually, roysh, she puts down her spoon, takes off her scrunchy, slips it onto her wrist, shakes her hair loose, then pulls it back into a low ponytail again, puts the scrunchy back on and then pulls four or five or strands of hair loose. It looks exactly the same as it did before she did it. She goes, 'Ross, there's something I want to ask you,' and I'm there, 'Shoot,' and she goes, 'Okay, I'll come straight out with it. Will you come to the UCD Orts Ball with me? Just as, like, friends?' I'm there, 'But neither of us is in UCD.' She's like, 'Emma's got me two tickets. Please?' I go, 'Why don't you ask lover-boy? That Jamie O'Connell-Toss Features.' She's like, 'He's a loser, Ross.' I'm there, 'And what about this Josh tool?' She goes, 'Look, I'm asking *you*.' I let her sweat for a few seconds and then I go, 'Okay. But just as friends.' I'm dying to be with her, roysh, but I'm not getting into that whole going-together scene again.

She takes out a pack of Marlboro Lights and I go to squeeze the lizard. I wash my hands, splash some water on my face and then, like, take out my mobile. I have four new messages. Keeva phoned to say she is SO embarrassed and she's never done anything like this before, but she got my number from, like, Christian and she's probably making a TOTAL spa of herself but she really enjoyed that night, we're talking the night we were together, and she wondered whether I wanted to go out to her house in, like, Clonskeagh to maybe watch a DVD, or, like, go for a drink, or maybe something to eat, or the cinema and she leaves her number, roysh, and she tells me I can phone her back, but not on Saturday morning because she has, like, hockey. And I'm thinking, yeah she's right, she is making a total spa of herself. The next two messages are hang-ups, but I can see that they've both come from Sian's number, one at half-eleven last night and the other at, like, a quarter-to-nine this morning, which means she's probably been up all night brooding over the fact that I haven't rung her, the focking sap. The fourth call is from some bird called Claire who says she's, like, Sian's best friend and she tells me I'm a total orsehole for the way I treated her and she doesn't know why Sian is constantly falling for dickheads like me. Then she screams 'DICKHEAD' down the phone four times and tells me that any girl who has ever been with me says I have a small penis. I snap the phone shut and check myself out in the mirror again. I have to say, roysh, I'm looking pretty well. Then I go back to the table where Sorcha is handing the waitress her credit cord and asking her can she bring her a glass of Ballygowan. She goes, 'Still.'

XXX

Fionn goes, 'Ross, can I ask you something?' and I kind of know what's coming. I'm there, 'Shoot.' He goes, 'Did you say something to my old pair the other day?' Of course quick as a flash, roysh, I'm there, 'Like what?' and he goes, 'I don't know. They've just been acting really, I don't know, weird around me. They just keep smiling at me all the time. And the old dear keeps telling me that if I ever need someone to talk to ...' I go, 'She's probably just being, like, supportive. It's a difficult, confusing time for us all, Fionn.'

XXX

Erika always looks as though she's in a fouler, roysh, and I can actually picture her face when she answers her mobile. I'm there, 'Hey, it's Ross,' and I get nothing back. I'm there, 'Erika, it's Ross,' and she goes, 'So you know your own name, great. What do you want?' I'm like, 'Just, like, a chat,' and she's there, 'What kind of an idiot are you, calling me while I'm horse-riding? The ringing could have panicked Orchid,' and I'm there, 'Well if the phone scares the horse, why do you bring it with you when you're on him?' and it's probably in case Brad Pitt calls, or Matt Damon, or one of the other five men in the world she'd *actually* be prepared to sleep with. But she doesn't answer, roysh, she just goes, 'This conversation is boring me,' and she hangs up.

XXX

I need a sheet of paper, roysh, so I turn to the back of my copybook and rip out the last page, which of course means the first page comes out with it, though that doesn't matter a fock because I haven't written squat all year, even though it's, like, January. I write on it,

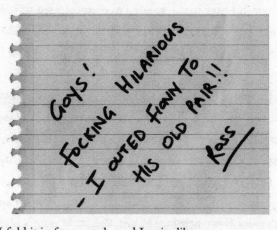

And I fold it in four, roysh, and I write like,

OISINN

on the outside and I hand it to Christian beside me and I tell him to, like, pass it down the line to Oisinn, totally forgetting that Fionn's sitting next to him and when he's handed the note to pass on, roysh, he's too engrossed in the lesson to look at the name that's on it, roysh, and he opens it while still looking at the blackboard and then he looks down and – FOCK IT! – he reads it. Then he turns it over, roysh, and he sees Oisinn's name on it and he looks back up the row and he knows it's from me. He just, like, gives me a filthy, then rips it up into, I don't know, fifty pieces.

The next thing I hear, roysh, is Ms Cully – we're talking Bet Down City, Idaho here – and she's going, *'Cad a bhí ar siúl nuair a fógraíodh na comhbhuaiteoirí don Duais Nobel in Oslo i 1998?'* and I'm just sitting there, roysh, staring at her, not having a focking bog whether this class is, like, French or Irish or what, but of course everyone's looking at me, roysh, waiting for my answer, so I take a gamble that it's Irish and I go, *Tá me on the S,'* which I have to say, roysh, I'm pretty pleased with. Everyone cracks their holes laughing and she ends up asking some swot, Fionn actually, who's her focking pet. He's like, *'Bhí sé in mbun oibre i nDoire ag seoladh plean eacnamaíochta don chathair agus David Trimble ag filleadh abhaile ó thuras geilleagrach i Meiriceá nuair a fógraíodh in Oslo gurb iad a bhuaigh Duais Nobel na Síochána i 1998. Luach saothair a bhí ann do John Hume agaus dá bhean, Pat, as ucht na hoibre eachtach a rinne siad le triocha bliain anuas,'* and it's all *an bhfuil cead agam dul go dti an focking leithreas* to me. Ms Cully's there, *'Ceart go leor,'* and Fionn's gone, *'Go raibh maith agat,'* and then she's like, *'An bhfuil tusa ar an S freisin?'* and he's like, *'Sea,'* and I don't know what the fock's going down here but she just, like, looks at me and shakes her head.

So after that, roysh – him basically making me look stupid – I decide there's no way I'm, like, apologising to him over the note, blah blah blah, so I decide to just, like, brazen it out, if that's the word, and after class I end up walking down the corridor behind him and I'm going, 'My name is Fionn. For Irish, press one. For French, press two. For Spanish, press three,' ripping the piss out of him basically, and of course he ends up flipping the lid, roysh, he spins around and he goes, 'What are you going to do when you finish school, Ross?' and the question catches me sort of, like, unawares, roysh, because I was expecting him to call me a tool or a knob or something like that. A spa or a wanker. Or a dickhead or a tosspot. Or a penis. I go, 'Em, nothing, I suppose,' and he nods his head and he's like, 'Just live off your old man's money? You don't aspire to anything better than that, Ross? You don't want something more for yourself?' I'm there, 'That's easy for you to say. You've got brains to burn,' and he goes, 'We've all got focking brains. It's how we use them that's different,' and I end up telling him that the only reason I give him such a hord time is because I always feel as thick as pigshit when I'm in his company and I'm probably jealous because he's amazing at rugby and at, like, learning.

I go, 'Look, I'm sorry about telling your old pair you were a steamer. There'll be no more of that shit, I promise. Are you coming down to the canteen? I'll shout you lunch, just to show there's, like, no hord feelings,' and he goes, 'I'm gonna skip lunch. I've got a meeting with the French Exchange Club,' and I have to bite my lip to stop myself calling him an Activities Nerd. He goes, 'Why don't you come along?' He senses my, like, reluctance, if that's the right word, and he goes, 'Come on. You never know what you'll get out of it.' So I end up tagging along, roysh, and on the way down to B6 I turn to him and I go, 'Fionn, can I just check with you – that wasn't French we were talking in that class back there, was it?' and he's there, 'No, that was Irish,' and I'm like, 'Thank fock for that. I thought I might have made a total tit of myself there for a second.'

So we head in, roysh, and it's like a focking Fionn lookalikes club in there, all glasses and anoraks and A4 pads on the table with blue and red biros and different coloured highlighter pens at the ready. It's the focking Valley of the Dweebs. This complete tool, roysh, I think I actually gave him a wedgy when we were in transition year, although he's obviously managed to blank out the experience because he turns around to me and he goes, '*Mon dieu*, a new member,' and straight away I go, 'Hey, don't get your hopes up. I'm just checking out the vibe.' He goes, '*Comment vous appellez vous?*' and I look at Fionn and he goes, 'He's asking you your name,' so obviously I'm like, 'Ross.'

Aidan's the tosser's name and I'm actually pretty insulted that he doesn't know who I am. He's obviously got no interest in rugby, the weirdo. He goes, '*Ah, Ross. Vous dites, "Mon nom est Ross", ou "Je m'appelle, Ross". Et je m'appelle Aidan. Bienvenu.*'

I'm just, like, staring the focker out of it. Everyone in the room's just, like, smiling at me and it's freaking the shit out of me. Fionn turns around to him and he goes, '*Il fait parti de l'équipe de rugby,*' and Aidan, who two years ago was down on his knees in the lobby, roysh, begging me not to hang his boxers off the Christmas tree in the library, suddenly thinks he's, like, shit-hot with his, '*Ooh la la! Nous devons parler plus lentement,*' and Fionn goes, '*Non, non. Il faut que nous parlions en Anglais.*'

Aidan goes, 'Ross, have you an interest in participating in the French Exchange Programme?' which I recognise as English, just about. He's even got me answering in this focking froggy accent. I'm there going, 'What *ees* involved?' like the tool that I am. He goes, 'Well, in collaboration with the languages laboratory, we've devised a ...' and I decide I've already heard enough of this shit and I go, 'Some frog comes to live in my house with me and then I go over there and live in his house with him?' He thinks for a few seconds and then he goes, 'Essentially, that's it,' and straight away I'm like, 'Not eenterested, *hombre*,' which is pretty good, I have to say, and I get up to go because my stomach's rumbling and I'd eat a scabby dog at this stage.

The next thing, roysh, Fionn slides this, like, file in front of me and goes, 'Aren't you going to at least look?' and I just throw my eyes up to heaven and I open it, anything for an easy life, and – HOLY! FOCK! – I cannot believe it. I go, 'You never said there'd be ... birds involved,' and Fionn goes, 'But of course if you're not interested,' and as he reaches over to take the file back, roysh, I grab it with both hands and I go, 'I never said that.' He smiles, roysh, and he's there, 'Beautiful, isn't she?' and I have to say she is, roysh, she's totally babealicious, a ringer for Natalie Imbruglia, and she's wearing this, like, swimsuit thing, huge top tens, and I've an old Woody Harrelson just looking at her. Fionn goes, 'Her name is Clementine,' and I go, 'I'll take her.'

Of course that's not good enough for this Aidan tool. He laughs, roysh – he's looking to get decked – and he goes, 'It's, er, not as simple as that, Ross,' obviously planning to bail in there himself. I'd love to see her face when she walks through the Arrivals gate and sees Bill focking Gates looking back at her. She'd be on the next plane back to, I don't know, Paris or wherever the airport in France is. It turns out, though, he knows he's out of his depth. He goes, 'First, you have to write a letter to her, to introduce yourself, let her know something about you. And she will write to you and you can decide whether you are suitable,' and I'm looking at the picture and I'm thinking, 'She's suitable alroysh.'

I stand up and pick up the file and I go, 'Fionn, you'll help me write the letter, will you?' and he goes, 'Absolutely,' and I'm there, 'Alroysh, I'm in. Now you're going to have to excuse me because I'm absolutely Hank at the moment. So I'll leave you to get on with whatever it is you do in here. *Asta la vista*,' and then I'm out the door.

XXX

'*Tommy Girl* really is the any-time fragrance,' Oisinn is going. And there's, like, three or four birds around him – we're talking total stunners here – and they're hanging on his every word. He takes the tester down off the shelf, roysh, and he takes this bird's hand – you'd say it was Sharleen Spiteri if you didn't know better – and sprays a little bit on the inside of her wrist and he's going, 'It's a blend of Cherokee rose, camellia and blackcurrant flowers, cedar, sandalwood ...' I'm thinking the dude has GOT to be making this shit up. He's going, 'Wild heather, apple blossom, mandarin, tangerine, Dakota lily, jasmine and violet.'

Then suddenly this, like, announcement comes over the air, roysh, and it's like, 'Would all passengers on Aer Lingus flight EI102 to New York please proceed immediately to Gate 26, where your flight is now boarding and is about to close,' and one of the birds, roysh, she goes, 'We'd better be quick. Our plane is going to go without us,' and it's only then I realise they're Septics. I'm about to try and bail in, roysh – give it a bit of, 'New York, huh? The Windy City' – but I know they're, like, too engrossed in Oisinn's act to listen to any of my killer lines. Actually, I'm too engrossed myself to even use them.

He goes, 'Now *Sensi* is, in my humble opinion, the flagship of Giorgio's fleet, and I once told him as much. It's the fragrance that combines Oriental romance with Italian spirit, a rich blend of akazia, kaffir-limette, orgeat, jasmine, palisander and – who can forget? – benzoe.' *Who can forget? – benzoe?* I'd rip the piss out of him later in front of the goys if these birds didn't look like they're all about to jump his bones. He goes, '*Sensi* is a fragrance that's as warm as love itself.'

Fffzzz. He sprays a bit on one of the other bird's wrists – we're talking Nigella Lawson except sexier – and she smells it and she looks at Oisinn and I swear to God their eyes sort of, like, linger. This is *Oisinn* we're talking about. He's fat and ugly and I've just seen him send four total stunners weak at the knees. He ends up selling them a shitload of perfume, we're talking seven bottles between them, and off they go like they've just met focking Tom Cruise.

He doesn't seem to have been aware of me standing there. I go, 'Look at Tom Cruise there,' and he looks at me and goes, 'Ross, how the fock did you get through Departures without a boarding cord?' and I'm there, 'Remember that security pass that you thought you lost?' and he's like, 'Yeah,' and I go, 'Well, you didn't ... Have to say, Oisinn, when you told me you were going back working Saturdays, I couldn't focking understand why. To be honest, I always thought this job was a bit ... faggy. My eyes have been opened here this morning.'

He checks out these two air-hostesses who walk in – not Ryanair, decent-looking ones. He goes, 'There's no jobs going, Ross,' crapping it in case I try to muscle in on what he's got going here. I'm there, 'You know me, Oisinn. Not really interested in working. Although the hours you spent studying that shit are really paying off. Actually, seeing those Septics hanging out of you reminded me that we're both doing pretty well on the old foreign bird front at the mo.' He looks, like, intrigued, if that's the right word, and he goes, 'Do tell.' I'm there, 'Oh, it's nothing really, just that I'm going to be getting it together pretty soon with a French exchange student with the biggest airbags you've ever seen. Looks like that bird who used to be in 'Neighbours'. We're talking Natalie Imbruglia. Gonna be some hot lovin' going down.'

He goes, 'Yeah, I heard you were in with the Nerd Herd yesterday. Fionn set that up for you?' and I'm like, 'Fair focks to the goy, Oisinn. I mean, I know we've not always seen eye to eye – probably a bit of jealousy on his port because of my rugby skills, success with the fairer sex, etc, etc – but he's, like, sound. Looks after his mates.' Oisinn goes, 'Pity that,' and I'm like, 'What?' and he goes, 'Just saying it's a pity you two are all palsy-walsy again. I've a focking geansaí-load of women's cosmetics and fragrance catalogues that I've got to throw out. I was going to suggest that you maybe slip them under his bed next time you're in his gaff for his old dear to find,' and I go, 'He's doing me a serious turn here, Oisinn. Wouldn't be fair to do it to the goy,' and we both look at each other and break into a smile and I'm there, 'Go on, then. Give them to me.'

So he bends down under one of the checkouts, roysh, and he storts reefing all this stuff out – we're talking brochures and shit – when all of a sudden one of the Septics is back – it's the Nigella Lawson one – and her face is, like, really, really red, and at first, roysh, I'm wondering is it, like, an allergy to the perfume or something, but then I realise it's, like, embarrassment. She runs down, roysh, and she hands Oisinn this, like, piece of paper and she goes, 'I have never done anything like this in my life before. But that's, like, my phone number? And my cell's there too.'

Hand it to him. The goy's a ledge.

xxx

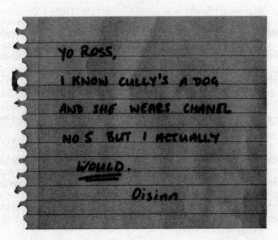

XXX

Okay. It's the third week in January. It's what, four-and-a-half to five months to the Leaving? I decide to knuckle down to a bit of study. There's no basic rule that says you can't play rugby *and* get a decent Leaving. Okay, Physics. No, fock that. History? Boring. Sorcha's doing it anyway. I'll get the notes off her the night before the exam. English. Yeah, not a bad idea. English is easy. It's just, like, reading, roysh? Where to stort is the problem. There's, like, a stack of books, we're talking poetry and plays and all sorts of bullshit. I pick up my book of past papers and just, like, open it at a random page.

'Kavanagh's poetry concerns itself with what it means to be a poet; a poet in a sometimes indifferent and ultimately beautiful world.' Consider his poetry on your course in the light of this statement. Your answer should be supported by relevant references or quotations.

Fock that.

XXX

In *Gay Times* this month the magazine's cinema critic asks why there aren't more romantic comedies with a gay theme. There's an article on gays in the Premiership and a feature on how the Internet has revolutionised the sex lives of hundreds of gay men. I wait until the shop has cleared out, then I go to pay for it, putting it face-down on the counter. The old goy in the shop goes, 'It's Ross, isn't it? You're Charles O'Carroll-Kelly's boy, aren't you?'

Fock!

I'm there, 'Can you just take for this?' and I slap ten bills on the counter and I'm like, 'Keep the change,' and I go to pick up the magazine but the focker's too quick for me. He's there, 'Let's see what it is first,' and he flips it over and he goes, 'Oh dear. What have you got yourself involved in?' I'm there, 'I haven't got myself involved in anything. It's not *for* me.'

'None of my business,' he goes, flicking through it. He storts reading out the focking headlines, roysh, at the top of his voice, going, 'THERE'S NOWT AS QUEER AS FOLK! SINGER-SONGWRITER TOM ROBINSON ON WHY HE'S RETURNING TO HIS TRADITIONAL ROOTS.' I'm there, 'HELLO? I said it's not *for* me.' He goes, 'FAIRY ACROSS THE MERSEY! AN EXCLUSIVE NO-HOLDS-BARRED REPORT ON THE GAY SCENE IN LIVERPOOL.' I go, 'Will you keep your focking voice down.' Two birds I know to see from Loreto Foxrock have just walked in. He goes, 'COTTAGE BY THE SEA! HOW LONELY MEN ARE FINDING LOVE IN THE PUBLIC TOILETS ... OF MORECAMBE.'

The two birds are over at the popcorn. The goy's like, 'Does Charles know you're out of the broom cupboard or what's this they call it?' I just, like, snatch the magazine off him. I go, 'It's not for me, you focking brain-dead tool. It's for a friend of mine.' He just, like, taps the side of his nose and goes, 'Mum's the word.' I'm there, 'I want a large brown envelope as well.' He goes, 'Got them right here under the counter.' I stick the magazine into the envelope, roysh, then I borrow a pen off the goy and write Fionn's name and address on the outside. Then I rip the envelope a bit so the word GAY is showing. The goy goes, 'Whatever are you up to, Ross?' I'm there, 'HELLO? Will you focking butt out? Do you sell stamps?' He goes, 'I've a book of local ones, Ross. Letter rate. I've no scales, though, to weigh that. I wouldn't have a notion how much it'd cost to post something like that.' I'm there, 'Just gimme ten locals then.'

He gives me the stamps. The birds arrive down at the counter. One of them asks if he has any popcorn other than cheese popcorn. I think Oisinn was with one of them once. The goy says no, he just has what's there and the two birds throw their eyes up to heaven and go down the back of the shop to get a bottle of Volvic each. I stick the stamps on and turn around to the goy. I'm there, 'There's a postbox outside, isn't there?' He just, like, nods. I throw the tenner at him.

I'm on the way out the door and he goes – the birds *had* to have heard him – he goes, 'Being gay isn't the end of the world, Ross. I know they're old, but your parents can always try for another child. Or adopt.'

✗✗✗

We're in Annabel's, roysh, and I've got these two Mounties eating out of my hand, we're talking Zara and Eloise, both absolute babes. Zara's a *little* bit like Angel from 'Home and Away' it has to be said, and Eloise is a total ringer for Julia Roberts and I've pretty much decided, roysh, that it's Eloise I'm going to be with. She's actually giving it loads, roysh, going, 'I saw you play against Gonzaga. I thought you had a great game,' and I'm going, 'You're not just saying that because you want to be with me, are you?' and she takes it the way I meant it, roysh, as a joke and she sort of, like, slaps the top of my orm and tells me I am SO big-headed it's unbelievable.

Zara decides to get in on the act then, roysh, and she asks me if I remember her and I ask her where from and she goes, 'HELLO? I'm on the Irish debating team. We had a debate against your school, like, two months ago?' and I'm there, 'Hey, yeah. Your speech was amazing,' even though I don't remember ever clapping eyes on her before in my life, roysh, and even though I haven't a focking breeze when it comes to Irish and the only words I know are, like, *tá* and *sea* and *agus* and it's pretty hord to make a sentence out of them.

Eloise tells Zara that she is SO going to have to stop reminding her about, like, school, because she basically hasn't done a tap all year and OH! MY! GOD! if she hears the words 'trigonometry' or 'vectors' again she is going to ohmygod scream and I'm standing there, roysh, trying to work out what subject she's actually talking about and whether I'm taking it as well. She says her parents are giving her SO much hassle over, like, studying and shit? And she's applied to do, like, International Commerce with French in UCD but it's, like, OH! MY! GOD! SO many points. On top of everything, she says, she's also deputy head girl this year and she's been asked to, like, arrange the music for the graduation, because she plays the piano, even though her playing has SO gone to seed since she got mono – 'we're talking, like, glandular fever?' – and she still doesn't know what song she's going to choose as their farewell song, roysh, or whether it's even up to her, but it's definitely going to be either 'Never Forget' by Take That, 'Hero' by Mariah Carey, or 'Wind Beneath My Wings' by that Bette Midler, which is OH! MY! GOD! her favourite song of, like, ALL time.

So she asks me which one I'd choose and like any great outhalf, roysh, I'm quick to see the opening. I go, 'Hero,' and she asks me why, roysh, and I tell her it's because I like love songs. She goes, Oh my God, I wouldn't have had you down as a romantic,' and I can see her, roysh, trying really hord to believe it. I get another pint in and ask her if she wants another vodka and Diet 7-Up and she's there, 'Cool.' Zara saw the odds were stacked against her and focked off somewhere. I go, 'You've probably heard a lot of bad stuff about me from other girls,' and she doesn't answer. I'm there, 'It's all bullshit, Eloise.' Fock, I nearly called her Zara. I'm giving it, 'They all want to get to know the real me, you see. And I'm not prepared to open up until I find the girl I truly love and want to spend the rest of my life with. Can I kiss you?' She looks like she's going to, like, die of focking happiness. Before she can answer, roysh, I move in and throw the lips on her and there we are basically wearing the face off each other for twenty minutes until I get bored and stort wondering what the goys are up to. I tell her I have to drain the snake, then I head off to look for Christian and Oisinn.

When I find them, roysh, they're having a toast to the greatest rugby team in the world – us, of course – and how we're going to total Sker-ries in the second round of the cup next week and when we say total we're talking totally total. Then Oisinn and JP, roysh, break into a cho-rus of, like, 'WE'VE GOT ROSS O'CARROLL-KELLY ON OUR TEAM, WE'VE GOT ROSS O'CARROLL-KELLY ON OUR TEAM ...' and everyone in the whole club is, like, looking over and we're just there, 'OH MY GOD! we SO rock.'

Christian tells me I'll have to leave my droids outside because they don't serve their kind in here and before I can ask him, roysh, what the fock he's bullshitting on about, Fionn – *oooh, my face is sponsored by Weatherglaze* – goes, 'Goys, do we know anyone called Julian?' and of course I have to turn away to stop myself cracking up in the dude's face. Fionn goes, 'Ross, I swear to God, if I find out you're ...' and I'm there, 'What?' playing the innocent. He goes, 'We had a truce, Ross. I'm sorting you out with a hot, seriously French Natalie Imbruglia lookalike and all you can do is ...' and I'm like, 'What the fock are you talking about?' and he goes, 'Some goy keeps ringing my house looking for me. Always when I'm out. Keeps leaving the name Julian,' and Oisinn goes, 'Well, he's got to be a bender with a name like that,' and I'm there, 'Don't look at me,' but Fionn just stares at me, like he's trying to make up his mind whether to believe me or not, and I have to get the fock away before I laugh, so I head off to the can. After six or seven Britneys, the old back teeth are floating.

So there I am at the trough, roysh, and the next thing Oisinn appears beside me, with this big focking grin on his face. He goes, 'I take it that was you,' and I'm there, 'You think I'd be capable of doing something like that?' and he's like, 'You're pure evil, Ross O'Carroll-Kelly,' and I'm there, 'Hey, careful with that thing, you're focking splashing my Dubes.' He goes, 'Sorry about that. Hey, gimme your mobile.' I'm there, 'Why, are you going to have a hit and miss on that as well?' He's like, 'Just give it to me.'

I hand it to him, roysh, and he flicks down through the old directory and presses Fionn's home number. His old man answers, roysh, focking Ned Flanders himself. He's like, 'Heeee-llo?' and Oisinn, roysh, he puts on this, like, faggy voice and he's like, 'Oooh what a lovely masculine voice – as the chorus girl said to the disgraced bishop of Galway. Is Fionn in residence?' I can hear Fionn's old man going, ''Fraid not at the minute. Expect he's out with his chums,' and Oisinn's there, 'I bet he is. I bet he *is*.' I'm up against the wall, roysh, holding my sides I'm laughing so much.

Oisinn goes, 'I'm ringing from Toni & Guy, the ladies' hairdressing people, just to let him know that we received his application for the trainee stylist's job. I've given it the once-over – as the chambermaid said to the elderly peer with the pronounced limp – and we'll be calling him for an interview next week,' and I can hear Fionn's old man going, 'That's wonderful! Andrea, come and share this wonderful news ...'

By the time he hangs up, roysh, I pretty much need oxygen I'm laughing so much and when we head back out to the goys, of course,

neither of us can look at Fionn without cracking our holes and I'm
pretty relieved, roysh, when someone suggests grabbing a load of cans,
hopping into a Jo and heading out to Donnybrook to Simon's free gaff.
His old pair are in New York for the week. His pad is amazing, roysh, a
big fock-off one on Ailesbury Road. He actually looks quite shocked
when he opens the door. He was probably upstairs having an Allied
Irish, but when he sees the cans, roysh, he's going, 'Welcome to my
humble abode,' then he goes, 'Anyone score tonight?' and I'm like, 'I
nipped that Eloise one. She's wanted me for ages. I was always going to
give in, in the end,' and he nods and goes, 'Darned Mounties. They always get their man.'

I high-five the dude, roysh, and then we hit the kitchen and get stuck
into the cans and it turns out to be an amazing night. We're all sitting on
the floor of his sitting-room, roysh, knocking back the Britneys, then
we move onto the shorts, we're talking vodka and Red Bulls to stort
with and then Simon produces a bottle of Sambucca that his old man
brought back from, I don't know, Greece or somewhere.

Oisinn says he ended up with Ellie Whelan last week, roysh, and of
course we're all going, 'As in first year Agriculture in UCD, used to be
head girl in Loreto on the Green?' and he goes, 'Ugly *as* sin,' like it's a
plus point, and we're all there, 'Yeah, it's the same Ellie Whelan alroysh.' Turns out, roysh, he nipped her in Annabel's last Friday night
and he rings her up on Saturday and asks what she's doing that night
and she's like, 'I don't have any plans,' which was pretty obvious, roysh,
because with a face like that she'd hordly be expecting Brad Pitt to stop
by. So Oisinn takes her into town, roysh, lashes the old wheels into the
old man's porking spot just off Baggot Street and they hit Café en Seine
and she's, like, knocking back the Bacordi Breezers and of course

Oisinn's drinking Coke because he's, like, driving? One o'clock in the morning, roysh, they head back to the jammer, Oisinn lashes on the Love Affair on Lite FM and they stort getting hot and bothered in the back. So anyway, roysh, Oisinn drops the hand and Ellie pushes him away and he asks what the Jackanory is, does she not, like, fancy going to heaven and back, and she says it's not that, roysh, it's just that, well, she's up on the blocks at the moment.

Oisinn goes, 'I flipped, of course. I said, 'You never told me that before I spent the best port of thirty sheets on drinks for you.' I'm there, 'So what did you do?' Actually, this Sambucca is going down a bit too well. Oisinn goes, 'What do you think? I threw her out of the cor. Wasn't moving, of course.' Fionn's like, 'Oisinn, that is the most callous thing I've ever heard. You left a girl in town on her own, late at night, just because she was menstruating?' and quick as a flash, roysh, Oisinn goes, 'What do you take me for, Fionn? I dropped her down for the Nightlink. I'm nothing if not a gentleman,' and I crack my shite laughing and I high-five the dude and Christian high-fives him and then I high-five JP and then he high-fives Christian and Christian high-fives me.

So we're all hammered off our tits, roysh, and of course the games stort then. First it's, like, Chariots of Fire, roysh, which – if you've never played it before – is where everyone gets a long strip of jacks roll, roysh, and you shove one end up your orse and then, like, light the other end, and the last one to pull theirs out is basically the winner. Then there's, like, Mince Pie, roysh, which is where everyone whips down their kacks, puts a mince pie between the cheeks of their orse and then there's, like, a race? Everyone had to peg it to the bottom of the gorden, roysh, touch the wall and get back to the house, without dropping the pie of course. Then you had to squat, roysh, over your pint and drop it in. The last one to do it has to drink the pint of the goy to his immediate roysh. I end up losing one game of that and three games of Soggy Biscuit, which is ... no, forget it.

I wake up the next morning, roysh, on the floor of, like, Simon's room, still wearing the clothes I went in last night, except there's vom all over them. I must have been borfing my ring up. I open my eyes a little bit, roysh, and I can see three figures standing over me. From their voices, roysh, I know it's Fionn, JP and Simon. JP's going, 'Is he still alive?' and Simon's like, 'Yeah. A miracle. I've never seen anyone eat so many soggy digestives.' Fionn's there, 'I suppose we'd better wake him up. Double biology in half an hour. It's that test today on the respiratory system,' and I'm listening to this, roysh, but I haven't even got the strength to go, 'Yeah, roysh!'

XXX

Eloise leaves a message, roysh, and says she knows it's, like, the second time she's phoned this week and – OH! MY! GOD! – she doesn't want me to think she's a stalker – she SO doesn't – but she forgot to say in her last message that she really enjoyed the night we were together and if I want to call her, here's her number.

I'm like, Take the hint, girl.

XXX

'Skerries,' Fehily goes. 'SKERRIES! The very name evokes a sense of misery ... and of dread. God created the Earth and he did it in seven days. But man ... MAN CREATED SKERRIES. Who else but iniquitous man could have conceived of a town where winds and rains not seen since the time of Noah bring misery to thousands of people huddled inside their holiday homes? Where fishermen return from another fruitless day on the over-fished Irish Sea to find solace in solvent abuse, where heroin is distributed free to children as young as two, and harlots – common whores, my children – walk the main street, offering their sorry wares as early as nine o'clock on weekday mornings and ten-thirty at weekends? Verily I tell thee that unto thee falls a great responsibility today.' Fehily's giving us his usual pre-match pep talk and I have to say, roysh, it's real lump-in-the-throat stuff.

He goes, 'Does not the Book of Revelation prophesy what will happen at Belfield this very afternoon? Does Revelation 17:1 not tell us: *And there came one of the seven angels which had the seven veils, and talked with me, saying unto me, Come hither; I will shew unto thee the judgement of the great whore that sitteth upon many waters.* Is the village of Skerries not that whore?

'Does Revelation 19 not relate to us the bloody crimes committed by the great whore? And when it speaks of the King of Kings, the Lord of Lords, is it not Castlerock College – this holy, sanctified institution – that is being referred to? I quote Revelation 19:11: *And I saw heaven opened, and beheld a white horse; and he that sat upon him was called Faithful and True, and in righteousness he doth judge and make war. His eyes were as a flame of fire, and on his head were many crowns; and he had a name written, that no man knew, but he himself. And he was clothed with a vesture dipped in blood: and his name is called The Word of God. And the armies which were in heaven followed him upon white horses, clothed in fine linen, white and clean. And out of his mouth goeth a sharp sword –* YOU, MY CHILDREN, TAKE THY MARK – *that with it he should smite the nations –* AS WELL AS MISERABLE FISHING TOWNS IN NORTH DUBLIN – *and he shall rule them with a rod of iron: and he treadeth the winepress of the fierceness and wrath of Almighty God. And he hath on his vesture and on his thigh a name written, KING OF KINGS, AND LORD OF LORDS. For true and righteous are his judgements: for he hath*

judged the great whore, which did corrupt the Earth with her fornication, and hath
avenged the blood of his servants at her hand.'

It's like, Whoah! Major round of applause. He just raises his hand, roysh, and with, like, a flick of his wrist, the room is silent again. He goes, 'Verily, I say unto thee that great will be the temptation to keep the score down to double figures today, as a mark of sympathy for a group of players who should in truth be playing more Earthly games, such as soccer. Don't give into temptation. Don't give the devil a foothold that he might gain a stronghold.'

Another round of applause. He goes, 'The army which we have formed grows from day to day; from hour to hour it grows more rapidly. Even now I have the proud hope that one day the hour is coming when these untrained bands will become battalions, when the battalions will become regiments and the regiments divisions, when the old cockade will be raised from the mire, when the old banners will once again wave before us: and then reconciliation will come in that eternal last Court of Judgement – the Court of God – before which we are ready to take our stand.

'Then from our bones, from our graves will sound the voice of that tribunal which alone has the right to sit in judgement upon us. For, gentlemen, it is not you who pronounce judgement upon us, it is the eternal Court of History which will make its pronouncement upon the charge which is brought against us. The judgement that you will pass – that, I know. But that Court will not ask of us: "Have you committed high treason or not?" That Court will judge us ... who, as Germans, have wished the best for their people and their Fatherland, who wished to fight and to die. You may declare us guilty a thousand times, but the Goddess who presides over the Eternal Court of History will, with a smile, tear in pieces the charge of the Public Prosecutor and the judgement of the Court: for she declares us guiltless.'

XXX

The Skerries match turned out to be a piece of piss. All through the game, roysh, their fans – so-called fans, there was only, like, ten of them there – they were giving it, 'DADDY'S GONNA BUY YOU A BRAND NEW MOTORCAR,' and of course quick as a flash, roysh, our goys were like, 'SKANG-ERS! SKANG-ERS! SKANG-ERS!' and if that doesn't fock their heads up enough, roysh, we ended up scoring ten tries – three from man-of-the-moment, me – and I also kick seven conversions and, like, six penalties and we win basically 82-6.

I have a shower, roysh, and throw on my threads for going out, we're talking my blue and white check Dockers shirt and my Armani jeans. Sooty tells us we were a credit to ourselves today and to our race and then he goes, 'But don't forget, goys, you're only in the quarter-finals. Don't go too mad on the beer tonight,' and of course we all, like, cheer, as if to say, Yeah, roysh!

Christian got, like, a box in the face off one of their goys – the focker never even got sin-binned – and he has, like, a huge shiner and he's looking pretty pleased with himself because it'll guarantee him the pick of the scenario when we hit Annabel's later. Some official dude comes in and he storts having, like, a chat with Sooty and then they go over to where Christian's sitting, roysh, and they ask him whether he wants to cite the skobie who pretty much decked him. He goes – and this is amazing, roysh – he goes, 'No. He comes from a disadvantaged background. Those people have enough problems putting food on the table while staying on the right side of the law. I don't want to add to that,' which I have to say, roysh, is a pretty amazing thing to say. I go, 'Not sure I'd be so forgiving. Fair focks to you,' and he's there, 'It's cool, young Skywalker.'

So we're heading out, roysh, and who's waiting outside the dressing-room – for FOCK'S sake – only Knob Brain with his orsehole solicitor. He's there, at the top of his voice, roysh, going, 'HERE HE COMES! HERO OF THE HOUR! ANOTHER MILESTONE IN THE HISTORY OF IRISH RUGBY. AND NO SIGN OF GERRY THORNLEY. THE PAPER OF RECORD HAVE SENT A *FREELANCE!*' I walk straight up to him and I go, 'Will you keep your big focking foghorn voice down? Now give me some sponds.' He goes, 'Off for a celebratory beer or two with the chaps, are we?' and I'm there, 'It's none of your focking business where I'm going. Two hundred sheets should cover it.' As he's fishing through his wallet, roysh, Hennessy, the big focking oily sleazebucket, goes, 'A fine game, Ross,' and I just shrug my shoulders and go, 'Cool,' because it costs nothing to be nice. As he's peeling off the wedge the old man's giving it, 'I shall be placing a phone call to a certain Mister Malachy Logan Esquire in the morning; find out why it's wall-to-wall coverage of Ireland versus France and there'll be barely a word in tomorrow's sports pages about the Leinster Senior Cup second-round match at Belfield and the birth of a new star.' I trouser the sponds, roysh, and I turn around to him, in front of Oisinn, JP and a couple of the other goys, and I go, 'You are the biggest focking tool on the planet,' and then we hit Kiely's.

I see Fionn's already there talking to Sorcha's friend, Aoife, who he's been seeing since he broke up with Jayne with a y and Aoife broke up with Cian, our tighthead prop. She actually looks amazing – not a pick on her, I don't know what she's doing with him – and I make, like, a resolution to try to be with her in the not-too-distant future, if only just to fock his head up. I walk over and I go, 'Now that's what I call style.' She has, like, a Castlerock jersey tied around her waist. I'm totally turning the chorm on. She gives me a hug and she air-kisses me on both cheeks and goes, 'Congrats. You'd an amazing game,' and I go, 'Thanks,' even though I know she knows fock-all about rugby. She's there, 'Sorcha said she's SO sorry she couldn't come; she's up to her eyes organising this Lenten fast,' and I go, 'It's cool, she texted me,' but Aoife ignores me and she's like, 'She is going to be SO thin after it, the bitch.' She takes a sip out of her Ballygowan and I go, 'Aren't you going to introduce me to your friend?' because there's this bird – bit of a babe actually, not *that* unlike Libby off 'Neighbours' – and she's just, like, standing there on the edge of the group, like a spare one. Aoife goes, 'This is my cousin, Cara,' and straight away I'm giving it loads, roysh, playing it Kool AND the Gang, going, 'And where have you been?' as in where have you been all my life?, roysh, but she thinks I mean this afternoon and she goes, 'Me and Aoife took the afternoon off for the ATIM open day. I'm thinking of going there next year too. Then we came here to see Fionn play,' and I go, 'Cool,' and there's, like, two or three minutes of silence and I'm thinking this bird's got basically fock-all to say for herself. She's crashing and burning here and she doesn't even know it. She goes, 'Em ... you had a good game. How many, er, things did you get?' I go, 'Tries? We're talking three,' and just as I'm saying this, roysh, I notice these two crackers over the far side of the boozer and they're, like, staring over, obviously waiting to get some face time with the man of the moment. This Cara one knows she's losing it, roysh, and just as she's telling me that she hasn't done a tap all year and she SO has to pull her socks up if she's going to pass the Leaving, I go, 'I'm going over here to talk to these honeys.'

So Slick Mick moseys on over, roysh, and he's going, 'Hey,' and they're like, 'Hihoworya?' and one of them, we're talking the one in the pink sleeveless bubble jacket – Polo Sport – she goes, 'Oh my God! you had an amazing game. They wouldn't have won it without you,' and her friend – I'm pretty sure they're Whores on the Shore; kind of know them to see – she goes, 'Ohmygod, they SO wouldn't.' The one in the bubble jacket is definitely the better-looking of the two, roysh, we're talking Joanna – a total ringer for Chloë out of 'Home and Away' – and her friend, who's not bad looking either, says her name's, like, Keelin and that I know her cousin, we're talking Sara Hanley. I'm there, 'Why is that name familiar?' laying it on really smooth, roysh, and she goes, 'She knows you from Irish college last summer,' and I agree with her when she says that Sara's SUCH a cool person, one of the nicest people you could ever meet and one of the few people you could ACTUALLY call a true friend, even though I don't know who the fock she's talking about.

So we're standing there, roysh, chatting away, and all of a sudden this goy comes over, one of the Skerries heads, he's actually one of their second rows, and he's got one of his eyes closed, roysh, and he goes to shake my hand and he's like, 'Put it there, bud,' and I don't know whether he's ripping the piss or not, roysh, but I shake his hand – basically just to let him know I don't hold it against him, being a skobie and everything – and I'm there, 'No hord feelings. What happened to your eye?' and the focking orsehole goes, 'It got poked out by your bird's collar there.' Keelin's got her collar up, oh big swinging mickey. He just, like, bursts out laughing, roysh, then he walks back over to this crowd of CHVs who are also breaking their shites laughing and he tells them that he said it.

Of course there's no way I'm having that, roysh, so I'm straight over there and – this is actually me talking, roysh, nobody told me what to say or whatever – I just go, 'Why are you such a knacker?' but it seems to go over his head, roysh, because he just, like, cracks up laughing in my face. I'm there, 'I know you. You're that Damien O'Connor they were going on about in *The Irish Times* this morning. A stor for the future, my orse.' He laughs in my face again, roysh, then he turns around to his mates – all creamers, of course – and he goes, 'Listen to the way he talks, lads,' and one of them goes, '*Dad, I need five grand for my cor insurance*,' basically trying to take me off.

I don't even know how they got past the bouncers because they're clearly all Ken Ackers. I've got, like, Christian on one side of me now and Oisinn on the other, basically for back-up in case I need it, and I go, 'Stor for the future? The only thing you're going to be doing in the future is dealing drugs. You won't be playing much rugby, unless the Joy has a team, which I seriously doubt.' One of his mates goes, 'Batter the little poshie,' and Oisinn goes, 'The only that's going to be battered tonight is your dinner, chipper scum,' which is almost as good as my line.

I'm there, 'What are you doing here anyway? There's no birds with leggings and hoopy earrings in here,' and Oisinn gives it, 'Yeah, stick to your own side of the city. You never see me out in Tomango's trying to cop off with AJHs on Mickey Tuesday,' which is basically a lie, roysh, but I don't pull him up on it. This Damien tool, roysh, he looks at Oisinn and he goes, 'I'm here because I'm gonna royid your sister,' and I go, 'Well the joke's on you then because Oisinn's sister's a total hound,' and Oisinn nods.

Then the dickhead goes, 'Come on, lads, let's hit the good soyid of town,' and as they're heading out the door, roysh, leaving a trail of, like, fake *Adidas* aftershave after them, I go, 'Yeah, drown your sorrows and then fock off back to the Fleck Republic.'

Joanna shakes her head and she goes, 'I don't know even know how they got in here,' and Keelin's there, 'That's the first time I've ever seen a real sovereign ring. Oh sure, I've seen them on television and in photographs, but never in real life.'

Pretty much everyone's buying me drink all night, roysh, and at one stage I've got, like, six pints in front of me and I'm knocking them back, we're talking double-quick time, and after basically two hours I'm totally horrendufied. Anyway, roysh, we end up in a nightclub that looks vaguely familiar but I'm too shitfaced to recognise which one it is, and the next thing I remember is, like, Joanna and Keelin dragging me out onto the dancefloor for some, I don't know, Backstreet Boys song, maybe 'Backstreet's Back', and I can hordly stand I'm so off my tits. Then it's that 'I Believe I Can Fly' and Joanna, who's obviously decided she's going to try to be with me, is holding me up while we slowdance and then it's 'Two Become One' by the Spice Girls, which Joanna says she SO loves. So I end up throwing the lips on her on the dancefloor, roysh, and it has to be said, she's a pretty amazing wear.

Spinning around in circles is storting to make me feel sick, roysh, so I tell Joanna I have to sit down and I find a seat and end up overhearing Fionn having a borney with Aoife. She's totally hysterical, and we're talking totally here, and I can't make out a word she's saying, but Fionn is, like, trying to hug her and he's going, 'You're not fat. You're SO not fat,' and all of a sudden someone sits down beside me and I turn around, roysh, and it's Simon. He's like, 'You entering Kruffs this year then?' and I'm there, 'Say again,' and he goes, 'Just wondering what you're doing with the mutt,' and he points to Joanna, who is, like, gesturing, I don't know, wildly I suppose, with her hands and telling Keelin and some other bird I know to see from Loreto Foxrock that she is SO going to become a vegetarian, she SO is. I'm there, 'What are you talking about? She's a total honey,' and he goes, 'From a distance maybe. Like Mallin Head to Mizzen Head. In a thick fog,' which I know is total bullshit, roysh, because Simon tried to be with her ages ago but totally crashed and burned. I remind him of this, roysh, and he just, like, smiles and high-fives me and then he focks off.

Anyway, roysh, the night basically flies and at the end of it all the other goys have gone and it's only me, Oisinn, Joanna and Keelin left. Oisinn is with Keelin, as in *with* with, and I'm wondering is he still seeing Amie with an ie, though that would hordly matter to Oisinn, what with him being a total horndog. He must be able to read my mind, roysh, because he puts his orm around my shoulder at one stage and he whispers in my ear, going, 'An erect mickey has no conscience,' which is one of his favourite phrases. The four of us end up in Keelin's house in Monkstown, what with her having a free gaff with her old pair in Chicago for the weekend.

The next morning, roysh, I wake up early and my head is hanging off my shoulders. I'm there going, 'Oh my God, I actually *want* to die,' and we're talking totally here. I try to get dressed without waking Joanna, roysh, but she hears me as I'm, like, putting my shoes on and grabbing a pair of knickers to show the goys later, and she asks me where I'm going. I don't want to lie to the girl, roysh, but I end up telling her that I generally help out at a Simon Community hostel on a Saturday and she tells me that that is SO cool, helping homeless howiyas, and she says she had SUCH an amazing time last night and that I shouldn't worry about you-know-what and she sort of, like, looks at my crotch as she says it, and she says she'd SO love if we could see each other again, roysh, and I tell her I'll give her my number and then I say the first seven numbers that come into my head. She writes it with, like, an eyebrow pencil on the cover of *Image*, which she tells me has a photograph of one of her best friends in it, as if I give two focks. She storts, like, flicking through the pages, roysh, but I tell her I have to go and she, like, blows me a kiss as I'm leaving and I just, like, smile at her.

I have five messages. I don't know who the first one is from but I can pretty much take a guess, roysh, because that song 'Short Dick Man' is blasting out and someone is obviously, like, holding the phone up to the speaker, ha focking ha. The second one is from Eloise. I can hear someone in the background going, 'He's not worth it, Eloise. Don't give him the pleasure,' and then she's going, 'Hello? This is a message for Ross. You're a wanker. An absolute, total wanker,' and she bursts into tears, roysh, and before the phone is put down I hear her friend go, 'I SO knew this wasn't a good idea.' The next message is from Alyson, who also calls me 'an absolute, total wanker.' The fourth is from Sian. She's hammered, but at least she's original. She goes, 'Every girl around thinks you're, like, hot stuff? News flash, Ross. You're, like, a total loser,' and then she goes, 'LO-SER!' The last message is from some bird called Keeva, who I nipped in the rugby club recently and who now wants to know why I stood her up on Friday night and whether I think it's actually funny leaving her standing outside the Hat for, like, an hour and twenty-five minutes and why I haven't returned any of her calls since then and why I seemed so keen before but am now doing a total Chandler on her, whatever the fock that is.

I get the Dorsh to Dun Laoghaire, pick up the *Times* and the *Indo* at the station and, like, read the reports on the game while I wait for the

46A. Tony Ward's got, like, half a page on the match and it's like, 'The schools game is the bedrock of rugby in this country and MAKE NO MISTAKE ABOUT IT the performance by Castlerock College in the second round of the Leinster Schools Senior Cup yesterday was as fine an exhibition of how the game should be played as you are likely to see at any level. This team is simply awesome and the game against Skerries was a particular *tour de force* for young Ross O'Carroll-Kelly, who MARK MY WORDS is an undoubted star of the future.' *The Irish Times* had, like, six paragraphs on the game, which described my kicking as unerring – whether that's good or bad is anyone's guess.

So I get home, roysh, and the old dear doesn't even mention the fact that I didn't come home last night, which pisses me off big-time. She's sitting in the old man's study, roysh, and she's got her focking glasses on, which means she's probably writing to all the local councillors again about this halting site they're building down the road. I walk past and she doesn't even look up, roysh, just goes, 'You'll have to fix your own breakfast, Ross. I have to prepare for tonight's committee meeting.' I'm there, 'You mean Foxrock Against Total Skangers?' and she finally looks up and she takes off her glasses and she goes, 'That is *not* the name of it, Ross, as well you know it isn't.' I go, 'I couldn't give two focks what your anti-halting site group is called,' and she goes, 'We're not *anti* halting site. We just happen to believe it's not appropriate for an area like this,' and I just go, '*What*ever,' and I hit the kitchen.

CHAPTER THREE
'Cheeky and disruptive'

I'm in town with JP, roysh, just picking up a few new threads – a pair of cream G-Star chinos, which I might bring back tomorrow and exchange for Dockers and a light blue Ralph – and we go back to the cor and he's like, 'Going to make a bit of a detour on the way home,' and I go, 'That's Kool and the Gang,' because we drove in in his old man's beamer. So I'm not really paying any attention to where we're going, roysh, but the next thing I look up and I realise we're on DNS, as in De Nort Soyid, and I'm there, 'Have you lost your focking mind?' and he's going, 'Come on, Ross. Think outside the box for once,' which is one of these wanky expressions he's picked up from his old man, who's an estate agent. He drives for, like, ages, roysh, and further and further northside we go. I'm there, 'JP, it's still not too late to turn around,' but it's like the dude's got a death wish.

So anyway, roysh, we eventually pull up in this council housing estate and it's like hell on Earth, roysh, we're talking boarded-up houses, horses eating the grass in people's gardens and fat women in leggings sitting on walls and smoking. And right in the middle of all of this, JP stops the cor and actually gets out. He has lost his focking mind. He walks around to the passenger side and opens my door and he tells me he wants me to drive and I agree, roysh, because I'm thinking, 'At least if I'm in control of the wheel I can get us the fock out of here.'

He goes, 'I want you to drive slowly, Ross. We're talking five miles an hour,' and he winds down the window and as I let down the handbrake, slip her into first and then move off slowly, JP practically climbs out the window – he's standing up with only his legs actually inside the cor – and he storts shouting, 'THE BREADLINE,' at everyone we pass. That focker is going to get himself killed one day.

XXX

It's time to stort seriously love-bombing this French bird, so I meet Fionn in the library and he hands me a pen and an A4 pad. I'm there, 'I was actually hoping you'd write the letter for me,' and he goes, 'She's *your* exchange student,' and I'm there, 'Yeah, and I don't have a word of focking French!' He takes the pen and pad from me and he goes, 'Okay, tell me what you want to say in English and I'll write it out in French for you.' I'm there, 'Hey, I owe you one, Fionn. Roysh, what kind of shit do these French birds like to hear?' and he goes, 'It's not a case of ... Look, it's about letting her know who you are, and where you are in your life right now, and why you decided to become involved in the exchange programme. Answer me honestly, Ross, what do you hope to get out of this,' and I look at him, roysh, like he's got ten heads or something and I go, 'My Nat King.' He goes, 'Okay, be maybe a *little* less honest. What do you want her to think you want out of it?' and I go, 'Improve my French, blah blah blah,' and he's there, 'Good. But let's stort off by telling her a bit about you.'

My favourite subject. I'm there, 'I play rugby,' and he goes, 'Let's stort with your name. *Je m'appelle Ross O'Carroll-Kelly et j'habite a Foxrock.* Okay, what else?' I go, 'I can bench-press ...' and he's like, 'Ross, she doesn't want to know how much you can focking bench-press. Fock's sake ... it's just the relevant stuff. Okay. *Je joue au rugby et je suis un outhalf. Je joue pour Castlerock College, c'est mon école.* What about your family?' I go, 'My old man's a dickhead.' He puts the pen down and he goes, 'Ross, I'm talking about how many brothers and sisters you have. You can't say ...' and I'm there, 'Fionn, if she's going to be staying in my gaff, she's going to find out pretty quickly that he's the biggest tool who's ever lived. I don't want her walking out after one day saying I didn't let her know what to expect.' He just, like, nods, roysh, and he goes, *'Je n'ai pas des frères ou des soeurs et mon père est un ... homme inhabituel.* What would you like to do when you leave school?'

I go, 'Probably play rugby,' and he's there, 'Ross, you *do* realise that if this girl isn't into rugby, you're up Shit Creek.' I go, 'What'll I put then? Hey, put bank manager. Birds love that shit,' and he storts writing again and he goes, *'J'ai plusiers films pornographiques,'* and I'm there, 'Good,' and he's like, *'Je voudrais coucher avec toi,'* and I'm like, 'What the fock's that?' and he goes, 'My favourite subjects are Physics, Mathematics, History and Geography,' and I'm there, 'This is good. Make me out to be some kind of intellectual.' He goes, *'J'aime regarder les hommes le faire et j'adore ton derriere.* I am a member of many societies at school and also do a great deal of charity work in my spare time.'

I'm there, 'Fionn, you're, like, a genius, my man.' And he gets me to sign it, roysh, then he goes, 'Well, it's not exactly Rimbeau, but I think she'll get the general idea of what you're like.'

I don't believe it. By the end of March I'm going to be having hot sex with some frog bird. I take the letter off him, high-five the dude, then fock-off to get some nosebag.

XXX

I'm sitting there watching telly, roysh, trying to chillax, when all of a sudden the two focking muppets arrive in. The old dear goes, 'Feet off the table, Ross,' and I just, like, give her a look and she knows better than to say it again. The old man goes, 'Actually, we'd like a bit of a word, if we might,' and I ignore him and he goes, 'Would you mind lowering down the volume on the television?' and I throw my eyes up to heaven and switch the thing off altogether and I go, 'Satisfied now?'

The old man's like, 'It's about this parent-teacher meeting, quote-unquote, we went to today.' I'm there, 'What about it?' and he's like, 'Well, you've got seven teachers, Ross, and ... three of them have never heard of you.' I'm there, 'So?' and he's like, 'So? Ross, it's the end of February in your Leaving Certificate year and three of your teachers couldn't pick you out of a police line-up. You've never sat any of their exams, submitted any of their coursework or attended any of their classes, from what they can see.'

I'm there, 'I'm sure there's a point to all of this, is there?' and of course he hasn't a bog what to say to that. The old dear gets in on the act then. She's going, 'The four teachers who *did* remember you didn't have very nice things to say about you either. Rude, hostile, uncommunicative and arrogant, they said.' The old man goes, 'I told them. I said, "He didn't pick any of those bad habits up at home. It wouldn't be tolerated".'

I'm there, 'Is that it?' and they don't know what to say. I turn on the telly again and I go, 'Make yourselves useful and get the dinner ready. At least *pretend* to be proper parents.'

XXX

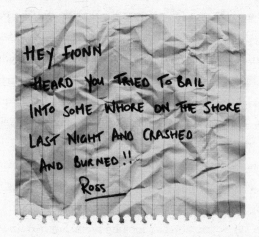

HEY FIONN

HEARD YOU TRIED TO BAIL

INTO SOME WHORE ON THE SHORE

LAST NIGHT AND CRASHED

AND BURNED !!

Ross

XXX

What's dirty, brown and ugly and hangs off the side of a satellite dish? The answer is a council house, roysh, and I've already heard it before but I couldn't be orsed telling Kenny, this total tosspot who Sorcha insisted we share a table with, just because she's in Amnesty with his bird, Helena – a total moonpig, before you ask. Helena's telling Sorcha that the media are OH! MY! GOD! totally ignoring what's going on in Rwanda, we're talking four years on from the genocide, with thousands of unarmed civilians being extrajudicially executed by government soldiers – 'It's like, HELLO?' – while almost 150,000 people detained in connection with the 1994 genocide are being held without, like, trial. She goes, 'I'm not even going to *stort* on the thouands of refugees forcibly returned to Burundi. It's like, do NOT even go there.' Sorcha's saying that President Pasteur Bizimungu SO should be indicted for war crimes if half of what she's read on the Internet is true. She's there, 'It's like, OH! MY! GOD!' but I'm not really listening, roysh, I'm giving the old mince pies to Amanda, this total lasher who's, like, second year Orts.

And of course it's not long before Sorcha cops it. She goes, 'Your chicken's getting cold, Ross,' but I just, like, blank her and keep staring. All week, roysh, I've been listening to Sorcha and her friends going on about this bird Amanda Cooper and how she was going to be wearing the famous Liz Hurley dress – *that* dress, the black Versace one with the safety pins – to the Orts ball. I heard Sophie and Chloë telling Sorcha that each pin cost OH! MY! GOD! eighty sheets. Now I know why everyone was so freaked out about it, roysh, because there isn't a goy in the room who can keep his eyes off her, and that's saying something considering the scenario that's here.

Have to say, roysh, Sorcha's looking pretty hot herself. She's wearing this, like, blue backless ball gown, I suppose you'd call it, and whenever anyone, like, compliments her on it she mentions that it's an Amanda Wakeley and then she goes, 'And do you like the shoes? Red or Dead.' I've pretty much stolen the show in my Ralph Lauren tux, which I borrowed from JP's brother, Greg – must get my own for when I'm in UCD myself – and one of those, like, novelty shirts, which is white, roysh, but has, like, cartoon characters on the sleeves. Sorcha has an eppo when I take my jacket off at the table, we're talking total Knicker-fit City here, giving it, 'Oh my God, oh my God, I am SO embarrassed.'

Oisinn is also here, roysh, with Rebecca, this friend of his sister, who's, like, first year Engineering, and he's also wearing a novelty shirt, though he's sitting at a different table.

The skivvies come to collect the food and I notice, roysh, that none of the birds at our table have, like, touched theirs and I hear the waitress – bit of an oul' one really – muttering under her breath about what a terrible waste of food it is and all of a sudden, roysh, this Helena one, at the top of her voice, goes, 'If you've got something to say, say it out loud,' basically like a teacher would say if he, like, copped you whispering to someone down the back of the class. The bird's there, 'I'm just saying, it's a terrible waste of food.' Helena goes, 'Your point being?' and old biddy's like, 'You cheeky little madam. There's young children starving in Africa,' and Helena's there, 'I doubt if they'd be interested in your Chicken Supreme.'

I have to say, roysh, I know this one works in the service industry and everything, but she doesn't deserve this. As she's walking away, roysh, Helena goes, 'Excuse me,' and when she turns around Helena's there, 'You see this girl here?' and she, like, points at Sorcha. 'Her father is Edmund Lalor. Of Edmund Lalor and Portners. He has all of his conferences in this hotel. He basically spends a fortune here. If you want to keep your job, I'd advise you to learn some manners,' and I'm about to stort clapping, roysh, as in *that told her,* but all of a sudden, roysh, Sorcha jumps up out of her seat and goes, 'How DARE you?' and I'm thinking, 'Okay, let's just see how this one plays out.' She's there, 'How dare you sit there pontificating about the terrible injustices happening in countries you've never been to and will never go to, then treat someone less fortunate than you in that way. You shallow, supercilious BITCH!' and she gets up and storms off to the jacks.

And it's at times like that, roysh, that I remember why it is I still love Sorcha, if that doesn't sound too gay. She has, like, principles, if that's the right word. She always stands up for what she believes in. Sometimes I wish I was more like her. Helena goes, 'What's *her* focking problem?' and I can feel everyone at the table just, like, staring at me, roysh, and I can't help it, I just shrug my shoulders and in a sort of, like, sneer, I go, 'Time of the month,' and everyone laughs and I hate myself for not having guts like she's got.

It turns out, roysh, that this bloke Kenny's a bit of a rugby head and he asks me if I've thought much about what club I'll sign with when I leave Castlerock and I tell him I haven't given it much thought, at the moment my main focus is on the Senior Cup and nothing else. He goes, 'The word is you guys have got a kick-ass team this year,' and I nod and go, 'Totally,' just as the dessert arrives. Only one bird at our table wants profiteroles – I think she's called Kerry – but just as she sinks her spoon into one, Helena goes, 'A moment on the lips, a lifetime on the hips,' and some other bird at the table who I don't know gives it, 'What you eat today, you wear tomorrow,' and she ends up eating one spoonful, then pushing the bowl away and lighting up a Marlboro Light.

I'm bored off my tits at this stage, roysh, and I'm casing the place to see can I spot Amanda Cooper, maybe bail in there, and I see her, roysh, on her own up at the bor and I decide it's time to give her the pleasure of my company. I'm straight up to her, roysh – fock, she's beautiful – and I go, 'Hey, babes,' and she just, like, looks at me, bit of a filthy if the truth be told. I'm there, 'Your dress is amazing,' and she throws her eyes up to heaven, like it's the fiftieth time she's heard that tonight, which it probably is. I'm there, 'Can I get you a drink?' and she's like, 'You're not going to come up with *one* original line, are you?' 'Out of the corner of my eye, roysh, I cop Erika, who came with some tool who's supposed to own his own yacht, and she's got this, like, smirk on her face, a real superior look, her usual look, and she's obviously loving watching me crash and burn. The borman comes over and Amanda asks him for a Coors Light, roysh, and she doesn't ask me if I want a drink. I go, 'Suppose I *better* lay off the sauce. Big game in a week's time. I play rugby, in case you didn't know.'

The next thing, roysh, I feel this, like, tap on my shoulder and I turn around and it's this total honey, and when I say total I mean totally to-tal, we're talking Teri Hatcher here, a dead-ringer. Of course Mister Shit Cool here goes, 'Hey, no fighting over me, girls. Play nicely,' as, like, a joke, and this Teri Hatcher one, who turns out to be Amanda's best friend, goes, 'Sorry, we're not interested in ...' and she looks me up and down and goes, 'schoolboys.' I'm there, 'No? Not even a member of the Castlerock College S?' but even as I'm saying it, roysh, I realise that it means basically fock-all to these birds. They're in, like, college. They're out of my league. Amanda goes, 'Run away back to your little rugby groupies,' and she turns her back to me and – total mare – I have to face the old walk of shame back to the table, where everyone's been watching me.

Oisinn comes over and he's like, 'I saw it, but I don't believe it. Was that a mission abort?' and I go, 'She's a focking lesbian,' and he laughs and we both high-five each other. That's when, roysh, out of the corner of my eye, I notice that Sorcha's back from the jacks – course she is, that was half a focking hour ago – and she's basically chatting to this complete tool over the other side of the room and even from where I'm sitting, roysh, I can see that the goy is hanging out of her. This, like, jealousy, I suppose you could call it, just takes over me, roysh, and I'm straight over there and I can hear the goy going, 'Murengezi is a lawyer who, for want of a better word, *disappeared* in Kigali in January. The Government ... Sorry, can we help you?' I don't know how long I was staring at him, but it must have been ages. I just ignore him, roysh, and I'm there, 'Sorcha, can I talk to you? *Alone,*' and she ignores me, roysh, so I grab her by the hand and pull her up and I'm just about to drag her away when this goy – glasses and this stupid focking quiff – he stands up and he's there, 'Hey, you are SO out of

order,' and I'm going, 'Do you want me to deck you?' and Sorcha's like, 'Stop it, you two! Paul, I'm really sorry about this, but I have to have a word with Ross,' and he's gone, 'Hey, don't sweat it, Sorcha. I'm right here if you need me,' like he's going to sort me out if I step out of line, and I'm thinking, 'Yeah, roysh.'

Sorcha is NOT a happy camper. *She* ends up dragging *me* to a table where nobody's sitting and she storts giving it, 'WHAT is your problem?' I'm there, 'Who's that tosser?' and she goes, 'His name happens to be Paul. And he's a really good friend of mine.' I'm there, 'There's something about him I don't like. I just don't want to see you get hurt, Sorcha.' She goes, 'I asked you a question, Ross.' It's only then that I notice how hammered she is. She's always been a total wuss when it comes to drink and she's only had, like, three bottles of Miller and she's already off her face. I'm like, 'What question?' and she goes, 'I asked you what your problem was with me talking to Paul.' I know the answer she's looking for and I give it to her. I'm there, 'I suppose I was, like, jealous.'

She goes, 'But we're not going out together anymore. You dumped me, remember?' I go, 'You were the one who broke it off,' and she's like, 'HELLO? Because you kissed, like, my best friend? I don't THINK I was being unreasonable.' I'm there, 'It was a mistake, Sorcha. I really miss you. Especially your friendship.' She goes, 'Bullshit! Ross, you didn't even stick up for me earlier when I had that row with Helena,' and I'm there, 'You should have heard me giving out yords to her when you were gone,' and she looks at me, roysh, like she knows I'm lying and she goes, 'You didn't even come after me to see was I alroysh.' I'm like, 'That's because ...' but I can't even look her in the eye, roysh, and I go, 'That's because ... because ... because I'm scum, Sorcha. You know it and everyone knows it,' and I can feel my eyes storting to, like, fill up and I'm hoping Oisinn hasn't copped me, roysh, but then suddenly the next thing I know Sorcha's thrown the lips on me and it's, like, amazing. 'A Million Love Songs Later' comes on – Take That or some shit – and we stop wearing the face off each other and Sorcha goes, 'Let's go upstairs.' I'm like, 'Where?' and she goes, 'I've booked a room in the hotel.'

I'm there, TOUCHDOWN! though I didn't say it, roysh, just thought it. I'm there, 'Okay, Sorcha, but only if this is what you really want.' She stops, roysh, just as we reach the elevator and she goes, 'It is what I want. But I am SO warning you, Ross, you better not mess me about this time. I don't want any of that rubbish you came out with before about wanting your freedom and not wanting to be chained down. If you still have commitment issues I want to hear about them now, as in this moment. I don't want you doing a Chandler on me again.'

I'm trying to remember if it was Keeva or Sian who said that to me the other day. We reach the third floor and the lift doors open. We find the room and as she pushes the key cord in the door she turns around to me and she's just like, 'It's a copy, by the way,' and I'm there, 'What is?' and she goes, 'Amanda Cooper's dress. It's not a real Versace. Her aunt is a dressmaker.'

XXX

We're all looking forward to kicking some serious St Mary's orse, roysh, but it's like the game is never going to come around. Doesn't matter what you're doing, roysh, it's there in the back of your mind the whole time. There's a place in the semi-finals of the Leinster Schools Cup up for grabs and no one needs to be reminded of the stakes. I'm in the gym at lunchtime with Christian – just working on basic strength really – and he tells me he's been pretty hord to live with the past couple of weeks, he's been snapping at his old pair and he's really going to make it up to them when all of this is over. I tell him I've probably been a bit short with mine as well the last couple of days, believe it or not, but once we get through Friday, then the semi-final and then the final, I can hopefully spend a bit of time with them and let them know what a couple of penises I really think they are.

Not that they've any interest in me or my life. It's still nothing but Foxrock Against Total Skangers at the moment. Meeting councillors and writing protest letters and trying to find someone in this day and age who's prepared to accept bribes. The old man was on the news last week, shouting his mouth off and making a total tit of himself outside the Dáil, going, 'What's wrong with my money? It was good enough for you last year.'

Christian tells me his old pair are having a lot of borneys lately, and we're talking MAJOR borneys here. I think his old man's a bit of a swordsman and his old dear is sick of him not coming home, or finding other women's numbers in his Davy Crocket. I tell him everything will work out, roysh, but only because it's the first thing that comes into my head and he nods and says, 'I know. I mean, it wasn't always hearts and flowers for Han and Leia, was it?'

I'm there, 'What have we got this afternoon?' and he goes, 'English. We're supposed to have *Waiting for Godot* read for today. Did you ...' and he realises it's a stupid question before he's even asked it. I go, 'Why don't me and you fock off for the afternoon, hit your gaff and watch the three *Star Wars* movies back-to-back,' and his face just completely lights up, roysh, and he goes, 'Like the old days,' and I'm there, 'Yeah, just like the old days.'

XXX

Fehily tells us that we are just three steps away from greatness. He goes, 'And pay heed, my children, to the significance of that holiest of holy integers. *Three* parts to the Blesséd Trinity. The Resurrection happened on the *third* day. But, oh, it is solemnly I tell thee that the path thou shall tread tomorrow is uneven and treacherous. St Mary's are a formidable enemy. Did the Good Lord himself not say before He crossed the Sea of Galilee, "Beware the team with the strong, mobile pack". But this is a battle we must win.'

He goes, 'And so, in all due modesty, I have just one more thing to say to my opponents – I have taken up the challenge of many democratic adversaries and up to now I have always emerged the victor from the conflict. I do not believe that this struggle is being carried on under different conditions. That is to say, the relation of the forces involved is exactly the same as before. In any case I am grateful to Providence that this struggle, having become inevitable, broke out in my lifetime and at a time when I still feel young and vigorous. Just now I am feeling particularly vigorous. Spring is coming, the spring which we all welcome. The season is approaching in which one can measure forces. I know that, although they realise the terrible hardships of the struggle, millions of German soldiers are at this moment thinking exactly the same thing ...'

XXX

An inappropriate gesture is what *The Irish Times* said I made to the crowd during the match and I'm there, 'An inappropriate gesture? HELLO? I just gave them the focking finger,' and it wasn't, like, inappropriate either. The crowd were giving me major stick all through the game, roysh, and we are talking MAJOR here. Mary's were a lot tougher than we thought, roysh, and I had a bit of a mare with my kicking, missing seven out of my twelve kicks. And of course their crowd, roysh, were loving it until Christian blocked down a drop-goal attempt about five minutes from the end, roysh, the ball fell to me and I pegged it seventy yords down the other end to score. Just threw the ball up in the air after that, roysh, ran over to their supporters and gave them the finger, as in who's in the focking semi-final now?

So I get up Saturday morning, roysh and the old man is on to *The Irish Times* sports desk and he's basically giving out yords, fair focks, tool and all as he is. He's going, 'Your representative said my son made an inappropriate gesture but made no reference whatever to the level of provocation he was subjected to,' but he's obviously getting nowhere with the goy on the other end of the phone, roysh, because the old man's going, 'It's quite evident from your coverage that you care nothing for the schools game. It strikes me that Mister Tony Ward Esquire from your main rivals is the only rugby writer in the country who appreciates the seriousness of it. I mean, where the HELL was Gerry Thornley on Friday?' There was this, like, silence, roysh, then the old man totally exploded, going, 'WELL GET HIM BACK FROM PARIS! WHO GIVES TWO FIGS ABOUT THE FIVE NATIONS?' and he finishes off by reminding the goy how much money he spends on, like, advertising in the paper every year and then he, like, slams down the phone.

XXX

It's Monday morning, roysh, and we've all been given the day off school today because we're, like, totally wrecked after the last few weeks. The training has been pretty intense, it has to be said, we're talking before school, at lunchtime and then after school as well, and weekends on top of that, so we're all focked at this stage. Anyway, roysh, because we all have the day off, me and goys decided to do something together, as a team, we're talking for morale? So we decide to head out to see the Irish team train, roysh. JP's had an offer to play for the Greystones under-19s next season, so it's an excuse to go out and check out the set-up and the facilities and shit.

There were six messages when I checked my phone this morning. Joanna rang to see how I was and to say she understood why I hadn't been in touch, that I must have been, like, SO focused on beating St Mary's and she wished me luck against the Gick in the semi-final and then she said that I'm capable of doing anything I want to in life as long as I put my mind to it, the focking sap. Then she said she'd, like, see me on Thursday afternoon, whatever the fock that means. The second and third calls were from Sorcha, who said she needed to speak to me about something and it was totally urgent and I feel a little bit bad for focking her around again. The fourth call was at ten o'clock last night and it was someone – again – playing 'Short Dick Man' down the phone, focking hilarious as it is. Zara and – this girl's a fool for love – Alyson, both phoned to say they saw *The Irish Times* on Saturday and they both wondered if I was alroysh and if I needed someone to talk to, blah blah blah.

I meet the goys at Blackrock Dorsh station and we're having the crack. Oisinn and Simon are on the other side of the platform, chatting up these two birds from Pill Hill, or *pretending* to, because they're both mingers and the goys are, like, totally ripping the piss out of them, Oisinn's giving it, 'This is the time of year when we turn our attention to who we're bringing to the debs. And I want you girls to know, you're candidates.' Of course the two birds are gagging for them, roysh, and we're all giving it, 'WE WILL, WE WILL ROCK YOU ...' across the platform, totally ripping the piss as well.

Of course the goys end up nearly missing the Dorsh, roysh, because they're so, I don't know, engrossed, if that's the right word, in talking to the two skobes that they don't notice the train coming and they have to peg it up the steps and over the bridge and they make it just before the doors close. It's, like, high-fives all round. Oisinn goes, 'I swear to God that girl was wearing *Blue Stratos*,' and we all break our holes laughing. Then it's, like, high-fives all around, roysh, and then of course the goys break into a chorus of, 'WE'VE GOT ROSS O'CARROLL-KELLY ON OUR TEAM, WE'VE GOT THE BEST TEAM IN THE LAND,' and this old goy, roysh, who gets on at Sandycove, he turns around and he goes, 'Excuse me. There are other people on this train. Would you mind keeping your voices down?' and quick as a flash, roysh, I'm like, 'Fock off back to Jurassic Pork,' and Simon calls him an old fort and when the train stops at Dalkey, roysh, the goy gets out and goes up to have a word with the driver, who obviously couldn't give two focks, roysh, because the next thing we know the train is moving off and the old tosser is just left standing on the platform, looking totally pissed off, and we're all there giving him the finger through the window, going, 'Yyyeeeaaahhh!'

We stop at Killiney, roysh, and JP jumps up all of a sudden and goes, 'Hey, Ross. There's Sorcha,' and I look over the other side of the platform and she's there with Aoife and they're obviously heading into town. Oisinn says it must be colder than he thought because Aoife's seems to be wearing two jumpers around her waist instead of her usual one, and we all crack up of course, but then we stop, roysh, because we remember that Fionn broke up with her not so long ago and Oisinn turns around to him and goes, 'Hey, no offence, man,' and Fionn pushes his glasses up on his nose and goes, 'Hey, it's cool.' They don't notice us looking at them for ages, roysh. Sorcha takes off her scrunchy, shakes her hair loose, smoothes it back into a ponytail, puts it back in the scrunchy, then pulls four or five stands of hair loose. Aoife looks pretty crap, it has to be said. She's lost basically shitloads of weight. She has a bottle of Evian in her hand and she storts scanning our train to see if she knows anyone on it. When she cops us, roysh, she waves and then she, like, nudges Sorcha and I can see her mouth the words, 'OH! MY! GOD! there's Ross,' and Sorcha, who's putting on lip balm, sort of, like, squints her eyes and when she cops me she makes the shape of a phone with her hand, as if to say, 'Ring me,' and she looks majorly pissed off, which is no surprise I suppose because, despite my promise that this time things would be different, I haven't returned any of her calls since the night we were together at the Orts Ball, and all the goys are giving it, 'Whoa! Who's in the bad books?' and then they're going, 'Leg-end! Leg-end! Leg-end!'

We get off the Dorsh in Bray, roysh, and we're waiting for the 184 to Greystones when all of a sudden this bird comes over to us – a Virgin on the Rocks – and she walks straight up to JP and goes, 'You're JP Conroy, aren't you?' and JP's there, 'The one and only. You're Lisa, right?' but she doesn't answer, roysh, just goes, 'You've been telling people you were with me,' looking seriously focked off. JP's there, 'Shurley shome mishtake,' trying to, like, defuse the situation with a bit of Sean Connery. She's having none of it. She goes, 'You told Esme McConville's brother that you were with me two weeks ago in the rugby club and that I've been gagging for you for ages,' and JP, roysh, he doesn't handle the situation very well, he ends up going, 'You HAVE been gagging for me for ages,' and she just, like, flips the lid, calls him an orsehole and, like, slaps him across the face. Then she storms off, roysh, and we're all there cracking our shits laughing, and JP is as well, fair focks to him. He's going, 'The girl's got it bad for me.'

One side of his face is still red when we get on the bus.

XXX

I text Erika, roysh, and it's like, **Wud u lik 2go4 a drnk?**

And she's there,

I'd rather be boiled alive in my own spit.

Which I take as a no.

XXX

I'm having a few cans in JP's gaff the other night and we're both bored, roysh, and I still haven't heard from this French one – Fionn probably told her I was a focking transvestite in that letter, for all I know – so I end up sort of, like, taking it out on him by ringing his gaff. I know he's not home, roysh, because he said he was going back to school to study after training, so I ring his number and his old man answers and I put on this, like, voice and I'm going, 'Hello. Am I speaking with Fionn's father?' and he's like, 'You most certainly are. And if it's about that book on the nitrogen cycle, it's my fault. He asked me to return it today and I just pure clear forgot. And what, pray tell, is the fine?'

I have to put my hand over my focking mouth so he doesn't hear me laughing. He's like, 'Hello? Is anyone there?' I'm going, 'Hello, sorry. No, I'm not calling from the library. I'm the father of, em, Jeff, who's Fionn's, shall we say, friend. And not to put too fine a point on it, I'm a bit worried.' JP's in the kitchen, listening in on the other line. Fionn's old man goes, 'Worried?' and I go, 'I'm worried, yes, that they might be a little bit more than friends, if you get my vibe.' He just goes, 'Oh, wonderful. That's great news. Andrea, come and hear.' I'm like, 'Did you say great news? They both disappear up to Jeff's bedroom at six o'clock every night and they stay up there for hours on end and you think that's wonderful?'

He goes, 'It's another world, I know. Andrea and I are really embracing it. The Internet's a wonderful resource. All sorts of sites that would open your eyes.' I'm there, 'But do you not think this kind of behaviour is wrong?' and he's like, 'Only according to social conventions.' I'm laying it on good and proper now. I go, 'Just because you don't mind your son going to hell,' and he turns around, roysh – real snotty now – and he goes, 'Do NOT quote the Bible at me. Our gay son is a gift from God! Good day to *you*, sir,' and he hangs up and I swear to God, roysh, me and JP laugh for the next three hours.

XXX

I finally get this letter back from Clementine, roysh, and it's all,

> Dear Ross,
>
> It was very pleasure to receiving your letter, the photograph of you in your rugby clothes and as well the newspaper writings about some of your matches. You must to be a very excellent player at rugby if it is to believed what the man Tony Ward writes about you.
>
> I am eighteen years of old also and I am in school also and will to do my last year exams in the summer times. My hobbies are to play the racquetball, to do the drawing, to dance, to collect the fancy paper and to play the clarinet. Also I like very much the music of George Michael. And I like too to meet the new people.
>
> It is with my mother and my father that I live in an apartment in Paris and I have two sisters which are Marie-France et Claudette. They are working at being the solicitors. When I am completed, I like very much to do the

fashion designing. I like very much to work for Calvin
Klein, but it is a dream!

I like very much also to go to Ireland to visit you. You ap-
pear like a very nice boy and I think something nice can
happen for us. I would like very much to come to Ireland
and get to know you very nice, you understand?

Write again to me in a very soon time. It is nice to be getting the letters.

Love, Clementine x x x

So of course I hop in the old dear's cor and I'm straight down to
Fionn's gaff, roysh, to find out my next move, him knowing more
about the French and what they're into than me. I ring the bell and it's
Ned Flanders who answers the door and he's going, 'Well lookie here,
it's Ross. Hey, Andrea, Ross has come to visit. Wonderful,' and it's, like,
hooray, get out the focking trumpets. So I'm brought into the kitchen
and I'm asked if I'd like a glass of pomegranate juice, whatever the fock
that is, and I say no and then Fionn's old dear sort of, like, winks at me,
and she goes, 'No announcement yet,' and his old man's there, putting
on the kettle, going, 'Give him time, Andrea.'

And she goes, 'It's not like there haven't been ... signs. Shall I show
him, darling?' and the old man's there, 'Yes, but *be* careful. He'll be
down those stairs any minute.' She goes to the kitchen door and looks
up the stairs, roysh, and then closes the door, pegs it across the
kitchen and opens this drawer. She goes, 'Lots of things have been arriving for him in the post. And we've found other *things* lying around
his room. There's been a lot of magazines. Lifestyle tips and all the

different positions these people can *do it* in. And the various toys. All very educational.'

The old man goes, 'I've told her she shouldn't be nosing around in there but she insists,' and she's like, 'Ewan, I'm taking an interest in my son. Anyway, Ross, the other day I was rummaging around in his sock drawer when I found this,' and she drops this brochure for the Mazda MX5 onto the breakfast counter. I'd completely forgotten I'd slipped it in there. Don't know how I kept a straight face, roysh, but I just go, 'It's worse than we thought,' and the next thing we hear Fionn coming down the stairs, roysh, so she lashes it back in the drawer and we crack on that we were talking about something else.

Fionn goes, 'Heard you coming in, Ross. Sorry, I was—' and quick as a flash I'm there, 'Trying to decide what to wear?' but it goes totally over his head. I'm there, 'I got a letter back from this French exchange hotty. Want you to have a look at it,' and we excuse ourselves from the proud parents and go into the sitting-room. I pull out the letter, roysh, open it up and hand it to Fionn. I'm like, 'Tell me what she's saying.' He sits down with it, roysh, reads about two lines, turns it over, then looks at the front again and goes, 'Ross, this is in English,' and I'm like, 'No shit, Sherlock.' He goes, 'Well, you can see what she's saying yourself. She likes racquetball and George Michael and ...' I'm there, 'Yeah, but I thought you'd be able to read between the lines, pick up the vibes. These French women are dirty bitches,' and he goes, 'Ross, there are no *doubles entendres* in this. She's interested in you. End of story. Why don't you write another letter to her?'

And I whip a pen and a piece of paper out of the pocket of my Henri Lloyd and I go, 'No, why don't YOU write another letter to her? You know what they're after, these French girls.' He sits there thinking for a few seconds, tapping the pen off the side of his glasses, then he goes, 'Romance. Okay, she's coming to Ireland to practice her English for her summer exams. But the possibility of falling in love gives it an extra *frisson*.' Him and his big words. He goes, 'You're going to romance this girl,' and he storts writing. I'm there 'Make sure she knows she's on for it,' and he's like, 'Leave the phraseology to me, Ross. You want to tell her that when you wake up in the morning her photograph illuminates your day. *Je voudrais coucher avec ta mère et ton père et tes soeurs*. And what about a bit of *Je voudrais caresser tes jambes*.' I'm there, 'What's that? No, keep writing,' and he goes, 'It means, I have never felt this way before. Is it really possible to fall in love with an image? *J'adore les grands hommes*. I am counting the days until you arrive. *Je voudrais manger ton visage*.

He finishes it, roysh, sticks it in an envelope and gives it to me to post. Oh yes, some hot French loving is winging my way.

XXX

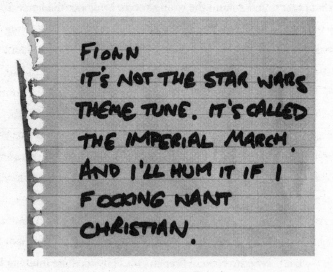

XXX

If the truth be told, roysh, I'm a little bit worried about my kicking so I stay behind for an extra half an hour after lunch to practice, just booting ball after ball between the posts from different angles. Anyway, roysh, where all of this is going is that I ended up being half an hour late for, like, double History, roysh, and it has to be said that tosser Crabtree's not exactly a happy camper when I decide to, like, show my face. The first thing he says to me, roysh, real sarcastic as well, he goes, 'You're late,' and of course I'm there, 'No shit, Sherlock,' giving him the same amount of attitude back. Everyone breaks their shites laughing. I sit down, roysh, and check in my bag to see do I even have my History book with me. He's not going to let it go though. He's there, 'Have you an explanation, boy. One you would care to share with me and perhaps your little band of cheerleaders down there in the back row?' I just, like, shrug my shoulders and I go, 'I was practicing my kicking,' trying my best to keep my cool with the focker. He goes, 'And too busy, no doubt, to consider more cerebral matters, such as the causes of the First World War, yes?' I'm there, 'What are you going on about?' He goes, 'You were to have learned this off by rote for today, boy.' I don't like the way he says that word. It's sort of, like, *boy*. He goes, 'What were the causes of the First World War?'

I sort of, like, lean back on the chair, roysh, with just the two back legs on the ground, which I know he hates, and I go, 'I don't think you understand. I'm on the S,' but he's straight down my throat, roysh, going, 'I don't care if you're the grand wizard in the Jessop County Clavern of the White Knights of the Ku Klux Klan. Answer the question.' I shrug my shoulders again, roysh, and I go, 'Well, I wouldn't exactly say Hitler helped,' and everyone in the class cracks their holes laughing and

I actually think they're laughing *with* me until Crabtree goes at the top of his voice, 'WRONG WAR, YOU IMBECILE!' and I'm looking at him thinking, You are SO totalled for that. He goes, 'That's the problem with you and your rugby friends. Too fixated on what's between your legs and no interest at all in what's between your ears. You are *still* the only one in the class who hasn't presented to me details of your special topic, so I have no other option but to choose one for you.' I'm just there, 'Enjoy the moment, orsehole.' He goes, 'The life and times of Gavrilo Princip. You know who Gavrilo Princip is, I presume?' and I go, 'I'm not focking stupid,' even though I haven't a bog and I'm, like, shitting it in case he calls my bluff and asks me who she is. Then it turns out to be a bloke. He goes, 'The Life and Times of Gavrilo Princip. Who was he? Where did he come from? His involvement with the Ujedinjenje ili Smrt and the opposition movement to Austro-Hungarian rule in the Balkans. The events, if any, that informed his political view in the lead-up to the events in Sarajevo in June 1914 as the great colonial powers of the late nineteenth and early twentieth century slid inexorably towards war. I want a full and detailed proposal on my desk at nine o'clock – no, seven-thirty – in the morning, also listing five reasons, based on European history, why you considered that this topic merited special study and naming all the sources you intend to consult for your information. That's all.'

That's all? No *please* or *thank you* or anything, but I don't pull him up on it, roysh, I'm there just staring at him, with that big focking smug look on his face, and I'm thinking, Oh my God, you are SO sacked it's not funny.

So when the class is over, roysh, I head up to Fehily's study and I tell him pretty much what happened and he goes totally ballistic. He's there, 'Do you mean to tell me that a member of the Castlerock College Senior Cup team was treated disdainfully by a member of the teaching staff?' I go, 'That's exactly what happened, Father,' and he's there, 'Well, I am NOT prepared to stand by and allow this to happen in MY school,' and he storms off, roysh, down to the staffroom and, according to a couple of fifth years who happened to be standing outside – one of them being a cousin of Fionn's – Crabtree ends up getting the balls chewed off him, we're talking the bollocking of a lifetime here. Half an hour later, roysh, I'm called out of Maths and Fehily turns around to me and goes, 'How far do you want to push this, Ross?' I'm there, 'What do you mean?' and he goes, 'Well, to my mind this is an open-and-shut case of gross misconduct. I can dismiss him immediately or suspend him pending a disciplinary hearing, or I can ...' and I'm there, 'No, it's cool. A simple apology from him will do. In front of the rest of the class, of course.' He goes, 'Oh, you'll get your apology, make no mistake about that. I'm just so very sorry it happened. We can't have members of our Senior Cup team made to look small by the hired hands. In the Year of the Eagle, of all years!'

CHAPTER FOUR
'Refuses to listen'

I'm walking down the corridor, roysh, and I cop this poster on the wall outside the drama room and it's only then, roysh, that I realise what Joanna meant when she said in her message that she'd see me Thursday afternoon. Turns out we're doing a production of *My Fair Lady* with the old Whores on the Shore and they're actually coming to the school today for, like, auditions. Of course straight away I'm going, 'Oh my God, I am SO going to rip the piss out of this.' I try to drum up a bit of crew for it, roysh, but Simon and Oisinn say they're going to the gym and Fionn's going to the library, the steamer, though JP and Christian are John B – JP because he wants to get talking to Gemma, who's, like, head girl and Christian because he fancies the orse off this bird Diardra, who's captain of the hockey team. He was with her once in the rugby club.

So two-thirty arrives, roysh, and everyone's packed into the assembly hall. Me and the goys wait upstairs in the library to see them arrive. Picture the scene, roysh, we're talking me, Christian and JP, each of us with a pair of binoculars, which I pegged home to get at lunchtime, and we're standing up on a table, looking out the window, watching them get out of their bus, pointing out the ones we've been with, or the ones we could have if we'd basically wanted them. JP goes, 'Diardra Lewsey. Nice rack. My compliments on your choice, Christian,' and Christian's there, 'Thank you, Obi Wan.' I'm there, 'Look at that goys. Four-in-a-row. Alicia what's-her-name, Carol Bennett, Ann Marie Taylor and that bird who goes to the School of Music. Plays the clarinet. I've had all four of them,' and JP's there, 'That's an accumulator,' and I crack up laughing and I high-five the dude. Then he goes, 'Christian, is that that bird you were with at Emma McNally's eighteenth?' and he's there, 'I think it is.' JP's there, 'She's a lot easier on the eye now, no offence to you, of course,' and I go, 'That's got to be fake tan,' and Christian goes, 'No, she goes to the Seychelles for a week with her old pair in January every year.'

I spot Gemma, roysh, a total lasher, no arguments there, a little bit like Angelina Jolie if you asked me to describe her, and I wouldn't mind bailing in there myself if JP wasn't a mate. He goes, 'Look at her, Ross. Look at the way she holds herself. Beautiful, and she knows it,' and then he storts going, 'Go girl, go girl ...' The two boys, roysh, it's like I've taught them fock-all over the years, they both hop down off the table and stort pegging it for the door and I call them back and I'm there, 'What's the focking rush?' JP goes, 'What's the rush? It's feeding time, Ross,' and I'm there, 'Goys, you must have learned something from the maestro here over the years. You don't want to look too Roy, do you?' and the goys – focking clueless, it has to be said – are there just looking at me. I go, 'Give it ten minutes. Let everyone sit down and get comfortable. Then – BANG! – we walk in. More impact.'

Which is exactly what happens, roysh. Ten minutes into the auditions, everything's really quiet, roysh – because they're basically knobs, the kind of people who go to these things – and all of sudden the doors swing open and in walk our three heroes, giving it loads, and we are talking totally here. The place is focking jammers and you can see all the birds, roysh, looking around as if to say, 'OH! MY! GOD! Who are they?' except they know who we are, roysh, because to them, being with a member of the Castlerock College Senior Cup team is even more important than the Leaving. They know it and we know it.

Old Battleaxe Kennealy, the drama teacher, she sees the three studs arriving, roysh, and she goes, 'Glad you lads could make it. Nice to see some of our boys are interested in the dramatic arts,' ripping the piss really, she's sound like that. All of the girls are cracking up laughing, roysh, and all of the blokes – nerds and benders most of them, Fionn will be raging he missed it – they're bulling, roysh, because suddenly the chances of them scoring any of the old Collars Up Knickers Down brigade have, like, gone out the window. Ms Kennealy – I actually think she has a thing for me – she tells us to come up and sit in the front row, which we don't mind, roysh, and we walk up, throwing serious shapes, like three male models on the focking catwalk, every set of mince pies in the place glued to us.

So anyway, roysh, Ms Kennealy asks for volunteers to, like, sing a scale and then to sing 'Amazing Grace' while she accompanies them on the piano, I suppose just to sort out the ones who actually want to be in the musical from those who are here to scope the scenario. So after a few minutes, roysh, Christian turns around to me and he goes, 'Ross, there's that bird you were with. What was her name ... Joanna?' I'm looking around me. He goes, 'Nine o'clock. Second row back, third from the left. She's wearing a pink scorf,' and I turn around, very subtly of course, and I go, 'I remember her. She's practically stalking me. Rings my phone all the time. Text messages, the lot.' JP goes,

'Bunny-boiler, huh? I thought you said she looks like Chloë out of 'Home and Away',' and I'm there, 'She does,' waiting for the punchline of course and JP turns around, has another look and goes, 'She looks more like focking Alf,' and he cracks up laughing to himself.

Of course Ms Kennealy knows the three boys in the front row are basically pulling the orse out of the whole thing, so she turns around to us, roysh, and she's there, 'Up you come, boys,' and we're there looking at each other going, '*Hello?*' She goes, 'Let's hear what sweet voices you have. Come on, up.' The goys are giving it, 'Oh my God, get me out of here,' but I turn around to them and I'm like, 'What are you, a pair of wusses? This'll be SOME crack.' So up we go, roysh – all the birds giving it loads, clapping, cheering, the whole bit – and Kennealy's there, 'Choose a song, boys. I'll accompany you on the piano.' Of course, JP, roysh, he's well up for it now. He's giving it, '*Laaahhh ...*' as if he's trying to find the right note and she's going, '*Laaahhh ...*' with him and whacking various, I don't know, keys on the piano to try to, like, find the note he's singing. After, like, half a minute of *laaahhhing*, JP all of a sudden breaks into, '*You can reach, but you can't grab it,*' and of course that's me and Christian's cue. We're going, '*You can't hold it, control it, you can't bag it.*' And we sing the whole of 'Discothèque', roysh, me looking straight at Ms Kennealy when we sing the line, '*You just can't get enough of that lovie dovie stuff*', to give her a thrill more than anything else, wouldn't say she gets much, like, action.

Of course, we go down like – what is it Oisinn says? – a Northside bird in a barrel full of mickeys. *But tonight, tonight, tonight. BOOM CHA. BOOM CHA. DISCOTHÈQUE.*' The whole crowd goes ballistic and I turn to JP and I go, 'We can have anyone we want now,' and JP nods and goes, 'It's an all-night buffet, goys.' We take a bow and stroll back to our seats and even Ms Kennealy's clapping and going, 'Excellent. Excellent. You might not be what we're looking for for *My Fair Lady*, but I'll see if I can think of a role for you ...'

Now it's just a case of sitting back and waiting for the bullshit to end. Up on the stage, roysh, it's all lah-de-dah, the whole song-and-dance routine, and after about an hour or so, they've found twenty or thirty people knobby enough to want to be in it. So when it's all over, roysh, me and the two boys stort working the hall, moving from group of girls to group of girls, like we're holding auditions of our own. Me and Christian end up talking to these two birds, one of which – Jill – has been giving him the once-over all afternoon. She's actually a total honey, the absolute spit of Janeane Garafalo. Her mate, roysh, I didn't think she was the Fred West when I saw her first, but up close she has a boat race like Gabrielle Anwar, and I tell her my name's Ross and she goes, 'I know,' and I'm there, 'Do *you* have a name?' and she goes, 'OH MY GOD! I am SO embarrassed. It's Evy. Short for, like, Evelyn?' and I'm there, 'It's an amazing name,' really laying it on thick. I'm sort of, like, eavesdropping on Christian's conversation as well, roysh, making sure he doesn't fock things up by saying 'May the Force be with you' in the first ten seconds, but the goy is playing it like Steve Silvermint for once. Jill's going, 'I saw your picture in *The Irish Times* last week,' because they'd a shot of him scoring our first try. She's there, 'I don't know anything about the rules of the game, but I know it was supposed to be a totally amazing try as well,' and I'm thinking, Don't say, 'Thanks, Princess,' but he doesn't, roysh, he just goes, 'I wish I'd had somebody to dedicate it to,' and the poor girl's knees nearly go from under her, the sap.

Evy's giving me loads at the same time, roysh, it's all, 'You go to the

Institute on a Friday night, don't you?' and, 'Do you not remember being introduced to me one night in Annabel's,' really coming on to me and eventually, roysh, totally out of the blue she goes, 'You were with Joanna Mulhall, weren't you?' and I'm there, 'Word gets out fast,' and she's like, 'Only because she told, like, the whole world.' Jill's ears have pricked up at this. Evy goes, 'I'm not being, like, a bitch or anything, but nobody could believe it when they heard you were actually *with* that girl. She's really nice and everything, but she's a bit of a–' Jill butts in, roysh, and she goes, 'A bit of a Wendel.' I'm there, 'A what?' and Evy makes an L shape with her thumb and, like, forefinger and she goes, 'LO-SER!' and Jill goes, 'Careful, Evy. She's over there.'

I turn around, roysh, and there she is, sort of, like, hanging around the outskirts, like a stale smell. Of course I make the mistake of making eye contact with her, which she takes as her cue to come over. She's there, 'Hi,' and the two girls are going, 'Hi, Joanna,' and Evy's giving it, 'OH! MY! GOD! Your hair is SO amazing,' even though she's actually ripping the piss, roysh, and when she's not looking Evy does that L thing behind her back again, which I have to admit is pretty funny.

Joanna says she is SO sorry we've been, like, missing each other lately and she says I never seem to have my mobile switched on, unless I'm screening calls, which is understandable because OH! MY! GOD! she's been pretty much doing the same thing herself, what with helping to organise the Debs and the whole drama over her CAO application and then netball as well. I'm there, '*What*ever,' and I can hear Evy and Jill sniggering, roysh. She goes, 'Em, I was wondering, if you're not doing anything, would you like to come out on Saturday night? It's my eighteenth and a few of us are ...' Straight away, roysh, I'm there, 'No,' and Evy actually laughs out loud, being a total bitch, which I like. But

Joanna, roysh, she cracks on she doesn't hear it and she tries to get out with her, like, dignity intact, if that's the right word. She goes, 'I understand. You're probably trying to focus on your game and ...' but I'm like, 'No, YOU don't understand. I was with you ONCE. A focking beer goggles job. I've no interest in you. You're a focking sap. I've no interest. Now fock off,' and she just, like, bursts into tears, roysh, and runs out of the place and one of her friends runs out after her and Evy goes, 'Well, someone had to tell the silly little girl,' and Jill's there, 'What a total retord,' but Christian doesn't look happy with me, roysh, it's like he thinks I went too far.

Anyway, we head off to find JP, roysh, and we spend the next half an hour working the room, just basically collecting mobile numbers off birds and then Jill and Evy come up to us and say they're heading off and me and Christian, roysh, we ask them if they're, like, doing anything later on, if they maybe fancy going for a few scoops, nothing too mad. Jill says she has no clothes with her and there's no way she's going all the way out to, like, Greystones and then heading back into town, but Evy says they can go to her gaff in Blackrock and she can borrow clothes from her and Jill goes, 'Cool. As long as it's your black Prada shirt,' and Evy goes, 'Eh, no,' and the two of them crack up laughing. Evy says she is SO going to wear that pink camisole top she got from Warehouse and then she phones her old dear, roysh, and asks her to come and collect them. Me and Christian tell them we'll see them later, and as we're heading off I hear Evy say to Jill that she doesn't want to be a bitch or anything, but she cannot BELIEVE how much weight Cliona Curran has put on.

XXX

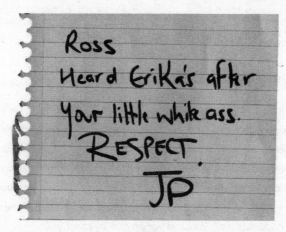

Ross
Heard Erika's after
your little white ass.
RESPECT.
JP

✗✗✗

I walk into History, we're talking ten minutes late, and Crabtree's going, 'What we'll deal with today is the reaction in the Dáil and in the country to the Anglo-Irish Treaty from the moment of its signing on the sixth of December 1921 right up to the outbreak of the Civil War.' He sees me, roysh, and he goes, 'Oh hello, Ross. Great to see you. Sit anywhere you like,' and I just, like, saunter down the back of the class, roysh, flop down on a chair and put my feet up on the desk. He cops this but knows better than to say anything. He goes, 'Em, now, in yesterday's class we discussed the controversial Oath of Allegiance,' and I'm like, 'Em, excuse me,' and he stops talking and he looks at me and I go, 'I think you've got something you'd like to say to me?' He goes, 'Em, yes, class, I'd just like to, em, apologise to Ross for the way I spoke to him here in class a couple of days ago. It was wrong of me and I'm, em, sorry.' I'm there, 'Louder,' and he's like, 'SORRY,' and then I go, 'Proceed.'

✗✗✗

I get another letter from Clementine and it's pretty clear, roysh, that she's gagging for me.

> **Dear Ross,**
>
> I received your letter just today and it make me very, very happy. I am love you too. I am think about you every time and it make me happy that I come to Ireland and meet with you. I will go to Ireland on 21 March arriving at six o'clock in the evening times. Is it possible please for you to meet with me at the airport and car me to your home? I hope it is. I am excited very much to meet you.
>
> **A lot of love, Clementine x x x**

I show it to Fionn down the back of, like, Maths and he writes this amazing reply, full of all this romantic shit, and it's like, '*Oui, je t'aime – oh oui, je t'aime. Moi non plus. Oh, mon amour. Comme la vague irrésolue. Je vais, je vais et je viens.*' Meaning, 'You are the first thing I think about in the morning and the last thing I think about at night.' Then it's, '*Entre tes reins. Je vais et je viens, entre tes reins et je me retiens. Je t'aime, je t'aime. Oh oui, je t'aime. Moi non plus, oh mon amour,*' which is obviously, 'I am counting the days until you come to Ireland. Thinking about you makes my mind race and my hort beat faster. You are my world. If you're passing through duty free on the way over, would you grab a couple of slabs of Brie for my mate Fionn's old dear.' Then it's, '*L'amour physique est sans issue. Je vais, je vais et je viens, entres tes reins. Je vais et je viens, je me retiens, non! Maintenant viens ...*' which is basically, 'I'll see you at the airport on March twenty-first.'

After class, roysh, I think about asking Fionn the French for, 'Make

sure to bring some sexy lingerie,' but it'd probably spoil the whole romantic vibe.

XXX

I wouldn't have bothered sitting my driving test at all, roysh, except the
old man said he'd buy me a black Golf GTI with alloys – we're talking
the ultimate babe magnet here – if I managed to get my full licence, and
of course Oisinn comes up with the bright idea, roysh, for me to do it in
some bogger county where it's supposed to be, like, easier to pass. So
anyway, roysh, I ended up applying to do it in Wicklow, of all places,
and there was no way I was waiting twelve months for it to come up, so
I got Dick Features to write me a letter saying I worked for him and
needed the cor for my job, bullshit, bullshit, bullshit.

So the day of the test, roysh, all the goys decide to come down to
Wicklow with me, supposedly to offer moral support, but basically to
go on the lash down in the focking wilds and score some complete ran-
domers. We check into The Grand in Wicklow Town, roysh, and the
goys are already on the beers when I head out for the test at, like, one
o'clock and they're all giving it, 'Kick ass, Ross,' and, 'We'll have one
ready for you when you get back,' which is all, like, positive stuff to
hear.

So there I am, sitting in the test centre in the town – had my inocula-
tions and everything – and I'm waiting for my name to be called, and
eventually this old fort comes out, roysh, and tells me to follow him
into this little, like, room, where he asks to see my provisional licence
and then storts asking me these totally dumb-ass questions. He's there,
'How do you know when you are approaching a pedestrian crossing at
night?' and I'm going, 'You just, like, keep your eyes open for, like, people,' and I can tell he doesn't like that. They don't like people who make

it basically sound simple because of course that does them out of a job. He goes, 'No, no, what I'm asking you is how would you know you are approaching one when it's dark,' and I'm there, 'I've already answered your question. Anyway, we're in the middle of Bogland. How many pedestrian crossings do you see in an average day down here?'

He just, like, stares me out of it, roysh, like he's trying to make out whether I'm serious or not, then he tells me to follow him outside and we get into my cor – well, the old man's Lexus – and he tells me to drive the way I normally would, which means he definitely has it in for me and wants me to fail. Before I put the key in, like, the ignition, I ask one question, roysh, and the dude flies off the handle. I'm like, 'Do you mind if I put a few sounds on?' and he goes, 'WILL YOU PLEASE JUST START THE CAR!' and I'm thinking, I am SO going to report this focker if he fails me.

We've been driving for, like, ten minutes, roysh, and I have to say I'm doing fairly alroysh until he asks me to do a turnaround on this, like, country lane. I'm there, 'HELLO? It's a bit narrow, isn't it?' and he's going, 'Please proceed with the manoeuvre.' A lot of these goys see you're driving a cor that's going to attract birds and they're jealous, roysh, and they want to keep you off the roads, which is portly the reason I lose the rag with him then. I'm there, 'Are you deaf or something? I said it's too narrow.' He goes, 'What would you do if you were in a situation where you HAD to turn around on this road?' and I'm there, 'I'd do what any focking normal person would do. I'd find, like, a driveway or something to turn into,' but he just can't leave it, roysh, he's going, 'What if there was no driveway? What if there were roadworks here and the road ahead was closed? What would you do then?' It's enough basically to wreck anyone's head so eventually I lose the rag with him and go, 'How often do you think I come down here? I'm only doing the test here be- cause it's supposed to be a piece of piss. That was according to Oisinn. He's totalled when I see him.'

I decide to let it rest then, roysh, and put the whole thing behind me and I have to say I end up actually driving really well for the next, like, fifteen minutes. We're on the way back to the test centre, roysh, when my mobile rings and it's, like, JP. From the noise in the background, the goys are already half horrendufied. I'm there, 'Yo, JP. Not a good time, my man,' and he's like, 'You're still doing it, then?' and I'm there, 'A- ffirmative.' He's like, 'How goes it?' and I'm there, 'Reasonably confi- dent,' and he goes, 'I'll get the borman to stick a pint of Ken on for you. Here, before I go, you will never guess who Oisinn was with in the Sugar Club the other night?' and I hear this big, like, roar from the goys. He goes, 'Esme. As in Esme O'Halloran?' and I'm like, 'As in second year Commerce UCD, plays hockey for Pembroke Esme O'Halloran?' and he goes, 'The self-same,' and I'm like, 'The focker. He knows *I* liked her.'

The next thing, roysh, I stort losing the signal, which is no surprise considering we're in the middle of focking *Deliverance* Country. I'm there, 'Can you hear me? JP, can you hear me?' and I snap the phone shut, roysh, and I turn to the tester and I go, 'Fock, I lost him.' The goy – OH my God, he SO has it in for me – he just goes, 'Will you bloody well concentrate on the road. Do you know how close you came to hit- ting that blue Micra back there?' and straight away I go, 'No way, José. I had plenty of room to overtake him. You better not fail me on that,' but he doesn't answer me.

Back at the test centre, though, he comes straight out with it. He's there, 'The bad news for you is that you haven't been successful,' and

I'm there, 'Was it the Micra, or was it that cow we hit? Because if it was the cow, I have to say I don't think he was badly injured,' but he just blanks me and storts filling in this piece of paper with, like, twenty or thirty things on it that I'm supposed to have done wrong. He hands it to me and I read it and then I tell him he's a tool and walk out.

'The goys are all at the bor when I arrive back. JP goes, 'How the FOCK did you not pass?' and I'm there, 'I don't know. They must have to fail x amount of people per day. It's the only explanation,' and Christian goes, 'Never mind, young Skywalker. Get this into you,' and he puts, like, a pint of Ken in front of me, which I knock back in, like, three gulps, then call up another.

By six o'clock, roysh, I'm as shit-faced as the rest of them and that's when we decide to hit one of the local battle cruisers, which turns out to be like the one out of *Star Wars*, the focking Wookie Bar or whatever it's called, except, as Fionn points out, the clientele in here are even uglier. Of course the whole place just goes silent the second we walk in the door, roysh, everyone stops talking and the music – 'Stand By Your Man', for fock's sake – just stops as though someone, like, pulled the plug on the jukebox. Everyone's just, like, staring at us. The men all look like they want to kick seven shades out of us and the women, if you could call them that, are looking us up and down and they're obviously thinking, Raw meat, happy days.

The state of them, though. The cardinal sin for birds with fat orses is wearing leather trousers, roysh, and let's just say there's a lot of focking cardinal sinners in there. How some of them managed to squeeze into them in the first place is, like, a mystery to me. They must, like, butter their legs or something.

I'm not making this up, roysh, but there's an actual bloke dressed up like a focking cowboy. He's got, like, a Stetson on and cowboy boots with actual spurs on them. And tight jeans. Anyone who's not wearing leather trousers is wearing tight jeans.

JP shouts, 'Five pints of your finest Heineken, innkeeper,' and the borman just, like, stares at him, roysh, like he's trying to make up his mind whether he should serve him or shoot him. Then he storts, like, pulling the pints and that's taken as a sign that we've been accepted, the music comes back on and everyone storts, like, talking again.

The Wicklow accent's focked-up, sort of goes up and down. 'So *what* has *yiz* down *in* Wickli?' this voice beside me goes. I stare at the person it comes from, looking for an Adam's apple, and there isn't one, roysh, so I take it for granted that it's a woman but with a moustache. I'm like, 'Sitting my driving test. Oisinn over there said it was easier to pass if you sit it in Bogsville. Full of shit, he is.'

I take a look over my shoulder, roysh, and three or four of the *law-culs* have taken Fionn's glasses off him and they're examining them like, I don't know, a bunch of aliens who've dropped out of space and have never seen a pair of glasses before. One of them goes, 'What *do* you *need* them *for?*' and Fionn goes, 'Reading, for storters,' and the four of them repeat the word and then, like, laugh and one of them goes, 'It's *reading* now, is *it?*'

Then I hear JP shouting, 'THE BREADLINE!' and I'm suddenly thinking there's no way we're getting out of here alive.

I go to get the round in, roysh, and I can feel someone lifting up the back of my Henri Lloyd sailing jacket, and of course at first I'm thinking some bogger's trying to, like, pickpocket me. But I turn around, roysh, and the bird with the moustache goes, 'Sorry, *just* having *a* look *at* your *arse*. It's *not* bad, *Sally,*' and suddenly there's this other bird behind me having a scope.

I'm probably the soberest out of the lot of us, roysh, so it falls to me to tell the goys that we're in serious danger of being killed here, but Christian is, like, locked in conversation behind me with these two guys who look like they're out of some American trailer pork and they're finding out the very subtle differences between the regular TIE fighter and Vader's model. Oisinn is – wait for it! – wearing the face off quite possibly the most hideous-looking bird in Wicklow, and that's saying something given the competition. Fionn is still trying to persuade his new mates to give him his glasses back and JP is raising a toast with a couple more locals who he's got shouting, 'THE BREADLINE!' with him, not realising they're taking the piss out of themselves.

I turn back and out of the corner of my eye, roysh, I can see the bird with the moustache trying to get her wedding ring off. I look at her and she smiles at me. She has two teeth. Another shout of 'THE BREADLINE!' goes up. Now I am very scared.

XXX

I've got, like, four new messages, roysh. Keeva says she's SO sorry for flipping out in her last message, that I must think she is OHMYGOD! SUCH a psycho and that I probably already have enough on my plate, what with the semi-final coming up, but when it's over maybe we could go for a drink, or to the cinema or something, that *Jerry Maguire* is supposed to be OHMYGOD! SO amazing, and then she says thanks for the advice that night on what song they should do for the graduation and that they've actually decided to do 'One Moment in Time' by, like, Whitney Houston, which wasn't her choice, it was Jade's, as in Rotary Club Jade, who is SUCH a lickorse that Miss Holohan would ACTUALLY take her word over the word of the deputy head girl, we're talking,

HELLO? Sorcha rang twice to say she needs to speak to me urgently and will I get my finger out of my orse and return her calls. And Oisinn rang to say he wants to meet up – as captain of the S – and have a chat about the game against the Gick, which is only, like, ten days away now.

I ring him back, roysh, and we arrange to go for, like, a sauna out in Riverview. His old man's a member. So I hop out of the sack, have a shower and grab a glass of orange juice while I'm deciding what to wear. I go for the old All Blacks jersey, black O'Neill's tracksuit bottoms and the old brown Dubes, but then I'm thinking, roysh, that maybe me and Oisinn will end up hitting town for a few scoops later on and I don't want to have to come back home, so I change into my navy Armani mock turtleneck, my tan G-Star deckpants, Dubes and my navy Henri Lloyd and, not being big-headed or anything, but I look shit-hot.

Meet Oisinn in the place. He high-fives me and we hit the bor, order a couple of Cokes, bit early to go on the batter. He asks me if I heard about Aoife, roysh, and I'm there, 'No,' and he says she totally flipped out in the rugby club on Friday night, storted going totally ballistic, telling Fionn he was this, that and the other. I'm there, 'That girl has totally lost it since Fionn red-corded her,' and he goes, 'She lost it long ago, Ross. That's why Fionn got rid. She was wrecking his head. She's very focked up. Sorcha's very worried about her.' I'm there, 'Sorcha? Must be why she's ringing me constantly. Needs a shoulder to cry on, if you know what I mean,' and Oisinn laughs and high-fives me and tells me I'm the man, which I have to say I am.

We hit the sauna then and Oisinn gives me this big major pep talk, which I really need at the moment. He reminds me how important the game against the Gick is, not just for the goys, roysh, but for the school and for the school's name, and he tells me how much is riding on my kicking. He goes, 'If you think about the S as one big machine and all of the players as, like, cogs, you are the most vital cog of all. So much depends on those two- and three-pointers, Ross,' and I'm going, 'I know, I know,' and he's like, 'I just wanted to make sure you're focused on your game, that the old pair, teachers, whatever, aren't on your case about, like, homework and whatever?' I'm there, 'Everything's Kool and the Gang, Oisinn,' and he high-fives me.

It's actually good to talk, though. We head off for a couple of frames of snooker then and Oisinn tells me he ended up snipping Wendy O'Neill on Friday night, as in second year Commerce in UCD – as in, 'She looks like Liv Tyler,' – which is a bit of a surprise really because he usually goes for mingers. He goes, 'I couldn't believe what she was wearing, Ross. It was a delightful fusion of vanity rose, fuschia and butterfly orchid – that much is true. But it had another, subtle, almost unspoken quality that captured the mood of a woman who will never accept second best.' I crack on that I know what he's talking about. I'm there, 'Is it going anywhere?' and he's there, 'She asked me to go to the Comm Ball with her, but, I don't know, I don't really want to get involved in that whole heavy relationship scene while we're still in the Cup,' and suddenly I feel guilty about hitting the old sauce so hord in the last few weeks. He has to pick his sister up from horse-riding, roysh, so he tells me he'll see me in school tomorrow and we high-five each other and, like, say our goodbyes.

XXX

I'm hopping into the cor, roysh – the old dear's Micra, SO focking embarrassing – and the next thing my phone rings and like a focking spa I end up answering it without checking my caller ID and who is it only Sorcha, and we're talking MAJOR hostility coming down the line here. It's like, 'Why haven't you returned any of my calls?' and I'm there, 'Chill out, babes,' and she's going, 'WHY HAVEN'T YOU PHONED ME, ROSS?' and I'm sorry, roysh, but this HAD to be said, so I just go, 'In case it's escaped your attention, we're not ACTUALLY going out with each other anymore,' and that storts her off, the old waterworks, and I'm thinking, Uh-oh! The Reds must be playing at home, because she always gets a bit, I don't know, emotional when she's got the painters in. She's there, 'You are SUCH an orsehole, you know that?' and I'm going, 'You don't OWN me, Sorcha. You might WISH you did, but, sadly for you, you don't.'

She goes, 'I told you there was something I needed to talk to you about and it was urgent. And you couldn't even be orsed ringing me back?' and I'm giving it, 'What is it? Make it quick, I've got a date to-night,' which is actually bullshit. She's there, 'HELLO? I CAN'T tell you over the phone. Call out to the house,' and I'm going, 'Like I said, I've something on. I'll call out during the week if I get a chance,' and she to-tally flips then. She goes, 'If you're not here by seven o'clock tonight, Ross, I'll say what I have to say to you in front of everyone in Anna-bel's. I'll make a TOTAL show of you, Ross, and I mean TOTAL,' and I know Sorcha long enough to know she's not bluffing, so I tell her I'll be out to her at about a quarter-past seven, just so she doesn't think she's getting her way completely.

It's only when she hangs up, roysh, that I remember that it's, like, our anniversary tomorrow, which she insists on celebrating, despite the fact that we've broken up, and the reason she's probably so keen to get me up to her gaff is that she's got, like, a present for me and I'm hoping that if it's aftershave it's, like, *Hugo Boss*. On my way home, roysh, I stop off in Stillorgan – mickey *marbh*, as the goys call it – and get a cord for her, then I go back to the gaff, roysh, go to the fridge and grab this massive box of Leonidas that the old dear got from one of the neighbours to thank her for her work with the old Foxrock Against Total Knackers group, the stupid bitch that she is. I tear off the message, write some shite on Sorcha's cord about being the only one who has ever truly loved her, then I go upstairs to get ready. I'm thinking about changing into the black Sonetti sweater that she really likes, roysh, and the Hugo Boss loafers she bought me for my birthday, but I don't want to look like I'm making too much of an effort; I'm pretty sure this one's in the bag.

I stick the cord and the chocolates inside my jacket, roysh, and I'm on the way down the stairs when – FOCKING great – the old pair walk in the door. The old dear goes, 'We've just had afternoon tea with Dermot and Angela,' who are, like, these orsehole friends of theirs from Sandymount. I'm there, 'Like I care.' She doesn't know what to say then so she goes, 'A girl called Suzanne phoned when you were out. Sounds like a lovely girl. Turns out her mother plays tennis in Monkstown. She wants you to ring her back today. After six, she said, because she's got hockey.' I'm just there, '*What*ever,' giving her focking daggers. Lainey focking Keogh.

The old man goes, 'Come on and have some coffee with your old dad and your old mum,' trying to get in with me. He's there, 'We're going to pop open that lovely box of chocolates that Helen bought your mother for her work with that Halting Sites Where They're Appropriate group of ours.' I go, 'The chocolates are gone,' and the old dear's there, 'Gone? Wherever have they gone, Ross?' I'm there, 'I'm giving them to a bird. I'd have bought a box myself but you two are too focking scabby to give me any decent pocket money.' The old man goes, 'A hundred pounds a week should be plenty for ...' but I hold up my hand in front of his face and I go, 'Talk to the hand.' I check the old Lionel in the mirror, roysh, probably needs a cut, and the old man's still moaning, going, 'That's a pity. We were rather looking forward to having one,' and the old dear's there, 'Oh, well,' and it's like, hint-hint, roysh, so to end all arguments I turn around to the old dear and I look her up and down and I go, 'Do you really think you need any more chocolate?' which shuts the two of them up.

Then I go, 'I'm out of here,' and the old man's like, 'Where are you going?' and of course I'm there, 'Sorcha's gaff. Are you focking stupid?' He goes, 'Just wondered how you were getting there,' and I'm like, 'I'm focking swimming, of course. You *are* stupid. I'm taking your car.' He sorts of, like, blows through his lips then and he goes, 'We've been through this before, Kicker. The roads around Killiney are far too narrow for the Lexus. Why not take your mother's?' I just give one of my dagger looks. I'm there, 'The spa-mobile? I am SO not arriving at Sorcha's gaff in a Micra,' and that's, like, my final word on the subject, roysh. He knows I've already taken the keys. He goes, 'Okay, well take the Lexus,' as if he has a focking choice, and he goes, 'but maybe drive it to Dun Laoghaire and perhaps get the train the rest of the way?'

AS IF!

I drive straight out to Sorcha's gaff – this amazing pad on the Vico Road – and her old pair obviously aren't home, roysh, because the only cor in the driveway is Aoife's, this convertible Merc, which is, like, shit-hot. I'm wondering what the fock she's doing in the house, roysh, but I guess she's probably giving Sorcha some last-minute advice on how to play it cool, make him work for whatever he gets, blahdy blahdy blah.

So I ring the bell, roysh, and it's, like, Aoife who answers, still not looking the George Best it has to be said, and I'm wondering is that the pink and white cheesecloth Tommy I bought Sorcha for, like, Christmas. She looks me up and down, roysh, and she goes, 'I don't even know why she's bothering to talk to you. You're an orsehole,' and I'm thinking she's obviously got some kind of problem with me, so I just go, 'Fock you, you fat bitch,' not because she is, roysh – she'd need to walk around in the shower to get wet – but because I know it's what'll really hurt her, roysh, and the second I've said it I regret it, but it's too late to apologise because she, like, pushes me out of the way and jumps into her cor.

I go into the house and Sorcha's, like, standing at the door of the kitchen. I go, 'Hey, Sorcha,' and she holds up a bag of popcorn and goes, 'Aoife forgot these. I'll text her if she doesn't come back.'

I can't help but notice, roysh, that she's wearing a white airtex with the collar up, blue O'Neill's tracksuit bottoms and a small bit of make-up – what is it they say? – thinly but carefully applied. The whole look – the clean white T-shirt, the bare feet and the, I suppose, understated use of foundation – they're the sign of a girl trying to look well without it looking like she's made an effort. Apparently this is, like, a trade secret among birds, but I overheard Sorcha telling Sophie about it in Kiely's one night. I go, 'Are your parents in?' and she doesn't answer. I go, 'Are they out for the night?' wondering if it'll have to be a quickie. She goes, 'They're *actually* in the Cayman Islands. Not that it's, like, any of your business.' I'm there, 'Tribunal shit, I presume? Yeah, my old man's got some loose ends he needs to sort out as well,' still playing it super-cool.

She goes, 'Don't pretend that you actually care,' and I'm there, 'I DO care, Sorcha. I care more than you'll ever know,' which is a bit gay, I know. I go, 'I really miss your friendship,' laying it on the line that I want to keep this, I don't know, plutonic, and making her do some of the spadework for a change. She goes, 'Do NOT go there, Ross. Do not EVEN go there.'

So I go to hand her the cord, roysh, and the chocolates and I go, 'I bought these for you. Happy Anniversary,' but she just turns away, roysh, and she walks out of the room and I'm left there wondering whether she's turned on the old waterworks, so I leave the cord on the table and the Leonidas – it's the big box as well, the ungrateful wagon – and I follow her into the sitting-room to try to offer her a bit of, like, I don't know, comfort. She's sitting on the sofa, roysh, and though the tears haven't arrived yet, they're in the focking post. She turns on MTV and I sit down beside her and she jumps up, roysh, like some total skobe has just porked himself down beside her on the bus with a six-pack of Dutch Gold, and she goes, 'Stay away from me! You make my flesh crawl!' and she moves over to one of the ormchairs and that's when I realise, roysh, that there's more than the usual playing-hard-to-get vibe going down here.

So we end up sitting there for ages, roysh, neither of us saying anything and All Saints come on and it's, like, 'Never Ever', and I'm about to ask her – to break the ice more than anything – which one Robbie Williams is throwing it into, when all of a sudden she goes, 'I heard you were with Evy Stapleton?' I'm there, 'Who?' and she just looks at me as if to say, you know damn well who. I go, 'Who told you?' and she's like, 'Word gets around,' and then she goes, 'So does she, I hear,' and she's all, like, pleased with herself. I go, 'You know her?' and she goes, 'I used to play tennis with her sister. She's an orsehole as well.' I'm there, 'I'm only *seeing* her,' not knowing why I'm suddenly explaining myself to her.

She gives me this sort of, like, pitying smile. She goes, 'You know she was with Gavin Cullen in the PoD on Saturday night?'

I just, like, shrug my shoulders, like, I couldn't GIVE a shit, which I couldn't if the truth be known. Then I go, 'Have you got a problem with me being with her?' knowing she has, roysh. She's there, 'I just can't believe you've, like, lowered your standards, that's all.'

Not being a wanker or anything, roysh, but I've been here for the best part of, like, half an hour, roysh, and there's not a sniff of a score, and I'm getting a bit tired of the whole Frigid Bridget scene so I'm thinking of hitting the road. As, like, a porting shot, roysh, I turn around to her and I go, 'Look, Sorcha. You're gonna have to get over *us*. We ended up being with each other at the Orts Ball – big swinging mickey. It was For One Night Only. There's no additional performances. You need to get over that fact. I can be with whoever I want,' and I'm just wondering, roysh, whether I've been a bit too hord and focked up my chances of a bit of the other, when all of a sudden she turns around to me and she goes, 'I'm pregnant.'

I can feel, like, my whole body go cold, roysh, all of a sudden. I can hear, like, the blood flowing in my ears, and it must be ages before I say anything because by the time I snap out of, like, the trance, Sorcha's changed the channel and now she's watching 'Porty of Five', and finally I go, 'You're WHAT?'

She goes, 'I'm pregnant, Ross. As in, *pregnant?*' I'm there, 'How?' and she's like, 'I know you're on the senior rugby team, Ross, and you probably haven't got your teeth into the biology syllabus yet, but I'm pretty sure you know the basics.' I'm there, 'But you said you were on the Jack and ... on the pill.' She goes, 'I *am* on the pill. But even with the pill, there's still an outside chance.'

I just, like, put my head in my hands and I go, 'Oh MY God, this is SO unfair.' She looks at me, roysh, and she's there, 'It might have been a thousand-to-one shot, but it's happened and it's a fact now.' I keep shaking my head. *Pregnant.* I can't take it in. I go, 'How come you're so, like, calm about it?' and she's there, 'I've had a couple of weeks to come to terms with it.' I go, 'Have you told your olds?' and she's like, 'Not yet.' I'm there, 'Thank fock for that. The fewer people know about this the better.' She looks at me like I'm focking Baghdad and she goes, 'HELLO? I think it's going to become a bit obvious after a while, don't you?' I'm there, 'Hold on. You're not actually thinking of HAVING it? Tell me you're not thinking of having it.' She goes, 'I'm going to have it, Ross. I'm having it.' I don't know what to say. I am SO not ready for this. I go, 'What about college?' and she's like, 'I can defer for a year,' and I'm like, 'Look, Sorcha, have you actually even thought that maybe *I* don't want to have a baby. I'm still only, like, eighteen?' and she's giving it, 'It's MY choice and my mind is made up.'

And of course I end up saying something I shouldn't have, roysh. I go, 'How do you know it's mine anyway?' and she goes totally ballistic, roysh, and we're talking totally here, giving it, 'BECAUSE I DO NOT SLEEP AROUND! BECAUSE I AM NOT SOME ... SLAPPER! I AM NOT EVY STAPLETON! THAT'S HOW I KNOW!' and then I make the mistake of going, 'Hey, take a chill pill,' which doesn't go down well either, it's fair to say, because she ends up slapping me across the face, roysh, and I have to hug her and tell her to, like, calm down and then I remind her that she's got, like, the baby to think about now.

When she stops having an eppo, roysh, I go, 'Whatever you decide, Sorcha, we'll deal with whatever we have to face together,' and she is SO not happy with that. She goes, 'We'll *what?*' and before I get a chance to answer she goes, 'Ross, I'm only telling you this because Aoife said you had a right to know. When this baby's born you're not going to have anything to do with it. I'm going to raise it myself.' I go, 'If that's what you want,' and she's like, 'It is. Now I want you to go.' I'm there, 'I'm not leaving you while you're this upset,' and she loses it again and goes, 'GET OUT OF MY FOCKING HOUSE!' which I do.

My head's, like, totally wrecked as I go out and get into the cor. I stort her up and just, like, drive, not even knowing where the fock I'm going. Sorcha's old pair are going to go spare when they find out, and I'm wondering how I'm going to tell mine.

I'm not even looking at the road at this stage, roysh, and I end up taking this narrow right bend at about, like, forty and at the last minute I notice this, like, Peugeot coming in the opposite direction and I have to, like, swerve to avoid it and I end up smacking into a wall. The goy in the Peugeot doesn't even stop, the tosspot, and I get out to check the damage. I've focking totalled the cor. The whole front of it is, like, wrecked and we are talking totally here. Of course I'm never going to hear the end of this from the old man, the penis.

The next thing this dickhead pulls up in a Ford Mondeo, this old fort who can't keep his nose out of other people's business, and he winds down his window and goes, 'That's some bang you've taken there.' There's focking steam coming from the bonnet. I'm like, 'No shit, Sherlock.' He goes, 'You'd want to be careful on these roads. Very narrow, you see. Probably a bit too narrow for a car like that.'

CHAPTER FIVE
'Academic application non-existent'

My head is focking fried. Just can't come to terms with what Sorcha told me. I'm not ready to be someone's father. Me with, like, a baby? It's like, I don't *think* so. But for some reason, roysh, everywhere I go, there's, like, reminders. Every time I open a magazine or turn on the television or get on a bus it's like,

```
THERE'S NO MILDER WIPE THAN A JOHNSON'S BABY
WIPE
```

and it's,

```
HiPP TODDLER RUSKS - GROWING UP NEVER TASTED
SO GOOD
```

and it's,

```
INFACOL RELIEVES INFANT COLIC AND GRIPING
PAIN.
```

And if it's not that it's,

```
SMA MEETS THE NEEDS OF EVERY LITTLE CHARACTER
```

Or,

```
PERSIL NON-BIO - FIRST CHOICE FOR BABY'S SKIN
```

Or it's,

```
CAPTURE THOSE MAGICAL MOMENTS WITH YOUR
LITTLE TREASURES WITH KODAK.
```

It's everywhere. And it's going to be SO, like, hord for me to concentrate on my rugby.

XXX

Evy sends me a text and it's just like, **ASSHOLE!**

XXX

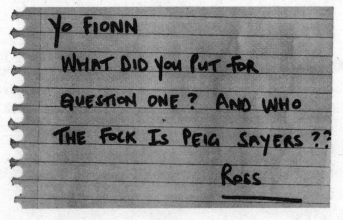

Yo FIONN
WHAT DID YOU PUT FOR
QUESTION ONE? AND WHO
THE FOCK IS PEIG SAYERS??
Ross

XXX

Us and the Gick: we've got, like, history. And we're talking a *lot* of history here. They've put us out of the Cup loads of times down through the years and there's always a bit of, like, needle between us. They basically think they're great, roysh, because, I don't know, some Taoiseach or some other tool went there, which basically means nothing, roysh, although Castlerock has never really produced anyone, unless you count people like my old man, which I don't.

Anyway, roysh, the last time Castlerock actually won the Leinster Schools Senior Cup was, like, twenty-five years ago, roysh, and it was the Gick they beat in the final, so Fehily has arranged for one of the stors of that team to come back and give us a bit of a talk, just for, like, inspiration.

So we're all sitting there, roysh, in the assembly hall, and Fehily's up there going, 'I want to introduce to you a man whose name is synonymous with success. In his day he was probably one of the finest rugby players of his age anywhere in the land. Now he is better known as one of this city's leading captains of industry ...'

Fionn leans over to me and goes, 'Tony O'Reilly didn't go to Castlerock, did he?' and I'm there, 'Don't think so,' pretending that I know who the fock Tony O'Reilly is. Fehily goes, 'He was the very foundation of the famous Castlerock pack in that unforgettable Cup-winning year. And it's no surprise that he should have gone on to make his living from, well, bricks and mortar. Yes, boys, I have great pleasure in introducing to you ... Edward Conroy of Hook, Lyon and Sinker Estate Agents in Donnybrook.'

Everyone claps. It's JP's old man. Out he comes, roysh, big Ned Kelly on him, and this giant turd of a cigar clamped between his teeth, which he's lighting as he's waddling out into the middle of the stage. As the clapping dies down, JP shouts, 'LEGEND,' ripping the piss, or at least I *hope* he's ripping the piss. Then he goes, 'THE BREADLINE!'

His old man just, like, raises his hand, as if to say, Enough, and then he goes, 'A lot can happen in twenty-five years. The first day I walked through the doors of this school was the year that man walked on the moon. The Vietnam War was still going on. Lennon and McCartney were still talking. And the price of a bribe to allow you to build something anywhere you bloody well liked was as little as twelve old pounds, and I can see you all looking at me in disbelief but that's what it was. Twenty-five years is a long time. But all the same, it's gone in the blink of an eye.

'There's not a day goes by that I don't think about the chaps, the ones I was proud to soldier alongside. Paddy Pemberton. Johnny Gilchrist with his dazzling runs on the wing. Lugs Lane. Roddy Allen. Sadly, we lost them all. Paddy signed for Blackrock the following season. Johnny and Lugs went down to Shannon, and Roddy – old Slaphead Allen – he fell on hard times and ended up playing League of Ireland soccer, Lord have pity on him.

'But they, like me, will never forget what it meant to win this school's first, and only, Schools Senior Cup. Castlerock's record since then, I am ashamed to say, is much the same as the houses I sell every day of the week – shit. That's not to put too fine a point on it. Terrible quality. You wouldn't put your worst enemy in some of the homes I sell to young newly-weds every day of the week.

'But that's beside the point. The actual point is that this school has waited twenty-five long and lean years for a team like this to come along. And if that makes you feel special, then that is understandable because special is what you are. In you – it makes me very proud to say – I see echoes of the last great Castlerock side.'

He notices that his cigar has gone out, roysh, and he takes out his lighter and gets it going again. He goes, 'I'm gonna make you kids an offer,' and I can see Fehily suddenly looking up, all interested. He's there, 'You're two games away from glory. Win them ... and I'll rent you the entire top floor of the best hotel in the city. For a weekend. Penthouse suites, boys. And ladies. Lots of very compliant ladies. Broads,' I can see Fehily running his finger across his throat, basically telling him to shut the fock up. He goes, 'I know people in this town. One phone call and – once it's illegal – I can have it for you in half an hour. I ring my man and pretty soon you're all going to think you're

Hugh Heffner. That's right. Take three or four into the Jacuzzi with you. Plenty for everyone. Fill your boots.

'That place in the final is yours. Don't let Terenure – of all schools – keep you from your destiny.'

XXX

I left eight messages on Sorcha's phone today and sent her six texts, but she won't return any of my calls. I just think we should, like, talk. I know now I was a bit, I don't know, hasty saying she shouldn't have the baby. I've had a bit of time to think about it and I think I'm ready to do the roysh thing. That's the only reason I'm so, like, desperate to talk to her. She told Sophie that I've turned into a total stalker and said she's thinking of changing her number.

XXX

It would not be an exaggeration to say that I am totally kacking it when Oisinn stands up to, like, make his speech, roysh, and I realise that having breakfast at the school this morning was SO not a good idea. We're all, like, SO nervous, roysh, that we can't keep anything down. JP is in trap one and Simon is in trap two, borfing their chicken and pasta back up, and Sooty is down on his hands and knees, roysh, slapping the floor and shouting underneath the gap in the bottom of the door, 'Cough it up, lads. Cough it up. Nerves are good. It's a matter of channelling that energy. Channel it, lads.'

Oisinn stands up, roysh, and he goes, 'Coach is roysh. Nerves are a good thing. This is a huge game. Gerry Thornley is out there today, which I think shows just how high the stakes are. Nerves show that you know it too. Terenure are a great side. You don't make it to the semi-finals of the Leinster Schools Senior Cup without being a great side. There are no soft touches left in the competition now. But we're so close, goys. We're so close now that we can almost smell it. So let's see off these orseholes today and make sure that it's us who's at Lansdowne Road on St Patrick's Day.'

After that, roysh, we all just shout out this big cheer and we all stort high-fiving and hugging each other. We go through the usual, like, rituals I suppose you could call them, to try and, like, psyche ourselves up. Oisinn's there, 'Okay, I want ten now, goys,' and we all count to ten. It's like, 'One, two, three, four,' blah blah blah. Then he goes, 'C. A. S. T. L. E. R. O. C. K,' basically spelling out the name of the school, roysh, and we give it, 'CASTLEROCK!' and then he's like, 'Pick the spuds,' and we all have to get down and pretend we're picking potatoes, roysh, and then it might be, 'Pull the chain,' and you basically all have to do the actions. It's all about morale and teamwork and shit. Of course by the end of this the goys are all going totally apeshit, kicking the walls and, like, punching the lockers, but I'm just sitting there with my towel over my head, trying my best to focus on my game.

Donnybrook is, like, jammers. We run out, roysh, and the crowd are, like, SO up for this game and even before it storts, roysh, they're giving it, 'ATTACK! ATTACK! ATTACK-ATTACK-ATTACK!' which is basically what they want us to do from the off. And it's what we end up doing. There's only, like, five minutes gone when Fionn – blind focker and all as he is – slices through a gap and gets over for a try, which The Master here converts. But then things stort to go wrong, roysh, when Simon goes and gets himself red-corded. There's a ruck, roysh, and he ends up stamping on the goy's head – I mean, the focker was offside – but his ear was pretty much hanging off and to be honest he made the most of it. Twenty or thirty stitches and it would have been back on, and even if the worst came to the worst you can get, like, prosthetic ones, if that's the word. But no, the referee totally over-reacts and sends Simon off and we're all there shaking our heads, wondering whether the rumours are true that the referee went to Terenure himself and that his nephew is actually Jonathan Palmer-Hall, their captain who, I don't think I've mentioned yet, is a complete tool who tried to be with Sorcha once and who hates me and the two are probably connected.

But Simon, roysh, is SO vital to our pack that once he's off, Terenure end up basically riding us. They score, like, three tries in the next fifteen minutes, roysh, and we are, like, SO lucky to be only 32-28 behind in the last five minutes, thanks, it must be said, to my kicking. So anyway, roysh, there's only a few minutes to go and they're murdering us down our end, looking for another try to, like, seal it, and our supporters are giving it, 'DE-FENCE! DE-FENCE! DE-FENCE!' but all of a sudden, roysh, one of their goys drops the ball and it lands roysh in front of me and I just, like, boot it and it must travel, like, forty yords down the field. But it stays in play, roysh, and I bomb it down the field after it, but who's pegging it beside me only this Jonathan wanker and we're, like, neck and neck, roysh, and I'm going, 'You haven't got the pace,' to him and I'm psyching him out of it. I'm there, 'Your legs are gone. You're never gonna make it, Jonathan,' and I get to the ball about a second before him, roysh, and give it another boot, which takes it just over the line and I dive on top of it, just as the dickhead lands on top of me. It's 33-32 to us and it's, like, game over. I just, like, push him off me, roysh, and I go, 'I said you didn't have the pace. On your knees and worship me.'

When the goys arrive at the other end of the field to, like, congratulate me, I'm still, like, sitting on the ground and I'm, like, holding the ball above my head and all the goys just, like, dive on top of me and eventually the referee – he's definitely Gick – he tells us he's adding on at the end any time we waste. But it doesn't matter how much he adds, roysh, it won't be enough because I add the points and we end up holding out for the last few minutes and after getting basically pissed on for most of the match we end up in the final. Unfair, I know, but fock them, they're Gick.

When the final whistle blows, roysh, all our fans invade the pitch. There's, like, four or five hundred from our school, then there's birds from, like, everywhere, we're talking Mounties, Alex, Whores on the Shore, the Virgin Megastore. I even saw one or two from Dogfood Manor – God loves a trier. So anyway, roysh, the whole crowd picks me up and they're, like, carrying me on their shoulders going, 'ONE ROSS O'CARROLL-KELLY, THERE'S ONLY ONE ROSS O'CARROLL-KELLY ...' and it takes me, like, half an hour to get off the field and back to the dressing-room. And of course who's waiting there when I do only Dick Features and that slimeball mate of his, looking a right pair of tools in their sheepskin coats and their trilby hats. Wankers, basically. The old man goes, 'Cometh the hour, cometh the man. Hennessy here said it, Ross. You're a big-game player. And he's Clongowes. So coming from him, it means something.' Hennessy goes, 'To survive as you did with your backs to the wall for so long and still to have the self-belief and the will to win that you showed ...' but I just ignore him, roysh, and I turn around to the old man and I go, 'Give me three hundred bills.' He goes, 'Three hundred? Em ...' like he thinks it's too much, the focking tightorse. I'm there, 'HELLO? I want to get hammered,' and he goes, 'You can get drunk on a lot less than three hundred pounds, Ross,' and I go, 'Well then I'm going to get VERY hammered.' He whips out this massive wad and he peels me off three hundred bills, and looking at how much money is in his hand, roysh, I wish I'd asked him for five hundred. Then I walk off.

As I'm going into the dressing-room, roysh, who do I bump into only Jonathan what's-his-face, who's on his way out. He's just finished with the niceties, the losing captain congratulating the winning team, saying he enjoyed the match and wishing the rest of the goys best of luck in the final. He sees me, roysh, and he goes to shake my hand – he ACTUALLY goes to shake my hand – but I just, like, pull away from him and stand there with my orms up over my head in sort of, like, triumph I suppose. He just, like, shakes his head, roysh, and he goes, 'You got lucky.'

Of course, I just smile at him and I'm there, 'No, I got the ball.'

XXX

Melanie is this slapper from Pill Hill who I was with two weeks ago, roysh, and she's left, like, a message on my mobile that's kind of, like, struck a raw nerve, if that's the right expression. It was left on Thursday night, roysh, in between two more of those 'Short Dick Man' ones that basically aren't funny anymore. Anyway, she says I'm, like, an orsehole for not ringing her and at least telling her I didn't want to see her again and that I don't give a fock about anyone's feelings except my own and that one day I'll meet someone who I really care about and they'll treat me like shit and then I'll know how it feels. And she's crying as she's saying this, roysh, and then I stort crying as well because I know she's basically roysh and it's already happened. This Sorcha situation is on my mind the whole time

If the truth be told, of course, the only reason I want her is because I know she doesn't want me and it's, like, wrecking my head at this stage. She won't, like, return my calls or anything. I thought she might ring after the game, especially after the stuff Gerry Thornley wrote about my performance – a star is born, blah blah blah – but she probably didn't even read it.

I make up my mind, roysh, to go and see her. It's, like, Saturday morning, which means she'll be, like, working in her old dear's shop – boutique, she calls it – out in the Merrion Shopping Centre. So I lash on my white Henri Lloyd, which I know she likes, roysh, and my bottle-green Timberland fleece, and I drive out there. I hang around outside for, like, ten or fifteen minutes, roysh, looking into the shop, obviously not wanting her old dear to see me, just in case Sorcha's, like, spilled the beans. It doesn't look like Sorcha's actually working today because I can see her old dear and her cousin, Clara, who's, like, first year International Commerce with French in UCD, but there's no sign of Sorcha. I'm about to head off, roysh, when I hear this voice behind him and it's like, 'OH MY GOD! *What* are you doing here?' and I turn around and it's, like, her and she's holding, like, three takeaway coffees, probably cappuccinos, because it's pretty much all she ever drinks.

I'm there, 'Sorcha, we have things to talk about,' and she's like, 'It's too late for talking,' and I'm going, 'I just came out to see how you've been?' She's there, 'As if you give a damn,' and I go, 'I do, honey,' and I'm trying to get a sly look at her stomach, roysh, to see if it's, like, storted to show yet, but her eye contact is, like, pretty intense, roysh, and I know I'm going to get sussed. Probably a bit early for her to be showing anyway.

I tell her she's looking well and she goes, '*What*ever,' and I ignore this and tell her I was a bit scared to go into the shop and face her old dear and she goes, 'Boutique. And I don't blame you.' I go, 'You haven't told her yet?' and she goes, 'With all she has on her plate at the moment? I don't THINK so,' and I ask her if her old man's still in the whatever-you-call-it islands and if she misses him and she goes, 'He HAPPENS to be there on business. Mum could end up losing the boutique, you know.'

I go, 'Sorry, I didn't realise ... how are you coping with ... I mean ...' and she goes, 'The baby? You can say the word, Ross. Actually, I'm not even thinking about it. I've got too much on my plate right now. The Leaving is, like, twelve weeks away and I'm SO far behind. Then there's this petition I'm doing for Amnesty to try to stop all these executions without trial in Rwanda – whatever she did or didn't do, time is running out for Virginie Mukankusi. And this whole Aoife situation is, like ...' and I go, 'I know, she doesn't look well,' and she goes, 'What the fock do you care?' and I go, 'I do care,' and she's there, 'You don't care about anyone but yourself, Ross. And that is why I don't want you having anything to do with this baby. You're an orsehole. And I don't want MY baby having an orsehole for a father.'

I look into her eyes and I know she means it. I search for something to say, roysh, something – anything – that might change her mind, but all I can think to say is, 'Did you hear we're in the final?' and she looks at me, roysh, as if she's just wiped me off the sole of her shoe and she goes, 'Grow up, Ross.'

Then she looks me up and down and says it again. She goes, 'Just GROW up.'

XXX

The old dear's left one of her birds' magazines on the table in the sitting-room, roysh, and I just sort of, like, pick it up and flick through it and I swear to God, every page I open has something to do with babies and pregnancy. It's either,

```
DO YOU BELIEVE IN SEX AFTER CHILDBIRTH? -
FROM EARTH MOTHER TO SEX KITTEN WITH THESE
TEN EASY TIPS
```
Or it's,
```
HOME FROM HOME - BEHIND THE SCENES OF A
NATURAL BIRTHING WARD
```
And if it's not that it's,
```
NOTHING BUT THE TOOTH - SURVIVING THE AGONIES
OF YOUR BABY'S TEETHING.
```

xxx

I've better things to be doing than listening to the old man crapping on about nothing, but when he calls me into the sitting-room, roysh, I make the mistake of actually going in. He's there, 'Ah, Kicker, there you are,' and I'm like, 'This better be important.' He goes, 'Well, I just thought, you know, big game tomorrow – big with a capital B, of course – St Michael's in the Schools Cup final and so forth, I just thought ...' and I'm there, 'Any chance of you getting to the point before I need to shave again?' which I have to say I'm pretty pleased with.

He goes, 'It's just, I wondered if you'd like to sit down with your old dad and watch a video. It's Ireland beating Scotland 21-12 to win the Triple Crown. Lansdowne Road, how are you? Twentieth of February 1982, thank you very much indeed. God, I remember it like it was yesterday. You wouldn't, of course, but we sat and watched it together. You must have been all of eighteen months old. We were in the old house then. Glenageary, quote-unquote.'

He's there, 'The tickets. Rare as hen's teeth, they were. Myself and Hennessy – he was doing his devilling that year if memory serves – we got our hands on a couple. Morning of the match, you got an attack of colic. Cried all day. Well, your mother felt one of her world-famous migraines coming on and she took to the bed. So I rang Hennessy and I said, 'Cockers' – because that's what we called him at school; Coghlan and so forth – I said, 'Cockers, I've got an emergency at home and it's one with a capital E. So you're going to have to tell Ciaran Fitzgerald and Hugo McNeill and old Ginger McLaughlin that they're going to have to do it without me.

And do it, they did. Ollie Campbell. Magnificent. Kicked twenty-one points that day. Six penalties and a drop goal. A record points haul for the master technician. Talk about grace under pressure. Five steps backwards, up and down on his toes and then – WALLOP – another one in your eye, so-called Scotland.

And you know what the oddest thing was? You stopped crying. There wasn't a peep out of you for the entire match. You just sat there, mesmerised by the great man. I knew then you were going to be a kicker. Your mother came downstairs not long after the final whistle. Said she was feeling a bit better. She had some work to do on some campaign or other. I think it was Travellers then as well. It was houses they were after in those days, but that's by the by. We'd just bought our first video recorder – they were new at the time – and I taped the game. Your mother asked me why on Earth I'd bothered recording a game I'd just watched. And I remember – it's like it happened yesterday – taking the tape out of the machine and telling her, "This, Fionnuala, is history."

So that night, Hennessy and I arranged to meet for a couple of celebratory brandies in the Shelbourne, which was where the Ireland players were staying. And I remember saying to him that night, I said, "Hennessy, that little lad of ours, he sat silently throughout that match today, transfixed by the performance of the great man. He's an outhalf, Hennessy, I can feel it." And I said to him, "Mark my words, he'll go on to play for Castlerock. And the night before the schools cup final, I'll pull out that tape and we'll sit down together, as father and son, and we'll relive the match that started it all." So what do you say, Kicker?' and he slaps the sofa cushion beside him to try to get me to sit down.

I go, 'I'd rather stick pins in my eyes.'

XXX

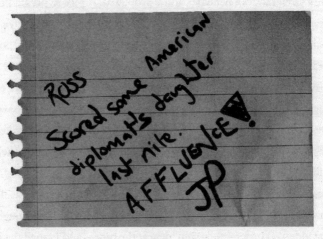

XXX

JP goes, 'Of course there is one major incentive for us to win tomorrow,' and we're all, like, totally clueless of course, and he goes, 'We'll all get a kiss off Oisinn's old dear,' and we're all, like, 'Yyyeeaahh!' The mother of the winning captain always gets to present the cup, roysh, and Oisinn's old dear is a total yummy-mummy. Oisinn takes this well, of course. He's giving it, 'No tongues, goys, I mean it,' and we all crack our holes laughing. Then JP leads us all into a chorus of, 'We're rich – and we know we are, we're rich – and we know we are ...' which is sort of, like, *his* song and at the end he storts shouting, 'THE BREADLINE!' over and over again and we're all cracking up. I have to say, roysh, staying over in the school dorms tonight was a really good idea, just to, like, boost morale and stuff.

Oisinn – you've got to admire his focus, roysh – goes back to his perfume catalogue, learning off all the shit about some new range or other, which he says keeps him from worrying about tomorrow. But of course I've got, like, Sorcha and the baby to do that. Christian knows that something's up, roysh. I know he's away with the, I don't know, Ewoks half the time, but he's actually good at sussing out when something's wrong. He catches my eye, roysh, and sort of, like, gestures at me to follow him outside, which I do and we go into the kitchen and straight away he goes, 'What's she done now?'

Of course I'm going, 'Who?' but there's no fooling this goy. He's there, 'Ross, did you know you've got two looks when someone's pissing you off – one for when it's Sorcha, the other when it's someone else.' There's no point in beating around the bush. I have to tell someone. Might as well be my best friend. I go, 'She's pregnant, Christian,' and even saying it makes my whole body go weak. He's there, 'PREGNANT? And you're the ...' I'm like, 'Father. I can say it now. Couldn't at first. I wanted her to have ... well, you know. It was just a shock, I suppose. But now I've actually storted to like the idea. Me and Sorcha and our little, I suppose, baby. Okay, it's not like I expected things to be but – Fock it - the old man will give us the money for a house.'

Christian goes, 'But I take it Sorcha wants nothing to do with you?' and I'm there, 'I don't blame her because of the way I, like, reacted. But it was just shock, Christian. My whole life was being turned upside down and ...' He goes, 'Have you ever thought that hers was too?' I look at him. He's there, 'All the things she was looking forward to after school – college, travelling, a social life, a life full stop – they've gone, Ross. And for what? Half an hour of passion?' He's being a bit generous there, but I just nod. He goes, 'I'm saying this to you as your best friend, Ross. Don't be too hord on her. What you're going through is probably only a quarter of what she's going through. Give her time. She'll come round.'

I love talking to Christian. I go, 'I've barely been able to think about anyone else. I've got that French bird coming next week. Haven't even got excited about that.' He goes, 'Ross, there's only one thing you should be focusing on right now and that's tomorrow's game. You don't need me to tell you how much the team relies on your kicking. If you're not roysh, then the rest of us aren't either. All these other things, Ross, they'll sort themselves out. Things have a way of working out for the best. You just need to focus on the here and now.'

I give the goy a hug, roysh, a really long one. Then he looks at me and he goes, 'You, a father. I can't believe it myself.'

Inside the dorm we can hear JP shouting, 'THE BREADLINE!' again and we both crack up. Then Christian goes, 'You must rest, Skywalker. You've had a long day.'

CHAPTER SIX
'Usually the ringleader whenever there's trouble'

Fehily says that education can go to blazes so long as a boy can outjump his peers in a lineout, punch his weight in the scrum, or kick a three-pointer from an obtuse angle deep in injury time. He's giving us our final pep talk before, like, the final. He's going, 'Books, education, learning – these things have their place in the life of young men, of course. But not in yours. Because you are the élite. You don't ask a pure-bred stallion to drag a cart uphill into town and similarly we here at Castlerock would never conceive of encumbering such fine athletic specimens as yourselves with such fripperies as schoolwork. The reproductive system of the earthworm, the fixed rhyming schemes of a Shakespearean sonnet and the principle industries of the Benelux countries should not matter a jot to you. Iambic pentameter, chlorophyll, Maginot Line, hypotenuse – such terms should have no relevance to your lives.'

Oisinn, roysh, he turns around to me and goes, 'Iambic what?' and I'm there, 'Don't ask me. I haven't been in Maths since, like, Christmas.'

Fehily goes, 'Your lives begin today. None of you know where you're going to be in ten years' time. But verily, I say unto thee, that you will always look back on this day and remember exactly where you were this afternoon. You can see your lives stretching out in front of you. Many of you will go on to play rugby for clubs and form new allegiances. A good number of you will meet a fellow at your new club who will get you a highly paid yet unfulfilling job that requires you to wear a suit – perhaps in a bank or some other such financial institution – where you'll open envelopes for fifty or sixty thousand pounds a year. Others will discover that the inability to spell the word lager is no hindrance to getting a job as a rep for a major brewing company if they happen to sponsor your team. Some of you will go on to manage your father's businesses.

'I think the point I'm trying to make here is that whatever you do and whatever you achieve in life you will always be Rock boys. Always remember where you're from. Did Jesus not utter those self-same words to His friends in the Garden of Gethsemane as he prepared to meet His Father?

'We don't have funny handshakes. There's no bizarre ceremonial rituals here. But we *are* a brotherhood. A fraternity. Call it what you will. But wherever you find yourselves in the world, and irrespective of what trouble you find yourselves in, all you need to do is make a call and you shall have succour, the same kind Jesus had as he prayed among the olive trees before going off to face his death, because you are Rock and Rock isn't merely the name of a school. It's an institution. A way of life. And it is underpinned by rugby and rugby – as the Good Lord told our friend from Cyrene as they carried the cross up to Calvary – is the very essence of brotherhood.'

I'm basically bawling here, roysh, and I have a sly look around and I notice that that isn't a dry eye in the place. He goes, 'From blood, authority of personality, and a fighting spirit springs that value which alone entitles a people to look around with glad hope, and that alone is also the condition for the life which men then desire ... It is not for seats in Parliament that we fight. But we win seats in Parliament in order that one day we may be able to liberate the German people. Do not write on your banners the word 'Victory': today that word shall be uttered for the last time. Strike through the word 'Victory' and write once more in its place the word which suits us better – the word 'Fight'.'

It's, like, totally amazing stuff, roysh, and we all suddenly burst into a chorus of 'Castlerock Above All Others', roysh, with Fehily just standing there with, like, his hands on his hips, nodding his head. Then when we're finished, roysh, he comes down to us and he shakes hands with every single one of us. Until, that is, he comes to me. He holds his hand out, roysh, but I don't shake it. I just hold mine up and he cops what I'm at, roysh, and he just, like, high-fives me. It's a totally unreal moment.

We arrive at Lansdowne Road about, like, half an hour before kick-off and the noise is already totally deafening. All our goys are up in the West Stand, roysh, singing all the Rock songs and we can actually hear them from the dressing-room as Sooty gives us a last minute bit of advice. Basically he tells us the things we already know, roysh, that Michael's haven't been in the final for, like, ten thousand years but they have a great team this year, wankers or not, and they are really going to be up for it. He tells us it's time to kick ass.

The butterflies are, like, SO bad as we leave the dressing-room and the roar of the crowd gets louder. We're standing there in the tunnel, roysh, and Christian turns around to me and goes, 'I have a bad feeling about this,' which is something Han Solo or some other goy says, and I go, 'The Force will be with us today,' and he turns around and he high-fives me and it's a great moment. Fionn looks at me and he goes, 'Ross, I know we don't always see eye to eye, but I'm proud to count you among my friends. I'd die for you out there on the field, you know that,' and I hug him and for a couple of seconds I actually regret sending that bunch of pink roses to his house with a cord saying, 'All the best, Ducky, from all the boys in The George,' with six or seven big kisses underneath it.

So there we are, standing in the tunnel, roysh, and out come the Michael's heads and they queue up beside us and I'm not sure if it's my imagination, roysh, but they are big fockers and very fit looking and I wouldn't say I'm alone in wondering whether we should have gone totally off the sauce this year. Some of them I recognise from Kiely's, the M1 and The Bailey, some of them I don't, all in their faggy jerseys. But they're actually very focking focused, roysh, so focused that it's actually, like, scary? They're not even looking at us, they're just, like, staring straight ahead, cracking on that the opposition don't even matter to them, that they're only concentrating on *their* game. So to ruffle their feathers, roysh, I turn around to their tighthead prop – I think his name's Risteard, a no-neck focker – and I go, 'You're a faggot,' and he turns his head to the roysh and he looks at me and goes, 'Repeat that, please.' I go, 'I said, you're a faggot,' and he turns his head again and it's like he's, like, weighing up what I've said, roysh, trying to decide what to do, then all of a sudden he takes a swing at me. Christian jumps straight in front of me, roysh, and he goes, 'You deck him and you're going to have to deck me first,' which I don't think would present much of a challenge for this goy – he's a focking animal – but then Fionn gets in on the act and then Oisinn and a couple of their goys as well and there's a bit of pushing and shoving in the tunnel, roysh, before a gang of stewards come and break us up and the referee tells us all to calm down and don't let the tension of the occasion spoil our enjoyment of the game.

We're told it's time to go and I turn around to the goy again and I'm like, 'Bent as a rusty nail,' and Oisinn goes, 'Let's kick FOCKING orse,' and then we run out onto the field and you can hordly hear yourself think, the noise is so loud. We head, naturally enough, for the South Terrace end of the ground and it's all, like, black and red striped shirts and the crowd stort chanting my name and I'm wondering whether Sorcha's in there somewhere and – this sounds bent, roysh – but if our little baby is kicking with excitement inside her. I can feel my eyes stort to water and I actually think I'm going to burst into tears, roysh, so I try to do what Christian says and just blank it out.

It's actually a bit of a relief, roysh, when the game storts, but you can tell that both sides are kacking it. It's full of, like, handling errors, turnovers, blah blah blah. Eunan's giving me shit ball and I end up giving Fionn a couple of hospital passes. JP's knocked on three times under, like, high balls and if it wasn't for Christian tearing them aport out wide and Simon and Oisinn kicking orse up front, we'd actually be behind.

The closest we get to a try, roysh, is when Christian sells their defence an unbelievable dummy and it looks like he's in. He's actually in the air, roysh, about to touch down, when one of their goys appears out of nowhere and drags one of his legs into touch and it's disallowed. We all call the referee a cheat, even though we know he's roysh. Basically, the first half turns out to be a penalty contest between me and their kicker, don't know the goy's name, but I know he sometimes drinks in the Wicked Wolf and he was with Sorcha's friend Sophie at Amie with an ie's eighteenth birthday porty. I get the upper hand, kicking four penalties from six, and we end up leading, like, 12-9 at half-time.

But it's hord-going, roysh. Oisinn has, like, a black eye – Risteard's revenge – and Simon's ribs are pretty badly bashed up and Sooty actually wants to, like, substitute the dude, but he just goes, 'I'll die before I'll go off injured.' The dressing-room is like a focking casualty ward, but hearing Simon say that, roysh, gives us basically the strength to go out there in the second half and go at them again.

Our supporters are giving it loads, roysh, fair focks to them because the match is probably kack to watch from a spectator's point of view. There's very little ball-in-hand stuff, it's all boot and rucks and solid defence. Twenty minutes into the second half, roysh, and the scores are still the same when one of their goys – a total penis who I'm pretty sure is Alyson with a y's brother – he kicks this big, long garryowen for their goys to chase onto, but JP's standing where he should be, roysh, and there's no wind, so he should catch it no problem, but I don't know what happens, he must, like, take his eye off the ball, and when he goes to catch it, it hits off his, like, forearm and spills onto the ground, and one of their goys – can't even see who it is, but there were enough of them there – jumps on it and they've scored the first try of the game. And of course they stort celebrating like they've won the focking thing already.

They miss the conversion, roysh, but even though we're only, like, two points behind, it's going to be hord now, because they're going to defend like their lives depend on it and in a close game like this it's unlikely that you're going to get a lot of tries, unless they're from mistakes. It's, like, backs to the wall time for them. This Risteard goy, I have to say it, roysh, he's having a focking stormer, the wanker, and he's obviously targeted me as the main danger man because he walks up to me, roysh, during a break in the play and he goes, 'I am going to cream you the next time you get the ball,' and I just, like, laugh in his face, pretending it's not, like, affecting me and shit, but as I go to run off he's there, 'Tell your friends not to pass to you. Seriously, next time you get the ball, you're going to see who's a faggot.'

I'm actually not intimidated, it that's the word, but about twenty seconds later, Eunan pulls the ball out of a ruck and takes half the focking day to give it to me and when he does it's, like, another hospital pass and Risteard – I swear to fock, I've never seen a goy that size move so fast – he comes from nowhere and just, like, clotheslines me. I am smack bang out of it for what must be a couple of minutes, roysh, and even when I come around I must have, like, concoction, if that's the roysh word, because my vision's blurry and I can only just make out the voices of the goys, standing over me, asking am I alroysh. It takes a few minutes before my head clears and the goys help me to my feet and before Oisinn has a chance to say anything to me, roysh, I go, 'I'm playing on, Oisinn. Don't want any arguments.'

But Michael's are unbelievable, roysh. It's, like, attack attack attack from us, roysh, but we can't get any nearer than ten metres from their line no matter what we do, and the goys are getting, like, frustrated. Oisinn decks their second row with the blond hair and luckily, roysh, the ref doesn't see it. The clock is winding down. Then the time's up. We're into whatever the dude's adding on, roysh, and we're still two points behind and ten metres from the line but we just can't make any more ground. And then suddenly, roysh, there's a ruck and Oisinn ends up on the ground and the goy that he decked, roysh, he can't help himself. He sees Oisinn lying there and WHACK! he stamps on the back of Oisinn's leg and you can hear this, like, TWANG, roysh, and it's his hamstring snapping, it's actually the sound of his hamstring snapping, and the ref blows for a penalty for us and it's, like, roysh in front of the posts, we're talking three minutes into, like, injury time, and all our goys are already celebrating. It's probably the last kick of the game.

But Oisinn is focked, roysh, They bring a stretcher on and, like, cart him off, but before he goes he says he wants to talk to me, so the St John's Ambulance dudes carry him over to me and he sits up on the stretcher and he grabs me by the back of the neck, roysh, and he puts his forehead up against mine and he goes, 'This is the most important kick of your life, Ross. You don't need me to tell you what it means. Now kick ass,' and I go, 'It's in the bag ... Captain,' and he's giving it, 'You the man, Ross! You the man!'

So I place the ball, roysh, run my hand through my hair, blow hord, take five steps backwards and four to the left, run my hand through my hair again, do a little dance on the spot and then ... It's silent, roysh, but then I hear something, a voice shouting and without looking, roysh, I know it's that Risteard dickhead and he's there, 'Hey, Ross. I was with Sorcha in The Queen's on Friday night,' and suddenly I can feel all the blood in my body go cold. My mind is, like, gone. I'm suddenly thinking about Sorcha and I'm thinking about what a good person she is and I'm thinking about our little child growing inside her and I'm thinking about that big focking ape with his hands all over her ... all over her stomach and his tongue in her mouth and ... and ... and ...

It must be, like, ages that I'm standing there, roysh, because when I snap out of it everyone's just, like, staring at me, wondering what the fock's wrong. I look at Christian, who's standing there with his eyes closed, probably trying to use The Force to get it through the posts. JP and Fionn are turned around, not able to, like, watch. Oisinn is sitting up on the stretcher on the sideline, waiting for me to knock this over so he can go to the hospital knowing he's got a Schools Cup medal.

And I'm still thinking about Sorcha and I just run at the ball and boot it and suddenly the noise returns and it's all, like, groans and I watch the ball as it sails high and wide of the posts.

The ref blows up straight away and the Michael's goys go mental. I just fall to my knees and then flat on my face and I lie there, roysh, with my nose in the ground, bawling my eyes out and all the goys – we're talking Christian, JP, Fionn – they're all coming over and telling me that it's not my fault, but it's not what I want to hear roysh now. I'm there going, 'I focked up. I focked it up for everyone,' and they're going, 'AS IF! We wouldn't even be here today, Ross, if it wasn't for you.'

Not being big-headed or anything, roysh, but it's actually pretty brave of me to go up with the goys to collect my medal, because my first instinct is to get the fock out of there as quick as I can. But I go up, roysh, and I collect it and Mary McAleese is there, 'You had a very good game,' and it's obvious she doesn't recognise me as the tool who threw the game away and I just go, 'Kool and the Gang,' and I trudge down the steps, wishing the ground would just, like, open up and swallow me.

I walk back out onto the field, roysh, and it's been invaded by Michael's heads and hundreds of birds, most of whom were cheering for us two hours ago but are now fans of the other side. I see Keeva and Sian and Evy and they're all, like, hanging out of the Michael's goys and Keeva sees me and makes an L shape with her finger and thumb and she mouths the word 'LO-SER' at me and I know she's roysh. Then we have to stand there and watch those dickheads go up and collect the Cup and we're all totally bulling.

I walk off the field, roysh, and Christian has his orm around me and I tell him I'm, like, really sorry for focking things up for everyone and he tells me not to be stupid, we lost it over the full eighty minutes and not on the one mistake I made in the entire match, and it's nice to hear even if it is total bullshit. I'm about to go into the dressing-room, roysh, but who's standing at the mouth of the tunnel only Orse Face himself. He's on the focking mobile, roysh, with the old dear standing beside him, hanging off his orm, six baby seals on her back, and when he sees me he goes, 'Hold on a second, Hennessy. Bad luck, Ross. Even Ollie Campbell had his bad days,' and then he goes back to his big focking chat, so I just walk roysh over to him, roysh, and stand roysh in front of him and give him the finger.

We go back to the dressing-room and it's like the world is about to end. Everyone has their heads in their hands. There's, like, tears, the whole lot. I ask Simon what he's going to do now, roysh, and he just, like, shrugs his shoulders and goes, 'Repeat, I suppose,' and I'm like, 'Again? Simon, they're going to suss sooner or later that you're over-age,' and he's like, 'I'm not leaving school until I get a winner's medal,' and I have to admire that. Then he goes, 'By the way, you're coming to my twenty-first on Friday night, aren't you?' and I'm like, 'I am SO there.'

The next thing, roysh, Fehily comes in and I'm expecting him to give us the kind of speech we usually get from him, sort of, like, uplifting and shit, telling us we did the school proud, that the Year of the Eagle will be forever remembered in the school, blah blah blah. But no. He walks in and he tells us that now that we're out of the Cup we'd better knuckle down and study because the mocks stort in, like, two weeks. Then he focks off.

But before he reaches the door, he turns around and he goes, 'Ross?' and I'm there, 'Yeah?' and he's like, 'Have that special topic report Mister Crabtree asked you for on his desk first thing on Monday morning.'

XXX

It's the day after the match and I haven't even looked at the papers to read the reports. I can guess the gist of them: Ross O'Carroll-Kelly Blows His Big Moment. I need to escape the old man and his, 'You'll play for Ireland by the time you're twenty,' bullshit and the old dear with her, 'I feel terribly sad for June (who's, like, Oisinn's old dear) because she was so looking forward to presenting the Cup; she bought a lovely new outfit,' and then all the goys ringing me to see if I'm okay and Ryle Nugent ringing me wondering if I'd like to share with the nation just what was going through my mind when I took that kick, and to be honest, I couldn't even begin to explain.

So I get the fock out of there. I grab two hundred sheets from the old man's safe and hit town for the day. So there I am, roysh, and I'm in the Stephen's Green Shopping Centre and something – I don't know what – just *something* drags me up to the mother and baby section on the first floor. There I am, standing on the escalator, roysh, not knowing what the fock I'm doing, but it takes me up and up, and all of a sudden it suddenly plonks me in the middle of this whole new world.

It's, like, Strollers and harnesses and sleepsuits and sterilisers and Moses baskets. It's EasiRiders and highchairs and baby monitors and potties and those gates that you put at the end of the stairs to stop babies snotting themselves. There's car seats and door bouncers. There's safety socket covers and bouncing cradles. And there's tiny pairs of booties and mittens and these little bibs with, like, Winnie the Pooh and Noddy and Tractor Tom and Boo and Bob the Builder and Fimbles on them. And this bird comes over to me, roysh, and she obviously works there, and she asks me if she can help me in any way, and then she asks me if I need to sit down because I realise that I've got, like, tears streaming down my face. I tell her I'm fine and she tells me not to worry because lots of men find walking into a baby store for the first time an incredibly emotional experience and that sometimes she feels more like a counsellor than a sales assistant. She asks me how far away is the big day and I count back the weeks to the Orts Ball and I tell her seven months. I wipe my eyes and she tells me that if I need any help to call her.

I wander around some more and I look at this Montreal Cot, which costs £129.99 and it's got a three-position base and teething rails that help protect delicate new teeth. Then I check out these freaky-looking things that turn out to be called breast pumps and it says on the box, roysh, that they enable mothers to express and store their breast milk quickly and discreetly for later use, and I put it down quickly in case anyone cops me and thinks I'm a perv. Then I look at the new Powertrack 360, a pushchair with a revolving front wheel that allows greater manoeuvrability in tight corners and a powerful disc brake that operates from the handlebor.

Then this woman walks by, roysh, and she's carrying her baby and I'm just, like, entranced by it, if that's the word. I look at its little fingers with its tiny nails. And the blond hair and the big blue eyes and this huge smile and I can feel myself storting to fill up again so I head for the escalator and just before I step onto it, roysh, the shop assistant I was talking to earlier goes, 'Excuse me, sir,' and she hands me this book and she's there, 'A little gift from us – the best of luck,' and on the front of the book it says, *Celtic Names for Children*.

XXX

The old man asks me where I'm going, roysh, and I am SO tempted to go, 'Who the fock are you? Bergerac?' but I don't, roysh, I try to be nice, I just go, 'The focking airport.' He's like, 'The airport? You're not flying somewhere are you?' I just, like, throw my eyes up to heaven and I go, 'We've got a French exchange student coming.' The old dear looks up from her speech for tonight's Foxrock Against Total Skangers EGM. She's there, 'Ross, you never told us ...' and I'm there, 'I'm telling you now, aren't I?' The only thing the old man can think to say is, 'I hope he likes his rugby, that's all I can say, because you know me and you once we get talking ...' I'm there, 'It's actually a *she*.' The old dear's still looking at me over the top of her glasses. She goes, 'Oh! Well I'd better air out one of the spare rooms, put some fresh sheets on the ...' and I'm like, 'No need. She's staying in my bedroom,' and the old man – I can't believe how slow he is on the uptake sometimes – he goes, 'But, where are *you* going to sleep?' I'm there, 'Do I have to draw you a focking picture?'

Probably sounds a bit, I don't know, rude I suppose. But I lost us the Schools Cup. I've lost Sorcha and our baby. I DESERVE some action with a French honey. So I lash on the old *cK One*, grab the Lexus – the old man's had the damage fixed – and I hit the airport. I check myself out in the rearview mirror – shit-hot – before I mosey on down to the Arrivals gates and even though I'm, like, pretty early, roysh, it's a bit odd that none of the other French Club geeks seem to be here yet. The plane's arriving in, like, half an hour. I try to get Fionn on his mobile, but it just, like, rings out.

I go to the bookshop on the Departures level and buy an A4 pad and a thick black morker. I grab a cup of coffee and I make this, like, sign and it's like,

with a few love horts around it, and then I think it looks a bit, I don't know, gay, so I crumple it up and make another sign and it's like,

and I then I end up putting the horts back on it. I check the time, knock back my coffee and peg it down to the gate. The Nerd Herd still aren't here and I wonder have I got the wrong date. I check Clementine's letter and no, the date's roysh. I check the flight details on the monitor and it is the roysh one and I see that it's landed. She's probably, like, waiting for her luggage as we speak. There better be a French maid's uniform in there somewhere, although you can get them on Capel Street.

I try Fionn's phone one last time but it's still, like, ringing out, then I just remind myself, 'Forget the focking Anorak Pack. Plough your own furrow, Ross.' So I'm standing there, roysh, holding up my little sign and all of a sudden there's this, like, little fat bloke standing roysh in front of me. Of course I'm there, 'Would you mind getting the fock out of the way. I happen to be waiting for someone,' and he goes, 'You are Ross, yes?' and I swear to God, at that moment, roysh, I just felt every hair on my body stand on end. It's, like, suddenly everything is clear to me. Fionn's stitched me up. He goes, 'Hello. I am Clement. I like it very nice to be here,' and he gives me a hug. Oh for FOCK'S sake, he's even got leopardskin suitcases. I don't say anything, roysh, I'm just, like, staring roysh through him.

He goes, 'You have big arms from playing of the rugby, yes?' and I go, 'Don't focking touch me. You wait here. We're talking five minutes. *Capisce?*' and I turn around and peg it up the escalator and on the way up, roysh, I try Fionn's phone again and this time he answers. I go, 'You are focking totalled.' He's there, 'I take it you've met Clement,' and I'm like, 'I hoped you'd at least *pretend* it was a mix-up. Who the FOCK is he?' Fionn goes, 'Well, I found his details on one of those lonely horts websites for gay men ...' I'm there, 'Yeah, I bet you spend a lot of time looking at those,' and he goes, 'I'm not the one who was standing in Arrivals five minutes ago waiting for his boyfriend to arrive. The love horts were a nice touch, by the way.' I flip the lid then. I'm there, 'You were actually, like, watching me?' and he goes, 'We all watched it – me, JP, Oisinn, Simon. I didn't tell Christian because I couldn't be sure he wouldn't tell you,' and I'm like, 'He *would* have told me. Because he's a *real* friend,' and then I'm like, 'Where the fock are you now?'

He goes, 'We're all still down here on the Arrivals level. Your boyfriend looks a bit upset, Ross. Probably thinks you didn't mean all those things you said in your letters,' and I'm there, 'I bet that was all benny talk as well, wasn't it? And where did you get that picture, the bird who looked like Natalie Imbruglia?' and he goes – real focking smort, roysh – he goes, 'Brace yourself, Ross. That *was* a picture of Natalie Imbruglia,' and I can hear all the goys cracking their holes in the background.

I'm there, 'Where are you? I want to meet you face to face,' and he's there, 'Ross, you've spent the last few months trying to convince my parents that I'm gay. Do you have any idea what it's been like living in my house? Asparagus and risotto for every meal. My old dear asking me for my opinion on nail varnish. My old man leaving Elton John CDs lying around my room.' Actually that was me, but I say nothing. He goes, 'And despite all the essays I've written for you in the past, all the homework I let you cog from me, all the exams that I coached you through, you forgot one important fact, Ross. I'm cleverer than you.'

I don't say anything. He storts laughing, roysh, and he goes, 'You should have seen your face when it dawned on you. I laughed so much I almost dropped the video camera.' I'm there, 'HOLY FOCK, you were actually *filming* it?' and he goes, 'That was actually Oisinn's idea. It was just one of those Kodak moments, Ross. You want to be able to enjoy it time and time again. And there were a lot of people who couldn't be here today who want to enjoy the moment of your humiliation too.' I go, 'What am I supposed to do with ... What is his focking name?' He goes, 'His name is Clement, Ross. Probably calls himself Clementine when he's camping it up. We're all still downstairs, Ross. I'll tell you something, he does not look happy. But do you know what's really funny in all of this? Clementine is actually the name of a fruit,' and he hangs up.

I ask this bird who passes me by in an Aer Lingus uniform where you can buy, like, a ticket to France and she points me in the direction of the Air France desk. I'm straight up to the desk, roysh, and I pull out the old man's credit cord, which I liberated from his wallet this morning, and I ask when is the next flight to, like, France. She says there's one seat left on the three o'clock to Paris and I tell her I'll take it. Five minutes later, roysh, she hands me the ticket and I'm back down the escalators to Arrivals, where Clementine, or whatever the fock he's called, is sitting there with a big face on him.

He sees me and his face lights up. I'm looking over my shoulder for the goys, but the place is, like, jammers and I can't see them anywhere. I don't give a fock as long as they get what I'm going to do on camera. He goes, 'Ross, there is no problem, I hope,' and I'm there, 'Only the fact that you're a focking bloke.' He goes, '*Je ne comp* ... I do not understand. You tell me you like to stroke my legs and you say you like to eat my face.' I'm there, 'I SO didn't say that,' and he goes, 'I bring some pornographic film as a gift for you, but the man at the, how you say, custom, he take them from me and he say I am lucky this time to be let go with just a warning.' I'm there, 'Can you get this into your thick skull, *ní mé* interested,' but it's in one ear and out the other. He goes, 'You say you like to do things with my sisters and my ... my family and I think perhaps this boy is a little, eh, *malade* – how to say – sick, yes? But I cannot get you out of my head. I like to watch the men doing it as well,' and I just lose it. I'm there, 'I never wrote any of that shit. It was a SO-CALLED mate of mine, basically ripping the piss. He set me up. You were SUPPOSED to be a bird.' He reaches into his bag, roysh, and – FOCKING! HELL! – he pulls out this big mass of, like, wires, roysh, with little pads on the end of them, obviously for blokes who are into, like, frying each other's nuts, and he goes, 'We have some amusement, yes?' and the whole focking airport is staring at us at this stage. He goes, '*Bzzz, bzzz,*' basically shaking the focking things in my face and making a buzzing sound, and I just throw the ticket at him and he bends down, picks it up and looks at it. He goes, 'This is ... I do not understand,' and I'm like, 'Understand this, then, you focking gimp. Check-in opened ten minutes ago,' and as I'm walking away, roysh, I look over my shoulder and I go, *'Bon voyage,'* which is basically French, roysh, for have a good trip, *adios* and Goodnight, Vienna.

XXX

I very nearly didn't go to Simon's twenty-first, roysh, but Christian basically talked me into it.

Emer says she SO has to change her mobile, roysh, because it's, like, SO last year and Sadbh reminds her that her old man only bought it for her, like, two months ago and Emer goes, 'Yeah but it only stores, like, forty numbers,' and Sadbh goes, 'Sorry, Miss Popularity,' and it reminds me that I must check my messages. But not yet. I'm actually thinking of trying to bail into Emer, this bird who's, like, sixth year Loreto on the Green and SO like Alicia Silverstone they might as well be, like, sisters. She's looking around the room now and she takes a sip of her vodka, soda and lime, sort of, like, screws up her face and goes, 'Why did Simon have to have it in the tennis club of all places?' Sadbh shakes her head and goes, 'OH! MY! GOD! I know. I do *not* need a reminder of how much I've let my game go since I storted going out with Alex.'

Fionn is over talking to Oisinn and JP. He waves over to me and I wave back, roysh, cracking on that everything's alroysh between us. He can wait. I've got a long memory. Actually, I don't. What I'm saying is, I'll bide my time. Even when all those orseholes I've never even clapped eyes on before come over and stort singing, 'Oh my darling Clementine' under their breath, I just go, 'Congratulations, you're the first one to think of that,' basically not rising to the bait.

Emer is going, 'It's not that, Sadbh. It's just that if it was in, like, a pub, you wouldn't have so many kiddy-nippers. I mean, Fiona Manning's little sister is here and she's, like, drinking? HELLO? Fake ID or what?' Emer mentions then that Fiona Manning got – OH! MY! GOD! – SO drunk and ended up making SUCH a fool of herself in the rugby club on Friday night and she ended up being with Jonathan Flood, who's, like, best friends with Adam Brannigan, who she was going out with for two years.

Anyway, engrossed as I am in all this, roysh, the next thing – I cannot believe my eyes here – Sorcha walks in. I'm like, 'What the FOCK is she doing here?' pretending to be pissed off but, like, secretly delighted. Simon hears me, roysh, and he puts his hand on my shoulder and goes, 'Chill the kacks, Ross. I know you two are finished but Sorcha's still a friend of ours,' and I'm there, 'Hey, I'm cool about it.' So she comes over, roysh, and she just, like, hugs Simon and air-kisses him and goes, 'Hi, happy birthday, are you having a good time?' and then she turns around to Christian and she gives him this big, long hug and tells him that she has SO missed him. She totally ignores me and of course I'm left standing there like a Toblerone, as in out on my own. So she heads over to Sophie and Emma who're over at the bor and I am SO pissed off I follow her, and she's in the middle of telling Sophie about the new black pencil skirt she got from, like, Karen Millen when I grab her by the hand and I go, 'I need a word,' and I drag her off to the side and she's going, 'Ross, what the fock is your problem?' Of course I'm there, 'What is YOUR problem?' and she's like, 'I don't have a problem,' being nice as pie now and she goes, 'How are you?' Of course this totally throws me and I'm there, 'I'm fine but ...' and she goes, 'Sorry about the match. Are you okay about it?' and I'm there, 'It was a bit of a bummer, but I'll survive,' wondering if she read Gerry Thornley's report that said I bottled it. I have to say, roysh, she looks drop-dead gorgeous tonight in this, like, blue satin dress. I go, 'How *are* you, if you know what I mean?' and I look down at her stomach and notice that she still hasn't storted showing yet. She goes, 'Fine. I got a pair of Marco Moreo shoes today for ...' and I decide not to beat around the bush any longer. I put my orm around her waist, roysh, and I go, 'Sorcha, what made losing the Schools final even worse was that I didn't have anyone to, like, talk to about it. That's when I realised how much I missed you.'

But she just, like, peels my hand off her and throws it back to me and she goes, 'Nice try. It might have worked once but I am SO over you now.' I'm there, 'Come on, Sorcha. We've got so much to look forward to. We can have an amazing summer together. And then ...' but she goes, '*Hello?* I'm going away for the summer,' and of course I'm just there, 'WHERE?' realising after I've said it that I'm actually shouting now. She goes, 'The States,' and I'm like, 'THE STATES?' and she goes, 'Calm down, Ross. I told you ages ago I was going to Myrtle Beach to work in my uncle's country club,' and I'm like, 'But what about ... I just presumed the baby would have changed all of that.' She looks at me like I'm off my bin, roysh, and she goes, 'Baby?' I'm there, 'Yeah. *Our* baby,' and she just, like, laughs at me and goes, 'HELLO? I'm not REALLY pregnant, Ross. I just told you that to fock with your head,' and then she just, like, walks off, roysh, leaving me standing there for ages, in total shock.

I walk out into the air and I bump into this bird who I've never met before in my life and she's totally hammered and she says her name is Grainne and she's, like, best friends with Carrie, or *was* best friends with her until Carrie threw herself at me, and the only reason was because she wanted to be with me, blah blah blah. I stort wearing the face off her, roysh, but she's ossified and her breath tastes of vom, so I end up just leaving her propped against the wall and she shouts after me, 'Carrie Fitzpatrick is SUCH a slapper, Ross. You know what we call her? Carrie Fitz Anything.'

I don't even look back, I just keep walking. I walk for an hour. Maybe two. I just, like, lose track of time. It storts raining, roysh, and I hail a Jo and when the driver asks me where I want to go I tell him Dalkey. I haven't seen Aoife since she got out of, like, hospital. I look at my watch, roysh, and it's half-ten and I wonder if her old pair are still up and if they'll let me see her. I ring the bell and her old man comes to the door. My old man plays golf with him the odd time. He goes, 'Ross. It's half-past ten at night ...' and I'm there, 'I just wondered how Aoife was,' and I can tell from the way he's looking at me that he's trying to work out how hammered I am. Then all of a sudden he opens the door wide and tells me I can go up and see her, but for five minutes only. As I'm heading up the stairs, he goes, 'And see can you get her to eat something.'

She's lying on the bed, outside the covers, and she doesn't look at me when I come in and sit down on the hord chair next to her bed. The walls are covered in pictures of Brad Pitt and – weird one – Will Carling. She carries on watching 'Friends', staring at the television without looking like she's actually watching it. Fionn said that a couple of weeks ago her old pair came home from the theatre to find her going through the family album with a scissors, cutting herself out of all the pictures. That's when they knew they had to get her in somewhere. There's a plate of, like, scrambled eggs on a tray on a chair on the other side of the bed. Looks like they're cold. I think of saying something about eating, but who the fock am I? We sit there for about ten minutes without saying anything, roysh, and eventually I turn around and I'm like, 'How long do you have to keep seeing the counsellor?' and she doesn't answer, she just goes, 'Have you got a cigarette?' and I'm there, 'I don't smoke, Aoife. You know that.'

Eventually, I give up trying to get a conversation going and I just sit there staring at the television with her and it's only then that I realise, roysh, how hammered I actually am. I can feel my cheeks all wet, roysh, and I realise that I'm *actually* crying again, like a focking benny or something. I'm like, 'Why are we so focked up, Aoife?' and she goes, 'Do you think Courtney Cox's hair would suit me?' and I can't take any more, so I just, like, get up and as I'm on the way out the door I hear her say, 'Bring cigarettes next time.'

CHAPTER SEVEN
'Poor attendance'

The Leaving Cert? Went pretty well, I thought. We're talking,

ENGLISH-HIGHER LEVEL-PAPER 1

I spent the entire time texting Sorcha, asking her what the fock I did to deserve what she did to me, but she didn't answer. Twice the – whatever you call her – the invigilator sussed me, but before she could get down to me, roysh, I slipped the mobile up my sleeve and when she went, 'Did I see you sending an SMS to someone?' I go, 'I don't even *own* a mobile,' and there's fock-all she can do about it. And I think she looks at my paper and sees that I haven't written a single word and there's, like, half an hour left of the exam, so she knows I couldn't be cheating.

ENGLISH-HIGHER LEVEL-PAPER II

This goes a hell of a lot better than Paper 1. I write my exam number on it and then I copy down the first question. It's like,

I. DRAMA

A. KING LEAR (Shakespeare)

(i) 'In King Lear, Shakespeare presents us with a world of

mental anguish expressed in physical terms.'

Discuss this statement, supporting your answer by quotation from or reference to the play.

<u>OR</u>

(ii) 'Gloucester's sons are far more interesting than the King's daughters.'

Discuss this view, supporting your answer by quotation from or reference to the play.

Then I spend the next two-and-a-half hours, roysh, writing out a list of all the birds I've been with in the past two years, with little stors beside the ones I threw a bone. Not all of them obviously, just the ones I can remember. The list takes up both sides of an A4 sheet and I sort of, like, debate over whether I should tear the page out or leave it in to give whoever's correcting it a thrill. In the end I leave it in and I write,
WHAT I DID IN FIFTH AND SIXTH YEAR:
across the top and JP says he was watching me throughout the exam and he can't believe how much I was writing. And then it was like,

IRISH-HIGHER LEVEL-PAPER I

Didn't even bother opening the question paper. Wrote *Tá*, which is, like, the Irish word for thank you, across every line on the first page of the booklet and it was like,

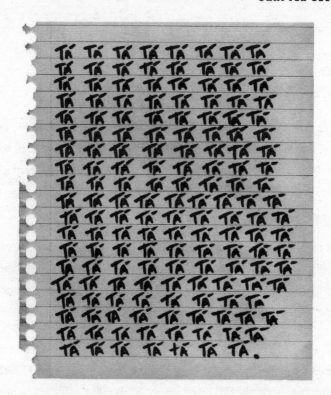

and then did the same on the second page. Halfway down the third page I storted to feel a bit Moby so I stopped and focked off home in time to see 'Home and Away'. And then it was like,

IRISH-HIGHER LEVEL-PAPER II

This was, like, really clever, roysh. I just wrote, 'I have decided not to sit this exam as a protest against the standard of refereeing in this year's Leinster Schools Senior Cup final,' and I try to show it to Christian, roysh, but he just ignores me because he's afraid of being caught. I stay however long it is you have to – half an hour, I think – and I'm back home in time to see the repeat of 'Home and Away' and it's getting to the stage that I can't even look at Isla Fischer without wanting an Allied Irish. The next day it was like,

MATHS-HIGHER LEVEL-PAPER I

Always wondered whether I was cut out for honours Maths, but I needn't have worried. Ruled every page in the booklet and then wrote out the lyrics to 'Sweet Child of Mine'. And after a well-deserved lunch it was like,

MATHS-HIGHER LEVEL-PAPER II

but I think the – what's the word Tony Ward used? – exertions of the morning had storted to take their toll. I was cream-crackered basically but I still found the energy from somewhere to write out the lyrics of 'Smells Like Teen Spirit'. So then it was on to,

HISTORY-HIGHER LEVEL

Got my second wind and used my time wisely, I felt. I just wrote out, like, really smort answers to all the questions. So if it was,

'During the period 1875–1886, Parnell came to dominate Irish politics and built up a strong and tightly disciplined party.' Explain how this came about. (80)

I was like,

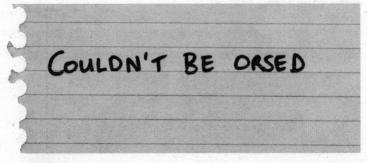

And then if it was like,

Discuss the developments in agriculture and industry in the period 1922–1939. (80)

I was there,

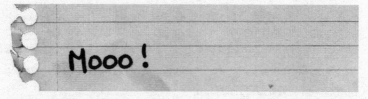

MOOO!

I was cracking my hole throughout the exam. Then, as far as I remember, it was,

FRENCH-HIGHER LEVEL

Bad memories. Didn't write a single word, unless you count the huge set of airbags I drew on the inside cover of the answers booklet. I mean, these correctors have a pretty shit time reading this stuff. Might as well put a smile on their faces. Left after half an hour, but I did much better in,

BIOLOGY-HIGHER LEVEL

when this bluebottle that had been annoying me all focking morning landed on my desk and – how many times has this ever happened to you? – I actually managed to swat the focking thing. SPLAT! Then I borrowed Fionn's ruler – that goy had better watch himself – and used it to smear the fly's guts and brains and whatever else was there all over the first page of my answers booklet. Then at the top of the page I wrote,

THE COMMON BLUEBOTTLE

And then underneath that I put,

DISSECTED THIS MORNING

and then I put, like, arrows pointing to different ports of what was left of him and things like, 'eye' and 'wing' and 'smeg'. Then I close the book over, seal it and hand it up.

Shannon, the character played by Isla Fischer, is having a difficult time of it lately, as do many of the birds who go through Pippa's foster home.

And then it's like,

ART-ORDINARY LEVEL

The hordest subject in the world to fail. If you took a shit in a mug, you could still find some focker who thought it was ort.

Anyway, roysh, the old man asks me how I got on and I go, 'I think I'm going to surprise a few people,' and he claps his hands together, roysh, and he goes, 'Trinity, here we come.' I swear to God, roysh, the sap thinks I'm some kind of misunderstood genius and of course I do nothing to, like, persuade him otherwise, but I *do* manage to persuade him to advance me the thousand sheets he promised me for passing the thing, which is a good job because I ended up failing miserably. JP's claim that you get an automatic pass just for, like, ruling your page and writing your exam number proved a bit wide of the mork. It was, like, *Ross O'Carroll-Kelly, nul points.* Twelve fewer than I kicked in the Schools Cup final, as Fionn pointed out to pretty much everyone.

XXX

To be honest, roysh, at that stage I didn't care. My head was, like, wrecked with everything that had been going on and the summer passed pretty much in a blur. So did the time up to Christmas. I saw little or nothing of the goys. After the Leaving we sort of, like, drifted aport. Happens. I did hear from Christian a lot. He went to Vancouver, where his aunt lives, just for the summer originally but he never came back, although he texted me pretty much every day, just to check I was alroysh and not thinking of doing anything stupid.

I heard that a scout from one of the big design houses – maybe Yves Saint Laurent – had seen Oisinn in action out at the airport and was involved in a catfight with Hugo Boss to sign him up as a rep. JP went to work in his old man's estate agency and was supposed to be doing, like, a morkeshing degree at night. Apparently he talks so much jargon now you need focking subtitles to understand him. Fionn went to UCD to do rocket science. He didn't really, although he probably had the points for it, because he got more than anyone else in the entire country. Had his picture in the papers and everything, and he ended up doing Psychology, which is, like, the mind and shit. He's still a nerd. It said in a notice in *The Irish Times*, roysh, that Simon's wife gave birth to their second child in August, which probably means he's not going back to repeat for a fourth time.

Sorcha went to the States for the summer and is now in, like, UCD doing Orts. She met my old pair in the Frascati Centre and she made sure to tell them she was going out with an amazing goy who's in her year and plays rugby for Blackrock, which makes him an automatic tool in my book. The last time I saw her she was on the 'Six One News' in, like, September or something? It was, like, some student protest or other, roysh, and she was going, 'Four years after the genocide, the Rwandan Government is perpetuating the cycle of violence. We must ensure that Virginie Mukankusi and Deogratias Bizimana did not die in vain. End the executions without trial now.'

She looked amazing.

Erika was rumoured to have married Pierce Brosnan, but it turned out to be total bullshit and she's doing Orts in UCD as well. Aoife got well again and she phoned me once to say she'd never forget the fact that I went to see her when she was ill and she told me I was a very decent person at hort, roysh, and that made me feel good, but then she went, 'Even *if* everyone thinks you're an orsehole,' and that made me feel crap again.

The old pair, of course, remained total dickheads. The council dropped plans for a halting site on our road, roysh, and the old dear became locked in a battle with Dearbhla, one of her friends from tennis, for the chairpersonship of the Foxrock Combined Residents Association, while the old man took most of the summer off to try to get his golf handicap down and became even more of a tool than he already was. Sian never rang again and nor did Alyson, Eloise, Joanna, Keeva, Zara, or Evy.

As for me, I spent most of the time on my own in my room, roysh, or that's how it seemed to me. I couldn't go out for a quiet drink. No matter what battle cruiser I hit, someone, somewhere would stort singing that focking song, 'Oh my darlin', oh my darlin', oh my daaarlin' Clementine ...' So I'd usually end up heading home early and the old pair would be like, 'Not like you to be in before ten o'clock, Ross,' and I'd just flick them the Vs, roysh, or sometimes just give them the finger and go up to my room and watch MTV and think of ways of getting back at Fionn, but I could never come up with anything to top Clementine. In the end I pretty much stopped going out altogether. The old pair were storting to get on my back about doing something with my life, when out of the blue I get a call from Fehily. I recognise his voice straight away. He's there, 'Hello, my child,' and it sends a shiver down my spine.

At first, roysh, I think it's about the damage I did to Crabtree's cor on Rag Day. Thought he might have got, like, I don't know, CCTV footage of me sticking the potato in his exhaust. I'm just about to tell him that he'll have to talk to Hennessy when all of a sudden he goes, 'I'd like you to come to the school, Ross. I have a proposal to put to you,' so I go to grab the keys for the Lexus, roysh, but Bog Breath has already taken it, so I end up having to go in the old dear's Micra, the famous spaz-mobile.

I arrive at the school, roysh, and the first thing I cop is JP's beamer – well, his old man's – outside and I'm there thinking, 'What's going down here?' So I go in, roysh, upstairs and head straight for Fehily's office. His secretary's outside – mad about me – and she goes, 'They're waiting for you,' basically flirting her orse off with me big-time and I'm there, 'Later,' and I go in. I have to say, roysh, I am SO not ready for what I find. The goys are all there. We're talking Oisinn (he's put on weight, impossible as that sounds), JP and Fionn. Oisinn turns around to Fehily and he goes, 'What's the Jackanory? You can tell us now,' and Fehily's there, 'One minute. I want Christian to hear this,' and he picks up the phone. He goes, 'He said he'd wait for the call,' and he dials this number – the dude's still in Vancouver – and he puts him on speakerphone.

Then he stands up and storts pacing the floor going, 'You five boys were part of something special. Something very, very special. You were the kernel, the core, the heart, the root, the essence of a team that brought this school to the brink of something historic and that is why I will believe, as long as there's breath in my body, that you were a gift from the Good Lord Himself.' No arguments there. He goes, 'Unfortunately, the Good Lord has proven something of a miser with regard to this year's gift. The Senior Cup team this year is – not to put too fine a point on it – bloody woegeous. The very words – I think you'll find if you check your scriptures – Jesus himself used to describe Nicodemus's line of patter as he tried to lead him into temptation in the wilderness. I trust you all read about the defeat to Pres Bray in a friendly before Christmas? Tried to stop the papers from publishing it, of course, but to no avail.'

I'm thinking, 'Get to the focking point,' when Fionn – the snake – goes, 'I have a lecture this afternoon, Father ...' and JP's like, 'Yeah, you called this mind-share. Give us the bottom line.' Fehily goes, 'I'm *getting* to the point. I want you boys – all five of you – to come back to the school, with a view to winning ... what is rightfully yours.' Of course all hell breaks loose then. Straight away, roysh, I'm like, 'Repeat the Leaving? Have you TOTALLY lost your mind?' and Fionn's there, 'You want me to drop out of college for the sake of a medal?' and through the speakerphone I can hear Christian going, 'Not for all the Tibanna gas in Cloud City.'

But JP, roysh, he's giving it, 'Just think *in* the box for a moment, goys. Sounds very much to me like there's a highly resourced, precisely targeted results drive going down here,' and Oisinn, the only one in the room who knows what the fock he's talking about, goes, 'I'd just like to say that, for me, not winning a Schools Cup medal is something that's going to haunt me for the rest of my life. Ross, I know you and Fionn have had your differences. But let's not forget that when you played rugby you made the sweetest music together.'

I'm there, 'I'm big enough to put the past behind me if Fionn is. But it's not just him. What about *him*?' and I point at Fehily. Of course *he* looks at me all innocently, cracking on he doesn't know what I'm talking about and I go, 'One day you're telling us we're the chosen ones. We lost one match and everything changed. I ended up having to actually sit the mocks. When I went to you to complain, you said you'd never seen me before in your life.' He goes, 'I was upset, Ross,' and I'm there, '*I* was upset. I missed the penalty that cost us the Cup and for ten months you've let me believe that everyone blamed me,' and he's there, 'I wasn't thinking straight.'

Christian goes, 'What's in it for us?' So much for *all the Tabanna gas in Cloud City*. Fehily goes, 'Apart from an opportunity to mesmerise the crowds again with your fancy footwork?' and Christian goes, 'Eh, yeah,' and JP's there, 'I think the dude wants you to run the numbers, Father. Personally, I think the idea's got core competency, but we all need a bottom line. Ballpark.' Fehily doesn't blink an eyelid, roysh. He goes, 'You'll each be paid five hundred pounds a week. There will be no requirement on you to sit your exams or even to attend classes. In your case, Ross, some of the teachers have asked that you don't. All that is required of you is that you train and play. No more than that.'

Oisinn says he's up for it. JP says we're talking ticks in boxes as far as he's concerned. Fionn takes me by total surprise by saying that he can defer the rest of first year and he tells Fehily to count him in. Then he looks at me, roysh, but I've still got issues here, not knowing whether I could ever, like, trust either Fionn or Fehily again. I'm about to say no, roysh, when all of a sudden Oisinn goes, 'If we do this thing, Father, it's important that you know that I've no interest in being, like, captain again. In fact I'd like to propose that this time Ross leads us,' and straight away, roysh, Fionn goes, 'Seconded,' and I swear to God, roysh, I actually thought I was going to burst out crying there and then. I actually feel like getting up and hugging Fionn – if he wasn't such a queer. And gay as it sounds, roysh, I can't even speak at that moment. Fehily goes, 'Well, Ross? It's down to you. This thing won't work without you, Ross,' and all of a sudden, roysh, I hear Christian's voice coming from practically the other side of the world and he's going, 'You say yes, Ross, and I'm on the next flight home. We're like Chewie and Han, me and you. I'm always by your side.' JP goes, 'Sounds like a strategic fit to me, Ross,' and of course what can I say then, roysh, except, 'Lock up your sisters. The Man is back.'

XXX

Grafton Street is, like, SO packed it's unbelievable, roysh, and I actually shouldn't have bothered my orse agreeing to meet Eimear, this bird I was, like, stringing along for a few weeks because I thought she looked like Calista Flockhart, which she actually doesn't. So much for the light in Annabel's. Anyway, roysh, I ended up accidentally answering the phone to her yesterday, roysh, and being basically too nice for my own good, I found myself agreeing to meet her for lunch in the Powerscourt Townhouse Centre. As it turns out, roysh, she's also meeting some bet-down mate of hers called Tara, who's doing, like, auctioneering somewhere in town and when she finds out I'm repeating in Castlerock she storts that crap of name-dropping people and when it turns out I know them, roysh, she reacts like we're living in, I don't know, China, or some country where there's shitloads of people. She's there, 'OH!

MY! GOD! I can't believe you know Sean Tyner,' and total idiot that I am, roysh, I'm playing along with it, going, 'He's playing in the second row for us this year,' and she's going, 'Is he still going out with Rachel Butler?' and in the end I couldn't be orsed answering her.

I tell the birds I need to drain the lizard and I end up just heading off, hoping Eimear takes some kind of hint from this. I check my phone. I have one new message and it's from Beibhin, who's, like, sixth year Whores on the Shore and who I ended up wearing the face off last week, at Glenageary Dorsh station, believe it or not. Long story, but she was on her way home from violin practice with a couple of her mates, roysh, and I was on my way home from training, and they're all, like, giggling and giving it, 'Are you Ross O'Carroll-Kelly?' and of course one thing leads to another and I end up being with her, although I don't remember giving her my number, roysh, so she must have got it by stalker means. Anyway, in her message, roysh, she says exactly the same thing she said in the one she left yesterday, which is that I mustn't have gotten her last message and she presumes there must be something wrong with my phone or maybe *her* phone and could I ring her later but not after eight because she's got practice again tonight, or if I want to I could meet her outside Pearse Street Dorsh station afterwards, she'll be finished at, like, seven and she'll give me until, like, half-seven to show up and if I didn't she'd presume I wasn't going to, but she hopes I get this message. And I'm thinking, You're the one who's not getting the message, girl.

So I'm heading down Grafton Street, roysh, and who do I bump into only, like, Sorcha and it's actually the first time I've seen her in person since ... well, since all that shit, and I can tell she's not sure what kind of a greeting she's going to get from me, but what can I do, roysh, only give her a huge hug and tell her she looks amazing, which she does. I go, 'Did you have a good time in the States?' and she's there, 'OH! MY! GOD! Martha's Vineyard is, like, SO amazing. If you *ever* get a chance, *Oh my God,* SO go. I mean, we worked, like, really hord, but we went out loads. The social life was, like, really hectic.' I know this is all for my benefit. She goes, 'I came back without a penny to my name, of course. *Oh my God!* I turned into SUCH a pisshead. We nearly got arrested one night. Me, Aoife, Sophie and Claire. You know Claire, my friend from Bray?' I do actually. She was a focking howiya until she met Sorcha through Amnesty or Vegetarians Are Us or one of that shower and suddenly she talks like she's next in line to the focking throne.

I ask whether she wants to go for, like, lunch, seeing as I left the last one I bought on the table in the Powerscourt Centre, and she says she's meeting her old dear outside Pamela Scott's at two and she has, like, an hour to kill. So we hit Fitzer's Café, roysh, and I end up ordering a beef and vegetable stirfry teriyaki and a Coke and Sorcha has a brie and camembert baguette which she doesn't touch, spicy wedges which she picks at and a Diet Coke. She goes, 'I heard you're repeating?' and I'm there, 'Bit of a bummer, but it's a chance to try and put right what happened last year.'

She goes, 'Your mum said you were looking at LBS,' which is a college, roysh, I say *college,* but all the goys say it stands for Loaded But Stupid instead of Leeson Business School. It's, like, six grand a term or something, though at the end you get a degree in morkeshing from the University of, I don't know, Bulgaria or something. I tell Sorcha that that plan fell by the wayside when I heard they had this, like, push on, roysh, to try to get State recognition for it as a legitimate third-level university. And the rumour was that the lecturers wouldn't be giving out the summer exam papers in November, as was the tradition, because they were sick of being treated as a joke by the Department of Education. So suddenly they're not giving out the papers until the end of, like, January, which gave people only, like, five months to go to the library and learn someone else's essay from the previous year off by hort. Sorcha says that sounds SO unfair, but I can tell from the way she says it that she's actually ripping the piss. Anyway, in the meantime the place went bankrupt, so it doesn't matter a fock.

We hordly say anything while we – sorry, I – eat and I realise that, whatever happened last year, I'm actually not over Sorcha yet. I have to prove to myself as well that I could basically still have her if I wanted her, so I turn on the old chorm and stort giving it, 'I've really missed you. Okay, I wasn't exactly an angel while you were away in the States, if you know what I mean, but I did think about you a lot while you were away.'

She thinks about this, roysh, as she takes off her scrunchy, slips it onto her wrist, shakes her head, pulls her hair back into a low ponytail, replaces the scrunchy and pulls four or five strands of hair loose. Then she pushes her food away and takes out her Marlboro Lights and goes, 'Are you seeing anyone?' and the, I don't know, directness of the question sort of, like, throws me. I go, 'Kind of,' and she shakes her head as she plucks a cigarette from the box and goes, 'That was always your problem. You either are or you aren't, Ross,' and I'm there, 'Well, I was sort of seeing this bird – Eimear. Met her in Annabel's,' and I think of her sitting in the Powerscourt Centre, focking steaming when she realises that I've left her with, like, the bill. Sorcha's like, 'Eimear who? As in, what's her second name?' and I'm there, 'You wouldn't know her,' and she goes, 'I bet I do,' and I'm like, 'Eimear O'Neill,' and Sorcha goes, 'Small, thin, straight blond hair? Went to Loreto Foxrock?' and I'm there, 'How do you know her?' and she goes, 'She was on the Irish debating team. She was actually SUCH a good debater.' Like I *give* a shit?

She goes, 'So, you're only, like, seeing her?' and of course I'm there, 'Well, I've been kind of going out with her really,' trying to make her jealous. I'm going, 'I don't know. I'm still searching for *the one*,' and she goes, 'Well, I've found *the one*. I met someone and he's, like, the perfect goy,' and like the fool that I am, roysh, I actually think she's talking about me. I go, 'Oh yeah?' and I'm about to reach over, roysh, to touch her hand when all of a sudden she goes, 'Brandon.' I'm there, 'Who?' and she goes, 'His name's Brandon. Brandon Oakes,' and quick as a flash I've gone, 'Brandon Oakes sounds like a focking retirement home.' She finally lights up her cigarette and she goes, 'Well, he's actually the nicest goy I've ever gone out with. Met him in the States. He has SUCH an amazing body. He plays, like, American football,' and I'm there, 'Hold on, hold on. Can we just rewind a bit? You're telling me that you met this goy in America last summer, we're talking six months ago. And now he's over there and you're over here and you're still, like, going out with the loser?' which I know is out of order the second I've said it. She stubs out her cigarette – she's only had, like, one drag off it – and she goes, '*You're* the loser, Ross,' and she looks at her watch, which is the pink Baby-G I bought her for her birthday last year and she goes, 'My mum is going to go TOTALLY ballistic,' and she gets up and goes, roysh, and it's only when she's gone that I realise that this time it's me who's been left sitting with the bill.

XXX

The old man calls me when I'm passing by his study, roysh, and when I stick my head around the door he looks all pleased with himself. He says he's just been on to *The Irish Times*, roysh, and he's going to be sponsoring their schools rugby coverage and in future they're going to give it, like, two pages. He goes, 'It'll be a bit like their Bulmers Total Golf pages except it'll be called Total Schools Rugby Totally, or some such. We haven't worked out the finer points yet, but isn't it exciting? Hennessy and I are playing golf with Malachy Logan this very afternoon.'

I'm just there, 'Yippee-doo.'

XXX

Fionn's telling us all the difference between the Id and the Ego – fascinating, I don't think – and I go up to get the beers in and while I'm up there, roysh, who sidles up to me only Fionn himself, going, 'No hord feelings,' and I shrug, but I refuse to shake the goy's hand. He goes, 'Ross?' and it all comes out, roysh, I'm there, 'You ruined my focking life,' and he goes, 'You ruined mine. My old pair *still* think I'm a knobber because of you. I could have Linda Evangelista, Claudia Schiffer and Liz Hurley up in my room and they'd be convinced we're just exchanging colouring tips.' I'm there, 'How many copies of that focking video are doing the rounds?' and he goes, 'I only made twelve. I can't take responsibility for any unauthorised copies that are in circulation,' and I'm there, 'Half of focking Dublin has seen it. Him pulling out those electrodes that he wanted to use on my town halls. Total focking strangers have been laughing at me in the street.'

The borman puts the bevvies down on the bor. Fionn goes, 'Why don't we just agree that we both suffered? Look, Ross, we're never going to be bosom buddies, we know that. But when we play rugby together ...' and he sort of, like, lets it hang in the air? I just go, 'Pure magic,' and he repeats what I say, he's like, 'Pure magic.' He goes, 'It's

January. We've got, what, three months together? Three months to work for something that we both want so much. After that we need never look at each other ever again. But the question is, Ross, are you big enough to put our differences aside to win that Cup,' and I think about it for a few seconds, roysh, even though I don't really need to. I just go, 'Let's play rugby,' and we shake on it and then we're back over to the goys with the pints.

JP goes, 'You goys look like you're dovetailing again,' and I'm there, 'We just want to play the beautiful game,' and JP's like, 'Sounds like a win-win situation to me. Oisinn here's just been telling us about his year. Fionn, I know you were doing alroysh scenario-wise in UCD and the Blankers-Koen is wall-to-wall in my game, but I don't know how you're still alive, Oisinn.'

This is all by way of introduction for Oisinn's act. He goes, 'I don't either, Fionn. I ended up having two mobile phones. I'd be selling some bird *Ultraviolet,* or *Escape for Women,* or *Angel.* Bit of seductive chitchat about the smell, sensuous being a key word, couple of squirts and the next thing I knew they were practically begging me for my number. The Motorola was for birds over thirty and the Nokia number was for birds under thirty. You know how it is, some nights you fancy a bit of old and some you want them young. The two were ringing constantly. By Christmas I had the two of them switched off. I'd shagged myself out.'

I tell the goy he's still a legend and Christian says he'll second that and before we know it I'm, like, raising my glass and suggesting a toast to the best team in the land. And whatever did or didn't happen at Dublin Airport is, like, all forgotten now and all I can think about, roysh, is how great it is just, like, catching up with each other again. We're like, 'THE BEST TEAM IN THE LAND ...' and I know that before the night is out, we're going to be looking for a twenty-four-hour garage that sells mince pies.

XXX

Ultra-resistant. Fantasy ribbed. Studded. Lubricated. Luminous. Extra sensitive for her pleasure. Orange. Strawberry. Fruit of the focking forest. I know I've been out of the game for the guts of a year, roysh, but I can't believe how many choices there are nowadays. I drop three pound coins into the slot, roysh, and choose a three-pack of extra-sensitive, gossamer, ribbed ticklers, which sound up to the job. On the way out the door, roysh, I check myself out in the mirror and I have to say I'm looking good tonight and the black eye actually suits me. Then I go back out to Angel, this bird from Clonskeagh who's in, like, first year Law in Portobello.

I ask her if she wants another drink and she says OH! MY! GOD! if she drinks any more there's no way she'll be able to get up for water aerobics in the morning and I go, 'There's only one kind of aerobics you're going to be doing in the morning,' and of course I'm kicking myself for coming across so, I don't, sleazy, roysh, but from the smile on her face, she doesn't seem to mind. Her best friend, Ana with one n, wouldn't mind a shot at the title as well. In fact it was her who tried to get in there first, giving it all, 'Congrats. You had SUCH a good game today.'

We basically hammered CBC Monkstown into the ground in the first round, me, Christian and JP all getting two tries – a brace apiece, as One F in *The Stor* called it – so me and the goys are back in Kiely's living off the glory, roysh, and it's like we've never been away. There must be, like, a hundred, maybe a hundred and fifty birds here and they all want a piece of the focking Dream Team. Like I said, roysh, I've been out of the game a long time and I very nearly make the mistake of taking the first thing that comes along. Ana with one n wants me and I'm actually entertaining serious thoughts of nipping it when I cop Angel, who's like a young Cameron Diaz, and straight away I know that in two hours' time I'm going to be conkers deep in this one.

Ana with one n knows it as well, roysh, because she's resorted basically to being a bitch to Angel and within twenty seconds of me coming back from the can with the jimmie hats she's going, 'I cannot BELIEVE you ate two of those Weight Watchers dinners. That's like, OH! MY! GOD!' and Angel looks at me, roysh, to get my reaction, and of course I couldn't give two focks what she had for dinner, even though I'm going to be tasting it myself soon enough. Angel goes, 'I only ate half of the salmon mornay. It was SO disgusting,' and Ana with one n is there, '*Hello?* That's why I told you to have the chicken in peppercorn sauce in the first place. Instead you had to have, like, two,' and Angel goes, '*What*ever,' and Ana with one n takes her lip balm out of her miniature backpack, gives her a filthy, then focks off to the jacks and when she's gone, roysh, Angel goes, 'I wouldn't mind, but they're MY buckled-back flared jeans she's wearing. You think SHE can afford to shop in Jigsaw? I don't THINK so. Her shoes are from Nine West, but they're the only decent pair she has.'

When she shuts the fock up, I manage to persuade her out onto the dancefloor, roysh, and it's 'Praise You' by Fat Boy Slim and I am giving it absolutely loads. I'm dancing with Angel, roysh, but I'm also flirting my orse off with this bird who Fionn knows from UCD and her name's, like, Rebecca and she's, like, first year Social Science and so like Liz Hurley that you could *actually* be looking at her. So, more to make Angel jealous than anything else, I cruise over beside her and I give it, 'You're a pretty amazing dancer, has to be said,' and she just, like, wiggles her little finger at me, which presumably means she's heard I have, like, a small penis, which I don't.

So then it's back to Angel of course and she obviously hasn't copped what just happened because she goes, 'I'd say that becomes SUCH a pain,' and I'm there, 'What?' and she's like, 'Girls, like, bothering you all the time. Propositioning you and stuff,' and I've gone, 'I'm not exactly fighting *you* off, am I?' and I throw the lips on her. Twenty minutes of deep throat exploration and she's, like, fishing in her bag for her cloakroom ticket and before we know it we're back at her gaff in Clonskeagh, and get this, roysh, she doesn't live with her old pair. They actually *bought* her this gaff so she could study in peace and quiet for the Leaving. We're talking big bucks here.

Much as it pains me to say it, it's ten months since I had my Nat King Cole, roysh, so when she asks me if I want a cup of tea, I don't even answer, I'm just, like, bailing into her, ripping the clothes off her and she's going, 'Be careful, Ross. These combats are Hobo,' but twenty seconds later, roysh, we're both in the raw, on the floor of her sitting-room and she's gagging for me and we're talking seriously gagging here. Five minutes of foreplay – she better not tell anyone or they'll all want that – and I'm ready to do the bould thing but she goes, 'Do you have any protection?' and of course I've got the old Johnny B Goodes in my sky rocket.

So I reach for my chinos, roysh, and I stick my hand in the back pocket and I pull out the little box. And of course I'm there in the dork, roysh, trying to find the little flap in the cellophane that lets you get into the box, but it takes me, like, five minutes and of course I'm worried all this time that the old snake chorming act's gonna fall flat. As it happened, roysh, he held up his end for once. But that's when it all went basically pear-shaped. When I got the cellophane off the packet and tore

off the top of the box, what fell out weren't johnnies at all, but – I CAN-
NOT FOCKING BELIEVE THIS – a comb and a length of, like, dental
floss and a tiny toothbrush and the smallest tube of toothpaste you've
ever seen. And of course straight away the performance is over as far as
the old pant python is concerned. She looks at all the stuff, roysh, and
she storts laughing, not normal laughter, roysh, but evil, Wicked Witch
of the West laughter. And I haven't been so humiliated since, well, since
Fionn made me look like George Michael trying to pick up some homo
at the airport, which is less than a year ago, so I suppose it's not so long.
I end up just making my excuses and getting the fock out of there as
quick as I can.

XXX

I'm just in from practicing my kicking when Erika rings, and I'm there
thinking, to what do I owe this pleasure? But of course I know. Now
that I'm on the S again I'm just about worthy of scoring as far as she's
concerned and she is SO going to show Sorcha that she could have me if
she wanted. She goes, 'I drove past you about half an hour ago. You're
not actually looking all that bad. I don't think it's going to be as painful
as I thought,' and I go, 'What isn't?' and she's like, '*Puh-lease*. I don't find
that Little Boy Lost act the least bit endearing. I'm going to *be* with you,
Ross. Not yet. It's still a total no-no for someone like *me* to be with
someone like *you*. Especially since I'm in UCD and you're still in school.
But if you win this rugby ... thing that you're playing in, you move up a
place on the social acceptability scale. I've never been a rugby groupie
but I've known Sorcha long enough to know how it works,' and I play it
Kool and the Gang, roysh, I really do.

   I'm there, 'I'm actually seeing someone at the moment,' which is total bullshit but it doesn't matter, roysh, because she just, like, ignores it

totally. She goes, 'I've looked up the fixtures and it seems you're playing Pres Bray tomorrow in Greystones. If you beat them, it's not a terribly big deal. I think I'm going to leave it at least until you reach the final before I'm with you.' I'm like, 'Do I have a say in all this?' and I'm picturing her right now – a total and utter goddess – and I know I don't.

She goes, 'You're going to get the night of passion you've always dreamt of and then we'll see how high and mighty your little girlfriend is,' and I'm about to tell her that Sorcha's not my girlfriend when all of a sudden she goes, 'That's the vet at the door. Orchid's got a twisted testicle,' and when she hangs up, I'm wondering whether she had anything to do with it herself.

XXX

The thing I forgot to mention, roysh, is that Fehily himself is coaching us this year. Sooty got sacked from the school after we lost the final last year, roysh, though not *because* we lost the final. He basically did an interview with the school magazine in which he said that people who live in council houses are paying for the sins of a previous life. Fehily goes, 'Merit as there was in his point, once the Dublin 4 media got their hands on the story, he had no choice but to go.'

I actually don't think Fehily's much of a coach, roysh, but it's like he said, once me and the other goys from last year are firing on all cylinders, the team basically runs itself. As captain, he's also given me a pretty big role in deciding, like, tactics and team selection. To be honest, roysh, he came to me the day before we lashed CBC Monkstown out of it, hands me a blank sheet of paper and asks me what team I'd pick if it were down to me.

Now I'm not the brightest, roysh, but I knew what was going down here. He was basically asking me to pick the team and the first thought that, like, occurred to me was that there were one or two old scores I could settle at the stroke of a pen. I seriously considered dropping Fionn, roysh, but I know the goy's too good a rugby player to leave out, though I'd never admit that to his face. I *do* drop Laurence Leahy, our inside centre who Wardy was bulling up in that morning's *Indo*. Let's see who's a Genuine Star In The Making now. I also end up drop-kicking this tool who plays in our second row, we're talking Rory Smyth. The main, I don't know, stumbling block with him is that he fancies himself as a bit of a ladies' man and had the balls to tell me a couple of weeks ago that New Castlerock – as in the bunch of losers who lost a friendly in Bray before Christmas – would out-score Old Castlerock – as in me and the goys – in the old scenario stakes. The reason he was easy to drop is that he's crap.

Of course he comes to me the morning we played Monkstown, roysh, just after Fehily broke the bad news to him, and he tells me that he's very disappointed not to have even made the bench, and I tell him he needs to keep his head down, lay off the scoops, ease off on the old nights out and keep plugging away. I tell him he's close, so close he can smell it, knowing full well in my mind that as long as I'm picking the team the only chance he has of playing for the school is if he joins the basketball team, which is basically for knobs. He goes, 'Thanks for the advice,' and he focks off, the tool.

The morning of the return game against Pres Bray – which has become a bit of a grudge match – he comes to me again and he goes, 'I want to play today, Ross. When their coach said what he said in the *Bray People*, about Castlerock being a fading power in the Schools Cup competition, I took it personally, because I was one of the players who under-performed that day. You've got to tell Fehily, Ross. I am SO up for this match,' and then Laurence Leahy arrives over and storts throwing in his two-pence worth, giving it, 'We should at least be offered a chance to put things roysh.' I don't know how I don't just, like, crack up laughing in their faces, roysh. Instead, I give them this, like, solemn look and I go, 'This is no time to be taking risks on goys who never delivered in the past. It's a day for men, not boys.' The poor fockers have been breaking their balls in training. I'm there, 'Keep up the hord work, goys, and you never know, maybe you'll make the bench for the quarter-final,' and they go off *actually* looking grateful to me.

Fehily gives us this, like, no-nonsense speech, all about Bray being famous for nothing more than slot machines and inbreeding. 'But last year – owing to the local Presentation College's, it shames me to say it, *victory* over this proud institute of education and social advancement – Bray emerged like an ugly, weeping sore on the face of schools rugby. And this, my children, is the cure.'

He holds up this huge plastic tub, roysh, which it turns out is full of, like, white powder. He goes, 'Fifty milligrams stirred into a glass of water five times a day,' and, almost thinking out loud, roysh, I go, 'Is it creatine or something?' and he's there, 'Creatine is last year's buzz. You don't NEED to know what this is. Just that it works,' and he sends Magahy – the total wanker who coached us as juniors – around the dressing-room, giving us each a tub of the stuff. We all stort, like, pouring it into our water bottles and knocking it back.

Fehily goes, 'What happened before Christmas should shame you all. Yes, there have been some changes since then, some old friends have come back to help us in our hour of need. But even my old friend Matt Talbot never knew the kind of shame that you heaped onto this school by losing to that shower before Christmas. The time for vengeance is at hand.'

He goes, 'First will come honor and then freedom, and from both of these happiness, prosperity, life: in a word, that state of things will return which we Germans perhaps dimly saw before the War, when individuals can once more live with joy in their hearts because life has a meaning and a purpose, because the close of life is then not in itself the end, since there will be an endless chain of generations to follow: man will know that what we create will not sink into Orcus but will pass to his children and to his children's children.'

This is in the dressing-room, roysh, and when he's finished there's no, like, cheering or anything. I just go, 'Come on, goys. Let's go to work,' and we go out there and basically kick ass.

They actually fancy themselves a bit, roysh, obviously got, like, notions about themselves. Their hooker, roysh, William something or other's his name, he comes up to me and he goes, 'Bit sad, isn't it? You lot, I mean, having to leave college to come back and bail out your school,' and without even thinking, roysh, I go, 'This time it's for real,' and he ends up having a mare of a game and couldn't hit a cow's orse with a banjo. We're, like, lording it over them in the lineout and knocking seven shades of shit out of them in the scrum. They hold out for, like, fifteen minutes and then suddenly it's, like, raining tries. Christian scores two absolute crackers. Fionn got one and the Stud Muffin here goes and scores three. After the third, roysh, I shove the ball up my shirt and walk up to this photographer who I think takes the pictures for *The Irish Times* and I stand in front of him and, like, point at myself as if to say, 'Who's the man?'

We're actually ripping the piss at the end, just basically enjoying ourselves while we're waiting for the final whistle, and when it goes, roysh,

I head straight for the press box, roysh, at the side of the field and I go, 'Anyone here from the *Bray People*?' and all the press, roysh, they look up from what they're doing, sort of in, like, shock. One F is obviously on the phone to *The Stor* because he's going, 'Pres Bray ... will remember ... this one ... as fondly ... as a tour of duty ... in 'Nam, full point,' and when he hears what I say he points at the dude behind him, who's like, 'Yes, I'm covering the game for the ...' and I just butt in, roysh, and I go, 'Some fading power, huh?' It must be that powder Fehily gave us that's making me so angry. I'm going, 'You know, by St Patrick's Day you're going to be looking at this team and all we've achieved and you're going to say it was a pleasure to see your team lose to us.'

✗✗✗

I get up, roysh, and the old man's in the kitchen, looking like somebody's pissed on his Corn Flakes. He goes, 'I take it from the equanimity of your mood that you haven't seen it yet?' and I'm there, 'What are you shitting on about now?' He hands me a copy of the paper, roysh, and they've printed the photograph of me with the ball up my shirt and underneath it says, 'Ross O'Carroll-*Kenny* salutes the crowd after scoring his third try in Castlerock's victory over Pres Bray in Greystones yesterday,' and Knob Head picks up the phone and before I can tell him to cop himself on he's giving out yords to some dude on the end of the phone and in the end the goy promises to print a correction. The old man's like, 'I want it on the front page, too. And you can bloody well print the photograph again as well. Otherwise you'll be hearing from my solicitor.'

He slams down the phone and tells me not to worry because Wardy – a *real* journalist – managed to get my name roysh. He's there, 'Wait until you read what he's written about your performance. A cracking prospect. *His* words, Kicker. Not mine.' And as he leafs through the paper to try to find the page, he suddenly stops and he goes, 'A girl called for you this morning. About nine o'clock. Hope you don't mind, I told her you were in bed, recovering from battle. Beibhin she said her name was. Nice girl. Said she'd call you later on your mobile.'

XXX

I'm on the Stillorgan dualler, roysh, and I hit a red light at Cornelscourt, so I check my messages. Some bird called Jennie with an ie rang and said I gave her my number in the rugby club on Sunday night and she hoped I remembered because we were both SO drunk, but she hoped I didn't mind her ringing and she just wondered whether I was, like, doing anything later in the week. Beibhin rang to say that – get this – she read my horoscope in the paper this morning and OH! MY! GOD! she couldn't BELIEVE what it said. Then she storts, like, reading it into the phone, going, '*Hobbies and pastimes bring enjoyment and success.* That's obviously the match against Pres Bray. *But be more prepared to show your softer side. You are about to woo and win the heart of someone close. Prepare yourself for sweet nothings and sentimentalities.* This is the amazing bit. *Strong attractions towards Cancerians,*' and then she lets out this, like, squeal and she goes, 'My birthday's on, like, June twenty-eighth. OH! MY! GOD!' and I'm wondering how focking gone in the head she is that she can believe what Fergus Gibson says and ignore the fact that I've never returned one of her calls since I nipped her that day, the sad bitch.

There's also a message from Angel, who doesn't seem to have been put off by the whole Travel Hygiene Kit incident and wants me to phone her.

The last message is from Sorcha, who says she's SO sorry she hasn't been in touch, roysh, because she's been rushed off her feet with this whole Khemais Ksila situation, which, at a guess, involves some black dude in some shithole of a country who's in the clink for acting the dick and is about to get snotted.

I've a wood on me like a focking broom handle. It must be this stuff we're taking. I lie on my bed, staring at the ceiling, trying to decide whether I should have an Allied Irish or ring Sorcha back.

CHAPTER EIGHT
'A pleasure to have at the school'

Ultan Mac An tSionnaigh is giving me filthies, roysh, and Christian
comes over and asks me how I'm feeling and I tell him that I'm about to
deck that tosser if he looks me up and down like that again. Christian
tells me not to do anything stupid because we need to be calm, roysh,
but he knows there's bad blood there, involving, not a bird – unusually
enough – but Ultan basically taking my place on the Ireland schools
team for the tour of Argentina last summer. I know I focked up in the
Schools Cup final, roysh, but the word on the street was that I was still a
shoo-in, what with our Junior Cup coach – that tosser Magahy – being
on the selection committee. This Ultan orsehole is, like, Belvo. How far
did they go in the competition last year? He's obviously repeating as
well, roysh, which I'm happy about because he's going to see that I'm
basically twice the player I was since I storted taking that white shit,
whatever it is.

So I've no need to go losing the rag with the dude. Wardy said in the
paper this morning that it's, like, a red letter day for Castlerock College
and Belvedere in the Leinster Senior Cup, although I tell the goys, as JP
gets ready to boot the ball into the air, that it's actually a kick ass day.
Probably sounds a bit weird, roysh, but we're so relaxed that every time
there's, like, a lineout in the first fifteen minutes, JP keeps turning

around to our crowd behind the goal and conducting the singing, which obviously pisses the Belvo goys off big-style.

At the same time, roysh, nobody's doing anything stupid. The quarter-final of the cup is no place to be taking risks and it's, like, twenty minutes I think before we give away the first penalty of the day with the scores still tied at, like, 0-0. Ultan – what were his parents thinking? – he steps up to take it, roysh, and Stevie focking Wonder would knock this over, that's how easy it is, twenty yords out, a little bit left of centre. Of course that's without Paul McKenna here focking with the dude's mind. I walk up to him, roysh, just as he's taking his five steps backwards – he ripped off his whole technique from me – and I go, 'There's a bit of a wind blowing. Keep it left,' and their prop-forward – Gavin's his name, he's going out with one of the Clerkin twins, both lashers – he drags me away, roysh, thinking he's all that *and* your bus fare home. I could have decked him if I'd wanted to and of course Oisinn came steaming in to get him out of my face, but I'd already done the damage I wanted. There's no wind at all, roysh, but I've put the idea in this retord's head that there is and now he can't make up his mind whether it's, like, a bluff, a double-bluff or a double-double-bluff. His head is totally wrecked and he ends up, like, kicking it wide.

Ten minutes later, roysh – it's one of the worst matches I've ever played in – we win a penalty of our own and I have to say, roysh, it's from a pretty difficult position. Of course I'm drinking the Kool-Aid. Forty yords out close to the left-hand touchline? No problem to me. I look around for Ultan and I stort, like, pointing to my eyes, roysh, telling him to watch how the master does it. Then I run my hand through my hair, roysh, blow hord, take five steps backwards, four to the roysh, run my hand through my hair again, do a little jig on the spot and then put the ball over the bor. When he passes me again a few minues later, I go, 'DID YOU SEE HOW IT WAS DONE? DID YOU? WATCH THE MASTER AND LEARN,' and he looks pretty, I don't know, taken aback by how angry I am.

And that's it basically for the first half. We're playing pretty good stuff, roysh, but their defence is, like, SO solid and there's not even a sniff of a try for either side. We go back to the dressing-room and Fehily's, like, pacing the floor, going, 'Now, people of Germany, give us four years and then pass judgement upon us. In accordance with Field Marshal von Hindenburg's command we shall begin now ...' But of course none of us is, like, listening to the dude. Like pretty much everyone else I go straight to my bag, get out my little box of powder, tip a small mountain of the stuff onto the palm of my hand and stort, like, eating it. The thing nearly chokes me, roysh. I'm so keen to get it into me that I forget to take it with water and half of it ends up in my focking lungs. I tip some more straight into my mouth and take a drink straight from the tap. Fehily's going, 'May God Almighty give our work His blessing, strengthen our purpose, and endow us with wisdom and the trust of our people, for we are fighting not for ourselves but for Germany,' but we don't need any half-time pep talks, we're straight back onto the field, so John B to get stuck into Belvo again that we're out there, like, four or five minutes before they've even left the dressing-room.

Ultan Dickhead has had a total mental meltdown, roysh. He misses another penalty early in the second half and – total mortification for the dude – they end up taking him off kicking duties and when they win another, roysh, it's actually their scrumhalf who takes it and he knocks it over from, it has to be said, a difficult angle, despite being a Ginger.

But, like, nothing's going to stop us today, roysh. Ten minutes later we hit them like a steamroller that's gone out of control. It's, like, recycle after recycle and it's, like, relentless if that's the word, and they're focked, you can see it in them, we've got the extra strength. Ball comes to me and I don't even see the three goys in front of me, roysh, just the line and it's, like, twenty yords ahead and I hold the ball to my chest and crash through the tackles and I am not exaggerating, roysh, I take the last five or six steps with a player holding on to either leg and another hanging on to my waist. I get the try and the crowd goes ballistic. I knock over the conversion but we don't really need it.

I'm walking off thinking if that's what I can do on, I don't know, one hundred and fifty milligrams a day, imagine what I could do on three hundred.

XXX

'SHE COULD HAVE LOST HER EYE.' That's what Fehily's saying to us, roysh, at the top of his voice. He's going, 'IT'S DIFFICULT ENOUGH TO BELIEVE THAT CASTLEROCK STUDENTS WOULD BEHAVE IN THIS WAY, BUT MEMBERS OF THE SENIOR RUGBY TEAM?' which we KNOW is total horseshit, roysh, because pelting the birds from Pill Hill with eggs is, like, a tradition at this stage. We actually didn't do it last year, roysh, but there's a few of us sitting around in the common room, bored out of our bins basically, when I turn around to JP and I'm there, 'Let's go yoke the scobes,' and he says he's on for it. What he actually says is, 'I'll take that off-line,' and so we set off for the Home Ec. room, where all the blokes who should have actually been birds are making Rice Krispie cakes and sewing aprons. We storm in, roysh, and JP creates, like, a diversion by shouting, 'SAME-SEX MARRIAGES, HERE WE COME,' and I basically lift a shitload of eggs and when old Bender Bentley, the teacher, tries to stop us we just, like, give him the finger and he knows that because we're on the S there's pretty much fock-all he can do.

So off we go, roysh, and on the way we end up picking up Oisinn and Christian – 'morching into the detention area is not my idea of fun. It's more like … suicide' – and head down to the convent. It's, like, half-one, roysh, and we spot these three total howiyas coming back from whatever they were doing at lunch, probably shoplifting. So we wait behind these trees, roysh, quiet as a focking mouse, and when they pass by we basically pelt the shit out of them. They're actually in too much shock to run away, roysh, and they're just, like, sitting ducks basically. Anyway, roysh, we leg it, but wouldn't you focking know it, one of the eggs hits one of them in the eye and apparently it's all, like, bloodshot and the nuns – the Little Sisters of Perpetual Sexual Frustration – they have a knicker-fit and end up ringing the school.

Of course Fehily knows straight away who's in the frame, but we all know he's going to do fock-all about it. He goes, 'As you are all members of the senior rugby team and the final is now only four days away, we can put this little episode down to pre-match tension. You won't be punished this time and I'll send this girl a pre-emptive solicitor's letter, just in case she's any notions of looking for damages of some description or other. I'll get Hennessy onto it immediately.' Hennessy's their focking brief! He goes, 'Fiends for compensation, these kinds of people,' and then he, like, gives us a wink and tells us to go in peace.

XXX

'We should open up, like, a pool,' JP goes, 'or a book, or whatever the fock you want to call it, but everyone on the team puts in, like, fifty sheets and whoever ends up scoring her at the debs takes the pot.'

We're basically talking about Miss Roland, the new French teacher, roysh, who actually *does* look like Uma Thurman and, according to a few of the goys who had her in St Columba's, bangs like a barn door in a force ten gale, and whether it's bullshit or not, I'm going to be the one to find out. Oisinn goes, 'This is presuming, of course, that only one of us ends up with her,' and JP's there, 'No it has to be the *first* one to nip her,' and I tell the goys to get with the programme and to forget about the debs because I'm basically going to end up being with her at the Leaving Cert Results Ball at the end of, like, August?

We've just come from, like, Saturday afternoon training, roysh, which was hord, even though none of us is supposed to be on the beer this year. I decide to up my dose of the white stuff to one hundred milligrams five times a day, just to see do I finish training any less wrecked. Anyway, roysh, after training, I – as team captain – suggested we all head out to the driving range in Kilternan, just to, like, beat off the cobwebs and to, like, do something together as a team. And I have to say, roysh, it's one of my better ideas because after a couple of hours everyone's back in the land of the living and having the crack and of course one thing leads to another and before we know it we're in the middle of a session in Johnnie Fox's. I know the semi-final's only, like, a week away, roysh, and I know it's St Mary's, but we really need to cut loose. It's funny but without the distraction of actually having to go to classes, there's that bit much more pressure on us this year because we all know that it's, like, win or bust. This is what I'm telling the goys as I'm knocking back my sixth pint of Ken and suggesting we hit town. The whole gang of us – we're talking Oisinn, Fionn, JP, Christian, the whole crew – we end up in, like, Café en Seine of all places, which is where I tell them that on the night of the Results Ball, roysh, I'm not going to throw the lips on Roland until we hit Buck Whaleys, which is just to, like, lull them into a false sense of security. I've already decided to make my move in the Berkeley Court as soon as we've finished the meal because, according to my information, supplied by a goy I know who claims to have been with her, after two glasses of wine she is literally anybody's.

My mobile phone rings and the caller ID says it's a private number and I answer, roysh, half-expecting to hear the old man's voice. But it's, like, a bird. Very sexy as well. She goes, 'Hey, Ross. It's Jemma with a j.' Forget I said that. I throw my eyes up to heaven and I'm there, 'What a surprise. I don't remember giving you my number,' and she goes, 'I got it from Claire Croft. She's in my furniture restoration class,' and I'm actually not going to ask the obvious question. I haven't a focking clue who Claire Croft is.

But I know who Jemma is. She's a head-wrecker basically. Met her in the M1 a couple of weeks ago and it was, like, the usual story. Her old pair were in Beauvoir-sur-Mer for the week and I ended up giving her the night of her life back in her gaff in Monkstown. Not bad looking and the bod was alroysh. But of course the next morning I was, like, Wile E Coyote, chewing the orm off myself to get out of there without having to give her my number. But she has it now.

She goes, 'I just wanted to get some, like, advice from you. I'm on the organising committee for our debs.' She goes to Our Lady of Perpetual Blob Strop in Templeogue, if anyone's interested. She's there, 'The big argument at the moment is whether we should stort off with, like, a drinks reception in the school itself. Or if we should just have the debs totally away from the school, maybe Powerscourt House,' and I know what she's getting at, roysh, she's basically dropping me bits of bait to see if I'm, like, interested, but of course I'm not biting. I'm there,

'Sorry, Jemma, you're breaking up. Hello? Hello?' and I blow into the phone, then hang up and switch it off.

So three or four vodka and Red Bulls later and we hit Reynords, roysh, and who do I bump into there only Sorcha, who gives me a big hug and tells me she's SO sorry she hasn't been in touch but she's been, like, SO busy and she goes, 'Isn't it SO amazing about Augusto Pinochet being arrested?' and I agree, not having a bog who he is obviously, and she asks me did I sign her e-mail petition and pass it on to someone I knew and I say I did, which is a complete and utter lie.

She's with, like, Sophie and Chloë, roysh, and they're both flirting their orses off with Christian, basically trying to get him to buy them drinks, and he's such a focking soft-horted kind of guy that all of a sudden I feel like telling them to stop taking advantage of him. But Sorcha, roysh, she's got the *Issey Miyake* on and her eyes are locked onto mine and we both know what's going to happen here. She tells me her old dear is opening a new shop – sorry, boutique – in the Powerscourt Townhouse Centre – and that's my cue to move in. It's like all the passion between us has been bottled up for so long and now someone's, like, popped the cork and we're all of a sudden eating the face off each other and I can hear Sophie going, 'I SO knew we shouldn't have come here tonight. It was obvious she wanted to be with him again,' and I can hear Christian going, 'What's wrong with that?' and Chloë going, 'Because he's a bastard basically,' and then Christian going, 'That's my best friend you're talking about,' fair play to the goy.

I don't hear any complaints from Sorcha, though. But I have to say, roysh, once I've nipped her and pretty much satisfied myself that I could have her tonight if I wanted her, I stort to get bored and – this is probably a bad reflection on me – I stort thinking about maybe going on to Lillies, to see if there's any scenario there. Of course Sorcha thinks this is, like, Happy-Ever-After now, which is the thing about her that always frightens me off. She's already going, 'OH! MY! GOD! I can't WAIT to see Erika's face when she hears we're back together,' and then she says she wouldn't mind, like, heading off because she's, like, wrecked after a long week in college, which is basically code for, 'Let's hop on the good foot and do the bould thing.'

Call me a gentleman if you will, roysh, but I don't want it when it's this easy so I go outside with her, intending to walk her, Sophie and Chloë up to the taxi rank then put myself back in the morketplace. So we're all walking up Dawson Street, roysh, me and Sorcha up ahead and Christian lagging behind with the other two, when all of a sudden Sorcha storts all this, like, crying. I nearly end up putting my orm around her she's so upset. She's going, 'OH MY GOD! I'm supposed to be going out with someone. I am SUCH a bitch,' and it's only then that I remember Brandon, or whatever that Septic's name is. I'm there, 'You don't have to tell him,' and she stops crying, pulls a tissue from her sky rocket and storts, like, dabbing at her eyes. She goes, 'No, Ross. It's only fair that he knows about us.' I have to nip this in the bud, roysh, as sensitively as I can, so I go, 'What's all this *us*, Kemosabe?' and that's when she freaks.

Well, first she sort of looks at me all confused for about ten seconds and then she goes, 'You told me you loved me in Reynords.' Actually, I probably did. Heat of the moment, blah blah blah. But then she storts, like, bawling her eyes out, telling me I'm this, that and the other, making a complete orse of herself in front of half of town. She goes, 'Why were you with me if you don't have any feelings for me?' and that's a question I hate birds asking me. The truth is, roysh, I do really have feelings for this girl, but after all that *I'm having a baby* shit last year there's probably a port of me that wants to hurt her and that's the port of me that goes, 'I just wanted to prove to myself that you still want me,' and Sophie, who's caught up with us, tells me to get out of her sight before she does something she'll regret and Chloë tells Sorcha I've always been a bastard to women and she should have known better than to have anything to do with me.

Then me and Christian hit Burger King.

XXX

'Talking about me again?' The old dear nearly craps herself when she sees me, roysh, and she's *actually* going to deny it when the old man stands up and goes, 'Your mother and I are worried about you, Ross,' and of course I'm there, 'That's a first,' which he just ignores. He's like, 'You're quiet, moody, irritable, secretive. You're showing all the classic signs of someone who's – I'm going to have to just come out with this, Fionnuala – on drugs.'

The old dear goes, 'Things have been going missing from the house, Ross. Your father's golf trophy–' and straight away I'm like, '*What* golf trophy?' and I turn to the old man and I go, 'You're shit at golf,' and he's like, 'The one I won in the Pro-Am out in Portmarnock. Playing with Ronan Collins and Christy O'Connor Junior, thank you very much indeed. It's gone, Ross,' and I'm there, 'And you think I stole it to buy drugs? You two are MAJORLY focked up. If you must know, I focked it out the window the night you brought it home. You came in thinking you were so shit-hot, so I thought, 'I'll show the focker.' The old man goes, 'You're missing the point, Ross. The trophy is replaceable. Especially if I keep playing the way I'm playing. We just want to find out what's troubling you lately.'

The old dear's still shovelling food into her face, that's how concerned she is. I just lose the plot, roysh. I'm there, 'Hey, I'm not the focking criminal in this family, remember? I'm not the one who refuses to answer the door in case it's a writ. It's not me who jumps six feet in the air every time the phone rings in case it's the Feds. I'm not the one who's been to the Cayman Islands so often they're thinking of naming the new terminal after me.' He goes, 'That's Hennessy's joke, Ross, and well you know it.'

The old dear goes, 'It's just that we've noticed ...' and I'm like, 'Noticed? I'm surprised you've noticed anything with your focking campaigns. Ban Poor People from the National Gallery. What are you focking like?' and she's like, 'There you go again. Over-simplifying things. That is not what we're about at all. We simply feel that if they're going to allow schoolchildren in, they should be a bit better behaved and not let run amok. One morning per week. That's all the girls and I want,' and I just look at her with total contempt, roysh, and I'm there, 'You and your focking coffee mornings,' and she goes, 'You want me to catch head-lice off these children, is that it?' and then the waterworks stort and I have to get the fock out of there. I go, 'When was the last time either of you knew what I wanted?' and even though I don't know what I meant by it, it sounded pretty good, it has to be said.

I go upstairs and throw on some new threads – my red and white striped Polo Sport rugby shirt, my navy Dockers and the old brown Dubes. I have, like, four voice messages, roysh, but I delete them without even bothering my orse to check who they're from. I head downstairs, roysh, and as I'm opening the front door, the old pair are still, like, at it. The old man's going, 'You just don't know these days, Fionnuala, it could be these blasted mobile telephones. Electromagnetic waves and so forth. The atmosphere is full of them. Full, I tell you, with a capital F. I was talking to that Alex Garton at the regatta last week. He's Hennessy's physician, you know? For his sins! Anyway, he said there's so many people using these phones that getting the 46A bus into town now is the equivalent of putting your head in a microwave oven for seven-and-a-half minutes.' She's going, 'I'm not giving him my Micra, Charles,' and he goes, 'No, of course not, darling.'

XXX

Me and the goys are having a few scoops in the M1, but I'm just really, like, bored, and I end up going to the can and snorting a shitload of the magic powder. Then I decide to call out to Sorcha's gaff, not because I regret the way I treated her the other night, roysh, but because I am totally gagging for my end-away and I'm actually storting to believe Fionn, who said he got his cousin, who works in the lab in UCD – another geek obviously – to test the stuff we've been taking and it turns out it's, like, pure focking testosterone, which explains one or two things, like the horn you could use to beat a donkey out of a quarry.

So I hit the Vico Road, roysh, and I know my game plan. I'm going to give it all that, 'I'm really nervous about the game. It's the biggest day of my life. You're the only one who truly understands me and the pressure I'm under,' blah blah blah, basically all the horseshit birds love. So I arrive up at the door, roysh, hit the bell and it's, like, her little sister who answers it, Afric or Orpha or whatever the fock she's called. I'm there, 'Is Sorcha in?' and she goes, 'No, she's at, like, the orthodontist?' and I go, 'Can I come in and wait?' and she goes, 'Sure.'

We go into the sitting-room, roysh, and she's watching MTV and it's, like, Robbie Williams, roysh, and she says she thinks he's, like, SO cool and she asks me did I see him interviewed on 2TV last weekend and I say no and she goes, 'OHMYGOD, he SO cool.' *Stars connecting our fate*, blahby blahdy blah.

She's a total focking airhead, roysh, but she's actually turned into a bit of a honey, although I have to say this is the first time I've ever actually looked at her in that way. No one really pays any attention to little sisters, roysh, and then one day – *whoosh* – they've suddenly got top tens and a great boat race and you're thinking, 'Yeah, I actually would if the opportunity arose.'

She's a Mountie as well, roysh, and I think she must be in, like, fifth year now, because she was definitely in transition year last year, because she did her work experience in my old man's company, although she had a brace on her Taylors and so many Randolph Scotts that she got charged three hundred bills into the cinema last week – this is JP's joke, by the way – because it was three quid a head. Now, though, she's a little focking hortbreaker and unless I'm very much mistaken, roysh, that's the black fur-collared cardigan Sorcha pestered me to buy for her in Morgan when we were, like, going out together. And she's wearing her *Contradiction* as well. I think she's like a young Anna Kournikova.

So I'm there racking my brains, roysh, to come up with a couple of lines that'll get me in there. I'm like, 'You used to play tennis down in Glenageary, didn't you?' and she's like, 'Oh my God, how did you know that?' and quick as a flash – I'm the Kool-Aid dispenser, man – I go, 'I never forget a pretty face.'

Twenty seconds later, roysh, I'm wearing the face off her and she's an amazing kisser and I'm giving her, 'All the time I was with Sorcha, I was actually thinking about you?' thinking we might end up taking this upstairs in a minute, but all of a sudden she pulls away, roysh, and says she has to finish her homework. And I'm there, 'Your homework?' and she goes, 'I'm supposed to be preparing my debate,' and I don't even bother asking her what the topic is, roysh, I just get up off the sofa, head out into the hall and tell her that it's probably best if Sorcha doesn't, like, find out about this. She goes, 'OH! MY! GOD! Sorcha would be SO pissed off if she found out,' and if there was, like, an edge in her voice, roysh, I didn't cop it.

But I get home, roysh, and I swear to God I'm in the door, like, five minutes when the mobile rings and it's, like, Sorcha. Of course I make the mistake of, like, answering it and she's spitting nails. She's going, 'I KNEW YOU WERE A BASTARD, ROSS, BUT I CANNOT *BELIEVE* YOU WOULD DO SOMETHING LIKE THAT,' and I go, 'I don't know what you're talking about,' playing the total innocent. She goes, 'She told me everything, Ross. You were WITH her.' This could still be one of about fifteen birds. She goes, 'My SISTER, Ross.' Fock. She goes, 'I cannot believe either of you would do something like that. She is SUCH a bitch, Ross. She only did it to get at me. Did I really hurt you that much last year that you want to keep doing things like this to me?' but I don't answer, roysh, because I'm actually feeling bad about what I did, weird as it sounds. She tells me I'm a bastard to girls and that she should have listened to Sophie and Chloë and Aoife and even Claire and then, like, the line goes dead.

XXX

All the Mary's crowd are giving it, 'DRUG-GIE, DRUG-GIE, DRUG-GIE,' and Christian comes over to me, roysh, and he tells me not to listen, to stay calm and to stay focused and I think the dude's worried that I'm going to go apeshit or something because of the way I was, like, booting holes in the walls and punching dents in the lockers in the dressing-room, though that was just a sign of how up for this game

I am. The game kicks off and the crowd are still giving it loads, it's all, 'WHERE'S YOUR SYRINGE GONE?' and all that, roysh, but it's a pity their team aren't so clever.

They're actually such a pushover, roysh, that the first half is a bit of an anti-climax. Christian danced right through their defence to score, like, two tries right under the posts in the first, like, eight minutes, roysh, and we were, like, 23-12 up by half-time and already dreaming about March seventeenth at Lansdowne Road. We go back to the dressing-room and Fehily's in there waiting and he goes, 'As Joshua said at half-time in the Battle of Jericho ...' and I just, like, push him out of the way, roysh, and I go, 'Goys, we let this slip last year and we've got to make sure we don't do it again. We owe this to ourselves, goys. Just keep telling yourself, we've earned this,' and we go straight out there again.

And the second half is an even bigger piece of piss. Oisinn and Fionn both get tries, which I also convert, and the Mary's crowd end up, like, taking their frustration out on me, going, 'WHO'S THE JUNKY, WHO'S THE JUNKY, WHO'S THE JUNKY IN THE RED?' meaning me, roysh, but I have the last laugh when I slip two tackles and sell one of their backs an amazing dummy, even if I say so myself, and I get over for a try. Then, roysh, for my celebration, I get down on my hands and knees and stort, like, snorting the white line, which does NOT go down well, but we're in the final, against New-bridge of all schools – crowd of muckers – so I couldn't give two focks.

XXX

It's Fionn who sees the white powder on the front of my jumper, roysh – we're talking my black, vertical ribbed Sonetti – and he storts looking at me suspiciously. I'm there, 'Do you have a problem?' and he pushes his glasses up on his nose and goes, 'No, but you obviously do.' I'm there, 'Are you a doctor or something?' and he's like, 'Let's just say I know enough to know when to stop taking that stuff. You're snorting it now, aren't you?' and I lose the plot then and I make a grab for the goy. But Oisinn hops up, roysh, and he tells me that, captain of the S or not, I'm out of order, in fact I'm BANG out of order and I should go for a walk to, like, sort my head out. I realise, roysh, that everyone in the sixth year common room is, like, staring at me, so I go, 'What the FOCK are you lot looking at,' and I boot the wall and my foot goes right through it and I just, like, walk out.

I must have had, like, seven hundred milligrams of the stuff already today and it's only, like, lunchtime and now my head is throbbing like nobody's business. I need to get some tablets and maybe something else, I don't know what, to try to get me calm because I feel like just …

So I walk down as far as the Merrion Shopping Centre and go into the chemist. And there I am, roysh, looking through all the various boxes and bottles and tubes, not knowing what the fock I'm really looking for, when all of a sudden I feel this, like, tap on my shoulder. I spin around, roysh, and it's, like, Sorcha. She's there, 'Hi,' and I'm like, 'What are you doing here?' and she's like, 'Working. HELLO?' Her old dear's shop. Of course.

She looks incredible. I blurt it out. Not *that*. I just tell her that her shirt's nice and she tells me it's a Scott Henshall and she tells me it goes really well with the black wool shrug she bought in Morgan that day we went shopping together and I just nod. She goes, 'I heard you played really well against St Mary's. Congrats,' and I'm there, 'It's Newbridge in the final and it's going to be tough, boggers or not,' and she smiles and says I'm probably glad that she's not around this year to fock things up for me again and I don't answer.

She doesn't even mention what happened with her sister. It's like she's blocking it out, roysh, but she says she's SO embarrassed about what happened that other night in town. She's like, 'I can't believe I was actually with you. I met the girls for a quiet drink after hockey practice and we ended up going on the complete lash and, well, I hadn't eaten all day and ...' and I just say, 'It's cool,' and I'm about to ask her whether she told her so-called boyfriend that she was sucking the lips off me last week, but I don't because I wouldn't give her the satisfaction of thinking I GIVE a shit one way or the other.

She goes, 'Preparation H? You haven't got piles, have you?' and I look down at the tube in my hand and I end up going, 'No, I'm in looking for, em, condoms,' and I can see her face drop, roysh, and I pick up five packets of johnnies and then after a few seconds I pick up two more. She goes, 'I heard you were with Angel,' and I'm there, 'What's that got to do with you?' and she goes, 'Nothing, I suppose. Just glad to see you're taking precautions these days,' and she goes off and I swear to God, roysh, she was on the point of bursting into tears.

XXX

I get a text from some bird called Hazel and it's like,

> hey ross its hazel, just wondring did u realy mean wot u sed last nite cos i ben doin sum tinkin n I tink I feel d same way

Who the FOCK is Hazel?

XXX

The old dear's sitting at the kitchen table, roysh, reading the National Gallery's response to her suggestion that their staff be armed to deal with, as she put, 'the riff-raff element,' and I take it from her expression, roysh, that they're not exactly Roy on the idea. She's just going, 'Terribly disappointing,' over and over under her breath, the stupid wagon, and when she finally notices that I'm actually in the room, she looks at me over the top of her glasses and she goes, 'Oh, hello, Ross,' and I know straight away that she's after something. She goes, 'The big match, eh? Won't be long now. You must be excited. *I'm* excited,' and I'm there, 'What have *you* got to be excited about?' and she goes, 'Well, I'm the mother of the Castlerock captain. If Castlerock win, I get to present the Cup ...'

HOLY FOCK! I should have thought of this.

She's there, 'Going to go shopping for a dress tomorrow. Andrea's going to come with me. We might try Sorcha's mother's place. See what she has,' and straight away I go, 'There's no point.' She's still looking at me over the top of her glasses. She's like, 'No point, is that what you said?' and I'm there, 'There's fock-all wrong with your hearing, don't worry. The old dear of the winning captain doesn't present the Cup anymore,' which of course is total horseshit. She goes, 'Oh,' and then, 'I'd better ring Andrea,' and then, 'When did they stop it because Ois-inn's mother told me ...' and I'm going, 'They stopped it last year. Too many old bags making complete tits of themselves.'

I'll tell everyone she's got, I don't know, some contagious disease or other, and get Christian to ask his old dear, who's actually pretty tasty, to present it to me instead.

XXX

Ana with one n – now there's a voice from the past – she leaves me a message to say she has tickets for the Lighthouse Family if I want to go and I'm wondering does Angel know she's ringing. Then I cop it, roysh, that the two of them have had a row because next there's a message from Angel herself and she says she's SO sorry she hasn't been in touch but Ana with one n is being SUCH a bitch and OH! MY! GOD! I will not BELIEVE the shit she was coming up with this morning, TRYING to make her feel guilty for eating, like, a packet of Hula Hoops, which is, like, three-and-a-half points, we're talking, HELLO? I don't even listen to the full message. I just, like, flush the chain, make sure it's not a floater and then go back to the old scratcher, where Elinor – this total Claire Danes lookalike – is fast asleep beside me. I'm only getting about two hours' kip a night since I storted taking this shit.

Me and JP actually did well last night. He pulled her best mate – as in Melanie – and she must have known a few tricks, roysh, because I could hear him through the walls going, 'QUALITY DRIVEN!' and 'CLIENT FOCUSED!' and that went on for, like, half the night. Have to say, roysh, it was a bit of a blow to the old ego to hear that, especially with me doing it during the ad break in 'Ally McBeal', though Elinor's not gonna complain. For her it's just BEING with Ross O'Carroll-Kelly that matters, nothing more, nothing less.

We're actually in JP's house, roysh, because his old pair are in, like, Chicago for the week, shopping. So there I am, roysh, lying there, actually in the mood for another round of the other, and I'm trying to come up with an excuse to wake Elinor up, when all of a sudden JP bursts into the room, roysh, and he goes, 'ROSS, QUICK! AL AND KAY GUY ARE AT THE DOOR!' and of course I'm like, 'Fock! The ones who caught–' and he's like, 'MICHELLE SMITH! YES! QUICK, EAT

THE EVIDENCE!' so he pegs it back to his room, roysh, and I grab the tub of powder out of my chinos, which are in a ball on the floor, and I stort wolfing it back and washing it down with the bottle of Evian that Elinor left on the bedside locker.

I'm thinking that if they ask to drug-test me, roysh, I'll tell them I'm already the most tested schools rugby player in Leinster and you only have to look at me to know that ... And then I'm thinking, what the FOCK is JP at, telling me to eat this shit if they're going to be asking me for, like, a piss sample? I look up, roysh, and he's standing at the door, cracking his hole laughing. He goes, 'You have to admit, I got you there, Ross.'

XXX

As if I need to be reminded what this match means, roysh, Erika phones me up the night before and she goes, 'What aftershave do you wear?' I'm like, 'Don't I even get a hello?' and she goes, 'Don't wear *Cool Water* or anything by Davidoff if you want to be with me. It's an allergy I have,' and she hangs up.

XXX

'Newbridge are a bunch of total boggers who have no business being in the final of a competition like this.' None of us can disagree with Fehily when he says this. He goes, 'These people are muck savages. Not a laywer's son between them. I don't think any person of sound mind would disagree that their appearance in the final denigrates the entire competition. But ... it is solemnly I tell thee, they came through the various rounds of the competition to get here and the rules are the rules. Until a fairer way can be devised to stop schools from the country from progressing in the competition, we just have to play by the rules, imperfect and all as they are. But you owe it not just to your school but to your class, your people, your way of life, to ensure that every single upper class one of you stands up and makes himself count this afternoon,' and before he has a chance to say anything else, roysh, we're all stamping our feet in the dressing-room and I'm leading us in a chorus of 'Castlerock Above All Others'.

Then we morch out onto the field in single file, roysh, with the cheers of our fans ringing in our ears. Fehily was roysh what he said to Tony Ward in this morning's paper, that the famous Castlerock roar is like having a sixteenth man on the field.

This year, roysh, we've left nothing to chance. We watched, like, videos of Newbridge's quarter-final and semi-final, roysh, and Fehily and me – as captain – went through the various ways in which we thought they were weak.

I've decided, roysh, to give my pre-match speech not in, like, the dressing-room but out on the field. And judging from the reaction of the goys, roysh, it's actually mind-blowing stuff, better than any drug. We all get into a huddle, roysh, and I go, 'This is the biggest day of our lives, goys. We've been through a whole lot of shit together but we'll probably never be all here together like this again. When we leave Castlerock, most of us will go on to five-grand-a-term private colleges, where we'll be given qualifications without having to sit exams. We'll all get jobs through people we share a shower with at the rugby clubs we play for. We'll keep on scoring the birds,' and that gets a roar and I'm like, 'until we reach our mid-thirties. Then we'll marry the youngest and prettiest of them and continue to sleep with all of her friends. We all have big futures to look forward to, because we are the élite. But today is the last time we will ever have to work hord for anything in our entire lives. So let's make it count this time. Let's do it for Fehily. Let's do it for Castlerock. But most of all ... let's do it for us.'

I swear to God, roysh, those goys would have walked through focking walls for me by the time I finish. I have to say as well, roysh, that I have never heard such an atmosphere at Lansdowne Road, not even for internationals, and the Newbridge goys, you can see it *by* them, they're crapping it. I make sure to walk up to them one-by-one as they're doing their warm-up, roysh, and I go, 'History,' and they're all bricking it, I can see it in their eyes.

They've brought a bit of a crew up with them from, I don't know, Kerry or wherever the fock Newbridge is, but the best they can do is, 'DADDY'S GONNA BUY YOU A BRAND NEW MOTORCAR,' and straight away, roysh, our goys are like, 'DADDY'S GONNA BUY YOU A BRAND NEW COW,' which we can actually hear on the field.

We just know, roysh, that we are not going to be denied. I've never actually seen Christian play a better match. He's dancing around them like Michael Flatley, roysh, but he's also putting out fires everywhere in, like, defence. Even Fionn, roysh, who I'd have had difficulties giving any kind of compliment to in the past, I turn around to him halfway through the first half and I go, 'Rugby is actually an easy game to play when you've got goys like you on your side,' and he high-fives me and it's just like, RESPECT!

JP scores our first try, roysh, running pretty much the whole length of the field to score after an intercept ten yords from our line. I pop over the points and within five minutes we basically flatten them with our rolling maul, shoving them from pretty much halfway, right to the other end of the field for Oisinn to put the ball down. Then Christian gets one and suddenly we're storting to relax and, like, enjoy ourselves.

A very funny thing happens in the second half, roysh. I grab a couple of tries myself, flukes I kept telling people afterwards, the whole false modesty bit. But to score the second, roysh, I basically have to run for, like, thirty or forty yords with one of their goys pegging it after me. And I have to say, roysh, he's fast this goy, but I've got a headstort on him and I know I've got just about enough in my legs to carry me over the line before he can, like, get in a tackle on me. Anyway, roysh, as he's chasing after me, I'm talking to him, giving it, 'Come on, catch up. You really need to eat more bacon and cabbage,' and then I'm going, 'Are they rugby boots you're wearing or wellies?'

Anyway, roysh, we end up beating the focking muckers 46-12 and it's, like, big-time celebrations. We really, like, deserved this and we're all bawling our eyes out and hugging each other. They go up to get their medals, roysh, and I end up standing at the bottom of the steps and I say to each one as he comes down, 'Fock off back to Bogland.' Then I go up to get the Cup from Christian's old dear. I ended up telling her that my old dear broke both her legs playing tennis, which was more wishful thinking than anything else. She hands me the Cup, roysh, and she kisses me, not on the cheek, roysh, but actually on the lips and I'm thinking ... No, forget it. I just grab the Cup in, like, both hands, roysh, and I go, 'FOR FEHILY! FOR ROCK! FOR GOD!' which probably sounds a bit wanky, roysh, but it was the first thing that came into my head and the crowd didn't seem to mind, they went totally ballistic.

We peg it back down the steps, roysh, and we do a lap of honour and then Wardy comes up to me and he asks me can he have a few words with the winning captain for tomorrow's paper. I'm there, 'Shoot,' and he's like, 'Okay, first of all, how do you feel?' I'm there, 'Can't really put it into words, Tony. This has been our dream now for two years. And today that dream became a realisation.' He goes, 'I notice you had a word with each of the Newbridge players as they came down the steps with their medals. What did you say to them?' and I'm there, 'I just told them they did themselves, their school and their way of life proud. I told them that the people who said they had no right to be here had been proven wrong and that it was actually our toughest match of the whole campaign.'

He goes, 'And finally, I suppose you and the goys will be having a quiet night in this evening, Ross?' and straight away I'm like, 'Yeah, roysh. AS IF!'

XXX

Picture the scene, roysh. It's two o'clock in the morning and we're in, like, Annabel's and Erika is wearing the face off me, but I'm pretty much numb from the amount of drink I've knocked back and I couldn't tell you whether she's a good or a bad wear. But I suspect it's bad. There doesn't seem to be any, like, passion in it. We both seem to be just, like, going through the motions. After about fifteen minutes, roysh, she finally pulls away and she goes, 'You're nothing to write home about, Ross. I don't know what your little girlfriend's been talking about all these years. I had tickets for the National Concert Hall tonight. The Lyric Opera production of *Nabucco*.'

XXX

Relinquishing testosterone addiction. Stage One, Preparation. For this you will need: one room which you will not leave for the entire month of April; one mattress; roast pumpkin and hickory bacon soup, ten tins of; Marks and Spencer green Thai curry soup, eight tins of, for consumption hot; ice cream, triple chocolate dream, one large tub of; Pringles, sour cream and chive, eight pipes of; mouthwash; vitamins;

mineral water; Lucozade Sport; photographs of Isla Fischer and Bianca Luyckx; one bucket for, like, crap, one for piss and one for Huey; one television; two parents who will basically wait on me hand and foot and get me whatever the fock else I want.

And now I'm ready. All I need is a final hit to soothe the pain while I'm waiting for the old dear to bring me my focking dinner.

XXX

All the goys have been wondering why I decided to bring Fiona, as in one of the O'Prey triplets, to the Leaving Cert Results Ball when (a) she's not exactly catwalk material and (b) she generally says fock-all from one end of the evening to the other, having no basic personality to speak of. Picture, No Sound, the goys call her, but it's when we're all piled into the limo on the way to the Berkeley Court, roysh, that the goys see the method in my madness. Oisinn's with Anna Cotes, a total honey who was head girl in – of all places – the Virgin Megastore in Rathfarnham and at this precise moment in time she's, like, straightening his bow tie and picking bits of fluff off his tux jacket, we're talking maximum attention here. JP brought that Anita Prentice, this bird from, like, Loreto on the Green, who he's already asked to our actual debs, even though it's only the end of August and the debs is still, like, two or three months away, the sap, and there's a major boyfriend-girlfriend vibe going down there. Fionn's brought some focking hound he met at some UCD open day or other and they're busy crapping on about whether or not Clinton should be, what was the word, impeached – your guess is as good as mine – and they haven't a clue what's going on around them. And Christian seems all loved-up with Sophie, a mate of Sorcha's who we've all been loved-up with at one stage or another.

What I'm basically saying here is that the field is pretty much clear for me to walk away with the top prize tonight, as in Miss Roland, this new French teacher who's as loose as, I don't know, Oisinn's trousers would be on me. JP pours me another brandy from the minibor, then slides the little hatch across and asks the driver to go twice more around the block. Fiona tries to, like, link me, roysh, but I shake my orm free and give her a look, to basically remind her she should be grateful just to be here and that I've no interest in going into this race with a weight handicap.

We're on the way in, roysh – red corpet, the works – when Oisinn pulls me back and he goes, 'I know what you're thinking, Ross,' and I'm there, 'You do?' and he goes, 'You think you're going to lick the pot. Just to let you know, I'm not out of the game and neither is JP,' and I end up high-fiving him, as if to say, I don't know, may the best man win. So we morch into the ballroom, roysh, totally ignore the seating plan and all decide to sit at this table smack bang in the middle of the room, which means telling these two Chess Club geeks and their ugly birds to basically hop it. One of them, roysh, a little tosser with glasses – a mate of Fionn's probably – he actually has the cheek to turn around to me and go, 'These places have been pre-assigned,' and without even having to think, roysh, I go, 'Now they're being reassigned. To the stars of the Castlerock senior rugby team,' and I rip off his glasses and drop them into his drink – a Coke for fock's sake, to celebrate his Leaving Cert results? – and the four of them fock off, muttering something about reporting us and we're all like, To who?

The meal arrives, roysh, and all the birds at the table are doing the usual, seeing who can eat the least. Christian, JP and Fionn are too busy knocking back the beers to think about food, but Oisinn wipes every plate on the table clean, roysh, basically breaking the world record for the most Chicken Supremes eaten in an hour. Then he eats everyone's Tiramisu and a few from the next table as well. Fiona's struck up a bit of a conversation with Anita, which is good because I want her to have SOME happy memories of the evening.

Miss Roland's sitting at the next table, roysh, and of course we're all trying to get a good eyeful without actually getting snared. She looks basically incredible. I might have mentioned that she's the spit of Uma Thurman, we're talking twenty-four, maybe twenty-five, and she looks hot tonight in this, like, black dress, which is, as Fionn points out, showing off an unwise amount of cleavage for a teacher taking her first step on the career ladder. I can see Fehily giving her a talking-to about it next week.

There's only one reason, of course, why a teacher would come to a school ball looking that good. She has the hots for, like, someone. Can't be one of the other teachers, roysh, because they've all either got BO, flaky skin, comb-overs, or all three and there isn't one of them under fifty. So she must have it bad for one of us and, not being big-headed or anything, but the smort money's on me, especially given the way she's, like, looking over. That cabbage-breath focker Crabtree's boring the ear off her, probably about Hitler or history or some other horseshite, and I catch her eye and she sort of, like, smiles and waves at me and I give her this, like, disapproving look, as if to remind her that us students are, like, forbidden fruit as far as she's concerned, just, like, focking around of course.

Haven't mentioned it, roysh, but I'm drinking the old non-alcoholic gerbil's piss, determined to keep a clear head. The other goys are already half hammered. We all want the same thing here basically, but I'm the only one with a game plan and the big-match temperament. Hope I'm not coming across as, like, arrogant or anything, roysh, but there's a reason why I always get the girl and it's the reason I'm the best young kicker of a dead ball in Ireland, according to Wardy, and that reason is focus. I suppose you could say that the goalposts in this case are Miss Roland herself and the ball is my ... whatever.

When she catches my eye again I give her a little wink and she sort of, like, blushes, and I know she's basically putty in the hand. Oisinn is asking Christian how much money he'd give him if he lit one of his forts, which means he's pretty much out of the game, roysh, while JP is shouting, 'EAT THE POOR!' which suggests to me that he's in no frame of mind to basically chat anyone up either.

Fiona turns around to me and she goes, 'I still can't believe that out of all the girls you could have invited here tonight you asked me,' obviously thinking she's in the big-time frame for the ACTUAL debs in November here, so I go, 'Don't read anything into it. I'm using you. I basically needed a Plain Jane who wasn't going to distract my focus. Not being a bastard or anything, but there's no attraction whatsoever,' and of course on go the focking waterworks then. Birds do my head in when they stort that shit so I hit the bor for another bottle of piss – Fiona's got half a vodka and Diet 7-Up there, she can make do with that – and who's up there, roysh, only Miss Roland herself and she's pretty locked from the way she's pouring that white wine into her glass.

I'm there, 'Hello there. Looking good,' playing it totally Kool and the Gang, and she looks up and goes, 'Oh! Hello Ross. How are you?' and I'm there, 'All the better for seeing you here tonight. What can I say? You look ... really well,' and she goes, 'I'll take that as a compliment,' and of course I'm wondering what other focking way she could possibly take it but I don't say that, I just go, 'I got into UCD,' and she looks at me as if to say, you know, did you accidentally get someone else's Leaving Cert results or something? To be honest with you, I didn't even bother my orse sitting the Leaving this time around because, well, I got the offer pretty much straight away after the Schools Cup final. I'm there, 'It's, like, a scholarship? We're talking sports management? You don't need, like, brains or anything,' and she nods like she understands. The thing is, roysh, I couldn't stay at Castlerock forever either, and I did the old maths – UCD, we're talking ten thousand students, more than half of them female – and I was like, Lemme at 'em.

Miss Roland goes, 'How was your summer? Did you get a chance to practice any of your French?' and instead of going, 'I don't focking have any to practice with,' which is what I was SO tempted to say, I go, 'As a matter of fact, yes. I spent the whole summer in ... what's the capital again?' and she's like, 'Paris,' and I'm there, 'How could I forget?' and it's all total bullshit, of course. I basically spent the summer in Kiely's, Annabel's, Reynords and the Club of Love, bringing pleasure to the lives of attractive women. That was a major, I don't know, incentive to get clean again. There I was, locked away in my room, and hearing all these stories about Oisinn and JP and Fionn – Fionn, for fock's sake – scoring all around them, roysh, and I just decided basically that I wanted the old Ross back. The birds had been too long without me.

Miss Roland goes, 'So you worked there for the summer?' and we're talking full eye contact here, the big-time hots for me. I'm like, 'No, I was mostly chilling actually, just basically doing French shit.'

Then there's this, like, lull in the conversation, roysh, and I end up going, 'Can I be honest with you, Miss Roland?' and she's there, 'Stephanie,' and I'm there, 'Okay, Stephanie then. I'd like to be with you,' and suddenly, roysh, she drops the whole flirty act and she's, like, looking over her shoulder to see if anyone's, like, listening. She goes, 'I can't believe you ...' and I'm there, 'Don't play the innocent. You want me as much as I want you,' and she goes, 'Ross, I could lose my job,' and I'm going, 'So you're not denying you're attracted to me.'

She storts, like, fidgeting with the wine glass. I go, 'I've got a room booked at the Radisson,' and she looks at me and she goes, 'For you and whoever you happened to pick up tonight?' and I'm like, 'No. I booked it in the hope that it would be me and you basically going back there.'

She doesn't say anything for, like, twenty seconds, roysh, then she just knocks back the rest of her wine and goes, 'I'll leave now. Follow me at a discreet distance. And I mean DISCREET, Ross. No one can know about this,' and I'm like, 'Hey, I'm not the type to kiss and tell,' and she's like, 'I hope not,' and she heads outside. Of course I'm straight over to the goys, roysh, putting my orms up and going, 'HE SHOOTS, HE SCORES!' and of course they're practically focking dizzy it happened so quickly. I'm there, 'At this moment in time, she's in the cor pork waiting for me.' Oisinn goes, 'You mean Roland?' and I'm like, 'Please. It's Stephanie.' JP goes, 'What's the deal? You said you were leaving it till Buck Whaleys?' and I'm there, 'Love doesn't work to a timetable, JP.' Out of the corner of my eye I can see Fiona bawling her eyes out on Anita's shoulder. I go, 'Anyway, I've entertained you losers long enough. I'm off to make mad passionate love to a member of the teaching staff. *Asta la vista*,' and I head out with chants of, 'LEG-END! LEG-END! LEG-END!' coming from our table and three or four others as well.

I go outside, roysh, and she's, like, waiting for me. She goes, 'Are you sure no one saw you leave?' and I'm there, 'Hey, I've got a bit more class than you're giving me credit for,' and she goes, 'I'm sorry. It's just, I really love my job and I don't want ...' and I just go, 'Ssshhh!' and I go to throw the lips on her. She goes, 'Wait till we get to the hotel,' and I'm like, 'Your wish is my command,' the one-liners just falling out of my mouth tonight.

She goes, 'The Radisson? You really believe in pushing the boat out, don't you?' and I think, 'FOCK!' and while I'm driving, roysh, I'm sending a text to Christian, and it's basically:

> **Yo! Ive a techer here who wants my dck bad. Ring d radison in stilrgan n book me a suite. Quick. She wants me NOW!**

And of course twenty seconds later I get a reply, roysh, and I realise I've actually sent it to my old man by mistake, what with Dick Features coming immediately after Christian in my phone. I open his reply and it's like,

No probs, Kicker

the tool that he is. So there we are, roysh, pegging it down the Stillorgan dualler, Stephanie in the passenger seat, Lite FM's Friday Night Love Affair on the radio and me texting the goys, roysh, telling them all the various things I'm going to do to her when I get her back to the hotel, when all of a sudden – OH! FOCK! – I hear this, like, siren behind and sure enough it's the focking Feds. I pull over, like you're supposed to, roysh, and in the old rear-view mirror I can see the copper putting on his hat and, like, walking towards the cor and of course Stephanie's losing the rag, roysh, going, 'If they ask, I was giving you grinds,' and I'm there, 'In that dress? Just leave the talking to me, hon,' thinking I'm basically fireproof tonight.

I wind down the window and I can't believe my focking luck, roysh. It's the same cop who was gonna lift me here before. I remember him from his thick neck and his big cabbage head, the focking bogger. I'm just hoping he doesn't recognise me. I wind down the window and I'm there, 'What seems to be the problem, officer?' but he's in no mood for my shit. He goes, 'Have you your licence?' and of course I know that if I show it to him he's sure to remember me from before, so I just go, 'It's at home. I'll present it at my nearest Gorda station within ten days. Is that everything?' and he's writing away in this little pad, roysh. He goes, 'Is that everything? Let's see. Driving at sixty miles per hour in a forty-mile zone. Texting while in charge of a vehicle. That comes under ... driving without due care and attention. I think that's everything, yes. Oh and there's a smell of alcohol on your breath. I'd like to breathalyse you. Unfortunately, the equipment I've here with me is a bit banjaxed, so I'm going to have to ask you to accompany me to the station.'

I'm like, 'I SO haven't been drinking. The smell is just ... I've been drinking that non-alcoholic shite all night. Look, whatever the fine is for the texting and the speeding and whatever, don't worry, my old man's good for the money,' but I make the mistake then of appealing to him sort of, like, man to man. I'm there, 'Look, I'm kind of on a promise here,' but that just makes him determined to lift me.

He goes, 'There's a reception area in the station. She can wait for you there. Otherwise, one of our officers can drop the lady wherever she wants to go.' Stephanie leans across me and goes, 'Garda, I was just giving him grinds. I'd really appreciate a lift back to Harold's Cross,' and he's like, 'That'll be arranged.'

I still don't know whether the focker recognises me from the time I gave him all that lip. He storts, like, writing in his notebook again, roysh, going, 'Now, name?' and I decide, fock it, I'll give him a false one, roysh, because I'll be out of there the second they find out I haven't been drinking. I end up just going, 'The name's Fionn—' but he just cuts me off and goes, 'Ross ... O'Carroll ... Kelly ... you said I'd remember it. Looks like you were right.'

Fock.

The Temple of Academe

of

2 BOOK SPECIAL

Book 2

The Teenage Dirtbag Years

You know the Jackanory, ROYSH. School rugby legend, babe magnet. All-round TOP DOG. And with my old pair to fund the lifestyle I, like, totally deserve, who needs further education? Turns out you CAN'T do the Leaving Cert four times, which is, like, a total focking bummer. But a Sports Scholarship – you don't need, like, brains or anything.

ROSS O'CARROLL-KELLY

'A man of great taste and sophistication, not unlike myself. Yet he still finds time for the simple pleasures in life – loose cors, fast women ... fast food.'
OISINN

'Stupid, vain and a total orsehole. And certainly not the great lover he pretends to be. Three minutes, if my memory's right. You could boil an egg by him. As long as you like your eggs soft.'
ERIKA

'Yeah, the dude stayed in my house in Ocean City. Made shit of the place. Paid the rent though. Knew what'd happen if he didn't. Said to him, "I got a pair of concrete shoes outside. One size fits all. You wanna see are they waterproof, ya leprechaun fock?" Yeah, a good kid. The broads loved him.'
PEASEY PEE

'One of the best rugby players this country has ever produced. Ever, with a capital E. Hennessy agrees with me. If it wasn't for injuries, bad luck and so forth, he'd have played for Ireland.'
CHARLES O'CARROLL-KELLY

'Who?'
EDDIE O'SULLIVAN

PAUL HOWARD is as working class as curry sauce, processed cheese slices and borrowing money from the credit union. He wouldn't know one end of a rugby ball from the other and has been turned away from Lillies a record forty-seven times. This is the first book he's written with more than five hundred swear words in it. His parents think he works in a bank.

The Teenage Dirt-bag years

Ross O'Carroll-Kelly

[As told to Paul Howard]

Illustrated by Alan Clarke

THE O'BRIEN PRESS
DUBLIN

Dedication
For Karen

Acknowledgements
Thank you Mum and Dad for making laughter compulsory at all times growing up. Thank you Mark, Vincent and Richard for so many happy days. Thank you Karen – you know this guy's as much your monster as mine. Thank you Paul Wallace, Alan Kelly and Peter Walsh – hey, only we know how much of what's between these covers is fiction. Thank you Rachel, an astute and uncompromising editor who worked me like a kulak during the rewriting stage and is responsible for most of the decent storylines that I'll be claiming credit for when this book is published. Thank you Emma and Alan for making these books scream from the shelves. Thank you Michael and everyone at O'Brien Press for taking a chance on an obnoxious rich kid from the south side. Thank you Caitríona and take a raise. Thank you Ger Siggins for being generally inspiring. Thank you Maureen Gillespie and Deirdre Shearin for always being encouraging. Thank you Matt Cooper and thank you Jim Farrelly, Paddy Murray, Mark Jones and everyone at the *Sunday Tribune* for your support. And thanks to all my friends – I know who you are, and I know where you live.

Contents

Shit the bed, is it my imagination, roysh, or am I getting better looking every day? Hord to believe I've just crawled out of the sack. I stare at myself in the mirror for, like, three or four minutes. There's no doubt that face is going to break a lot of hearts this year.

I hop into the shower. Lash on some of the old Ralph Lauren shower wash that Sorcha, my ex, who's doing the DBS in Carysfort, brought me back from the States. While I'm rubbing it in, I check the old abs and pecs. The bod's in pretty good shape considering what I put it through over the summer. I wash my hair using the *Polo Sport* two-in-one daily shampoo that Sorcha bought me for my, like, birthday and shit.

I jump out. Dry myself off. Check myself out again. I run my hand over my face. Need a shave. I lash on the old *Armani Emporio* shaving gel that Sorcha gave me, I can't remember when, and give myself a really good, close shave. I lash on some of the old *Escape for Men* aftershave balm, roysh, and go back to my room.

Can't stop thinking about Nell McAndrew. No time for an old Allied Irish, though. Not this morning. I lash on the *Tommy for Men* deodorant and hop into the old Hilfiger boxers. Only dilemma now is what to wear. My old Castlerock shirt, that goes without saying. The Blackrock goys will be wearing their shirts, so will Clongowes and the Gick. Orseholes. Have to wear your colours, though. I also go for the beige Ralph Lauren chinos, black socks and, like, Dubes.

I pull out my class schedule – 'Sports Management, 2000–2001' – and fock it in the bin. Only thing I'm gonna need this year is a map to the focking bor.

I lash on some sounds. We're talking the old Snoopmeister here. *'Gin and juice up this bitch, yaaah.'* I go back to the bathroom. Run my hand through my hair. Needs a cut. My quiff is going curly. Should have got a blade one at the sides as well. Might go later. Gel's gonna be fock-all use. It's a job for the heavy duty wax. I lash on the old Dax Wave and Groom. Check myself out again. Look-ing-good, no arguments.

'I'm on Interstate Ten focking with this Creole.' Go, Snoop.

I grab my mobile, the Nokia 8210 – we're talking dual band, thirty-five ringtones and 210 minutes of battery talk-time – and, like, ring Oisinn. He answers, roysh, with his mouth full. *Always* focking eating. He goes, 'Ross, my man. What's the *scéal?* Ready for your first day at college?' I go, 'Pretty much. Can't make up my mind what aftershave to wear, though.' He's there, 'So you've come to the man who speaks fluent Fragrance.' Oisinn worked in the Duty Free shop at the airport for the summer, roysh, and he has the whole focking spiel off by heart. Of course the birds go mad for it.

He swallows whatever it is he has in his mouth – probably

lard, the fat bastard – and he goes, 'The challenge, as I told Christian only a few moments ago, is to find a scent that's suited to the course you're doing. For instance, he's doing film studies. The birds on that course are going to be your Lillies, star-focker crew who still think they're going to marry Matt Damon. So, what Christian needs is something for an affirmed man who *totally* assumes his virility with the expression of a liberated, frank and provocative personality.'

I go, 'Are we talking *Body Kouros* by Yves Saint Laurent?' He goes, 'We most certainly are, my fast-learning friend.' I've heard this shit a million times before. He goes, 'We're doing sport, roysh? So ask yourself, what's going to push the girls' buttons on our course? Something that captures the fun and energy of an active life, a liberating fragrance that exudes cool. We're talking *Freedom* by Tommy Hilfiger, or *Polo Sport for Men*.' I'm like, 'See you later.'

I lash on the old *Polo Sport*, then wonder whether I've overdone it. Fock it, it's Kool and the Gang. Better skedaddle. There's ten thousand birds in UCD and I don't want to disappoint them. Couldn't live with that on my conscience. Head into the bathroom on the way downstairs to check myself out one last time. Looking great. Smelling great. Feeling great. There's gonna be a lot of broken hearts this year. And mine's not going to be one of them.

Ross O'Carroll-Kelly, you handsome focking bastard.

CHAPTER ONE
'Ross is, like, SUCH an arrogant bastard.'
Discuss.

Orlaith with an i, t and h Bracken. Fock me, haven't seen that bird since … must be three years. She played hockey for Alex. and tonsil hockey for Ireland. I was with her once or twice. She was pure quality then, but now she's an absolute cracker, roysh, we're talking Natalie Imbruglia but with bigger baps, and none of the goys in the class can, like, take their eyes off her. I catch her eye, roysh, and I mouth the word, 'Later,' to her, and I'm wondering whether she remembers that porty in her gaff when I puked my ring up all over her old dear's off-white Hampshire sofa and, like, focked off without saying anything. And she makes a L-sign with her thumb and her finger, as in '*Lo-ser*', and I take it she remembers it alroysh.

Her loss. It's no skin off my nose, and anyway, roysh, she's small change compared to some of the other birds in this class. Me and Oisinn struck gold when we got on this course. This bird walks in – blonde hair, amazing bod, you'd swear it was Nicola Willoughby, we're talking perma-horn material here – and she sits roysh in front of us and storts, like, fanning her face with her hand. Then she takes off her tracksuit top, roysh, and when she turns around to put it on the back of her chair, she goes to me, 'It's hot, isn't it?' and quick as a flash, roysh, I go, 'It is from where I'm sitting,' and I'm just there hoping it didn't sound too, like, sleazy and shit, but she smiles at me, roysh, and turns back around and I'm thinking, that one's in the bag anyway.

Oisinn goes, 'We are going to have some fun working our way through this lot,' and I'm there, 'I'm hearing you, big goy. I'm hearing you.' This lecturer dude comes in, don't know who the fock he is, don't care either, and he storts, like, telling us the Jackanory, what the course is about, the lectures we have, exams and loads of other boring shite, but of course I'm not listening to a word. There's another bird up the front, roysh, wearing a baby blue airtex and a dark blue baseball cap and I wish she'd turn around because I think it's, like, Samantha what's-her-name, went to Loreto Foxrock, amazing at athletics, alroysh looking, incredible pins, kicked Sorcha's orse in an Irish debate a few years ago, even though Sorcha was in sixth year and Samantha was in, like, transition year. I had to crack on, of course, that I thought Sorcha's speech was better, but then she copped me basically trying to chat this Samantha bird afterwards and she cracked the shits. I think she might be my first port of call because being with her would SO piss Sorcha off.

The next thing, roysh, everyone's suddenly standing up to go and the lecturer's giving it, 'Everyone enjoy Freshers' Day. And don't drink too much,' and this big roar goes up, as if to say, Yeah roysh, *as if!* Me and Oisinn head out and meet Christian and Fionn, who's blabbing away to some moonpig – a bogger by the sounds of her – about the connection between psychology and the biological and sociological sciences. Kathleen, he says her name is. Red hair, the whole lot. He goes, 'Goys, this is Kathleen,' and straight away I'm like, 'Fionn, we said this was gonna be just the lads,' and I turn around to this *thing* and go, 'Why don't you fock off back to Ballycabbage-and-potatoes, or wherever the fock you're from? You're not wanted,' and of course Fionn leaps straight to her defence, that's how desperate for his bit he is, the ugly bastard. He goes, 'I'm sorry about him, Kathleen. Somewhat lacking in the social graces is our Ross. I think a certain Swiss psychologist and contemporary of Freud would have a word for him,' and the two of them crack their holes laughing, roysh, basically trying to make me feel like a tit, which I do.

They're, like, saying their goodbyes, roysh, and I feel like I'm about to vom, so I head off towards the bor and Oisinn and Christian follow a few steps behind me. I can hear Oisinn asking Christian whether he wore *Fahrenheit* instead of *Body Kouros*, like he recommended, and Christian saying yeah, and Oisinn telling him that live florals mixed with balsamic notes are a bit 1997 and frankly he wouldn't use the stuff as paint-stripper. Then Oisinn puts his orm around him and asks what his course is like, some film shite he's doing, and Christian goes, 'I feel just like George Lucas did on his first day at USC,' and Oisinn goes, 'Should see our class. I feel just like Hugh Heffner does every time he gets up in the morning.'

I get to the bor first, order four pints of Ken. I turn around to the goys and I go, 'College life, huh? Freedom from school,' and the next thing Fionn's beside me and he's giving it, 'What the *fock* is your problem?' I'm like, 'What the fock is *my* problem? Who's the focking kipper?' He goes, 'She happens to be part of an experiment I'm conducting,' and I'm there, 'What, see can you finally lose your virginity?' He goes, 'Oh, someone bring me a corset, I think my sides have split. I'm investigating a theory actually,' and I'm like, 'This should be good,' him and his focking theories, and Christian's like, 'What is it, Fionn?' encouraging the goy. He goes, 'My theory is, redheads who come from a whole family of redheads are invariably bet-down,' and we all go, 'Agreed.' He's like, '*But* ... when you get one redhead in a family of non-redheads, she's usually a cracker.'

I go, 'Well, your friend obviously has a lot of brothers and sisters with the old peach fuzz. Now can we drop the subject? I want Freshers' Day to be a day to remember,' and Oisinn goes, 'No, no, no, my friend. Freshers' Day should be a day you're *not* able to remember,' and we all go, 'Yyyeeeaaahhh,' and high-five each other.

And then ... Fock it, I'll go into it another time.

✳✳✳

Women have peripheral vision, Emer goes, which is why they always know when a goy is, like, checking them out and why goys never know when they're actually being, like, checked out themselves. She can't remember where she read this, might have been *Red,* or *Marie Claire,* or some other shit. I'm not really listening. I'm waiting for my food to arrive and throwing the odd sly look at Sorcha, who's looking *totally* amazing, just back from Montauk, the pink Ralph Lauren shirt I bought her for her

birthday showing off her, like, tan. Aoife asks her if she thinks
Starbucks will ever open a place in Dublin, roysh, and Sorcha
says OH! MY! GOD! she hopes they do because she SO misses
their white chocolate mochas, and Aoife says she SO misses
their caramel macchiatos, and they both carry on naming
different types of coffee, roysh, both in American accents,
which is weird because they were only in the States for, like, the
summer and shit.

The food takes ages to arrive, roysh, and when the total
creamer of a waitress we've been given finally brings it she for-
gets the focking cutlery, and Oisinn turns around to her and
goes, 'I suppose a fork is out of the question?' The waitress,
roysh, we're talking complete focking CHV here, she's like,
'Wha'?' and I just go, 'Are we supposed to eat this with our *focking*
hands?' and she stands there, trying to give me a filthy, roysh, but
then she just, like, scuttles off to the kitchen and Oisinn high-
fives me, and Christian high-fives Fionn, and Emer and Aoife
shake their heads, and Zoey, who's, like, second year commerce
with German in UCD, SO like Mena Suvari it's unbelievable, she
throws her eyes up to heaven and goes, 'Children.'

Emer knocks back a mouthful of Ballygowan and goes, 'OH!
MY! GOD! I am SO going to have to get my finger out this year,'
and I stort asking her about her course, we're talking
morkeshing, advertising and public relations in LSB, *totally* flirting my orse off with her and watching Sorcha out of the corner
of my eye going, like, ballistic.

Then, completely out of the blue, roysh, Fionn launches into
this new theory he has about why public toilets are so, like,

gross. He goes, 'You have to be pretty desperate for a shit to use a public toilet in the first place. And let's face it, a desperate shit is never a pretty shit,' and Zoey, roysh, she holds up her bottle of Panna and goes, '*Hello?* Some of us are trying to *eat* here.'

Erika arrives then, roysh, total babe, the spit of Denise Richards, and she throws her shopping bags onto the chair beside me and goes, 'Is it my imagination or have the shops in town storted hiring the biggest knackers in Ireland as security guards?' Emer says something about the Celtic Tiger, roysh, about them not being able to get, like, staff because of it, and Erika goes, 'I'm sorry, I will *not* be looked up and down by men with focking buckles on their shoes,' and then she orders a Diet Coke and storts texting Jenny to find out what she's doing for Hallowe'en weekend and I basically can't take my eyes off the bird, roysh, and I make a promise to myself that if I'm going to score anyone between now and Christmas, it's going to be her.

Sorcha takes off her scrunchy, slips it onto her wrist, shakes her hair free and then smoothes it back into a low ponytail again, puts it back in the scrunchy and then pulls, like, five or six strands of hair loose again. It's been two-and-a-half years, but there's no doubt the girl still has feelings for me, the focking sap. I ask her how college is going and she goes, 'Amazing. Fiona and Grace are on the same course.' I'm like, 'Cool. Are you still thinking of going into Human Resources?' playing it - *totally* Kool and the Gang, and she gives it, 'I don't know. Me and Fiona are thinking of maybe going to Australia for the year. When we're, like, finished.' She's checking me out for a reaction, roysh, but I don't say anything and she eventually goes, 'I heard you got into UCD,' and I'm like, 'Yeah, the old dear said she met you,' and she goes, 'A sports scholarship, Ross. Congrats.' I can't make out whether she's being, like, a bitch or not. I'm just there, 'Yeah, it's the Sports Management course,' and she goes, 'That's supposed to be a *really* good course. It's only, like, one day of lectures a week, or something.' She's being a bitch alroysh. I pick up my tuna melt and I'm like, 'I don't give a fock what the course is like. I'm just looking forward to getting back playing good rugby again,' which, like, so impresses her.

Erika finishes texting Jenny, roysh, takes a sip out of her Coke and, like, pulls this face. She pushes it over to me and goes, 'Taste that. That's not Diet Coke, is it?' I take a sip, roysh, but she doesn't wait for my answer, just grabs the waitress by the elbow as she's passing by and goes, 'I *asked* for a *Diet* Coke.' The waitress is basically having none of it, she's there going, 'That *is* Diet Coke.' And Erika's like, '*Hello?* I think I *know* what Diet Coke tastes like.' The bird picks it up and says she'll, like, change it, but Erika, roysh, she grabs her by the orm, looks her up and down and goes, 'If I was earning two pounds an hour, I'd probably have an attitude problem as well.' I'm like, 'Well said, Erika,' trying to make Sorcha jealous and, like, *totally* succeeding.

Zoey's talking about some goy called Jamie from second year Orts who is so like Richard Fish it's unbelievable, roysh, and Sorcha and Emer stort having this, like, debate about whether Richard Fish is actually sexy, or whether it's just because he's a bastard to women, when all of a sudden the manager comes over and tells us he wants us to leave. We're all there, 'You needn't think we're paying,' and as we're going out the door the waitress goes, 'Snobby bastards,' under her breath, roysh, and Erika gives her this, like, total filthy and goes, 'Being working class is nothing to be proud of, Dear.'

✳✳✳

It's, like, two o'clock on Sunday afternoon, roysh, and the traffic on the Stillorgan dualler is un-focking-believable, we're talking bomper to bomper here. I mean, *what* is the point of having a cor that can do seventy if forty is the fastest you're allowed to go? Mind you, roysh, get above seventy in this thing – the old dear's focking Micra – and bits stort to fall off, not that there's much danger of that happening with this bitch in front of me. She is SO trying to fock me over, roysh, driving really slowly and then, like, speeding up when she sees the traffic lights on orange, trying to make me miss the lights. I turn on the radio and flick through the presets but there's, like, fock-all on. Samantha Mumba is actually on three different stations at the same time and I'm wondering if this is, like, a world record or something, and Helen Vaughan says that 'raidworks continue to operate on the Rock Raid saithbaind between the Tara Hotel and the Punchbowl, and the Old Belgord Raid is claised to traffic immediately saith of the junction with Embankment Raid.' And three goys in a silver Peugeot 206 pass me and they all have a good scope into the cor, roysh, obviously thinking it's a bird driving it because it's, like, a bird's cor – I have to admit, I get that all the time – and when they see it's a goy they all, like, crack their shites laughing, roysh, so I just give them the finger.

✳✳✳

What the fock sociology has to do with sport I don't know, but
Oisinn says it's on the course, roysh, and if it's on the course it
means we probably should check it out, suss out the talent
again and let the birds see what's on offer. As it turns out, roysh,
my mind wasn't playing tricks on me on the first day. The
talent's focking incredible, and I'm just thinking, roysh, I might
actually come back to a few more of these lecture things, when
all of a sudden who walks in only Aisling Hehir, as in
former-Holy-Child-Killiney-head-girl Aisling, as in plays-
hockey-for-Three-Rock-Rovers Aisling, as in here's-my-tits-my-
orse-will-be-along-in-fifteen-minutes Aisling, and we're all
there, 'Oooh, baby!'

I've never actually been with her before, roysh – despite her
best efforts, it has to be said – always thought of her as a bit of a
BOBFOC, the old Body Off 'Baywatch', Face Off 'Crimewatch'
sort. I don't know where the fock she was last summer, roysh,
but she's got the Peter Pan and she's, I don't know, done something with her hair, highlights or some shit, and she looks focking amazing, it has to be said: white Nike top, pink Juicy
tracksuit top tied around her waist, Louis Vuitton gym bag over
her shoulder. Everyone's eyes are, like, out on stalks when they
see her and – unbelievable, roysh – don't know how I missed
her on Freshers' Day, but she gives a little wave to me and
Oisinn, the two of us up the back playing Jack the Lad.

Of course this doesn't go down too well with the Blackrock
goys, roysh, who've been giving us, like, filthies since we got in,
especially that dickhead Matthew Path who can't handle the fact
that I scored his bird during the summer while he was off in

Ibiza on a post-Leaving Cert porty, roysh, getting his jollies off a load of ugly English slappers while I'm rattling his stunner of a girlfriend, Kate I think her name was. The word is he's taken her back, which to me lacks dignity, roysh, and the next time he turns around and tries to stare me out of it, I give him the L-sign.

Goes without saying, roysh, that the lecture is one big focking bore, the goy's up there blabbing on about Emile Durkheim, whoever the fock she is, and I turn to Oisinn's cousin, Kellser – he's a Mary's boy, but still sound – and I'm like, 'Are we really in the roysh lecture hall?' and he goes, 'Amazingly, yes. Can't see myself coming back, though. Hey, check out Aisling Hehir's rack.' I'm like, 'One step ahead of you, my man, one step ahead.'

Of course what happens then, roysh, but the lecturer, I don't even know what his focking name is, he totally snares Kellser and he's like, 'You up there. No, not you. Behind you. The boy with the blue shirt, white star on it.' Kellser's there, '*Me?*' and the goy's like, 'Yes, you. Would you like to come down and talk to us about dialectical materialism?' Of course Kellser goes, 'Eh, no,' and the goy's there, 'Okay, we'll cut a deal then, I'll stay down here talking to the class about Emile Durkheim and you stay up there with your mouth shut.' I turn around to Kellser and I'm like, 'Sorry, man,' and he goes, 'It's cool.'

Don't know what Oisinn's at, he's saying fock-all, just sitting there with his head down and for a minute, roysh, I think he's actually listening to the lecture, but then my mobile beeps twice and I realise he was sending me a text message and it's, like, a Limerick, roysh, and it's:

> THERE WAS A YOUNG ROCK
> BOY NAMED ROSS, WHOSE
> LIFE WAS A BIT OF A DOSS,
> UNMATCHED WAS HIS DIZZI-
> NESS, BUT HIS DAD OWNS A
> BUSINESS, AND ONE DAY HE'LL
> MAKE ROSS THE BOSS!

I'm about to send him one back, roysh, but he's, like, really good at them, the fat bastard, and I can't think of any words that rhyme with Oisinn, so I just send him back a message and it's like, **RETORD!** Pretty happy with that.

So there we are afterwards, roysh, arranged to meet Christian at the Blob, when all of a sudden this goy comes up to me – glasses, real nerdy head on him, I'm thinking, He's got to be a mate of Fionn's – and he goes, 'Didn't see you at the meeting, Ross.' I'm like, 'And what meeting is that?' He goes, 'Young Fine Gael. You joined up on Freshers' Day.' Freshers' Day, that's a story in itself. I go, 'Listen, I said and did a lot of things on Freshers' Day. If I joined whatever focking club it is you're talking about, I did it to take the piss. Now fock off,' and he calls me an intellectual pygmy or some shit, then does as he's told and focks off, and Oisinn high-fives me and tells me I'm the man.

Christian eventually comes along and he's talking to this total honey, who's apparently on his course, and he's telling her that General Carlist Rieekan was one of the best commanders the Rebel Alliance ever had and that, far from a defeat, the abandoning of the rebel base at Hoth was an inspired tactical retreat that didn't receive the recognition it deserved until he became Leia Organa's second-in-command on the New Republic Council, and the bird's nodding her head, roysh, but looking at him as though she's just walked into her bedroom and caught him trying on her best dress.

She focks off – no introductions, Christian lives in his own little world – and Fionn goes, 'What's the *scéal?* Looks like the *Fahrenheit* is working after all,' and Christian goes, 'Thanks, young Skywalker,' then he turns to me and he's like, 'What did you goys have?' I'm like, 'Sociology. It's, like, the mind and shit. I need a pint.'

We decide to hit the bor, roysh. I get the first round in and we bump into Fionn, who's doing Orts – we're talking psychology and Arabic and we're basically talking brains to burn here – and he's sitting up at the bor with these two birds who are in his class and he's telling them that, personally, he thinks Starbucks is far from the benign face of corporate imperialism that it pretends to be, that the company so beloved by liberal sophisticates for the cosy, aromatic, comfy-cushioned, *ennui*-inducing, 'Friends'-style world it has created is actually no different from McDonalds in its corporate structure and ideals, and is a major player in corporate America's plan to culturally homogenise the world. The birds are nodding their heads and telling him he is so roysh, and there's pretty much nothing I can contribute to this conversation, so I change the subject, roysh, and say I bought the new U2 album, *All That You Can't Leave Behind*, and I tell them it's *way* better than, like, their first album. One of the birds – she looks a bit like Elize du Toit except with longer hair – she looks at me funny and goes, 'Their *first* album? Which was their first, Ross?' I'm like, '*Pop*. It's way better than *Pop*,' and everyone in the group just breaks their shites laughing, roysh, including Christian, who's supposed to be my best friend, and Fionn goes, 'Anyone with information on the whereabouts of Ross O'Carroll-Kelly's brain, please contact Gardaí at Cabinteely,' and I haven't a clue what's so funny and it's only later that I remember about *Zooropa*.

✱✱✱

I get home from town at, like, four o'clock in the afternoon, roysh, and the old man's standing in the hallway, white as a sheet, and we're talking *totally* here, and he's just there, 'Ross, you're home.' Of course I'm like, 'No shit, Sherlock,' and he goes, 'Come into the kitchen and sit down. I've got some bad news.' I'm there, '*What* are you crapping on about?' and he goes, 'They're moving the Irish rugby team, Ross. They're moving them to … God, I can't even say it … the *northside*. The northside, Ross, I'm sorry.' Don't know what he's bullshitting on about, roysh, but there's a stink of whiskey off his breath and a huge whack gone out of the bottle of Jameson he got off his golfing mates for his fiftieth, the bunch of tossers. He always tries to be real palsy-walsy with me when he's locked. I'm, like, *totally* storving and I'm there, 'Where's that stupid wagon?' He's like, 'Your mother's out. She has coffee every Thursday afternoon with the girls. You know that,' and I'm like, 'What's the focking story with dinner?' but he totally ignores me, just goes, 'I've been trying to catch her on her mobile since two o'clock, but of course she's in the National Gallery, she's not going to have it on. She's a strong woman, your mother. Heaven knows I need her now …'

He pours himself another drink, roysh, sits down at the table and puts his head in his hands, so I get up, grab a pack of Kettle Chips and a handful of, like, funsize Mars bars out of the cupboard and stort moseying up to my room. Then I hear him, like, crying. *Hello?* I should have just ignored the attention-seeking bastard, but, of course, I'm too much of a nice goy for that. I'm like, 'What the *fock* is your problem?' and he goes, 'Lansdowne Road, Ross. It's over. They're building a new stadium. In … Abbotstown.' I'm like, 'Where the *fock* is Abbotstown?' Don't know why I'm actually bothering to sound interested. He's there, 'A million miles away from the Berkeley Court, that's where. Two million miles from Kiely's.' I'm like, 'So what? The Dorsh goes there, doesn't it?' He just, like, shakes his head and goes, 'Think again, Ross,' knocks back his drink, pours himself another and carries on blubbering to himself, the total sap.

There's a David Gray CD on the table, we're talking *White Ladder*, which Sorcha lent to the old dear. She is SO trying to get back with me, roysh, it's pretty much embarrassing. The old man's blabbing away again, going, 'It's all about votes, of course. Oh yes. Oh yes indeed thank you very much. Oh you should have heard that blasted Bertie Ahern on the one o'clock news, so bloody smug. A national stadium. Quote-unquote. And all to boost his popularity out in, what's this you and your pals call it … Knackeragua?'

He goes, 'Some of the guys are coming around tonight. Hennessy's four-square behind me. Going to set up a pressure group. KISS. Stands for Keep It South Side. And I am going to put myself forward as chairman. Or maybe president sounds better.' Then, next thing I know, roysh, the stupid bastard's up on his feet, practicing the speech he's planning to make tonight, going, 'Think of the northside and you immediately think of un-married mothers, council houses, coal sheds and curry sauce. You think of cannabis, lycra tracksuits and football jerseys worn as fashion garments. You think of men with little moustaches selling *An Phoblacht* outside these wretched dole offices, mothers and fathers in the pub from morning till night, 'Fair City', entire families existing off welfare and – sadly – the twin scourges of drugs and satellite dishes.' I'm like, 'Sit down, you're making a *total* dick of yourself,' but he just carries on, giving it, 'There are some people in this country who want our community to be-come a mirror of that. And that is why every white, Anglo-Saxon one of us has to stand up and treat this northside stadium non-sense for what it is: an all-out attack on our way of life. You can mark my words, this is just the thin end of the wedge. What's next? A methadone clinic in Foxrock?'

I hear the front door opening, roysh, and it's, like, the old dear, and for the first time in my life I'm happy to see the bitch. Or I am until she bursts into the kitchen and storts going, 'Charles, oh darling, I came as soon as I heard,' and the two of them stort, like, hugging each other, complete knobs the two of them, him pissed off his face on whiskey, her doped off her head on, like, cappuccino. And they both totally blank me, roysh. And we are talking TOTALLY here. She's like, 'What are you going to do, Charles?' He goes, 'We, Fionnuala. What are *we* going to do?' and she's there, 'Yes, of course. I'm with you, you know that,' and he goes, 'I'm going to fight it. Tooth and nail. Some of the chaps are coming over here tonight.' She goes, 'Oh I'm so proud of you. And because I knew you'd need cheering up, guess what I bought?' and she, like, pulls out this focking Gloria Jean's bag, roysh, and just, like, dances it up and down in front of his eyes, going, 'Colombia Narino Supreme,' and he's like, 'My favourite. I'll fill the percolator,' and she goes, '*And* I went to Thornton's,' and she pulls out this box, and I'm about to borf my ring up listening to this shit. He's got this, like, dopey focking smile on his face and he's there, 'Are they cherry almond charlottes, perchance?' and she nods and goes, 'And … walnut kirsch marzipan.'

He gets out the cups. *Two* cups. He's like, 'I've cheered right up now. I thought I was losing my mind before you came home.' Not a mention, of course, of me trying to cheer him up. He takes a filter from the packet and then stops all of a sudden and he goes, 'Why didn't I think of it before? You are *such* an inspiration, Darling,' and the old dear goes, 'I know that look … you're going to write a letter to *The Irish Times*, aren't you?' and he's like, 'You're damn right I am,' and she goes, 'I'll go get your pen.'

I'm standing at the kitchen door, roysh, still being completely ignored. The old dear brushes straight past me to go into the study and doesn't, like, say a word to me. The old man goes, 'Get my good one, Darling. The Mont Blanc.' The old dear comes back, roysh, and puts the pen and some of the good writing paper on the table. He hands her a cup of coffee and he goes, '*The Irish Times* will be behind me. Hell, I might even get in touch with Gerry Thornley,' and she's like, 'Remember what the judge said, Charles. Two miles.' He goes, 'No, no, no. That'll all be forgotten about by now … How was the gallery by the way?' and she goes, 'Oh, we went to the Westbury in the end. Change of scenery.'

And they both sit down at the table, roysh, and I just give them a total filthy and I go, 'You two are as sad as each other,' and I head up to my room and the old dear shouts after me, 'Don't go far, Ross. Dinner will be an hour. It's soba noodles with chicken and ginger.'

✳✳✳

We're in town, roysh, standing in some focking nightclub queue, so horrendufied I don't even know the name of it, and the birds are giving out yords to me and Christian, roysh, telling us to sober up big time or we're SO not going to, like, get in. Emer says that if we don't get in here we should head to Lillies, and Sophie says she was there last night and OH! MY! GOD! Jason Sherlock was there and so was Liz what's-her-name from 'Off the Rails'. Emer says she was there with Alyson with a y and *Oh My God!* she's thinking of going to Australia for the year, and Sophie goes, 'Yeah, after she, like, finishes in Mountjoy Square, Carol told me.'

Erika shoots Sophie a filthy, roysh, why I don't know, but then again Erika never needs a reason, not a proper one. She'd pretty much take offence at anything when the mood takes her.

But she's looking mighty fine, it has to be said, wearing a black Donna Karan dress that looks like it's been shrink-wrapped onto her, roysh, shows off the old melons really well.

We get up to the door, roysh, and there's no way the bouncers are going to let us in, me and Christian are SO struggling to hold it together, we're totally hanging, especially Christian who was really knocking back the sauce in SamSara, but suddenly Sophie goes, '*Oh my God!* I think I know one of the goys on the door,' and when we get up to the front of the queue she, like, flashes a smile at this big focking gorilla, roysh, and goes, 'OH! MY! GOD! Hi-how-*or*-ya?' as though they're, like, long-lost friends, and she gives him a peck on the cheek and a hug, and the goy hasn't a clue who she is, but he goes along with it, roysh, he's getting his jollies, the old sly-hand-on-the-orse routine. He goes, 'Lookin' lovely tonight, ladies,' the total focking howiya that he is.

Sophie goes, '*Oh* my God! I've put make-up on your shirt,' and she storts, like, rubbing his collar, roysh, but the goy goes, 'Don't worry about it. You can put make-up on me any time you like, love,' and all the girls laugh, roysh, all except Erika, who is SO not impressed, she's got, like, her orms folded, really pissed off at being kept waiting.

Of course the bouncer, roysh, he pushes it too far, tries to get a bit of physical contact going with the rest of the birds, and he goes to hug Erika next – I SO want to deck the focker at this stage – but of course she doesn't respond, roysh, just stands there stiff as a focking tree. And when he picks up on the vibe, roysh, he pulls away and Erika asks him what the fock he thinks

30

he's doing, and he says he's just being friendly. He goes, 'Ine just tryin' to be your friend, love,' and she looks him up and down and goes, 'You're sexually frustrated. Why don't you get a dirty magazine, take it to the men's room and stop making a nuisance of yourself out here.'

I'm falling in love with the girl.

✳✳✳

Most of Freshers' Day is a total blur. And we're talking TOTALLY here. I remember bits, roysh, but I was basically off my tits by about four o'clock in the afternoon, so I don't know what was, like, real, and what I, like, imagined. I remember millions of people milling about the place. All these tossers standing up on stages trying to get you to, like, join stupid societies. And freebies. They gave us, like, tubes of toothpaste, roysh, and we ended up having fights with them, covering each other with the focking stuff. Blue shit. And someone else was handing out packets of johnnies. The old love zeppelins. Packets of six, yeah they're goinna last a long time, I *don't* think!

Join Fianna Fáil. Join the World Wildlife Fund. Join the Drama Society. Join the dots to reveal a good-looking goy who's only here for the beer and the birds and thinks you Society wankers should get a focking life. Big time. And we're talking TOTALLY.

Another double vodka and Red Bull. And then ... Pretty much the only part I can remember after that, roysh, is chatting up these two Mounties in some focking marquee or other, don't have a clue how we all ended up there. I remember the birds coming up to us, we're talking me, Christian, Oisinn and Fionn,

and one of them, roysh, I think she's first year Social Science, she goes, 'OH! MY! GOD! did you hear about Becky?' and I'm like, 'No, what's the story?' obviously not cracking on that I don't have a focking clue who Becky is. She goes, 'OH! MY! GOD! She drank half a bottle of vodka *straight*, had to be brought home in an ambulance. Her mum is SO going to have a knicker-fit.'

I don't actually remember when these two birds focked off, roysh, but I'm sort of, like, vaguely aware that Oisinn said something totally out of order to one of them. I think he pointed at one of them and went, 'Halle Berry,' then pointed at the other and went, 'Halle Tosis,' and then the next hour is, like, a blur. I fell asleep at one stage, with my feet up on the chair opposite me, and then I woke up maybe half an hour later with all, like, spit dribbling down my chin, and this other bird, who I've never laid eyes on before, roysh, is sitting beside me, boring the ears off me about some bullshit or other. She has my mobile, roysh, and she's, like, flicking through my numbers, going, 'Keyser. Is that Dermot Keyes? *Oh* my God! I can't believe you know Dermot Keyes. I was going to bring him to my debs,' and then it's like, '*Oh* my God! You know Eanna Fallon. I kissed his best friend in Wesley when I was, like, fourteen. OH! MY! GOD! That's, like, SO embarrassing.' This goes on for quite a while, roysh, although I completely conk out again after about, like, five minutes. I don't know what the fock happens then because the next thing I know she's bawling her eyes out and asking me if I think she's fat, but all I can see is Christian across the far side of the bor and he's, like, calling me over, and he reminds me about this plan we had – didn't think we were being serious at the time, roysh – to rob this, like, ten-foot-tall inflatable Heino can from outside the student bor and hang it off the bridge over the main road.

So I just, like, get up and leave the bird there, roysh, the stupid, sappy bitch, and the next thing I know, me, Christian, Oisinn, Eanna, and I'm pretty sure Fionn as well, are trying to smuggle this, like, big fock-off can out of UCD, trying to avoid the security goys who were, like, driving around in jeeps. I remember Christian saying it was just like the time Princess Leia tried to sneak Han Solo out of Jabba's Palace dressed as the Ubese bounty hunter, Boussh, then getting totally, like, paranoid and going, 'I'm not gonna be no dancing girl in your court, you slimey Hutt,' and we have to calm the mad focker down, roysh, before we can cross the road over the bridge with the thing.

I remember hearing Fionn go, 'Is that noise what I think it is?' but I'm basically too busy trying to decide the best way to, like, attach this thing to the railings, but then, all of a sudden, roysh, I notice that the goys are gone. They've focking pegged it, I can see them in the distance and they're halfway to focking Stillorgan. Of course, in my shock, roysh, I end up letting go of the focking Heino can and it just, like, falls over the side of the bridge and lands on the road, and this black Fiat Punto has to, like, swerve to avoid it. That's when I hear the siren, and I'm instantly focking sober.

So the next thing I know is the Feds are asking me for my name, my address and my phone number. Obviously, roysh, I don't want my old pair to know that I focked this thing onto the dualler – still hoping the old man will give me the shekels to go skiing at Christmas – so I give them my name and Sorcha's address and number because I know she's actually the only one in her house at the moment, roysh, because her parents and her sister are in, like, the south of France for a couple of weeks.

I try to play it cool like Fonzie, roysh. I go, 'Is there a problem, Ossifer?' but the cop who's arrested me, roysh, he's on the radio, all delighted with himself for having lifted someone, and it's then that I stort thinking about basically pegging it, which isn't a good idea because I don't know if I can trust my legs, but I chance it anyway and I get about ten yords before the cop grabs me – must play focking bogball – and slams me up against the railings. And he's back on the radio, roysh, going, 'Assistance, assistance,' and he snaps the old bracelets on me and makes me lean over the railings, looking down onto the dualler, a mistake because I feel like I'm going to borf my ring up, and I'm made to stay like that until the van arrives and I'm thrown into the back of that.

Seems I'm not the only person who's been a naughty boy tonight either. There's this cream cracker in the back as well, roysh, who insists on trying to talk to me. He's going, 'What are you in for, Bud?' and straight away, roysh, I'm like, 'Let's get one thing focking straight: I'm *not* your *Bud*, roysh. We've both been arrested on the same night. That's all we have in common. I live in Foxrock. You live at rock bottom. I'm wearing *Polo Sport*. You're wearing the same clothes for a week. I was holding a giant, blow-up Heino can over the edge of a bridge. You were holding up someone with a syringe.' He looks at me like I'm talking in a foreign language, which I suppose I am to him. He goes, 'I hit a bouncer a dig,' and I'm there thinking, He's not all bad then, and for two seconds I'm almost sorry for giving the creamer such a hord time.

I go, 'Please don't breathe near me. I hate the smell of turpentine,' and he smiles then, roysh – four focking teeth in his mouth – and he goes, 'You have to watch out for me, I'm a bit of a character.' I go, 'Why did you hit the bouncer?' and he's there, 'Wouldn't let me in. Said he didn't know me face. Says I, "You'll remember it de next toyim."' I go, 'I suspect it had nothing to do with not knowing your face. You were turned away because you're a skobie. You dress like a scarecrow and you smell of piss. You are one hundred percent creamer. I'm no fan of bouncers myself, but us regulars have the roysh to go to a night-club without having to be deloused afterwards.' He's sitting there with his mouth open. With the language barrier, you could say anything to him. I go, 'You piece of vermin.'

He goes, 'D'ya tink you'll end up insoyid?' and I'm there, 'I *seriously* doubt it. I don't make a habit of being arrested, you know.' He goes, 'Don't worry, Bud, just tell the judge you're going back to do yisser Junior Cert. Dee love dat. Improving yisser self. Mustard.' I'm like, 'I *don't* think so. My old man's solicitor will get me off.' The goy goes, 'Ah, I'm on dee oul' free legal ayid meself,' and I'm there, 'No shit.'

We get to the cop shop, roysh – think it's Donnybrook – and we're brought in and this total focking bogger takes my details again, while the one who arrested me is, like, muttering under his breath with all his 'endangering the lives of road-users' bullshit, roysh, and I'm just there, 'Spare me the lecture, will you?'

So the next thing is, roysh, the copper who takes my details, he tells me to, like, turn out my pockets and hand over my belt and shoelaces and I'm like, 'Why do you need those?' and he goes, 'In case you try to hang yourself.' I'm like, '*Hang myself?* Whoah, who the fock owns that Heino can? Is there something I should know here?' and he tells me I have a big mouth and it's going to get me into trouble one day and I'm like, 'Spare me.'

The reason I can afford to be so Jack the Lad about it is that I know the old man's dickhead of a mate will have me out of here in ten seconds flat. So before they stick me in the cell, roysh, I tell them I want to make a call and they give me a phone and I ring his number. He answers pretty much straight away. He's like, 'Hennessy Coghlan-O'Hara,' and I'm like, 'Hennessy, it's Ross. I've been arrested. If you tell the old man, I'll tell your wife about that time I saw you in Angels. Where are you?' and he goes, 'Outside Donnybrook Garda Station.' I'm there, 'Holy fock, that was quick. Who told you?' He goes, 'No, I've been arrested myself. It seems you can't even hold a conversation with a prostitute these days without being accused of kerb-crawling. The Gardaí have had to take stern action to stem the tide of people being civil to those less fortunate than themselves.'

The next thing the door swings open, roysh, and there he is, a cop either side of him, and he marches straight up to the counter and goes, 'Can you explain to me why the criminal justice system is squandering vital resources that could be used in the war on crime?' One of the Feds beside him goes, 'You have been charged with performing a lewd act in a public place. Do you understand the charge?' and he goes, 'I was asking the girl for directions, for heaven's sake,' and I'm like, 'Hennessy, your trousers are open,' and he looks down, pulls up his fly, fastens his belt, winks at me and goes, 'The little minx.'

I tell the Feds I am SO not sharing a cell with him, or with the goy from *The Commitments,* roysh, and they put me in one by myself and it's a bit of a hole. I lie on the hord, wooden bed and read some of the graffiti on the wall, and after a while one of the Feds comes into me and he goes, 'That number you gave us, who's there now?' I'm like, 'Sorcha. My … em … sister.'

So he goes off to ring her, roysh, obviously planning to let me out, probably needs the cell for some real criminals, but Sorcha takes her focking time getting here, we're talking *two* focking hours, and when they finally let me out of the cell, I can see why. She's, like, *totally* dressed to kill, the sad bitch, wearing the Burberry leather knee-high boots, in cognac, that her old dear bought her in New York, her long black Prada skirt, her black cashmere turtleneck sweater, we're talking the Calvin Klein one, and her sleeveless, faux sheepskin jacket by Karen Millen – as if I'm supposed to believe she always looks this well at, like, three o'clock in the morning. I'm SO glad to see her though, and I give her a hug and go to throw the old lips on her but she just, like, pulls away from me, roysh, and I'm just there going to myself, *Oh* my God, this one is in a Pauline now.

The cops decide not to charge me, roysh – happy days – but they say they'll keep the incident on file and if I'm ever arrested again, blah blah blah. They give me my shit back, but I'm still too shit-faced to put my, like, shoelaces back into my shoes, roysh, so I just stuff them into my pocket, while Sorcha spends about ten focking minutes apologising to the cops for my behaviour, totally overdoing it with the Mature Young Adult act, and we're talking *totally* here. Then she walks on out to the cor, like she's in a hurry and in no mood to take shit from me.

I see this bird arriving, roysh, dirty blonde hair, big hoopy earrings, leather jacket, denim skirt, bare legs, white stilettos – we're talking straight off the 'Jerry Springer' show, roysh – and she marches up to the desk and goes, 'Here to pick up me fella,' and I know straight away, roysh, that it's the goy who was in the back of the van with me. I just walk up to her, roysh, and I'm like, 'Your boyfriend's one hell of a goy. You're a lucky girl,' and she looks at me, roysh, real aggressive, and she goes, 'Who the fook do you tink you are?' and I'm like, 'Sorry, I've been assigned to his case. I'm his social worker,' and the stupid sap believes me, roysh, she shakes my hand – she's more sovs on her than Jimmy focking Saville – and then I turn around and go, 'I'll be in touch,' and head for the door. She shouts after me, roysh, she goes, 'He's not goin' back insoyid, is he?' and I turn back to her and I'm there, 'He's gonna get ten years. I'm sorry, there's nothing I can do,' and I can, like, hear her shrieks from outside.

Sorcha tells me to hurry up. We get into her cor, roysh, black Rav 4, we're talking amazing here, and the nagging storts straight away. She's like, 'Well, you've certainly made an impression at UCD. It was certainly a day to remember, wasn't it?' I just, like, totally blank her, which really pisses her off, but she just keeps it up, going, 'Don't worry, Ross, you'll grow out of it.'

On the other side of the road, roysh, there's, like, two or three buses turning into the bus depot in Donnybrook, and I realise that it's actually a lot earlier than I thought it was. What the *fock* was I drinking? Sorcha goes, 'By the way, that was a stupid thing you did back there. In the police station,' and I'm like, 'What?' and she goes, 'Trying to kiss me.' I'm like, 'You *love* it,' and she goes, 'You *told* them I was your sister.' I'm like, 'Incest, the game for all the family.'

Blah blah blah blah blah. She goes, 'You owe me. *Big* time.' I'm like, 'What do you mean, *owe* you?' She goes, '*Hello?* Do you think I've nothing better to do at eleven o'clock at night than drive all the way from Killiney into town to get you out of a police cell?' I'm there, 'What were you doing when the Feds called?' and she looks at me, shakes her head and goes, 'I *have* a life, you know,' which means she was doing fock-all.

I spend what seems like the next hour falling in and out of sleep, roysh, but it must only be a few minutes because when I open my eyes we're only at, like, the Stillorgan crossroads, and I realise that it's actually Sorcha's shouting that's woken me up. I keep sort of belching, roysh, and there's, like, baby sick on my chin and my jacket and Sorcha's going, 'If you borf in my cor, Ross, I am SO going to kill you.' I wipe my face on my sleeve, tell her I love her when she's angry and go to kiss her on the cheek, but she tells me that if I even think about it she'll break my orm, so I don't.

After a few minutes, roysh, completely out of the blue, she goes, 'I'm seeing someone.' She's totally dying for me to ask who, roysh, but I don't say anything and after a couple of minutes she goes, 'He's in my class. He's *actually* twenty-eight. The goys in Carysfort are SO much more mature than the goys in UCD.' She takes the roysh turn at White's Cross and she's there going, 'I am SO over you, Ross. I look back now and I'm like, *Oh my God*! what a mistake.' I don't say anything. She goes, 'I mean, is the proposition of monogamy such a Jurassic notion to you?' I'm just like, 'Okay, Joey,' and she realises that I'm not as shit-faced as she thought I was and she just goes really red and doesn't, like, say anything else for ages and I'm, like, totally laughing my orse off.

She turns up the CD then, roysh, and I hadn't even realised that she had it on. I'm just like, 'What is this shit?' and she throws her eyes up to heaven and goes, 'It's Tchaikovsky, Ross. 'Dance of the Reed Flute'. It's from *The Nutcracker*. Oh my *God*, Ross, when are you *ever* going to get with the programme?' The cover from the CD is on the dashboard, roysh, and it's like, *The Best Classical Album of the Millennium … Ever!* I turn up the sound really high, roysh, until it's blasting, and then stort, like, conducting the music, swinging my orms around the place and Sorcha goes, 'You are SUCH a dickhead.' We pull up outside my gaff and I get out of the cor and, like, stagger up to the gates of the house, and I must have left the passenger door open because I hear Sorcha getting out and, like, basically cursing me under her breath, then slamming the door shut, and the next thing I know I'm waking up and it's, like, the middle of the after-noon the next day, and I still have my Castlerock jersey and my chinos on and I'm in the total horrors. And we're talking big style.

✲✲✲

Me and Oisinn, we skip our eleven o'clock, roysh, and we're sitting in his gaff watching the telly when my mobile rings and I, like, make the mistake of answering before checking who it is, roysh, and who is it only the old man, basically checking up on me, he's like, 'Hey, Kicker, how's college?' and I'm there, 'Not a good time. I'm watching 'The Love Boat',' and I hang up on the loser.

✲✲✲

Huge row in the bor the other night, roysh. Erika was going on about the National Lottery, which she said was basically for skangers, and Claire, who basically *is* a skanger, roysh – a Dalkey wannabe who actually lives in Bray – she goes, 'But what about my mum? She buys scratch cards. That doesn't mean *I'm* a skanger.' And Erika goes, 'I'm not changing the rules to accommodate you, your mother, or anyone else in your family. Scratch cords are actually worse than doing the Lottery. Face it, Dear, you're peasant class,' and Claire storts going ballistic, roysh, screaming and shouting, telling Erika she's the biggest snob she's ever met, which Erika would actually consider a compliment, roysh, and she just smiles while Claire makes a total tit of herself in front of everyone, and eventually Sorcha takes her off to the toilet to calm her down and, like, clean up her make-up and shit, which totally pisses Erika off, roysh, I can tell, because she looks at me and goes, 'Sorry, *whose* best friend is Sorcha supposed to be again?' Then she gets up and leaves the boozer without even finishing her Bacordi Breezer.

I actually felt a bit bad for her, roysh, so the next morning, I decide to head out to her gaff in Rathgar, just to, like, tell her I thought she was in the roysh, about time someone put Claire in her place, blah blah blah, basically just trying to get in there. I check my jacket pocket to see have I any johnnies left. We all got, like, a free six-pack on our first day, roysh, off some focking Society or other, and I turned around to Christian and I'm like, 'Six? Well that's the first weekend looked after,' but that turned out to be bullshit because they're still unopened.

Anyway, roysh, I peg it out to Rathgar and her old dear opens the door – bit of a yummy mummy; with a daughter who looks like Denise Richards, of course she is – and she says Erika's not in, she's actually down with her horse, she goes, 'She spends half her life with that animal,' but I might be able to get her on her mobile if she has it switched on, which she probably doesn't because it freaks out the horse. I tell her I'll, like, head down to the stables myself to see can I catch her.

The cor pork is full of really cool cors and I'm actually embarrassed porking the old dear's Micra there, but fock it. I mooch around the place looking for her, and when I eventually see her, roysh, she's carrying this, like, bucket of I-don't-know-what, basically some type of shit she feeds the horse, and I'm straight over, playing the total gentleman, going, 'Erika, let me carry that for you,' flexing the old biceps as well, of course.

When I go to take it from her, though, she shoots me this total filthy, roysh, so I just hold my hands up and go, 'Hey, no offence.' I follow her into the stable and she puts the bucket down and goes, 'Your girlfriend has a serious attitude problem.' I ask her who she means, roysh, and she goes, 'Sorcha,' and I tell her that Sorcha isn't my girlfriend, that I'm young, free and single and I want to mingle, which she just ignores. She goes, 'I SO love her little friend, the one with the Rimmel foundation. Made such an impression in The Queen's last night, didn't she? That's what you get when you go dredging for friends in Bray.' I'm like, 'That's actually what I'm here for, Erika,' and she goes, 'What *are* you here for, Ross?' I'm about to tell her that I thought she was really badly treated last night, roysh, when all of a sudden she goes, 'Do you want to be with me? Is that why you're here?' and even though she makes it sound sort of, like, sleazy, roysh, I tell her yes and she goes, 'Okay then, let's go.'

So I basically just grab her, roysh, and stort doing, like, tongue sarnies with her, and I have to say, even though the boots and the jodhpurs are a major turn-on, she's not actually as good a kisser as I remembered from the last time I was with her two years ago. I open my eyes a couple of times, sort of, like, mid-snog, roysh, and notice that she has her eyes open the whole time, and this sort of sounds, like, weird, roysh, but it was like kissing a dead body and the only response I actually get out of her is when we fall backwards into the hay and I try to go a bit further than just snogging – can't blame a goy for chancing his orm – and she just looks over my shoulder and goes, 'Get off me. I have to feed *Orchid.*'

✳✳✳

Out this particular Friday night, roysh, and me and Christian make the mistake of hitting Boomerangs, got the old beer goggles on, of course, spot this gang of birds, roysh, obviously out on a hen's night, we're talking easy pickings here, mosey on over, give them a couple of killer lines, though I wouldn't have bothered if I'd known they were skobies. This one bird, roysh, she looks like Kelly Brook, but she talks like something off 'Fair City', and she has a laugh like a focking donkey getting taken out with an Uzi.

I go up to her, playing it cool like Huggy Bear, roysh, and I go, 'I know what you're thinking. Great body, amazing-looking, dresses well – and yet he's got something else. The X factor,' and this bird, she turns around to the bird beside her and goes, ''Cinta, have a listen to dis fella,' and I think Christian's the only one there who cops the look of, like, pure focking horror on my face. He turns around to me, roysh, and he goes, 'Jesus, Ross, these people are working class,' – can be difficult to tell these days, every slapper in town's wearing Ralph since TK Maxx opened – and I'm going, 'Play it cool, Christian. Play it nice and cool and I'll get us the fock out of here.'

She going, ''Cinta, have a listen to um,' and she turns to me and she goes, 'Go on, young fella. Say it again.' I'm not gonna be a performing seal for any skobie bird, so I just give her a different line this time, show her I'm not a one-trick pony. I'm there, 'We wouldn't be true to ourselves if we denied that there's an attraction here,' and she's off again – nah-ah-ah-ah-ah-ah-ah, hee-haw – and 'Cinta's cracking her hole as well, as are all the other birds. 'Cinta goes, 'Does de voice great, doesn't he?' and another one of the birds – focking cat – she goes, 'Ah Jaysus, he's veddy good.'

The bird who, until ten seconds ago, reminded me of Kelly Brook, she goes, 'Where are yiz from den, lads?' and I go, 'I'm from Foxrock. Upmorket area on the south side,' and they all break their shites laughing again and 'Cinta goes, 'Dee can't be serdious for foyiv minutes, can dee?' Kelly Brook Gone Wrong goes, 'Are yis gettin' dem in, lads?' We're all drinkin' Ritz, 'cept for Pamela dare who's on pints of Carlsberg and so is Anee-eh.' I go, 'Fine. We shall return presently,' and 'Cinta's going, 'Dare gas, ardent dee,' as me and Christian head off in the general direction of the bor, but take a long detour out the focking emergency exit and up the road without looking back once.

✳✳✳

I phone up Erika, roysh, on her mobile, and ask her where she is, but she doesn't answer, she just goes, 'What do you want?' so I get straight to the point. I'm there, 'Just wanted to talk to you about, you know, what happened between us,' and she goes, 'Make it quick. I'm in Nine West.' I'm like, 'Well, I just wanted to let you know that I won't say anything to Sorcha. About, you know, me and you being with each other. I know she's your best friend,' and there's this, like, silence on the other end of the line. I'm like, 'Are you still there?' and she goes, 'The line is perfect, Ross. Is that all you want to say?' and I'm like, 'Well, I just wondered whether *you* were going to say anything to her,' not that I actually give a shit one way or the other, just wanted an excuse to ring her, see if there's any chance of another bit. She goes, 'Do you think being with you is something I'd actually *brag* about?'

CHAPTER TWO
'Ross is, like – OH MY GOD! – so shallow.'
Discuss.

Me and Oisinn skip our three o'clock, roysh, and we're in his gaff watching 'Countdown' and he tells me it's my turn to go to the fridge and get the beers, so I head out to the kitchen, roysh, and, HOLY FOCK! I'm like, 'What the ...' There's this, like, life-size statue of, I don't know, some dude with long hair, big fock-off wings and no mickey. I go back into Oisinn and I'm like, 'What the *fock* is that thing out there?' He goes, 'The bacon? You didn't throw it out, did you? It's only a week past its sell-by date,' and I'm like, 'I'm talking about that focking statue. Looks like the one in the paper. The one that was stolen from the Classics Museum on Freshers' Day.' Oisinn just looks at me.

I'm like, 'Are you focking *mad?* I can't believe it was you,' and he's like, '*Me?* Ross, do you remember Freshers' Day?' I'm there, 'I told you already, I was rat-orsed, pretty much the whole day is a blank.' He goes, '*You* stole it, Ross. This is *your* shit. You asked me could I mind it for you. And thanks for reminding me, you're going to have to take it with you. My old pair are storting to ask questions.'

I've a few focking questions of my own. He goes, 'It's *Eros* apparently.' I'm like, '*Hello?* I need a little more information than that …' He's there, 'Well, Fionn said he was the son of Aphrodite. Fired magic arrows at people's hearts and made them fall in love.' He doesn't even turn away from the television when he says this. He goes, 'Actually, I thought it was Cupid did that. Consonant, Carol.' I'm like, 'You know what I mean. When did I steal it? No, why? No, how?' He goes, 'Pretending you don't remember. Cute.' There's no focking way I'm letting him pin this one on me. I'm like, 'I'm sorry, Oisinn. I didn't steal that thing. You're gonna have to prove it.' He turns around, roysh, calm as anything, and he goes, 'Ross, you were wearing the face off *Eros* in front of the UCD webcam as a dare. There was about thirty of us sitting in the computer lab watching you. I've actually got it on disk. And you mooning.'

I'm actually storting to feel faint. I sit down. I'm there, 'Is that the lot? I mean, did I do anything else that day?' He thinks for a bit and goes, 'Some ugly bird was looking for you in Finnegan's Break yesterday morning. Think you might have joined the Chess Society.' I'm there, 'I am SO never drinking again.' He goes, 'Fock me, Gyles, you're roysh, draughts does have eight letters … I'll help you carry it out to the cor.'

***

I ask for a large latte, roysh, and the bird behind the counter, who's, like, French or some shit, she says they have no large, so I ask for a small instead and she goes, 'No small.' I'm like, 'What *have* you focking got?' and she goes, 'Only *grande*, tall and short,' and at this stage, roysh, I'm so confused I don't know what the fock to ask for, so I head back to Melissa and ask her what she wants, roysh, and she just looks me up and down and goes, 'Will you *grow* up. This is focking serious,' and for a couple of seconds I think she's talking about the coffee, roysh, but when she stands up and, like, storms out of the place, I finally cop that she's actually talking about what happened at the Traffic Light Ball. Or should I say, afterwards.

I peg it after her, but she's already across the other side of the road, up by the Central Bank, and the lights are red, but I leg it across anyway and this orsehole in a blue Nissan Almera beeps me, so I just give him the finger. I catch up with her and touch her on the shoulder, roysh, but she just, like, spins around and goes, 'Nicole was SO right about you,' and I'm going, Who the fock is Nicole? to myself, of course, and she's there, 'You are *such* an orsehole. That's what she told me, Ross. And she was right.' I'm suddenly all, like, defensive now, I'm there, 'Hey, I said I'd meet you this morning and I did,' and she goes, 'You just want to make sure I go through with it.' I'm there, 'Not true, I wanted to be here with you. This is something you shouldn't have to go through on your own.' She goes, 'You are SO full of shit. You're just thinking about what your parents would say if they found out I was ...' I'm like, 'Bullshit. Anyway, you're not,' and she turns around and storts walking again, off through Temple Bar, and I, like, follow her from a safe distance.

There's a goy busking in the archway outside Abrakebabra, roysh, and it's like, 'Don't Look Back in Anger', and as we're waiting for the lights, roysh, I tell Melissa that that song has been SO ruined by every busker in town playing it, but she just ignores me, as she does when I ask her why they're building a new bridge next to the Ha'penny Bridge. She just, like, shakes her head, roysh, and I am SO tempted to point out that this is only, like, fifty percent my fault, that it takes two to tango, but I know it'll only make things worse if I do.

The place is next door to Pravda, and Melissa presses the button on the intercom, says she has an appointment and the next thing, roysh, there's a bird behind a desk asking her whether she's attended the clinic before, and Melissa looks her up and down and goes, 'Hordly!' Then we're sitting down in the waiting room and Melissa's filling out this, like, form and shit, which she gives to the nurse and then we just, like, sit there and wait. In total silence. I sort of look sideways at her a couple of times and I have to say, roysh, she's actually a bit better looking than I thought she was last night, a little bit like Charisma Carpenter, except with blonde hair. I only ended up with her because Christian wanted to be with her best friend, Stephanie, who actually does look a little bit like Natalie Portman, and he asked me to take a bullet for him, which, being the great mate that I am, I did. They're both, like, first year Orts.

Eventually, roysh, the doctor calls her into her office, and I'm not sure whether I'm supposed to, like, go in with her, but as I go to stand up Melissa tells me to stay outside and mind her stuff, which suits me fine. I'm sitting there, roysh, looking around and there's this bird sitting two seats down from me who I think I recognise from Annabel's, and she's a total nervous wreck, can't stop, like, fidgeting and shit.

All of a sudden, roysh, Melissa's phone storts beeping, so I grab it out of her bag and notice that she has a text message and it's from some bird called Gwen and it's like, **OMG**, which I presume means Oh My God, **RACHEL KISSED ROSS**, which I'm guessing is, like, a reference to 'Friends'. Two sad bitches, and we're talking TOTALLY here. I flick through her numbers, roysh, and notice that she knows four or five chicks I've been with before. I still don't have a clue who this Nicole one is, and I think about writing down her number, roysh, but in the end I don't bother. I lash her phone back in her bag and stort flicking through a copy of *Now!* that the bird two seats down has just put back on the table. Says you can achieve the Liz Hurley look by using this gel, lactic acid or some shit, to increase the flow of blood to the lips, making them look fuller.

About ten minutes later, roysh, Melissa comes out and it's all, like, thank-you this and thank-you that to the doctor, but her face changes when she sees me and she just, like, heads straight for the door and I follow her down the stairs. We walk back towards Grafton Street and even though I have no real interest in seeing her again, I ask her what she's doing later and she goes, 'Leaning over the toilet and getting sick, I would imagine.' I ask her what she's bullshitting on about and she goes, 'Do you have *any* idea what I've just taken?' and I go, 'The morning-after pill,' and she just shakes her head and tells me I haven't got a clue.

She says she's going down for the Dorsh, roysh, and I tell her I'm going to get the 46A. And I don't know why, maybe because I feel sorry for her, I ask her whether I'll see her in college tomorrow and she tells me not to get my hopes up, that she's seeing someone.

✳✳✳

The old man comes into my room and he's there, 'Ross, is there any reason why there's a Greek statue in the laundry room?' I just give him a filthy and go, 'You have SUCH a focking attitude problem.'

✳✳✳

I ring Sorcha, roysh, and tell her that the Castlerock debs is coming up at the end of November and, well, would it be alroysh if I called out to see her tonight because there's, like, something I really want to ask her. She's there, 'Of course. Make it after eight. Mum and Dad will be at the sailing club annual dinner.'

So after half-eight, roysh, I mosey on out to Killiney and Sorcha, roysh, she's made the effort, there's no doubt about that, she opens the door and she's wearing her black halterneck from Pia Bang, her black Karen Millen trousers and the black Prada boots I bought her for her birthday last year, and half a focking bottle of *Issey Miyake*.

She air-kisses me and asks me whether I want, like, marshmallows in my hot chocolate. I'm like, 'Cool, yeah,' and I follow her into the kitchen and we sit at the counter, roysh, sipping hot chocolate and making small talk and she's like a child she's so excited.

Eventually, I go, 'Sorcha … em … as you know, the debs is coming up. And it's weird, but I'm … em … a bit nervous asking you this.' Her face is all lit up. She's like, 'Go on, it's okay.' I'm like, 'Well, we've known each other since … forever, haven't we? You know you're very special to me. How's that goy you're going out with, by the way, the twenty-eight-year-old?' She's like, 'Cillian? I have to be honest with you, it's not really serious. We're only really, like, *seeing* each other.' I'm like, 'Good, good. Anyway, Sorcha, as you know, there's no one in the world who I value more than you. Which is why I wanted to ask you, with the debs coming up in two weeks, if you'd mind if I asked Erika to go with me.'

She's like, 'What?' and I go, 'Erika.' She's there, 'Erika? Erika as in my best friend Erika?' and I'm like, 'Have you got a problem with that?' She's, like, staring into space, trying to get her head around this, but of course she doesn't want to let herself down. She goes, 'No, I've no, em, problem with it. Ask her if you want.' I'm like, 'I will. I'm glad you're cool about it.'

She goes, 'Actually, I was hoping you weren't going to ask me. I know I said me and Cillian were only seeing each other, but I think he wants to be a bit more serious about things.'

Pathetic. I know I could have her now if I wanted her.

I finish my hot chocolate and get up to go. I'm there, 'I like that music, by the way,' and she goes, 'It's Bizet. It's from *Carmen*,' and she's trying her best not to cry, but I can see the tears in her eyes.

✳✳✳

JP sends me a text message, roysh, and it's like:

> **SCORED A JUDGE'S DAUGHTER LAST NIGHT! AFFLUENCE!**

✳✳✳

I'm in the bor, roysh, shooting some pool with Christian, two o'clock in the day and the two of us gee-eyed. Christian was locked when I met him at ten o'clock this morning, totally paranoid as well, keeps telling me that the UCD water tower is the secret headquarters of the Prophets of the Dark Side and I ask him who the fock they are – why I encourage the goy I don't know – and he tells me they're essentially a band of imperial operatives posing as mystics who are strong in the Dark Side of the Force, and whose real function is espionage. I go – quick thinking, this – 'They're probably listening to us now. Let's be careful what we say,' and he nods and goes, 'Well, they have a vast network of spies as well.' The goy is losing it.

Anyway, there we are playing pool, roysh, and this total twat comes up to the table – long black coat, black hair in a ponytail, looks like the goy out of the comic shop in 'The Simpsons'. So Christian, roysh, he holds his cue like a sword and he goes, 'Supreme Prophet Kadann sent you, didn't he?' and the goy goes, 'Hey, *The Lost City of the Jedi*. What a book, dude,' but Christian looks at him sort of, like, suspiciously and goes, 'Be careful. I think this one's a changeling.'

The goy goes, 'I'm actually here to see you, Ross.' I'm like, 'What the fock could we possibly have to talk about?' and the goy goes, 'The We Are Not Alone Society. I spoke to you on Freshers' Day.' Not another one. I go, 'Look, I was locked. It didn't mean anything. Now get over it.'

Then I tell him to fock off.

***

I send Erika a text message, roysh, and it's like, **w%d u llk 2go2 my debs?** and straight away I get one back and it's like, **GAL**, which I presume stands for Get A Life, because that's what she always says. She actually says it to everyone. It's like, '*Get* a life!'

***

Oisinn grabs me by the lapel, roysh, and smells my neck and goes, '*Bvlgari pour homme.* Notes of perfumed darjeeling with citrus and aquatic notes. Classic … and yet modern.' I straighten his bow-tie and I go, 'Oisinn, my man, looking good. Look-ing-good.' He goes, 'Yeah, I was quite surprised myself to discover that Hugo Boss does tuxes for goys of my generous build. So some of the credit for what you see here before you must go to Mr HB Esquire.' Then he turns around to the bird beside me and goes, 'And who, pray tell, is this little … beauty?'

The little beauty happens to be Elspeth Hadaway, who's, like, third year Orts in UCD, pretty decent-looking, a little bit like Catherine McCord, except in the old body department. It's a bit of a long story really. Erika knocking me back came as a bit of a shock, roysh, and didn't leave me much time to find an alternative – forty-eight hours to be precise. Then JP tells me about this bird he knows, plays tennis with his sister and was going out with this Trinity wanker – I knew him when he was in Terenure, a total dickhead – who, it turns out, did the dirt on her when she was in Germany for a year on Erasmus.

JP goes, 'We're talking about a mutual convenience of wants here, Ross. She wants the word to go back to this tosser that she's seeing someone else. And you want someone to go to the debs with so you don't look like a sad bastard.' I'm like, 'Thanks, JP.' He goes, 'Cheer up, it's a win-win situation. Let's throw this idea out of the 'plane, see does its parachute open.'

So I meet her the night before the debs, roysh, we're talking Eddie Rockets in Stillorgan. She pretty much insisted on inspecting the merchandise beforehand and, not being big-headed or anything, I think I can say she wasn't disappointed. And I have to say, roysh, I thought she was alroysh as well, no complaints, until she switched on the focking waterworks and storted telling me I'd never guess who it was her *so-called* boyfriend did the dirt on her with, we're talking Shauna, the girl who is *supposed* to be her best friend. I'm just there going, 'Bummer,' but on and on it goes, she's giving it, 'This is the girl who I actually helped through her break-up with Tadgh.' The girl's pretty much hysterical at this stage, roysh, and we're beginning to attract a bit of an audience, so I just go, 'Look, have you got a focking dress?' and she's like, 'I'm going to wear the one I wore to the Orts Ball two years ago. And I am going to look SO amazing. I'm going to–' I just go, 'Fine. Meet me at eight in the bor in the Berkeley Court.' That's where the gig was on. I'm there, 'And get all that focking crying out of your system tonight. Don't want you making a tit out of me,' then I drop a tenner on the table, which should cover my buffalo wings, chilli-cheese fries and vanilla malt, and I get the fock out of there.

Twenty-four hours later, of course, I'm regretting being such a dick to her – and leaving her to get the bus home – because she looks focking amazing in this, like, pink satin dress that she says is a Donna Karan original, and all the goys, roysh, their eyes are out on stalks when they see her. This bird lights up the room.

Oisinn's bird lights up a John Player. The goy has surpassed himself this time. We're talking Jo Brand with orange hair and a face full of double-u double-u dots. She's wearing a purple dress she must have borrowed from Fossett's circus. She is a *total* mutt, which seems to make Oisinn very proud. I introduce him to Elspeth and he introduces me to, Julia I think her name was, didn't get a chance to check her collar. He's like, 'Isn't she pretty?' and then, roysh, in front of her face he goes, 'Pretty *ugly*,' and Julia sort of, like, slaps him as if to say, You're terrible, Oisinn, like she thinks the goy's joking.

Fionn has brought Eilish Hunter, this total lasher from his class who looks a bit like Faye Tozer and who, for some bizarre reason, actually has the big-time hots for the boring, drippy-looking geek. And he's SO focking smug about it. He's giving it, 'Lots of girls have a thing about glasses, Ross. Especially since *Jerry Maguire* came out. They think if we have kids, they'll turn out like the kid in that film.' I'm like, 'Please. I'm gonna vom my lemon sorbet back up in a minute.'

Then, roysh, just to, like, rub it in, he goes, 'Heard yours was an *arranged* date,' and he tries to make it sound really sleazy. I look at Elspeth and she's chatting away to Oisinn, no way she can hear me, then I turn around to Fionn and I'm like, 'I think she's fallen for me. Big time,' which is total bullshit because she's been stressing the whole 'We're just friends' bit all night, but I'm not letting him get one over on me. Fionn goes, 'Catching a girl on the rebound can be fraught with problems, because you never know what angle they're coming back at you from,' as if I need advice from *him*. Then he turns to Eilish and they stort talking about some, I don't know, stupid intellectual thing.

I look over and I cop Aileen Hannah-Lynch, this bird I used to know – in the biblical sense – and she's getting up to leave with Andrew Beirne, and it looks like they're about to get to know each other in the biblical sense too, roysh, because Fionn says they've got a room booked and I'm there thinking, We haven't even had the main course yet. Jammy bastard.

The night drags. I'm on a shit buzz. Me and Elspeth have hordly said two words to each other, roysh, and I can hear Oisinn giving it the whole 'bouquet of floral, amber and powdered notes' bullshit, and he's got Elspeth and the hound he brought hanging on his every word.

I end up horsing down the Bailey's ice cream and focking off to another table to talk to Woulfie, Ed and Barser, three goys who were on the S with me, brains to burn the three of them, they're doing politics or some shit in Trinity, but they still like their rugby. So we're basically there shooting the breeze, roysh, when all of a sudden this bird comes over, Lia – nice boat-race, great rack – and she goes, 'Ross, have you seen Christian? Carol is, like, SO worried about him.'

I'd totally forgotten about Christian. He was in the bor earlier but I sort of, like, slipped away from him when he storted telling me that Tibanna gas is the best hyperdrive coolant there is and no one can blame Han for heading for Bespin like he did. You've SO got to be in the mood to listen to Christian's shit, and I wasn't, so I left him with Carol, who JP reckons looks like Susan Ward, though I don't see it myself.

I go off looking for the dude and, considering how shit-faced he was when I last saw him, roysh, my first port of call is the jacks. And he's there. He's standing at the sink, roysh, with his face pressed up against the mirror. I call his name, but he doesn't answer. I go, 'Christian,' again. Still nothing. I pull his head away from the mirror and I see that he's crying. He's bawling his eyes out. I go, 'Christian, what's the focking story, my man?' He looks at me, roysh, like he's trying to focus on me and he goes, 'I can't tell you, Ross.' I'm there, 'Too focking roysh you can. I'm your, like, best friend,' but he just bursts into tears again.

The dude is focked. I decide to take him back to my gaff, roysh, just to sleep it off. I'm having a mare of a night anyway, so it doesn't bother me to fock off so early. I manage to walk Christian out as far as, like, reception, plonk him in a big orm-chair, then ask the bird at reception to call us a Jo. There's, like, couples slipping upstairs and couples slipping outside, basically all doing the debs thing. Elaine – don't know her second name, I was with her once, second year Orts UCD – she's bet into some bloke, can't see his face, think it might be Kellyer, this tosser who was on the Castlerock second team and had big ideas about taking my place on the S.

Weird as it sounds, roysh, I actually feel a little bit bad about focking off on Elspeth without saying anything. But then all of a sudden, roysh, I can't believe what I'm seeing. Woulfie, the focking sly old dog, he's making a move on her and we're talking big time. Trying to bag off with *my* bird. They're behind this, like, pillar in the lobby, roysh, I can't see them but I can hear them, and Woulfie's asking her does she want to go for, like, a walk, we're talking along the canal.

Woulfie goes, 'We can look at the swans,' and Elspeth's like, '*Oh* my God! I SO love swans,' the slapper, and Woulfie's like, 'They represent hope for humanity, don't you think. They symbolise how everyone can grow into a beautiful creature and have a meaningful life.' He's a slick mick, I'll give him that. She pulls away and looks at him like he's focking mad or something and she's there, 'Everyone?' And he goes, 'Well, everyone with money.' She's there, '*Oh my God!* I SO want to be with you.'

And even though I want to go over and deck Woulfie at that particular moment, even though I SO want to deck the focker, I can't. I just have to admit, the goy's got class. The bird at reception goes, 'Taxi for O'Carroll,' and as I'm helping Christian up, I go, 'It's actually O'Carroll-*Kelly*.'

***

I bell JP on his mobile. Feel a bit sorry for the dude, he must be feeling a bit left out of things lately. I mean, me and the rest of the goys, we're all in college, roysh, on the beer everyday and basically screwing our way through every chick on campus, while he's stuck doing an MDB – Managing Daddy's Business – namely Hook, Lyon and Sinker Estate Agents. He's been left out of the loop a bit, so I give him a ring, roysh, and he's telling me he's just got four hundred thousand sheets for a gaff in Sandymount that's no bigger than a focking coalshed. I'm telling him all about the Traffic Light Ball, roysh, about me wearing a red spot instead of a green one – we're talking red as in No Go – and ending up scoring seven times, or eight if you count that bogger from Ag. Science, which I don't, and how it all goes to prove the theory that what birds really want is what they can't, like, have.

Then I mention to him that I've got my driving test the next day, roysh, and how I'm pretty much gicking it because I've, like, sat the thing more times than I've sat the Leaving Cert at this stage and, well, let's just say the last examiner told me that if there was a Certificate for *In*competence, I'd walk it. Of course, I never copped that he was taking the piss until a few days later.

JP tells me he aced his and he suggests we have a quick mind-meld, which, to those of us without a degree in Bullshit, means we should meet up, put our heads together, see can we come up with some way for me to pass this focking thing once and for all.

We meet for a coffee in Donnybrook. I tell the bird who's cleaning off the tables that I want an ordinary cup of coffee and she tells me I'll have to go up and order from one of the *barristas*, and I'm like, 'The what?' JP's there, 'I'll go. I speak reasonably good Coffee. A Long Black is what you're after,' and he comes back a few minutes later with two cups of ordinary coffee.

Anyway, roysh, to cut a long story short, fair focks to him, the dude has already come up with a plan. He asks me what test centre I'm doing it in, and I tell him Rathgar, and he tells me he knows where he can get his hands on a JCB. I'm there, 'What the *fock* has that got to do with the price of cabbage?' and he's like, 'The second you come out of the test centre, I'll pull out in front of you and drive at, like, fifteen miles an hour. You'll end up doing your whole test in, like, second gear.' I'm there, 'But he'll just get me to turn off somewhere to get away from you.' He goes, 'Soon as I see you indicate, then I'll turn that way too. Trust me, Ross, it'll work.'

I'm there, 'Well, I suppose it won't cost anything to try,' and then I cop the big shit-eating grin on JP's face and I go, 'How much?' He blows on his coffee, takes a mouthful and goes, 'Weighted with overheads this job, Ross. Got to pay the site foreman to turn a blind eye while the JCB goes walkies. There's my time. Danger money.' I'm like, '*Danger money?* You said fifteen miles an hour,' and he's there, 'Of course, you don't have to take the idea offline if you don't want to,' and he gets up to go and I'm like, 'Okay, okay. How much?' He goes, 'Five hundred bills,' and I go, 'Okay, five hundred bills it is.'

So the next day, roysh, I'm pulling out of the test centre and the examiner – no crack out of him *what*soever – tells me to pull out roysh onto the Orwell Road. So there I am, in first gear, nosing my way out the gate, and there's JP porked opposite the entrance, and I'm thinking the focker might have dressed down for the day because basically no one digs the roads in a two-thousand-lid Armani suit, Celtic Tiger or no Celtic Tiger, and I'm storting to think we're never going to get away with this.

JP sees me indicating roysh, roysh, and pulls out into the middle of the road and I slip in behind him and we're doing, like, ten miles an hour all the way up Orwell Road. Before we hit the lights, the goy tells me to hang a left, roysh, so I indicate left and in front of me, sure as houses, JP swings the big beast left onto Zion Road. The examiner tells me to hang a quick roysh onto Victoria Road, not leaving me much time to indicate, but JP slams on the brakes in front of me, makes the turn and I crawl over the speed bumps behind him in, like, first gear. Ten minutes into the test and so far, so good.

Then we hit what I think is a problem, roysh. The examiner goes, 'I want you to pull in just beyond this left junction here and show me your reversing around corners,' and I'm basically kicking myself for not copping this before. We're going to pull in, JP's going to carry on driving and this dude's going to find out that I can't drive for shit.

Probably should have had a little more faith in JP. He takes the left turn and I continue on and pork, then turn around in my seat, lash the gears into reverse and stort moving backwards slowly. The next thing, roysh, JP pulls up roysh at the corner I'm supposed to be backing around, blocking me off, and he hops down out of the JCB and pretends to be taking a big interest in the grass verge. He's got his Hugo Boss shoes on as well. I'm like, 'Must be a lot of money in pipe-laying these days,' trying to strike up a bit of banter with the dude in the cor, but he's having none of it, he has his eyes closed and he's, like, shaking his head and he tells me to turn around and go back down Victoria Road.

JP sees me indicating to pull out and he's back at the levers in, like, two seconds flat and he pulls out in front of me again, and we're heading back the way we came, going over two ramps so slow that if we went any slower we'd stop. Bottom of Victoria Road we hang a left back onto Zion Road and then a roysh at the lights onto Orwell Road.

The tester goy's like, 'Proceed to the test centre.' We've only been out, like, fifteen minutes. I'm there, 'You don't want to see my hill-stort?' and he goes, 'No, I've seen enough to make my determination,' and in my mind I'm going, YES! and I think about flashing my lights at JP, just to tell him, 'Piece of piss,' but in the end I don't chance it.

I hang a left into the test centre, pull into a space and the goy tells me to come inside, and I suppose it's just, like, procedure. I follow him in and he tells me to sit down on the opposite side of this table, roysh, then he sits down himself and goes, 'You've failed your test.' I punch the air. I'm like, 'TOUCHDOWN! YESSSS!' and I'm already planning to hire a big fock-off Porsche, head out to Erika's and impress the knickers off her. And we're talking *literally* here. The goy's like, 'You obviously misheard me. You *failed*.'

I'm there, 'Failed?' How *focking* embarrassing. I'm like, 'How could I have failed. I never got out of second gear.' He goes, 'Well, let's start with the questions I asked you.' I'm like, 'Go on, let's hear it, this'll be good.' He goes, 'When I asked you an occasion on which you might turn on your full lights ...' and I'm like, 'Go on,' and he's there, 'You said, "When some stupid bitch won't pull over when you're trying to overtake".' He's basically one of these nit-pickers. Then he goes, 'What was the first thing you did when you got into the car?' and I'm like, 'Stort the engine,' and he goes, 'No, you turned on the radio.' Of course I'm like, '*Hello?* There's a law against driving with the radio on now, is there?' and he goes, 'You changed a CD while you were driving.' Trust me to get one of those fockers who's trying to trip you up. Then he goes, 'And you didn't look in your mirrors at all.' I'm like, 'That's bullshit,' and he's there going, 'Sorry, you did. Once. To check your baseball cap was on straight.'

I stand up, roysh, and I'm like, 'You're going to be hearing from my old man's solicitor. Have you ever heard of Hennessy Coghlan-O'Hara?' He thinks for a few seconds and goes, 'Yes, matter of fact I have. I read about him in *The Irish Times* this morning. The Law Society are considering striking him off.' This focker's got an answer for everything. I'm like, 'I'm obviously wasting my time here,' and I go to leave, roysh, and just as I reach the door, he goes, 'He's a friend of yours, isn't he?' I stop and without looking at him I go, 'Who?' He's like, 'The guy in the JCB.' I'm there, 'You can't prove that,' and he goes, 'It's just that it's the fourth time it's happened in the past six weeks. Quite a little business he's got going obviously. You should tell him to be a little less conspicuous, though, change his routine. Maybe try a steamroller next time.'

JP dies.

✳✳✳

Been seeing this girl for about three weeks, roysh, Georgia's her name, you probably know her to see, she was one of the weather girls on, like, Network Two, a little bit like Laetitia Casta, but thick as a focking brick, and we're talking TOTALLY here. We're in Annabel's one night, roysh, and we're sitting with Wally and Walshy, these two goys I know from Castlerock, doing anthropology or some shit, total focking brainboxes, not really into rugby, but, like, sound anyway. So we're there and the Nice Treaty comes up in conversation, roysh, and I have to say I know fock-all about Northern Ireland, but I do know to keep my mouth shut in case I, like, embarrass myself. Georgia, of course, doesn't. She goes, 'OH MY GOD, I am SO sick of all these, like, referendums and stuff. I don't know why they can't just rip up the Constitution and just have one article that says, like, you know, *What*ever.' And the goys, roysh, fair play to them, they just stort, like, nodding their heads as though she's made an amazing point, but I can tell, roysh, they were looking at her going, 'What the *fock* is Ross going out with?'

I'd already storted to ask myself the same question – Oisinn and Fionn, roysh, they call her Clueless – and I'm seriously thinking about giving her the flick this particular night in Annabel's, having done the dirt on her three days ago with Heidi, this sixth-year Mountie who's so like Yasmine Bleeth they could be twins. Anyway, roysh, being the nice goy that I am, I don't actually have the heart to give Georgia the flick tonight because, as it turns out, RTÉ have done exactly that that same day. Why, I don't know, I was pretty shit-faced when she explained it to me and I really couldn't have been orsed listening, even though she was, like, bawling her eyes out.

Of course, coming up to the end of the night, roysh, when it's clear I'm not going to get my rock and roll elsewhere, I'm pretending to be all concerned, giving her hugs and kisses and shit and giving it, 'They must be mad, letting you go,' – she probably stuck a focking rain cloud on the map upside down or something – 'they'll regret that one day. You'll be the star they let slip through their fingers.' And she goes, '*Hello?* I have a degree in communications from ATIM, Ross,' – Any Thick Idiot with Money, we call it – 'I'm *hordly* likely to walk into another job.' I'm like, 'With your looks?' Of course this does nothing to cheer her up. She gives me this total filthy and goes, 'You think I'm an airhead, don't you? Good-looking with nothing between my ears.' And the tears stort again.

I stort going, 'Of course I don't,' but I'm struggling to keep a straight face, roysh, because I can hear all the goys – we're talking Christian and JP – and they're *totally* ripping the piss, giving it, 'Tomorrow will be a clidey day,' and 'There'll be scashered shars throughout the country,' basically taking off her accent, roysh, and I'm caught between wanting to look all, like, sympathetic to make sure I get my bit later on, while at the same time playing Jack the Lad in front of the goys, letting them know I'm actually ripping the piss out of her myself. It's a focking tightrope, but I manage not to burst out laughing in her face and all of a sudden, roysh, a couple of her mates arrive over – birds she knows from Loreto on the Green, JP was with one of them once – and they take her off to the toilets.

Oisinn comes over and high-fives me, roysh, and asks whether I heard about Fionn, and I say no, and he tells me he's copped off with *Georgio Sensi*, which could be a bird's name, though I doubt it, and I reckon he's talking about Olwyn Richards, who Fionn was chatting up at the bor at the stort of the night, the jammy, four-eyed focker.

Oisinn's off his tits. He's there, 'Where's the weather girl?' I'm like, 'Toilets,' and he goes, 'What was all that crying about? Did she find out about …' I'm like, 'No, no, RTÉ gave her the old heave-ho.' He nods sort of, like, thoughtfully, roysh, even though he hasn't really got a clue what I said, the music's so loud, and he goes, 'Bummer,' and I'm there, 'Total.'

'Shackles' comes on, roysh, and JP's giving it loads out on the dancefloor and he gives me the old thumbs-up, roysh, and I do it back – focker still hasn't given me my five hundred bills back – and Christian's chatting up some bird I know to see from the M1 and he's telling her that he senses a strange disturbance in the Force, which is his usual chat-up line, roysh, and she's sort of, like, leaning away from him, as though he's completely off his rocker, which he actually is. I'm worried about the goy, though, the way he's been tanning the beer lately.

The next thing I know, Georgia's back from the toilets and she's, like, tied her cardigan around her waist, roysh, and she's wearing this halterneck top, which is pretty revealing and it's only when she goes, 'Do you want to stay in Amy's house with me? Her parents are in Bologna,' that I realise she's a lot more pissed than I actually thought and I tell her I'll basically go and get my jacket. Probably a bit of a shitty thing to do actually, giving her an old rattle tonight, then the Spanish archer tomorrow, but as the goys always say, you don't put three weeks of spadework into a job and then give up when the treasure's in sight.

I knock back the rest of my pint, roysh, and I look up and – FOCK! am I cursed, or something? – you will not believe who's suddenly standing there in front of me. We're talking Heidi, the bird I was with three nights ago, the Yasmine Bleeth ringer, who may have got the impression, from some of the things I said, that me and her were an item now. I'm just there going, How the *fock* do I get out of this one?

Heidi looks at me and goes, 'Hi, Ross,' and Georgia, roysh, sensing another bird moving in on her patch, she sits beside me on the couch, or sort of, like, flops down, she's that off her tits, and she links my orm and Heidi – who I have to say is actually looking really well – she goes, 'Oh, I see you've moved on, Ross.'

I'm fairly well-on myself at this stage and I can hordly string a sentence together, it has to be said. I go, 'That's roysh, Heidi. Onwards and upwards,' which I'm kicking myself for saying because it's her I'd rather be with tonight. Heidi, roysh, she looks Georgia up and down and she goes, 'I'd *hordly* call that upwards.' And Georgia, roysh, she's having none of it, she turns around to me and she goes, 'Sorry, who is this ... *girl?*' Heidi, roysh, who's, like, well able for her, fair focks to her, she goes, 'I'm Heidi. And I know who you are.' Georgia goes, 'Oh, I recognise you now. What school was it you went to, Mount Anything?' And Heidi's like, 'Better than Collars-Up, Knickers-Down.'

I have to say, roysh, it's fascinating to watch. One says something really bitchy and just as you're thinking there's no coming back from that, the other says something even better. Georgia goes, 'You're in Emma's class, my *little* sister,' trying to, like, put her down, making out she's only a kid or something, but Heidi's there, 'Your sister is a knob, just like you.' Georgia stands up, roysh, and she goes, 'My sister is *not* a focking knob,' and Heidi laughs, roysh, shakes her head and goes, '*Oh* my God, she does supervised study, like, every night.'

At this stage, roysh, it looks like it might get ugly, so just, like, to defuse the tension, if that's the roysh word, I decide to go and get another pint in, maybe find the lads, but Heidi all of a sudden goes, 'Ross obviously hasn't told you about us, has he?' Oh fock. Georgia's like, 'I'm not interested in whatever mistakes Ross might have made in the distant past.' And Heidi goes, 'Distant past? Try Wednesday night.'

So Georgia's just sitting there, roysh, with her mouth open, like a fish, and she's storting to, like, hyperventilate, she can't get any words out, so she just picks up a bottle of Coors Light and, like, dumps the whole lot over my focking head, then runs out of the place bawling her eyes out. Heidi tells me I'm pathetic and focks off as well.

One of Georgia's mates, roysh – not the one JP was with, the other one, I think she's doing Tourism Management and Morkeshing in LSB – she comes over and tells me I'm an orsehole and, in my defence, I'm there, 'I wasn't going out with Georgia, you know. We were only seeing each other.'

I sit there for a few minutes, completely focking soaked, just knowing that my new light blue Ralph is going to reek of beer now, and I'm sort of thinking about maybe heading to the jacks to stick it under the drier and then going off to look for Heidi, but I'm so off my face at this stage I really couldn't be orsed.

I can't actually remember how long I'm sitting there when all of a sudden JP comes over, roysh, and sits down next to me and he goes, 'What the fock happened?' I'm like, 'Georgia found out about Heidi. You owe me five hundred bills, by the way.'

He goes, 'It's coming, my man. You were going to give Georgia the flick anyway, weren't you?' I'm like, 'Yeah, *totally*,' and he smiles and goes, 'Well then, every clide has a silver lining,' and I have to laugh.

***

I skip my three o'clock, head out to Oisinn's gaff and I find him sitting at the kitchen table with a scissors, a Pritt Stick and a stack of newspapers. I'm there, 'I didn't know we'd homework,' and he goes, 'Not homework. I've come up with a plan for the statue. Look at *this*.'

I go, 'Like it, Oisinn,' and he winks at me. I'm like, 'Is it gonna work?' He goes, 'You are looking at a criminal mastermind.' I'm there, 'Glad to hear it. I could do with the shekels. The debs cleaned me out.'

***

I get this text from Georgia, roysh, and it's like:

WE REGRET TO INFORM CUSTOMERS THAT THE EIRCELL NETWORK HAS GONE DOWN. HOWEVER THIS WILL NOT AFFECT YOU AS NOT EVEN A NETWORK WOULD GO DOWN ON YOU!

What a total bunny-boiler. I'm just, like, you know, 'Get over it, girl.'

CHAPTER THREE
'Ross is, like, such an orsehole to women.'
Discuss.

When Christian asked me to go with him to the premiere of that focking *Bridget Jones' Diary*, roysh, he never told me it was in the Savoy, we're talking on the focking *northside* here. Pork the cor in my usual spot in Stephen's Green, and as we're, like, walking down Grafton Street, I'm suddenly thinking, Hang on, what cinemas are on the southside?

Of course my worst fears are confirmed, roysh, when we cross over onto Westmoreland Street – that sort of, like, no man's land between *us* and *them* – and I realise the crazy bastard is actually thinking of bringing me the other side of the Liffey.

I stop, roysh, just before we cross over the bridge, we're talking O'Connell Bridge, and I go, 'You are *not* focking serious, I hope.' He's like, 'Don't centre on your anxieties,' and I'm there, 'Quit it with that Obi Wan bullshit, will you? Do you know what they do to people like us over there? These people aren't walking uproysh that long.' He just laughs and carries on walking and, well, the goy's my best friend, roysh, can't let him do this on his own, so I follow him across the bridge and I go, 'This is suicide.'

There's a goy selling newspapers who shouts something in Northside, which I don't understand, though I think I caught the word 'Hedild' in there somewhere. The whole focking street is just, like, burger bors, with all these peasants in them getting their dinner. We cross over onto this traffic island, and this goy – twenty-quid jeans and hundred-quid runners, the usual skobie uniform, and a big red inbreeder's face to go with it – he bumps me with his shoulder as he's passing me, we're talking on purpose here. I mean, there's two of us, roysh, and one of him, but he doesn't give a fock. I turn around, roysh, and he's come back towards me, going, 'Have you got a bleedin' problem?' I'm there, 'You just bumped into me. Did your old dear not teach you how to say sorry, or was she too busy on the game?' He looks totally, like, stunned by this, doesn't know what to say, roysh, he's obviously so used to people going, 'Oooh, no, I haven't got a problem,' and he just manages to get out the words, 'Are ye wantin' yisser go?' when all of a sudden, roysh, Christian hits him a box that comes from, I don't know, the next focking postal code – BANG! – and the goy's laid out flat on his back. I stand over him and go, 'See what you get when you fock with the Rock, you piece of vermin. You'll be selling your cigarette lighters tomorrow in a neck-brace.'

We head on, roysh, manage to get to the Savoy without any further incidents. Christian hands me my ticket outside and we head in and meet a few of his friends from his film course in the lobby, roysh – two blokes who are both complete dickheads and four birds, three of them are bet-down, the other I'd file under 'Ugly But Rideable'. Anyway, roysh, they're wanking on about how Hugh Grant has been typecast as the slightly repressed, upper-class, English fop and how this new role has opened up a whole new anti-hero persona that will allow him to explore his range as an actor. I just go, 'Yeah, roysh,' and head off for a wander, see if there's any scenario about the place.

So there I am, roysh, scoping this bird who looks a bit like Winona Ryder – or I Wanna Ryder, as I call her – when all of a sudden, roysh, there's all these flashbulbs going off outside and who walks in? We're talking Renée *focking* Zellwegger, and she looks incredible. I decide there and then, roysh, that I'm going to try to be with her, so I join this queue of all these film-industry tossers waiting to talk to her. About ten minutes later, roysh, I'm in front of her and I'm giving it, 'Hey,' and she's there, 'Hello,' and I'm like, 'You having a good night?' and just as she's about to answer, roysh – and I'm *really* pleased with this – I go, 'Shut up. Just shut up. You had me at Hello,' and she cracks her shite laughing, and I'm in, I am SO in.

She goes, 'It's great to see you again. How was Paris? Did you go to that restaurant I told you about?' and it's pretty obvious, roysh, that she thinks I'm someone else, and that's alroysh by me because she's focking quality and I'm there telling the old pant python to behave himself. I'm like, 'The restaurant? Yeah, it was Kool and the Gang,' and suddenly, roysh, everyone's going in to watch the film and Renée Zellwegger links my orm – links MY focking orm – and we're heading into the VIP area when this bouncer, the biggest creamer you've ever seen, stops me and asks me where my pass is. He goes, 'Where's yisser pass?' I'm there, 'It's alroysh, I'm with Renée Zellwegger,' and he's just like, 'No one gets in wirourra pass.' Stick a skobie in a monkey suit and give him a walkie-talkie and he thinks he's the focking Terminator.

Probably took the wrong tack with him, roysh, when I went, 'It'll be back to the dole queue and stealing fireplaces from building sites for you when Renée Zellwegger's people find out you've dissed her date for the night.' He goes, 'Couldn't give a bollicks,' and, of course, Renée Zellwegger's off talking to some other bloke now, this tit with a ponytail and, seeing the headlines 'Renée Zellwegger's New Mystery Man' slipping away, I make the mistake of going to step over the rope into the VIP section, roysh.

Next thing I feel this orm around my neck and my feet are, like, off the ground, and I can see Christian and his orsehole film mates staring in, like, horror as the skobie in the tux carries me out of the cinema and basically throws me out onto the street, in the middle of Knackeragua. He's there, 'You were warned,' and I just, like, dust the old chinos down and go, 'Your orse is SO fired.'

✳✳✳

To whom it may concern,

Many thanks for your recent ransom note. Please accept my apologies for the delay in replying. My secretary is away on maternity leave at the moment and I'm not very well organised. Your letter got mixed up in a stack of essays I was correcting and I've only this minute laid my hands on it again.

As to your request for £1,000, unfortunately the department doesn't have sufficient finance to undertake this kind of project at this time. We will keep your letter on file and, in the event of a budget being set aside for meeting extortion and blackmail demands, we will endeavour to contact you.

Can you please pass on the best wishes of everyone in the Classics Department to *Eros*. We all miss him.

Best wishes,

Francis Hird,
Classics Department, UCD

✱✱✱

Emer's parents' house is worth over a million, roysh, or so she tells us, but Sophie says that that's nothing because there's council houses, *actual* council houses, in Sallynoggin, we're talking Sally-*focking*-noggin here, which are going for two hundred grand. All of the girls go, 'OH! MY! GOD!' and all of the goys go, 'Crazy shit,' except me because I'm only sort of, like, half-listening. Erika is sitting opposite me, roysh, and she's looking pretty amazing I have to say, with that, like, permanent scowl on her face, that's what Fionn calls it – a permanent scowl.

Sent her a text message the other night and it was like, **U R my fantaC. C U l8r**, but she didn't answer it, don't know if she even got it, and now I'm trying to, like, catch her eye, roysh, maybe wink at her across the table, or blow her a kiss, something stupid just to say, you know, 'Me and you. Our little secret,' whatever, but she's totally ignoring the fact that I'm there.

When she finally does look at me, roysh, she goes – at the top of her voice, we're talking – she goes, 'Ross, why are you staring at me?' and I can feel myself go red and Sorcha, roysh, she stares at me and goes, 'How was the debs, by the way,' and it's obvious Erika's told her about knocking me back.

All the goys are cracking their holes laughing, roysh, and I'm so morto I don't know where to put myself, but Sophie rescues me by changing the subject. She goes, 'It's a pity you can't buy, like, a glass of boiled water in a pub,' and Emer's there, 'Oh my God, that reminds me, how many points is a muffin?' and Sophie's like, 'Five-and-a-half.' And Emer's there, 'There's no way that muffin was five-and-a-half,' and Sophie goes, 'Emer, it was an American-style muffin and an American-style muffin is five-and-a-half points. I told you you shouldn't have had it, so don't take it out on me,' and Emer just gives her daggers.

Fionn turns around to me, roysh, and he goes, 'Girls are obsessed with points, aren't they? When we were doing the Leaving, it was getting as many as possible. Now it's eating as few as possible,' which is way too deep for me.

Christian is, like, really quiet, roysh and I ask him if he's alroysh and he says he's cool, but he's tanning the Ken, knocking back two pints for every one I'm drinking.

The girls stort talking about some bird called Rachael who was in Loreto Foxrock and has put on SO much weight since she went on the Pill, and then they're talking about this big night out they have planned, they're going to see Vonda Sheppard, a girls' night out, even though Sophie thinks her latest album SO isn't as good as her last one. And Sorcha says she wouldn't know because she's been listening to mostly classical music lately, especially Elgar's 'Third Movement from Cello Concerto in E Minor Op 85'. Emer goes, 'Oh my God, have you got *The Best Classical Album of the Millennium ... Ever*?' and Sorcha, roysh, real defensive, she goes, 'Yeah, but I've got, like, loads of other classical albums as well as that.' And Fionn goes, 'You've probably got *The Best Classical Album of the Millennium ... Ever Two, Three, Four* and *Five*, have you?' and I high-five him, even though, to be honest, roysh, I don't really get the joke.

Sophie says she *loves* Pachelbel's 'Canon', and Sorcha says she *loves* Rachmaninov's 'Variation 18 from Rhapsody on a Theme by Paganini', roysh, and this pretty much goes on until Fionn asks whether or not we're going to The Vatican, and that's when we all grab our jackets and stort heading up towards, like, Harcourt Street.

We're pretty much halfway there, roysh, and me and Fionn are walking ahead of everyone, basically talking rugby – Ireland's chances in next year's Six Nations, whether I could be as good as Brian O'Driscoll if I got my finger out, all that – when all of a sudden, roysh, Sorcha shouts up to me, 'Ross, where's Christian?' and I turn back and I go, 'I presumed he was with you goys.' She's there, 'No, he was behind us.'

I tell them all to walk on up, roysh, and I head back towards Grafton Street and I find him outside Planet Hollywood, arguing with the bouncers. They've got, like, whatever they're focking called, C3PO and R2D2, in the window, roysh, and Christian, who's off his face, he wants to go in and touch the two robots, to see if they're, like, the real ones, the ones they used in the movie, which Christian reckons they're not, but the bouncers – you can't blame them – they're having none of it, they're trying to move him along, and all of a sudden he storts going ballistic at them, giving it, 'YOU DON'T OWN THEM! THEY BELONG TO THE PEOPLE!'

I grab him, roysh, and sort of, like, drag him up the street, but we only get, like, ten steps up the road when all of a sudden he stops and storts crying his eyes out, and I keep asking him what's wrong, roysh, but he's too upset to talk and he just grabs me and hugs me there on the street and I'm sort of, like, you know, looking around to see who's, like, watching, not wanting people to think I'm a steamer, obviously.

I'm like, 'What's wrong, Christian?' and he squeezes me horder, roysh, and I can hordly breathe at this stage, and I'm like, 'What is it?' and he goes, 'My parents are getting divorced,' and I can't think of anything to say to the dude, even though he's been my best friend since we were, like, four, and I just end up going, 'That's heavy shit, man.' He's lost it, he's bawling like a baby, going, 'I don't want them to break up. I don't want them to break up,' and I'm there still hugging him, going, 'This is SUCH heavy shit.'

✳✳✳

When we were kids, roysh, Christian's old pair brought the two of us to Lansdowne Road to see Ireland play. It was, like, a Five Nations' match, roysh, against, like, Scotland, and though I remember pretty much nothing about the game, roysh, I know we lost by, like, three points, or maybe it was six, but we lost anyway. Christian said Ireland were crap and his old man said they were far from crap, that if they had in their legs what they had in their hearts then they'd win the Grand Slam every time.

We waited in our seats until about ten minutes after the final whistle, roysh, then we headed around the back of the West Stand and Christian's old man decided we were going to, like, wait in the cor pork and cheer every Irish player onto the bus, to let them know that their courage was appreciated by at least some of the fans.

Me and Christian both had programmes, roysh, and his old man gave us a pen each to get the autographs of the players as they came out. I'm pretty sure it was raining and Christian's old dear put up her umbrella and, like, pulled the two of us under it. And what I remember about that is the smell of her perfume.

After about an hour, roysh, the players storted to come out in twos and threes and, like, make their way to the bus, but I didn't really recognise that many of them, except Brendan Mullin and Donal Lenihan and maybe Willie Anderson. Got loads of autographs, though. Brendan Mullin asked me my name and then he signed it, 'To Ross, best wishes, Brendan Mullin,' which I remember Christian's old man telling me he didn't have to do. He goes, 'A great ambassador for his sport and his country. Didn't have to do that, you know.'

Then Brian Smith came out, roysh, and pretty much everyone there wanted to get his autograph because he was, like, a major stor at the time, so there was all this, like, pushing and shoving to get at him, roysh, and I ended up falling over in this puddle and I was, like, soaking wet and my knee was all, like, grazed and shit. I was, like, bawling my eyes out, more out of embarrassment than anything else, roysh, and Christian's old dear helped me up and told this man who just happened to be standing beside me when I fell that he ought to be ashamed of himself, carrying on like that, and the goy told her he didn't push me, that I fell, and Christian's old dear just looked at him and shook her head.

I remember she rolled up my trouser leg and she took, like, a piece of tissue out of her pocket and used it to clean the blood off my knee. Then she used another piece to wipe my eyes and she, like, gave me a hug and Christian's old man asked us how we'd like a Coke and a packet of crisps, and we went to the Berkeley Court, or maybe it was Jury's, it was one or the other, and that's what we had, Coke and crisps. And me and Christian, roysh, we were, like, flicking through our programmes, looking at all the autographs we'd got, trying to make out who they all were, and I had this, like, squiggle that Christian didn't have and his old man asked to see it, roysh, and he told me it wasn't an Irish player at all, it was actually Gavin Hastings, and he told me I was a lucky man to get the great Gavin Hastings' autograph.

***

Sophie rings me, roysh, to tell me that she's going to be late – said I'd go Christmas shopping with her – but there's a signal failure on the Dorsh *again* and – OH! MY! GOD! – it's taken her an hour to get from Glenageary to, like, Booterstown. She goes, 'The Dorsh is a jake, Ross. A complete jake.'

***

It's the last day of term, breaking up for Chrimbo today, roysh, and I've got a letter from the head of the course informing me – 'we'd like to inform you' – that I've attended a grand total of ten lectures this term, which is news to me, I didn't think it was as many as that, roysh, but it's not a letter of congratulations. It's like, blah blah blah, doubts about your commitment to the course, bullshit bullshit bullshit, academic dimension to the course must be taken seriously, wank wank wank, monitoring your attendance over coming months. I go to Oisinn, 'Spoke too soon about freedom. School wasn't this focking bad,' and he's like, 'Come on, Ross, cheer up. We're out of here for *four* weeks.'

And you can tell it's the last day of term, roysh, because all the boggers are walking around with, like, rucksacks full of dirty washing, bringing them home to their old dears to wash over the holidays. I see Fionn saying his goodbyes to Kathleen with the peach fuzz. There's more to that than him sussing out a theory. He likes the bird. They're well-suited if you ask me, one's as focking ugly as the other.

She's wearing a Galway bogball jersey, roysh, and it turns out she's from a place called Gort, which I think we passed through on the way down to, like, Ennis two New Years' Eves ago, one of those shithole towns where old men with red hair stand outside the local supermorket on a Sunday afternoon with their mouths open and 'the wireless' up to their ears, going, 'You can never write off Cork,' to passersby. In fact, the red hair's storting to make a bit more sense now. Fionn kisses her goodbye, a big slopping wet one, on the lips, and when he comes over to me and Oisinn, I go, 'You'll need a shot of Ivomec after that,' which I'm pretty happy with because for once, Fionn has no focking answer.

We hit the bor and get off our faces.

✳✳✳

donT fOck About a graNd or well seNd It back to you in PiECeS

***

It's the day before Christmas Eve, roysh, and we're all having drinks in The Bailey, middle of the afternoon, and Sorcha hands Aoife a present, roysh, and Aoife goes, '*Oh my God!* I haven't got yours with me. I was going to wait until tomorrow night,' and Sorcha says it doesn't matter and Aoife opens the present and it's, like, a 'Friends' video. Aoife's face lights up and Sorcha goes, 'I hope you haven't already got that one,' and then Aoife's face drops, roysh, and she's like, 'Oh shit, I do,' and Sorcha's like, 'I don't believe it. I asked your mom to check whether you had Series 5, Episodes 17-20, 'The One Where Rachel Smokes', and she said you didn't.' Aoife goes, 'She is SUCH a stupid bitch, my mother. It's Series *3*, Episodes 17-20 that I don't have.' Emer, who's, like, first year Morkeshing, Advertising and Public Relations in LSB, she goes, 'Which one is that?' and Aoife's there, "The One With The Princess Leia Fantasy'.' Emer says that is SUCH a good episode, and Sorcha says it's okay because she kept the receipt, just in case.

Emer says there were three refugees outside her old dear's coffee shop all day yesterday, wrecking everyone's heads with their music, those bloody accordions, and Erika says she read somewhere that they're making up to a thousand bills a day – we're talking *each* – from begging and busking, and Emer goes, 'If you could call it busking.' I don't know why, roysh, but I turn around and I go, 'Why don't you lay off the Romanians,' and everyone at the table turns to me, roysh, and looks at me like I'm totally off my focking rocker, and I probably am because *I* can't believe I said it myself. Erika goes, 'Sorry, Ross, *where* is this coming from?' I'm like, 'I don't know. I mean, it's Christmas. Could we not be, like, a bit more, I don't know … caring?'

Erika goes, 'Caring? *Caring? Hello?* This *is* Ross O'Carroll-Kelly I'm talking to, isn't it? Most selfish bastard who ever lived.' I'm there, 'I'm not selfish.' And Erika goes, 'Aoife, tell Ross what Bronwyn told us. You remember Bronwyn, Ross? You were with her at the Loreto on the Green pre-debs.' Fock! I know what's coming next. Aoife's cracking her hole laughing, roysh, and she goes, 'According to her, Ross, you bought a packet of condoms. Ribbed, extra-sensitive, for *her* pleasure. Well, according to her, you tried to put one on … inside out.'

I'm there, 'That was a focking accident and she knows it,' but everyone's, like, cracking their shites laughing and I go, 'Look, all I'm saying is, you know, these refugees, they've lost their, like, homes and shit. I mean, how would you like it if you were suddenly dropped in the middle of, I don't know … Budapest,' and Erika goes, 'The capital of Romania, Ross, is Bucharest. And they have Prada there. And Amanda Wakeley.'

✳✳✳

Christmas in my gaff is a complete mare, and we're talking total here. I wake up in the morning, roysh, about eleven o'clock, feeling pretty shabby I have to say, a feed of pints the night before, hanging big style, and I can hear the old pair downstairs all-focking-over each other, we're talking *total* borf-fest here. It's all, like, squealing and, 'Oooh, it's just what I wanted,' roysh, and I go downstairs to tell the two of them to keep it down, my head hurts. Turns out, roysh, the old dear bought the old man a Callaway ERC2 driver and he bought her, like, jewellery, a shitload of Lladro and a mid-week break at the Powerscourt Springs and they're, like, hugging and kissing each other, roysh, and it's all, 'Happy Christmas, Darling,' and I'm finding it pretty hord to keep this toast down.

They've got me a cor, roysh, a Golf GTI, black, *total* babe magnet, or should I say they're *going* to get me one. I told them to wait until the New Year, roysh, to, like, get the new reg. So anyway, roysh, the old dear hands me this present and she's like, 'Oh, we wanted you to have something to open on the day,' and I'm like, 'What am I supposed to say, yippee-hoo?' but I open it, roysh, just to keep them happy and it's a phone, a *so-called* phone, a Motorola T2288, we're talking a crappy eleven ringtones, we're talking no vibration alert, we're talking only 210 minutes of battery talk-time. I'm like, 'Sorry, what is *this* supposed to be?' and the old man goes, 'It's a mobile phone, Kicker,' and I'm like, 'You are taking the *total* piss here. It's not even focking WAP-enabled,' and I fock it across the table and go upstairs to, like, get dressed. As I'm going up the stairs, I can hear the old dear asking the old man what WAP-enabled means, roysh, and then she says she's so sorry and she feels she's ruined Christmas and then she storts, like, bawling her eyes out, the attention-seeking bitch.

About, like, ten minutes later, roysh, the old man shouts up the stairs to me and he goes, 'Don't be too long, Ross. We're going to go to twelve Mass. As a family,' and I'm like, 'Get real, will you? You retord,' but I end up going anyway, roysh, anything for an easy life, and it's the usual crack, Holy Mary, Mother of God, blah blah blah, and I end up sitting there for the whole thing, texting Christian, Oisinn and everyone else I know to give them, like, my new number and tell them I might see them l8er.

Sophie actually phones me back straight away to say thanks for the Burberry scorf, which I bought her pretty much to piss off Sorcha, who was basically dropping hints to me that she wanted one herself. So Sophie rings, roysh, and I have totally forgotten that the ringtone is switched to, like, 'Auld Lang Syne', and when it goes off this old focking biddy sitting in front of me, she turns around and gives me a total filthy, we're talking daggers here, and I'm like, 'Hang on a sec, Sophie,' and I go, 'Turn the fock around,' and she does as she's told.

And *Oh my God*, roysh, you should have *seen* the state of my old dear, we're talking dressed to focking kill here, and it's, like, guess who spent a grand in Pia Bang yesterday? When she comes back from Communion, roysh, I hear her go to the old man, 'Ann Marie is wearing the same coat she wore last year,' and the old man goes, 'OH! MY! GOD!' out of the corner of his mouth.

Dinner is, like, majorly painful. Dermot and Anita, these dick-head friends of the old pair, roysh, they're invited around and, of course, the whole conversation is dominated by this new campaign they've storted, which is, like, Move Funderland to the Northside. I mean, we don't live anywhere near the focking RDS, roysh, but Anita lives on Sandymount Avenue and, of course, the old dear can't resist it, keeps saying that Anita was so helpful with the Foxrock Against Total Skangers Anti-Halting Site campaign, roysh, that she simply *had* to get involved. What a sap.

She's there going, 'I don't know how you cope, Anita. I really don't,' and Anita's there going, 'We've put up with it for twenty years, Fionnuala. Gangs of what can only be described as gurriers walking by, carrying giant elephants, urinating in our gardens, off to get the Dorsh to – what's this it's called? – Kilbarrack, and God knows wherever else.'

She's going, 'Now don't get me wrong, Charles. We're not anti-Funderland *per se*, are we Dermot? But somewhere like, I don't know, Ballymun, would be a far more appropriate place for it, surely.' The old dear goes, 'Now don't get upset, Anita.

Charles will print out those posters for you tomorrow. Have another drink.'

And Anita, roysh, you can see she's storting to get emotional, already half-pissed on Baileys and mulled wine, and she's going, 'I'm going to picket the RDS, Fionnuala. On my own if I have to. I'm going to flipping well do it.'

This goes on for ages and I basically can't take it anymore, roysh, and I end up going, 'Is this a family dinner or a focking campaign meeting?' and everything goes silent. The old man goes, 'Well, what would *you* like to talk about, Ross?' and I don't know what to say, roysh, so I just end up telling them what a bunch of tossers they look in their paper hats and the old man goes, 'Ross, if you can't keep a civil tongue in your head, I suggest you leave the table,' and I'm like, 'With focking pleasure,' and I grab three cans out of the fridge and head into the sitting room to watch the Bond movie.

So I'm sitting there, roysh, and it's, like, *Octopussy*, and I'm knocking back the beers, milling into the old Quality Street, and my phone rings and it's, like, Fionn, and I'm just like, 'Yo, Fionn, Happy Christmas, my man. Speak to me.' He goes, 'Having a great day here with the family,' – focking weirdo – he's like 'Greetings and felicitations to you and yours.' I'm there, 'What time did you leave the M1 last night?' and he goes, 'It was late. Hey, you won't *believe* who I ended up being with last night.' I'm like, 'Who?' and he goes, 'Esme.' This is the only reason he's ringing me.

I'm just there, 'Who's Esme?' knowing full well who she is, roysh, and he goes, 'Esme. *Hello?* Second year business in Portobello? Looks like Elize Dushku, or so you said.' I tried to be with her two weeks ago in Annabel's, totally crashed and burned, and we're talking TOTALLY. I go, 'I never said she looked like Elize Dushku,' and Fionn's like, 'I *know* you tried to get in there, Ross. No hord feelings. Turns out she goes for goys with glasses. Thinks they're a sign of intelligence.' I'm there, 'What an airhead ... I never said she looks like Elize Dushku,' and Fionn laughs and goes, 'Anyone with any information on the whereabouts of Ross O'Carroll-Kelly's dignity, please contact Gardaí in Dún Laoghaire.'

He goes, 'Christian ended up with this bird from Iceland.' I'm like, 'As in the country?' and he goes, 'No, as in the supermorket. Of course the focking country. What's wrong with you today?' I'm there, 'Sorry, man. Distracted.' He's like, 'Does this have anything to do with Sorcha? I saw her at Mass this morning. Wasn't a happy camper. Asked her whether she'd been talking to you and she practically storted crying.' I'm like, 'Starring role in a period costume drama?' and he goes, 'Maybe. I wondered if she found out about you and Erika.' I'm like, 'Erika. Now you're getting to it. Can't stop thinking about her, Fionn. Fock, don't know why I'm spilling my guts like this, sounds a bit gay, I know.'

Fionn goes, 'Take my advice, Ross. Do *not* go there.' I'm like, 'JP reckons she's saving herself for Ben Affleck,' and he goes, 'It's not that, Ross. She's into horses.' I'm there, 'And your point is?' and he's like, 'Take it from someone who's pissing his way through first year psychology. I know what I'm talking about. No girl who's into horses can ever truly love a goy.' I'm like, 'Is that because of the size of their–' and he goes, 'Ross, try to forget about your schlong for one minute, will you? Now think about all the girls we know who have horses. Alyson Berry. Amy Holden. Caoimhe Kelly.' I'm there, 'I thought you told me to stop thinking about my schlong,' but he ignores me and goes, 'Medb Long. Becky Cooper. Maggie Merriman. What have they all got in common?' I'm like, 'I've been with them all,' and he goes, 'Apart from that?' I'm like, 'Em, they've all got horses.' He goes, 'And they're focking wenches. Stuck-up. Moody. Selfish. Cold. Stubborn. Whatever. The very qualities you associate with horses. I'll make this simple for you. Horses aren't nice animals. They're not loyal. They're not friendly. And they don't need human love. They want apples and carrots and if you don't bring them, they go into a sulk.'

I'm like, 'I'm missing *Octopussy* here, Fionn.' He goes, 'Girls like Erika, they've been trying their whole lives to relate to these animals, to get love from them, but they can't. Erika knows that however much she feeds that animal, brushes him, cleans him, he's never going to feel the same way about her as she does about him. The first love of her life was unrequited. And that's focked her up. Goes for all girls whose daddys buy them horses when they're kids.'

I'm there, 'I've got to go. Bell you later.'

The next thing I hear when I get off the phone, roysh, is the old dear coming into the room, with a bottle of Sheridans in one hand and a big heart-shaped box of, like, Butler's chocolates in the other. I'm like, 'What do you want?' and she goes, 'Three o'clock, Ross. The Queen's speech,' and I'm there, 'If you think you're coming in here to watch that bullshit, you can think again.' She goes, 'It's only ten minutes long,' and I'm there, '*Hello?* There are six other televisions in this house. Watch one of them, you stupid wagon,' and she focks off.

I sit around for another, like, ten or fifteen minutes, just thinking about Erika, roysh, and about what Fionn said and whether I only really want her because she's the only girl in the world I can't have roysh now. I decide to give her a call. The best way to play it, I decide, is Kool and the Gang, so I phone her up, roysh, and I'm like, 'Hey babe, how the hell are ya?' She goes, 'Who is this?' sounding like she's pretty pissed off about something, which is pretty much the way she sounds all of the time. I'm like, 'It's Ross. Just wondering how your Christmas is going.'

She goes, 'Look, I'm going to save you a lot of heartache and save myself a major headache by telling you, *again*, that I have no interest in you.' I'm there, 'Hey babe, why so hostile?' and she goes, 'I'm only stretching this conversation beyond one sentence because I want you to get this into your head once and for all.' I'm there, 'Well, you seemed pretty interested a few weeks ago. The stables, remember?' She goes, '*Get* a life, will you. If you must know, I did that because I was pissed off with Sorcha.'

I'm like, 'Sorcha?' and she's there, 'Sorcha. You know, as in your girlfriend? *"All this subtext is making me tired".*' I have to say, she does the voice really well. I'm like, 'Look, why don't I call over to your gaff?' and she, like, breaks her shite laughing, roysh, and goes, 'You really think that under this hord outer shell there's a vulnerable, sensitive little girl who's going to melt into your orms when she hears all your bullshit lines, don't you?'

Not trying to be big-headed or anything, but I go, 'You did in the past,' and she's like, 'We were at school then. I was sixteen. That was back in the days when you *were* someone,' and I'm like, 'Meaning?' She goes, 'You were on the senior rugby team, Ross. Being with you was, like, a status thing. Who are you now? You're doing Sports Management, for fock's sake. You're not even playing for UCD.'

Below the belt. I go, 'Yeah, I've been mostly chilling this year. I mean, I SO have to get my finger out, I know that. The goy who has my place on the team, Matthew Path, he's shite. He's a focking Blackrock boy, for fock's sake. I could easily take his place. If I do, would you be interested then?'

She tells me I'm basically making a fool of myself, roysh, then says she has neither the energy nor the interest to continue the conversation further and she hangs up.

I think about calling her back, roysh, but she's left me a bit shell-shocked, to be honest. She's roysh. My name used to mean something. Every girl wanted to say she'd been with Ross O'Carroll-Kelly. Time has moved on, I guess.

In the kitchen, the old dear has put on her new Charlotte focking Church album and the old man gives one of his big false laughs to some obviously unfunny thing that, like, Dermot has said. I go into the study and grab the tape of the senior cup final, fast-forward it to my winning try and spend the next, like, twenty minutes watching it and then rewinding it and watching it over and over again. Rewind and play. Rewind and play. Then my interview with Ryle Nugent. 'That's a good question, Ryle. I can't take all the credit for this victory, though. Some of it has to go to the goys.'

And in the background, roysh, you can see all these blue jumpers. Mounties. We're talking hundreds of them. And I think I can even make out Erika – her hair was shorter then, still a dead-ringer for Denise Richards though – and she's hanging on my every word. I think I might have even been with her that night ...

I put the lid back on the Quality Street, knock back the last of the cans and make my New Year's resolutions. Get fit. Get on the UCD team. Get Erika.

Then I go into the kitchen and tell the old man to keep the fake focking laughter down.

✳✳✳

I call out to Sorcha's gaff on Stephen's Day, roysh, and it's the usual crack from her old dear, who SO wants me to get back with her daughter it's not funny. She's all over me, we're talking TOTALLY here. It's all hugs and kisses and I'm just there going, Guess who got a bottle of Chanel No 5 for Christmas? The gaff is full, of course. The Lalors always have, like, half the focking world around to eat the Christmas leftovers, and when the old dear's finished air-kissing and squeezing the shit out of me, she leads me around the house, introducing me to aunts and uncles and neighbours and clients of the old man and a few ladies-who-lunch types who, I presume, spend a lot of money in that boutique she has in the Merrion Shopping Centre. Sometimes she goes, 'This is Ross O'Carroll-Kelly, Sorcha's friend. He was on the Castlerock team that won the cup,' and other times it's, 'This is Ross, Charles O'Carroll-Kelly's son, very good friends with Sorcha.' Then she offers me, in the following order: a slice of banoffi, a glass of mulled wine, a turkey-and-stuffing toasted sandwich, a piece of plum-pudding, a can of lager, some Baileys and a home-made mince pie, and I say no to all of them and then there's pretty much nothing else to say, roysh, and we're both standing there like a couple of spare pricks, so she just tells me that Sorcha's in her room and to go on up to her.

She's lying on her bed, roysh, wearing her black Armani jeans and a white airtex with the collar up, and she's, like, flicking through the channels on the telly. She doesn't even acknowledge me and I just sort of, like, hang around in the doorway and I ask her whether she's pissed off with me about something and she goes, 'Why would I give a shit what you do with your life?'

Her room has actually been decorated, pretty recently I'd say, and I basically tell her that it's changed a good bit and she looks at me for the first time and goes, 'It *has* changed, Ross. The last time you were in here, you were with my little sister,' and I turn around and stort, like, heading downstairs, but she calls me back and says she's sorry and then she, like, gives me a hug and wishes me a Merry Christmas. She goes, 'I don't know why I insist on reliving, in excruciating detail, one of the most painful experiences of our lives. Maybe it's my perversely self-deprecating way of moving on. Or maybe I'm still trying to punish you.'

I sit down on the bed and she lies down with her head on my lap and asks me to, like, pet her face, which is something I used to always do when we were, like, going out together, and I can't work out whether she actually wants to be with me, or whether it's just, like, a prick-tease, but I do it anyway.

I ask her why she's not downstairs at the porty and she goes, 'Because I'm tired of my mother's projection fantasies,' and I don't have a focking clue what she's talking about, so I just go, 'Bummer.'

She says that the millennium turned out to be one complete bummer and that Cillian was the only decent thing that happened to her in the year 2000, and I'm like, 'Is this the twenty-eight-year-old?' and she nods and goes, 'I should say that Cillian and *you* were the only decent things that happened this year,' and all of a sudden, roysh, I'm pretty certain that I'm going to end up, like, getting my bit here and I stop petting her face and go, 'What do you mean, *I* was one of the decent things that happened?' She goes, 'Well, not so much *you*, Ross, as *us*.

After years of gratuitous self-examination, we've finally got past that whole relationship checkmate thing.'

Your guess is as good as mine, but I get the impression, roysh, she's trying to get across the point that she's not actually interested in me anymore, which is total bullshit because I notice she has *The Very Best of Ennio Morricone*, the CD I bought her for her birthday last year, on her bedside locker – I say *bought*, I actually robbed it off the old man – and I'm pretty sure that before I arrived she was listening to 'Gabriel's Homo', or whatever it's called, wondering whether I was going to call up.

But she's obviously playing hord-to-get, roysh, so I sort of, like, change tack and go, 'I was talking to Erika earlier,' but instead of getting jealous she goes, 'She's making a fool out of you, Ross,' and I'm like, 'Spare me.' She goes, 'Nothing that girl does bothers me anymore. You know what she said in the bor the other night? She said that wheelie bins are working class. I'd hate to see you get hurt, Ross. She's an orsehole. I should know, she's one of my best friends.'

We lie there on her bed for a couple of hours. We watch 'The Royle Family'. Eventually I tell her that I've got to go and she tells me she's SO happy I called up, that Christmas wouldn't be the same without seeing me and that she's glad we're over 'that whole relationship trauma'. I tell her I'm going back playing rugby and she tells me it's not going to change the way she feels about us. She goes, 'Me and Cillian are too strong.'

She takes off her scrunchy, slips it onto her wrist, shakes her hair free and then smoothes it back into a low ponytail again, puts it back in the scrunchy and then pulls five or six, like, strands of hair loose.

As I'm leaving, roysh, she asks me how Christian is. I go, 'Not good. You heard he was done for drunk-and-disorderly last weekend?' Sorcha's like, 'I can't *believe* his parents are splitting up. Trevor and Andrea? OH! MY! GOD! It's, like, SUCH a shock.'

I go, 'I know,' but I can't look at her when I say it. She gives me a hug and says that Christian's SO lucky to have a best friend like me and she knows that I'll be there for him. I go, 'I don't know what to say to the goy,' and she goes, 'Just be yourself and be there for him.'

CHAPTER FOUR
'Ross, like, so loves himself it's not funny.'
Discuss.

Hazel is this bird I met in the M1, roysh, a Montessori teacher and a total lasher, we're talking SO like Rachael Leigh Cook it's just not funny. There I was, roysh, sitting up at the bor with Christian and Fionn, just talking about, like, rugby and shit, when her and a couple of her friends – recognised one of them from The Palace, Orna I think her name is, second year Law in Portobello – they come up and they're, like, ordering drinks, roysh, and this Orna one picks up Fionn's mobile phone and, the usual, storts, like, scrolling down through his phonebook, going, 'Keavo? OH! MY! GOD! is that Alan Keaveney?'

I turn around to Hazel, who's paying for, like, two vodka and Red Bulls and a Smirnoff Ice, roysh, and stort chatting away to her, working the old charm on her. I ask her what Montessori actually is, roysh, but of course I'm too busy thinking of my next killer line to listen properly to what she's saying, though from what I can make out it's pretty much the same as, like, a normal nursery school, except that instead of giving the kids, like, paint and jigsaws and shit, they teach them focking Japanese and how to play the violin.

Of course, I'm there cracking on to be really interested. End of the night, roysh, Christian's focked off home, because his old man moved out of the house today and he wants to make sure his old dear is alroysh, I mean, I offered to go with him, but he said he wanted to be on his own, and it's just me, Fionn, Orna and Hazel left. Orna is completely off her tits, roysh, and she keeps telling us she has to have an essay in for Tort tomorrow and she hasn't done a tap on it and that the Law course in LSB is so much horder than it is in UCD, but when you tell people that – OH! MY! GOD! – no one believes you.

Eventually, roysh, Fionn leans over to me and goes, 'I'm going to drop the old Chief Justice here home,' and I high-five the dude and he helps her off the stool and out the door. Hazel, roysh, she shows no sign of following, so obviously I'm there thinking, I'm well in here. I go, 'So, where are you living?' still playing it Kool and the Gang, and she goes, 'Sandycove,' and I'm like, 'I've been known to find myself in that particular vicinity. Can I drive you home? We're talking Golf GTI. Black. *With* alloys,' and she goes, '*Oh* my God! Cool.'

So there we are in the cor, roysh, heading out towards her gaff, and I decide it's time to put on the old *Pretty Woman* tape, but I can't remember whether I've, like, rewound the tape to the stort of 'Fallen'. If I haven't, roysh, she's going to get an earful of Roy Orbison giving it, 'Whooooah-hoh, Pretty Woman,' which is actually a pretty good song, but a bit of a passion-killer.

So I'm basically taking a bit of a chance hitting the play button, roysh, but it's cool because the next thing I hear is, like, Lauren Wood's voice and Hazel goes, 'OH! MY! GOD! I don't believe it,' and I'm like, 'What?' cracking on to be all surprised. She goes, '*Oh* my God, this *has* to be fate. This is, like, my favourite song of all time,' and I'm like, 'Really? Who is it, Samantha Mumba?' She goes, 'It's from *Pretty Woman*. Is this a tape?' and I'm there giving it, 'No, it's just the radio,' and she goes, 'OH! MY! GOD! then this *has* to be fate. Every time I hear this song I'm going to think of you now.'

If only she knew how many locks I've picked with this tape.

So we pull up outside her gaff, roysh, massive pad, her old man must be minted, and she goes, '*Oh* my God, I said I wouldn't let this happen,' and I'm like, 'Let what happen?' and she goes, 'I promised myself that I wouldn't fall so easily again. Especially after Cian.' I'm like, 'Who's Cian,' as if I give a fock. I'm just getting ready to bail in here. She goes, 'You don't want to know,' and she's bang-on there.

She looks away and she goes, 'I got really hurt,' and of course I'm like, 'Hey, just go with the flow,' and I move in for the kill, roysh, but as I go to throw the lips on her she goes, 'What are you doing?' and I'm like, 'Hey, a little bit of what you fancy is good for you.' I hate myself for using Oisinn's chat-up lines, but it's fock-all use anyway because she pushes me away, just as Roy Orbison comes on as it happens. I'm wondering has she fallen to the communists, but she says it's just that she wants to, like, take things a bit more slowly. It looks very much to me as

though this could be a two-day job, which, under normal cir-
cumstances, roysh, would be enough to put me off completely,
but she asks me what I'm doing tomorrow night and, of course,
now I've got to face the old dilemma: do I cut my losses now
and just tell her I'm emigrating to Outer Mongolia, or do I go for
a second crack at it?

One thing is certain, roysh, this whole taking-things-a-bit-
more-slowly shit sounds like she has a potential relationship on
her mind, and even though I know it's a mistake, roysh, I end
up giving her my number, my actual *real* number, and she says
she'll, like, give me a call the next day. Which she does, the sad
bitch, she rings me at, like, eleven the next morning, roysh, a bit
too John B, and asks me whether I fancy going, like, bowling.
I'm like, Bowling? *Hello?* Is this bird a knob or what? Of course
I'm still in the scratcher when she rings, having skipped my
eleven o'clock, and I'm pretty much half-asleep, which is why I
end up agreeing to meet her in Stillorgan.

So that afternoon, roysh, I'm pulling into the cor pork, thinking, If any of the goys find out I'm bowling with a bird, I'm to-
taled. And this is where it all goes pear-shaped. Unbeknownst
to me, she's bringing her whole focking class with her, we're
talking a school trip here, with me roped in as a focking child-
minder for the day. We are talking total mortification and we are
talking TOTALLY.

I'm in such a Pauline, roysh, that I end up having a row with
the bird who gives out those crappy shoes. First of all, roysh,
she says I can't wear the old Dubes, even though they've got,

like, white soles. She goes, 'You have to use the house shoes,' namely these half-red, half-blue things that make you look like a complete knob. And then, roysh, she tells me she needs a deposit of, like, five bills. I'm like, '*Hello?* I've just handed you a pair of shoes that cost eighty bills. Do you honestly think I'm going to run off with these focking things?' and I point down to my feet, roysh, but she just goes, 'That will be five pounds, Sir,' like she's a focking robot or something.

And the kids, roysh, they're all little shits, brilliant at bowling of course, every focking one of them, probably part of the, like, curriculum, if that's the roysh word.

And Hazel, roysh, she keeps coming up to me going, '*Oh* my God, you are SO good with kids,' obviously morking me down as future marriage material. I'm there going, Do not even *go* there, girl.

She obviously didn't see me whacking one of the little spoilt shits around the ear. The little focker kicked me, roysh, and told me I was rubbish at bowling, so I hit him a sly little slap around the head, the kind the referee never sees, then bent back one of his fingers and told him he was a spoilt little brat and, of course, he goes bawling his eyes out to Hazel, who is such a sad bitch she actually believes me when I tell her he caught his fingers in the bowling ball, and the kid stays out of my way for the rest of the day, the clever boy.

Then, roysh, it's all across the road to McDonalds, me trying to talk to Hazel, to find out, obviously, if I've any focking chance of getting my bit at the end of all this, and her reminding me to keep my eyes on the ten or eleven little shits who are walking behind us. I feel like the old woman who lived in the focking shoe, sitting there in McD's with all these little fockers running around me. And they're all going, 'Are you Hazel's boyfriend?'

And this one kid, roysh, he sucks a load of Coke up into his straw, roysh, and I swear to God the little bastard's about to, like, spit it at me, and I go, '*Don't* even think about it.' And Hazel all of a sudden jumps up and goes, 'NO, ROSS!' and I'm like, 'What?' thinking, I haven't even hit the little focker yet. She goes, 'You're not allowed to use the D-word to the young people.' I'm like, 'What D-word?' She goes, 'The D-O-N-Apostrophe-T word. You're not supposed to say *Don't* or *Can't* to the young people. They're negatives, you see.'

I'm like, 'So what do you do then, just slap them?' and she looks at me totally horrified, like I've just shat on her Corn Flakes. She goes, 'You *never* hit young people, Ross. Nobody should live in fear of violence. When you're trying to stop a young person from acting in an anti-social way, you have to acknowledge that emotions are involved. So to stop Lorcan from spitting his drink at you, what you should say is, 'I understand *why* you want to do that and I understand that you are upset that I'm asking you *not* to do it, but I really feel that …' And as she's saying this, roysh, the little focker sitting next to Lorcan is squashing a bit of gherkin into the table.

I just get up and head for the door, roysh, wave at Hazel, and I go, '*Arrivederci*,' which, I remember on the way home, isn't actually Japanese, but I'm sure she got the message anyway.

✳✳✳

I'm in Stillorgan Shopping Centre, roysh, doing a bit of shopping, actually looking for a new pair of rugby boots, and I'm backing out of a porking space when the phone rings and it's, like, Keevo, a Blackrock head but sound anyway. He's like, 'Ross, I've a good one for you.' I'm there, 'Keevo, now is not a good time, my man,' and he's like, 'It won't take long.' I'm there going, 'What is it?' and he's like, 'Think of a number between one and ten.' And I'm like, 'Okay, hang on … roysh, got one.' He goes, 'Roysh, add four.' I'm like, 'Okay.' He goes, 'Now, double it.' And I'm like, 'Hold on, hold on … roysh.' He's there, 'Now, halve it. And I'm like, 'O-kaaaay.' Then he goes, 'Take away four,' and I'm like, 'Yyyeah,' and he goes, 'And you're left with six.' I'm like, 'No. I'm left with four.' He goes, 'Oh, roysh. No, it doesn't always work.' And he hangs up. And this so worries me, roysh, because Keevo is, like, second year theoretical physics.

✳✳✳

To whom it may concern,

Many thanks for your letter. It was a pleasant surprise to hear from you again. Please accept my apologies for the delay in replying. The college was closed for three weeks for Christmas holidays and I was off work for an extra week due to salmonella poisoning, which I contracted from a piece of turkey which hadn't been thoroughly re-heated.

I note with interest your threat to send *Eros* back to us 'in pieces'. Personally – and I'm not speaking for the entire Department here – I do not see this as a particularly bad thing. I'm not sure whether you have had a chance to view the *Venus de Milo* in the Louvre in Paris, but it has both upper limbs missing and this has merely added to not detracted from its charm.

You will also notice that *Eros* is already missing an arm, the consequence of a similar Rag Day prank, in 1978 I think I'm right in saying. The missing arm, I believe, has given it that classic, ancient look.

Notwithstanding all of this, I must repeat my earlier assertion that the Department does not have sufficient finance to become involved in a project such as this at this time. Incidentally, if you are experiencing financial hardship, as many students do, you might like to know that the college bookshop is currently having a sale. There's up to 30% off some titles.

Happy new year, and regards to *Eros*.

Francis Hird

Francis Hird,
Classics Department, UCD

***

Sophie takes five minutes to chew one mouthful of popcorn, roysh, and it is, like, seriously storting to wreck my head, and we're talking TOTALLY here, and when I ask her what the fock she's doing, roysh, she says she read in some magazine, maybe *Cosmo* or *InStyle*, that you don't put on as much weight if you, like, chew your food for longer. Chloë, who's, like, second year International Commerce with German, SO like Heidi Klum it's unbelievable – scored her at the Traffic Light Ball – she asks Sophie whether she's seen Valerie lately and Sophie goes, 'Valerie as in first year Strategic Morkeshing in LSB?' and Chloë nods and says she has put on SO much weight and, she's not being a bitch or anything, but OH! MY! GOD! she's actually a size sixteen, and Sophie asks her how she knows and Chloë tells her that she's storted working in Benetton, just to get money together for Australia if she decides to go for the year, and Valerie came into the shop last week. Sophie goes, '*Oh my God!* she used to be SO gorgeous. She brought Alex Gaffney to the Holy Child Killiney debs,' and Chloë's there, 'I SO know.'

I knock back the rest of my Coke, roysh, and I get up to go and Sophie asks me whether I've got a lecture this afternoon. I'm like, 'Had a ten o'clock, but I skipped it. I'm just going off to practice my kicking for a couple of hours.' She asks me whether I've been talking to Sorcha. I say no, roysh, so she tells me the plan for Saturday night has changed, that Gisele has decided to have her going-away somewhere in town, because the problem with Clone 92 is that if the bouncers, like, turn you away, then that's your night over, you're stranded in Leopardstown. She says that Erika won't go there anyway because she reckons it's full of skobies.

I bump into the goys at the Blob, we're talking Christian and Oisinn, and they're about to go on the serious lash with Fionn. Christian already reeks of drink and I'm not sure if it's from this morning or last night. Oisinn goes, 'Where are you going?' and I'm like, 'Training.' Oisinn's there, 'Training? What are you *training* for?' I'm like, 'Rugby. *Hello?* We are all doing *sports* scholarships, remember?' And Christian's there, 'Is this because of what it says on the door of the jacks?' Oisinn's there, 'Leave it, Christian,' and I'm like, 'What does it say in the jacks?' Oisinn goes, 'Just something about you being finished. Past it. You have had a lot of injuries, Ross. I know you were breaking your balls to get back.' Christian goes, 'They call you Tampax, Ross. One week in and three weeks out.' I'm like, 'They call me that?' and Oisinn, roysh, he looks off into the distance and goes, 'Some do. You've had very bad luck with injuries, though.'

So I head down to the gym, roysh, do some stretches, and then do half-an-hour on the treadmill, after which I'm, like, totally shagged. But I am SO determined to get fit, roysh, that I go roysh through the pain barrier. I do, like, half-an-hour on the bike and a few weights and then I head out with a ball to, like, practice my kicking. It's focking pissing rain. I basically hate January.

When I get to the field, roysh, who's there before me only Matthew Path, the knob whose place on the team I'm about to take, and he's, like, practicing his kicking as well, roysh, and when he sees me he storts totally gicking himself. I stand there and watch him for, like, twenty minutes, really psyching the goy out of it and in the end, and I'm not being a bastard here or anything, the goy couldn't hit a donkey's orse with a banjo. He's taking kicks from, like, different angles, roysh, and even in front of the post he goes and misses and he's getting, like, totally flustered, doesn't have the big-match temperament, as Sooty, our old coach, used to say. It's no wonder UCD are focked.

When he finally gets one between the posts, roysh, I just stort clapping, sort of, like, sarcastically, if that's the roysh word. Then I head over and stand in front of him and I've got my old Castlerock jersey on, roysh, and I point to the badge and go, 'You know what this means, don't you?' and he goes, 'It means you went to a school for wankers,' and quick as a flash I'm like, 'It actually means that you can go home now,' and then I go, 'You're excess baggage,' which, I have to say, I'm pretty pleased with, roysh, even though I don't know where I got it from.

He goes, 'You're living on past glories,' and I'm there giving it, 'Your girlfriend didn't seem to think so,' and then I push him out of the way and go, 'Learn from the master.' I stort spotting the balls, roysh, and kicking them at the goal he's been using and he stands there and watches me putting ball after ball straight between the posts from, like, every angle you can think of. I'm on focking fire. Doesn't matter what I do, I can't miss. He watches me for, like, ten or fifteen minutes and then I decide I've punished him enough and, as I'm leaving, I turn to him and go, 'Thanks for keeping my place warm, orsehole.'

I have my shower and get changed and it's, like, only three o'clock, so I phone Christian on his mobile, roysh, and he tells me they all ended up heading into town and they're in The Bailey, so I drive in, pork the cor on Stephen's Green and head down. I am in *such* good form. I walk in and I'm like, 'I'm back, goys. I am SO back,' and Oisinn goes, 'Pint?' and of course I give it, 'Orange juice.' And Oisinn makes this, like, wolf-whistling sound and then high-fives me. Christian, who's *totally* shit-faced, he grabs me around the neck and goes, 'Remember, if you choose the quick and easy path as Vader did, you will become an agent of evil. You must complete your training,' and I'm like, 'My training is complete, Obi Wan,' sort of, like, playing along with the dude. Then I go, 'I'm going to kick orse, Master.'

I knock back a couple of glasses of orange juice, roysh, but the goys are on a totally different buzz from me, so I end up heading off after a couple of hours and I'm in such a good mood I even think about phoning Erika on the way back to the cor, but it's, like, early days yet.

Fock this for a game of soldiers, my cor – we're talking my brand new Golf GTI here – has been focking clamped and I'm just there going, that is SO not on. I get onto the old man, roysh, and I go, 'Need your credit cord number. Now.' He goes, 'What for?' and I'm like, 'No time to go into all that. Just gimme the focking number.' The dickhead, roysh, he actually goes, 'It's a bit of an awkward time, Ross. I'm in a meeting,' and I'm like, 'Well just give me the focking number then and stop blabbing on,' which he does, the focking tosser.

I phone up the number on the notice that's stuck to my windscreen and I go, 'Yeah, you've put a clamp on my cor. Take the focking thing off. Here's my credit cord number. You've got fifteen minutes, otherwise I'll take you to the focking cleaners.' The dude on the other end of the phone, he takes down the number, roysh, and I go, 'And make sure you get all the glue off my windscreen, or I'll sue your focking orses.' He goes, 'Can I just take your name, Sir?' And I'm like, 'My name? It's Ross O'Carroll-Kelly. And if you haven't heard it before, don't worry. You will.'

✳✳✳

When we were in, like, first year in school, roysh, Christian's old pair split up for, like, six months or something, and though Christian never really spoke about it, pretty much everyone knew it was because his old man was basically knocking off this other bird who was, like, a portner in the same company as him, she was a barrister, or something. Anyway, roysh, while all this shit was going down, Christian was sent to, like, Castlerock to board, and his sister, roysh, we're talking Iseult, she boarded at Alex., just for, like, the year, while the old pair were working things out.

Christian said it was, like, the most amazing year of his life, but I knew he hated it. A couple of the goys I knew from the junior cup team said he used to cry pretty much every night when the lights were off and he thought, like, no one could hear him.

I used to stay back after school for a couple of hours, roysh, supposedly to do supervised study, that's what I told my old pair, but it was basically so me and Christian could hang out, mostly chatting about rugby and birds we'd snogged and birds we wanted to snog and birds who wanted to snog us, and *never* about his old pair. And even though, roysh, technically I shouldn't have still been on the school grounds at, like, half-seven at night, the priests never said anything to me because, well, basically I think it was because they knew the shit that Christian was going through and having his best mate there just, like, made it better for him. Sounds a bit gay, but it wasn't.

Anyway, roysh, this sounds a bit gay as well, but I hated going home because it was like he was in prison or some shit, and I was just, like, visiting him, and every night, roysh, when it was time for me to head off, he'd ask me to stay a bit longer and when I'd tell him that I had to get my bus, he'd say that there was a 46A every, like, ten minutes.

Seems so long ago now. I remember this one time, roysh, and this is going to sound totally weird, but we were hanging out at the rugby pitch next to the dorms, basically lying on the grass, watching the sky get dark, again talking about birds, probably Karyn Flynn and Jessica Kennedy, these two Mounties we were into. This thing, roysh, had been on my mind for about a week, so I turn around to him and I'm like, 'Christian, can I ask you something?' and he goes, 'What?' and I'm there, 'You know that thing they say about magpies? That it's, like, one for sorrow, two for joy, three for a girl ...' I can see him now, roysh, all of a sudden sitting up, so he's, like, leaning on his elbows, and he goes, 'Yeah. What about it?' And I went, 'I saw four the other day ... does that mean I'm ...' And he broke his shite laughing. Absolutely cracked his hole. He went, 'You are SO focking weird, Ross,' and he broke his shite laughing again. Then I broke mine.

***

STOP FOCkiNG Us aRoUnD this iS one of His feathers WEll accepT 500 lliDs Day oR the stAtue gEts it

***

What happened between me and Christian's old dear wasn't actually my fault. Okay, I didn't exactly fight her off, roysh, but basically she was the one who made a move on me and I'm the one, of course, who, like, ends up the villain. Christian's old man is basically an orsehole, roysh, who was doing the dirt on her for years and not just with that bird he worked with, there was also this other bird he played tennis with in Riverview and then this other one who was, like, Christian's old dear's best friend since they were, like, ten or something. Doesn't excuse what happened, roysh, but Christian's old man is basically a focking hypocrite if he tells Christian about it.

It happened at Iseult's twenty-first, roysh, we're talking Iseult as in Christian's sister here, about three years ago. The porty was in their gaff on Ailesbury Road and it was obvious that the old pair had had a massive row earlier in the day, you could tell from the atmosphere and the way the old dear was putting away the sherry. Basically, I don't know what Christian's old man had said to her, roysh, but the shit was *totally* hitting the fan.

I went to use the downstairs jacks and there was someone in there. I couldn't hold it. Knocking back the beer all day, my back teeth were floating, so I headed upstairs. The door wasn't locked, roysh, but when I pushed it there was something blocking it, a pair of legs, basically Christian's old dear, sitting on the side of the bath, bawling her eyes out.

I was a bit embarrassed, roysh, probably should have focked off back downstairs instead of going in. She was, like, off her face and suddenly she storts pouring out her whole, like, life story to me – what Christian's old man was *really* like and *that woman* who had the cheek to come into her home on this of all days, and I wasn't sure who she was talking about, though I presumed it was someone she'd found out the old man was rattling on the side. And that's probably what the row was about, him inviting her.

It's funny, roysh, I'd always had a bit of a thing for Christian's old dear. She was always a bit of a yummy-mummy, not quite as nice as Simon's, but I wouldn't have said no.

I sat on the bath beside her, roysh, and the next thing – it's focking stupid, I know, but I'd a few on me as well – we're suddenly, like, hugging each other and there's a bit of kissing going on and, well, I'll spare you the details, but basically one thing led to another and we did it, there on the floor of the bathroom, and there's me gicking it in case Christian, or his old man, or, fock, his granny even, came up to use the can.

When it was over she said it was lovely, she goes, 'That was lovely,' but I knew it was bullshit. It was too quick and too sleazy to have been lovely.

And that was it, roysh, we both got dressed and headed back downstairs to the porty and it was never, like, mentioned again. Even when I was in the gaff after that there was no, like, awkwardness about it. Sometimes I wondered whether she was too pissed to even remember because she basically acted like it had never happened and shit.

That was until this night, about three weeks ago, when she phoned me up, roysh, and says she told Christian's old man what had happened between us. She was really sorry, it was all bound to come out now, she said. I asked her why she had to say anything. I'm like, 'It was three focking years ago, for fock's sake.' She goes, 'And we're separated now. I know it shouldn't matter. But there's so much stuff going on. So much bitterness. So many bad things coming out. I found out today about this woman he was seeing. Two years it was going on. Right under my nose as well. We had a row about it. On the phone. And in the heat of the moment, I mentioned what happened between you and me.'

I asked her did she think he'd tell Christian and she said not for now, roysh, because Christian was refusing point-blank to see him or even, like, take his calls because he was, like, blaming him for the break-up and shit. But she was sure it would come out eventually. He would use it to try to worm his way back into Christian's good books. Nothing focking surer.

✳✳✳

The old man calls a meeting of KISS, roysh, what with all the stuff in the papers about rugby going to, like, Croke Park and shit, and you should see our driveway, it's like focking Maxwell Motors, we're talking Beamers, Mercs, Rovers, the whole lot. The old man's, like, in his element, of course, crapping on about the Berkeley Court and how the heart and soul of the game belongs at Lansdowne Road. He's there giving it, 'I don't care whether it's Abbotstown, Croke Park, or Áras-an-blooming-Uachtaráin, rugby will *not* be moving to the northside, certainly not as long as I have breath in my lungs and I'm chairman of Keep It South Side.'

I warned him not to make a focking knob of himself again, but of course the old dear was straight on my case, going, 'Please be on your best behaviour, Ross. Today's a big day for your father,' and it must be, roysh, because she's got the focking gourmet coffee out again and it's, like, I don't know, French Vanilla Supreme all round, and the old man's giving it, 'It's far from Wedgwood that Bertie Ahern was reared,' which gets a laugh off all his dickhead mates, and the old dear, who's standing there with the tray, goes, 'I say, how clever, Darling,' and she kisses him – on the *actual* lips – and I'm thinking, *Oh my God!* I am going to focking vom.

She lays the tray down on the dining-room table and she gives it, 'For heaven's sake, that man can't even speak properly, that Bertie Ahern.' And Alan, this total orsehole who's, like, president of Castlerock this year, he goes, 'You're right, Fionnu-ala. It's all Dis, Dat, Deez and Doze with that chap.' And Alan's wife is like, 'C as M. The man is simply C *as* M.'

The old man goes, 'But we're not allowed to say that, unfor-tunately. Not politically correct, quote-unquote. That's why we have to think out our strategy carefully. You mention unmarried mothers, tracksuits and satellite dishes and you're immediately labelled a snob. With a capital S.'

I'm standing at the door of the sitting room, listening to this shite and going, 'What a bunch of sad bastards,' under my breath. Eduard, this knob the old man knows from the golf club, he bangs his fist on the table and goes, 'What are we going to do then?' and Richard, this other complete and utter dickhead who's supposed to be helping the old man get his handicap down, goes, 'That's the frustrating thing, Eduard. We know what this is about. It's about Bertie Ahern getting votes in these Northside hellholes. That's what it's about ... I mean, some of these young girls, they're having these babies just for the money. Are we just going to sit back and accept that that's right?'

The old man goes, 'I think you've gone off on a bit of a tangent there, Richard, but your point will be noted in the minutes. But if we're to accept that we can't include anything about sovereign rings, little moustaches, or spice burgers in our argument, then I believe there's only one way for us to fight this nonsense. And that's by using the only language Fianna Fáil understands.'

Hennessy goes, 'I can raise a few hundred thousand. Might mean going to Guernsey, but it's feasible.' Eduard goes, 'You'd do that?' and Hennessy's like, 'This is an attack on our way of life, Eduard. I'd do that and a lot more besides.'

Richard goes, 'I've known Frank Dunlop for many, many years, and something tells me that simple bribery isn't going to work this time.' Eduard, roysh, he loses it then, jumps up and goes, 'Well, what do you suggest we do? For thirty-five years I've been going to rugby internationals. Thirty-five years. It's the Berkeley Court. It's the Dorsh. It's ... it's ... I mean, where is Abbotstown anyway?' Hennessy puts his orm around him, trying to calm the looper down, and he goes, 'Who knows, Eduard? Who knows ...?'

The old man's there, 'Can I just call this meeting to order for a moment and say that I think we've gone off the point slightly. This Abbotstown business, it's still some way down the line. The real, immediate danger at the moment comes from the GAA. If they vote to open up Croke Stadium, we could be in real danger. We'll be travelling out to north Dublin for our matches quicker than you can say, "What do you mean, you don't sell Courvoisier around here?" Now I think Richard is right. Frank Dunlop has been keeping his head down lately, and who can blame him?'

Hennessy goes, 'Kerrigan. He hates anyone with money,' and the old man's like, 'Let me finish, Hennessy. What I'm saying is, let's deal with the GAA *first*. If we need to bribe anyone, we've got to get a few of these Gaelic Association of … what does it stand for? Gaelic … I don't know, these GAA chaps. What I'm saying is, let's put together, say, £50,000 each and try to bribe a few of them. Get them to vote against it.'

Hennessy goes, 'Just think of all the bacon and cabbage and, you know, sports coats they could buy with that kind of money.'

And Richard's like, 'We can offer it to them, but they'd never go for it, would they?'

✳✳✳

JP asks me whether it's true I've been texting Lana, this Daisy Donovan wannabe who's doing fock-knows-what in Bruce. I go, 'I wanna say this just one more time. I did *not* have textual intercourse with that woman,' and everyone at our table cracks up, including Erika. Probably the funniest thing I've ever said.

✱✱✱

Usual crack in college, doing fock-all, just basically chilling, taking it easy and shit. I hit the sports bor in the morning, roysh, read Wardy's report on the Clongowes match, play a few frames of Killer with, like, Oisinn and Christian, head down to 911 for the old rolls, then to the computer room for the two hours of free internet access, which is mostly spent downloading pictures of Rachel Stevens, Carmen Electra and Lisa Faulkner.

After that, roysh, the afternoon's basically my own, so me and the goys are, like, sitting around in Hilper's with Chloë, who's, like, first year B&L, and Clodagh, who's repeating first year Orts, and everyone has, like, their mobiles, their car keys and, in the girls' case, lip balm on the table, and Oisinn's talking about some goy in first year Business who, he says, is a total faggot and we're talking a *total* faggot here, and all of a sudden, roysh, Chloë goes, 'What have you got against gay people?' and Oisinn's like, 'Nothing,' and Chloë goes, 'You better not have, because I've got *loads* of friends who are gay.' Clodagh says she has too, but Chloë says she doesn't have as many as she has and they argue about this for, I would guess, fifteen minutes.

I have to say, roysh, that Chloë is a total honey, we're talking really well-stacked here, former Virgin on the Rocks, so like Emmanuelle Béart it's unbelievable, while Clodagh is a complete focking moon-pig, though Christian told me in Annabel's last Friday night that he'd be prepared to take a bullet for me if I'd any chance of being with Chloë.

So we're sitting there, roysh, and Chloë is SO flirting her orse off with me it's unbelievable. She's there going, 'Ross, would you be a complete dorling and go and get me a cup of boiled water?' and I ask her why boiled water and she says that it's, like, good for your skin and anyway cold water just, like, slows down your metabolism. I have to say, roysh, she looks totally amazing in her pink Ralph with the collar up and a baby blue sleeveless bubble jacket. She goes, 'Would you be a complete dorling, Ross, and get it for me? And a packet of Marlboro Lights as well,' and of course I'm there, 'Does the Pope shit in the woods?'

After lunch, there's, like, fock-all happening, so the five of us decide to head out to Stillorgan to, like, see a movie for the afternoon. Clodagh says she really wants to see *Cast Away*, roysh, and Chloë says that is SO a good idea. Clodagh says they actually filmed it in two sequences, roysh, and that Tom Hanks basically lost three stone in eight months to play the port of a goy who's, like, shipwrecked on a desert island, and Oisinn says that three stone in eight months is nothing, that anyone from the cast of 'Friends' could do that in a long weekend, and even though I think it's, like, really funny, roysh, I notice that Chloë isn't laughing, so I tell him he's a knob.

So we're about to head off, roysh, when all of a sudden this goy, Dowdy, who's, like, second year Sports Management, ex-Clongowes boy and a total dickhead, he comes over and storts, like, chatting to the birds, asking them how they're fixed for the exams and shit. Clodagh says she hasn't done a tap all year and SO has to get her finger out of her orse it's not funny, and then he turns around and asks us the same question, roysh, and we all, like, totally blank him.

He's there, 'Oh, I get it, the old school-rivalry shit. All I'm saying, goys, is don't leave it too late to stort studying. I should know,' and I go, '*Hello?* We're doing Sports Management.' He goes, 'I know. You've still got exams,' and I'm like, 'I've been training my orse off for, like, two weeks. I cannot *believe* they are pulling this shit on me now. How many exams are we talking? There's only, like, three subjects on the course.' He goes, 'Well, there's actually seven subjects on the course, goys. You must have done exams at Christmas?' *Oh my God,* roysh, I'm storting to feel seriously dizzy. I'm like, '*Seven* subjects? Christmas exams?' He's there, 'Yeah, we're talking physiotherapy, computers, psychology …'

Me and Oisinn are there, 'OH! MY! GOD! you know what this means? If we've missed the Christmas exams, we're going to have to sit the summer repeats.' I'm there, 'I am SO not cancelling Ocean City.'

So we tell the birds, roysh, that we're going to have to postpone the flicks because this is, like, a major emergency, and me and Oisinn end up hitting the sports bor and knocking back a few pints, to get over the shock more than anything, and by seven o'clock we're totally shit-faced. We hit the M1 for a few more, then head into town to Mono.

Pretty much the next thing I remember is being out on the dancefloor, giving it *loads* to 'Beautiful Day', roysh, and the bouncers telling me and Oisinn that if we can't control ourselves we're going to have to take it outside, and I look around, roysh, and I notice that Fionn's here as well. That geeky-looking focker doesn't have to worry because he's doing Orts and he's focking brains to burn and he's chatting up this bird, blonde hair, big baps, a little bit like Stacey Bello, though not up close, and when I get up close she's asking him where he's from and he says Killiney and she's, like, totally disgusted all of a sudden and she goes, 'I am SO not getting involved in another Dorsh-line relationship,' and she focks off.

And that's pretty much the last thing I can remember, except I think I ended up being with this bird Carol, who's, like, first year accountancy in Bruce, really good-looking, so like Estella Warren you would actually swear it was her, but I wasn't with her for long because I could hordly stand, and I was so off my face I ended up giving her my number – we're talking my *real* number here – though that isn't the thing I was most worried about the next morning.

I don't know whether I imagined this because I was so horrendufied, and I can't get through to the goys to find out whether it really happened, but I could have sworn, roysh, that I was walking down Grafton Street, just before I blacked out, and I bumped into Hendo, the UCD coach, who said he'd been trying to contact me all day and seeing the state of me now he's wondering why he bothered at all, but I'm on the team for next week's match if I can manage to stay off the drink for that long and I'm a disgrace to the game of rugby and it's a pretty sad day for UCD that the team has to rely on the likes of me and I should get myself sobered up and get my act together and this is my, like, last big chance. And maybe it was the drink, probably was, but I could have sworn that he said the match was against, like, Castlerock RFC.

And of course I'm like, 'Fock.'

CHAPTER FIVE
'Ross thinks he's, like, too cool for school.' Discuss.

JP, roysh, he persuades Oisinn to borrow his old man's cor, we're talking a big fock-off Beamer here, and they head out to Tallafornia and drive around these real skanger estates, with JP sticking his head out through the sunroof, shouting, 'AFFLUENCE! AFFLUENCE!'

***

Valentine's Day was the usual crack – got four cords, two from, like, secret admirers, roysh, one from Jessica Heaney who's, like, second year Actuarial and Financial Studies in UCD, a big-time flirt and so like Natasha Henstridge you'd swear they were twins, and one other addressed to 'The goy with the smallest penis in UCD,' which is obviously from Keeva, or Amy, or some other bird I've given the flick to and is having a problem getting over it, maybe Emma, or Sinéad. Or Cara, or Jill. One of those orseholes. Or Sadch. Or Abhril. Or Teena with two Es.

Anyway, roysh, the good news was that Fionn got his hands on tickets for the Valentine's Ball, so there I am in my gaff getting ready, roysh, looking pretty well, I have to say, in my new beige chinos, light blue Ralph and Dubes, when all of a sudden there's this, like, ring at the door. I open it, roysh, and surprise sur-focking-prise, who is it only Sorcha, who hands me this cord, roysh, and this present and goes, 'Friends?' and I just, like, shrug my shoulders and go, '*What*ever,' thinking, *Hello?* Has this girl no, like, self-respect? Then she gives me a hug and goes, 'You smell SO nice. What are you wearing?' Everything with this girl comes with a focking hug. I'm like, '*Emporio He*,' and she goes, 'Giorgio Armani?' and I just, like, nod at her.

She's totally dressed to kill, roysh, and we're talking totally here, and she's there giving it, 'You going out tonight?' and I'm like, 'Going to the Valentine's Ball,' and she goes, 'Oh my God, where is it on this year?' and I just go, 'Town.' She is SO trying to get back with me it's embarrassing. She goes, 'Are you not going to open your present?' so I tear open the wrapping and it's, like, the new Radiohead album, which I've basically wanted for ages, and she goes, 'I hope you haven't already got it,' and I'm like, 'Yeah, I have actually,' and she says, OH MY GOD! she'll change it, but I tell her not to bother, that I'll give it to Megan, and she's like, 'Who's Megan?' and I go, 'This bird I've been see-ing. She's, like, first year B&L. You wouldn't know her. Looks like Holly Valance,' completely making it up, and the sad bitch nearly bursts into tears.

The next thing, roysh, the old dear decides to stick her fock-ing oar in, she comes out to the hall and goes, 'Sorcha! Come in, come in. Ross, why have you left her standing at the door?' and the two of them air-kiss each other and then, like, disappear off into the kitchen together, talking about the sale in Pamela Scott and whether or not Ikea will ever open up a branch in Dublin. I'm just glad the old dear has managed to tear herself away from Dick-features. They actually bought each other Valentine cords, roysh, how focking twisted is that, they're in their, like, fifties. It's that focking statue, I know it is.

I just, like, grab the cor keys. The old dear tells me to drive carefully and I tell her to focking cop herself on, and as I'm leaving I notice that Sorcha has actually got, like, tears in her eyes and she's hordly even touched the cappuccino the old dear's made for her and I'm like, *What* a total sap.

The Coyote Lounge is totally jammers, roysh. There's, like, a queue halfway up D'Olier Street when we arrive and everyone's there going, 'WE HATE C&E. WE HATE C&E,' and the Commerce and Economics Society goys are, like, *totally* bulling. After about an hour, roysh, we finally manage to get inside, but I end up having a pretty shit night, probably because I'm only drinking Diet Coke, what with me back playing serious rugby and all.

The only bit of crack I actually have, roysh, is watching Oisinn totally crash and burn when he chances his orm with Phenola, this complete fruitcake who's, like, second year B&L. He's chatting away to her, roysh, giving it loads, and that Destiny's Child song comes on, roysh, 'Independent Women', or whatever the fock it's called, music for cutting men's mickeys off to, and all of a sudden he makes a lunge for her and she slaps him across the face and tells him that trying to be with a girl while that song is on is SUCH a no-no. It's, like, SO funny seeing this big six-foot-five, seventeen-stone prop-forward getting slapped across the face by this little, like, squirt of a bird.

But then I end up getting cornered by Kate, roysh, this total knob who's, like, first year Orts, and we end up having one of those pain-in-the-orse conversations which storts off with her asking me who I know in Orts and I go, 'Lisa Andrews,' and she goes, 'OH! MY! GOD! I can't *believe* you know Lisa Andrews. She's one of my, like, best friends. Who else?' and I go, 'James O'Hagan,' and she goes, 'OH! MY! GOD! I can't *believe* you know James O'Hagan. I was with him at the Freshers' Frolic.'

I'm storting to lose the focking will to live when Fionn comes over and rescues me, roysh, and he points over to this bird, I think it's Bláthnaid, who's, like, repeating first year Counselling and Psychotherapy in LSB, and she's wearing half-nothing, and Fionn turns around to me and goes, 'Gardaí at Harcourt Terrace are seeking the public's help in tracing the whereabouts of Bláthnaid Brady's clothes.' I laugh, roysh, but I tell him that I'm going to fock off home because I have to be, like, up early the next morning.

The next day's a pretty big one for me. Castlerock College are playing their first match in the Senior Cup against the Logue, and Father Feely asked me to go back and give the goys on the S a pep-talk. I have to say I'm pretty nervous going back, roysh, especially with all the shit that's going to come down about next week.

The thing is, roysh, by some focking miracle the goys don't know this yet, but I'm making my debut for UCD next week and it's against Castlerock RFC, with mid-table mediocrity in Division Two of the AIL at stake. Someone at the school is bound to have heard. It's a mare. A total mare.

Anyway, as it turns out, roysh, I'd nothing to worry about, because I get an amazing reception at the school the next morning. I'm there giving the goys on the team my speech, roysh, all like, 'THIS IS THE GAME OF YOUR LIVES' and 'KICK ORSE, ROCK,' and as I'm leaving the stage, the whole assembly is there singing 'Castlerock Über Alles' and it's, like, really focking emotional.

But then, roysh, over comes Magahy, this total dickhead, he's one of the geography teachers, and he comes up to me, roysh, and asks whether it's true that I'm going to be playing against Castlerock in the AIL next week. Now this goy, roysh, is a total orsehole. He coached the Junior Cup team when I was in, like, first year, a total club man, he goes to all the matches and sits up at the bor thinking he knows everything about rugby when in fact he knows fock-all.

I *totally* hate this goy and there's, like, history between us as well. When I was in second year, roysh, I missed a pretty simple penalty and we ended up getting knocked out of the Junior Cup by focking Pres. Bray of all schools, and Magahy goes to me, as I'm leaving the pitch – now I probably should say I was a bit heavier in those days – he goes, 'You're going to be huge, Ross … especially if you keep eating the way you do.'

I so haven't forgotten that.

Anyway, roysh, he asks me if the rumours are true and I'm like, 'What's it to you?' and he turns around and goes, 'You're going to be a turncoat, then?' and I just, like, put my baseball cap back on, roysh, and go, 'No, Magahy, you dickhead. I'm going to be focking sensational.'

✳✳✳

The cor, we're talking the black Golf GTI, *with* alloys, it's in the garage at the moment – just thought if I'm getting serviced on a regular basis, roysh, then my wheels deserve the same pleasure – but the only downside is that I have to use the old public transport, the dreaded 46A. I'd totally forgotten how many Paddy Whackers use it. I'm sitting upstairs, roysh, and there's this, like, total fleck beside me, and he's smoking away there, roysh, and I'm thinking of saying something to him, not that I've any objection to smoking – Sorcha smokes, so do most of the birds – but I just want to basically say to the guy, Are you gonna be a knacker all your life?

I don't get a chance to say anything, roysh, because past the shopping centre in Stillorgan, he suddenly jumps to his feet, reefs open the window and shouts, 'Oi, Plugger. I fooked your mudder,' and this Plugger goy, roysh, he's standing near the bus stop looking up at the top deck, trying to spot who it was who shouted it, no doubt half of him thinking it's probably true, then he sees the goy and he goes, 'Alroy, Anto. Storee?' and the two of them give each other the thumbs-up. Then Anto sits back down and lights up again.

What the fock is the deal with these people?

***

A few months ago, roysh, before I decided to lay off the sauce and go back training, me and the goys – we're talking Christian, Fionn, Oisinn, all those – we were out on the lash, roysh, a Monday night in Peg's, pound a pint, the usual crack and when it was over we all headed back to Oisinn's gaff on Shrewsbury Road to get, like, food and a Jo Maxi. So there we were, like, in the kitchen, roysh, and I looked over at Oisinn – he's had, like, thirteen or fourteen pints at this stage – and the goy's eating a block of lard. We are talking focking *lard* here. At first, roysh, I thought it was the usual crack, you know, absolutely storving but too shit-faced to cook, I mean the goy would eat focking anything as it is, but then he tells us, roysh, that he's in training, and of course we're all there, 'What for?' and says the Iron Stomach contest that the C&E are holding.

To cut a long story short, roysh, Oisinn decided to enter after he met a bunch of Andrews dickheads in the Ass and Cart the previous weekend, all first year Commerce heads who recognised him and storted giving him loads about what a shit school Castlerock was, roysh, brave men it has to be said because Oisinn is a big focker. But it was all like, 'How many points did you get in the Leaving?' and, 'How many former *taoisigh* went to your school?' and what with one thing and another this goy, Keyser, who Oisinn came pretty close to decking, he ended up, like, challenging Oisinn to see who had, like, the strongest stomach.

So the day of the competition arrives, roysh, and we're all there in our Castlerock jerseys, giving it loads, and there's, like, seven people in the competition, all sitting in a row, a few from Commerce, a couple from Science, but all eyes are on Oisinn and Keyser, who are the big-time favourites, and we're all there giving it, 'You can't knock the Rock. You can't knock the Rock,' *totally* intimidating the Andrews goys.

So first, roysh, all the contestants are given a can of Holsten, which is, like, six months past its sell-by date and, while they're drinking that, they have to eat a Weetabix with, like, soy sauce and lemon curd on it. One of them, roysh, we're talking one of the Science goys, he borfs straight away, so there's only, like, six of them left and we're all there giving it loads as they hand out the next thing they have to eat, which is, like, a pot of cold custard with a spoonful of baked beans stirred into it, we're talking cold here, and a spoonful of treacle as well. *Oh my God*, I thought I was going to vom myself.

More Holsten. Then it's, like, a double shot of tequila, roysh, and then they all have to hit the deck and do, like, twenty sit-ups each. The next thing is a cold mince-and-onion pie with, like strawberry jam and Bonjela gum ointment on it, and this girl sitting beside Oisinn, a real Commerce head, she just goes totally green, roysh, and we're talking *totally* here, and she spews her ring up all over Oisinn, all over his chinos, all over his Dubes, all over everything. At this stage, I'm convinced that Oisinn is going to borf as well, but he manages to keep it in.

Then, roysh, we see one of the Andrews goys in the crowd, Henno, this total dickhead who's going out with Emma, not hockey Emma, we're talking Institute Emma, who I was sort of seeing when I was doing grinds. I look over at him, roysh, and give him the finger and he comes over and goes, 'Your goy is going to lose,' and of course I'm there, 'You seem pretty sure of yourself,' and he goes, 'There's something you don't know about Keyser. He has no taste-buds, man. Lost them a couple of years ago. An unfortunate accident involving a flaming Sambucca. Tragic really. He can't taste any of that shit he's eating.'

I'm like, 'OH! MY! GOD! that is *it*,' and I storm up to the front and tell Oisinn that me and the goys are pulling him out of the competition. He's like, 'No *focking* way.' When he says this, roysh, he has a mouthful of, like, beetroot and yoghurt, most of which ends up all over my jacket, we're talking my red Henri Lloyd sailing jacket here. I go, 'Oisinn, Keyser's a freak. The goy has no taste-buds,' and he thinks about this for, like, five seconds, roysh, swallowing what he has in his mouth, and goes, 'So? We're Castlerock, remember? We never quit.'

I have to say, roysh, I feel pretty emotional at that moment, but then I have to take a few steps backwards because all the other contestants stort, like, spewing their guts up all over the place, and suddenly there's only, like, Oisinn and Keyser left in it, we're talking a two-horse race. More Holsten. More tequila. A twenty-second squirt of, like, ketchup into each of their mouths. *Oh* my God, how they don't borf there and then, I don't know. Another double shot of tequila. Hit the deck, twenty press-ups and then, like, twenty sit-ups. Then they've got to, like, put their heads back while one of the C&E goys comes up behind them and feeds them, like, a raw fish. He holds it by the tail and just, like, drops it down their throats.

Keyser is looking so cocky at this stage, roysh, dancing to the music and everything. A glass of cooking oil with a squirty cream head. Pickled onions with ice cream. Mussels. A catfood sandwich with toothpaste and ketchup on it. Down they go. Keyser looks like he could go on at this all day, but Oisinn looks in trouble.

He's knocking back the beers, though, probably to take the focking taste out of his mouth, and when he finishes another – it's, like, his eighth – he turns around to Keyser and goes, 'Are you not drinking?' So Keyser, roysh, he's suddenly handed two cans by one of the C&E goys, who's noticed that he's only drunk, like, six, and Keyser decides he has to show off, he can't be seen to be drinking less than a Rock boy, so he shotguns the two cans and downs them.

Next thing, roysh, you can actually *see* that the goy is going to borf, his face goes white and it's like he can't catch his breath, roysh, and he just leans over and spews his guts up, we're talking all over the gaff, we're talking all that shite he's just eaten, and we're talking undigested here.

We all just, like, mob Oisinn, singing 'Castlerock Über Alles', the whole lot, then we're like, 'SPEECH! SPEECH! SPEECH!' and eventually, roysh, when he's, like, composed himself, Oisinn goes, 'Thank you very much. I have to tell you that I knew all along about Keyser having no taste-buds. It didn't bother me. For I also knew that Andrews goys can't drink for shit, therefore I believed that I could eat more than Keyser could drink. It was a gamble, but it worked.'

Christian turns to me, roysh, and goes, 'The goy's a focking legend, Ross. A *legend*.'

Oisinn heads off to Vincent's, roysh, and we peg it into town and tell him we'll meet him in the Temple later on. Ten o'clock, we're all still sitting around waiting for the man of the moment to arrive, and I think Fionn speaks for us all when he goes, 'How long does it take to pump a goy out?'

There's, like, loads of birds hanging around our table and shit and it's just like the night we won the Senior Cup, except they're actually wrecking our heads a bit because this should be, like, a night for the goys. And I'm just pretty much savouring this mo-ment, roysh, because it's only a matter of time before the goys find out I'm going to be playing against Castlerock next week and I get the feeling that things are going to change.

The second Oisinn arrives, it's definitely going to be a case of ditch the bitches. The saps are actually, like, in competition with each other to see who's going to end up being with him when he arrives. Sarah Jane, who's, like, repeating first year Law in Portobello, she goes, 'My cousin actually knows Oisinn's sister *really* well.' And the other bird, Bryana I think her name is, looks a bit like Naomi Watts, she goes, '*Hello?* I was in Irish college with Bláthnaid for two summers. She's one of my *best* friends.'

Chloë, roysh, who's, like, second year International Commerce with French in UCD and, like, really good friends with Sorcha she asks me what Oisinn had to eat and I tell her, roysh, about the cold custard, the beans, the Weetabix and the raw fish, the mince-and-onion pies and the strawberry jam, and she goes, 'OH! MY! GOD! that is SO gross. Can you *imagine* how many points that is?'

***

I bump into Erika in Finnegan's Break and she's, like, sipping a glass of hot water, roysh, I ask her what she's doing for the afternoon and she throws her eyes up to heaven and says she's going to the orthodontist, and I'm like, 'Have you heard I'm back playing serious rugby?' and she stubs out a Marlboro Light and goes, 'This affects me how?'

I ask her what time she's going to be finished at the dentist, and she says it's the orthodontist and I'm like, 'Same thing,' and she just looks me up and down and goes, 'Hordly.' Then she focks off.

I ring Oisinn on his mobile but there's, like, no answer. I ring Christian and it's, like, switched to his message-minder. I get the *Star Wars* theme tune and then it's like, 'A long time ago, in a Galaxy far, far away ... was a man with a message to leave. Beep.' I don't bother leaving one. I phone Fionn and he's not answering either. And it's obvious. Basically, the goys know about the match.

***

Simon is the first one over. Feel a bit sorry for Simon. He was captain of the S the year we won the cup and now he's the youngest ever captain of Castlerock RFC at, like, twenty years of age. The club is his life, and we're talking *totally*. But he comes up to me, roysh, and he goes, 'So it's true then?' and I'm like, 'What's true?' and he's there, 'You *are* stabbing us in the back.' I'm there, 'You are SUCH a sad bastard,' and he goes, 'I seriously didn't think you'd play. I knew you were training with UCD, but I presumed this was a game you'd skip. Out of loyalty. Looks like I was wrong,' and then he, like, pushes me in the chest, roysh, and calls me a turncoat and I switch my gearbag to my other shoulder, basically getting ready to deck the focker if he touches me again.

He goes, 'Whatever happened to Castlerock above all others? *"We'll shy from battle never. Ein volk, ein Reich, ein Rock"*?' I'm just there, 'We're not at school anymore, Simon. I'm playing for UCD now.'

He storts, like, shaking his head, roysh, going, 'No, no, no,' we're talking tears in the stupid sap's eyes here, the whole works, and he's giving it, 'You *never* leave Castlerock, Ross. And *it* never leaves you.'

I'm trying to reason with the goy, roysh, telling him that playing for UCD is, like, one of the conditions of my scholarship and shit, but he keeps bullshitting on about how pretty much all of my old team-mates off the S went on to sign for Castlerock and now, just when they're looking like pulling themselves out of the bottom four of the Second Division of the AIL, along comes one of their own to stab them in the back. He goes, 'You haven't played rugby all season, Ross,' and I'm there, 'That's why I've got a point to prove. Show them that the old magic is still there.' He goes, 'But why *now*? Why *this* game?' and I go, 'I've grown up, Simon. I think it's about time you did, too,' and I stort, like, heading towards the dressing-rooms and he shouts after me that I'm totalled, we're talking totally totalled and he's talking TOTALLY.

I get into the dressing-room and all the other goys are already there and Hendo, our coach, is giving this, like, major pep-talk about how we've, like, striven all season to finish mid-table and we can't let it slip through our fingers now.

I'm getting changed into my gear, roysh, when Hendo storts, like, looking at me and he goes, 'Any divided loyalties here to-day?' and I'm there, 'Are you talking to me?' and he goes, 'I saw you talking to Simon Wallace out there. Just want to know whether you're with us or against us today.' I'm just there, 'I'm kicking focking *orse* today,' and the whole dressing-room goes ballistic, roysh, everyone banging on the lockers, kicking the walls, giving it, 'YOU THE MAN, ROSS. YOU THE MAN.'

It's just like the old days, roysh, except that outside the door there's a couple of hundred Castlerock fans giving me total filthies when we go out, instead of, like, cheering me on, but I do see one friendly face in the crowd and it's, like, Christian, and I walk up to the dude and go, 'Hey, Christian. Looks like I'm public enemy number one around here.' He goes, 'Anyone hurts you out there today, man, and I'll focking kill them.' I go,

'I knew you'd understand. Us college heads have to stick to-gether, eh?' and he's there, 'No, that doesn't mean I'm on your side, Ross. I won't stand by and watch you get hurt, but that doesn't mean I agree with what you're doing.'

I'm like, 'What am I doing, Christian?' and he goes, 'You're turning to the Dark Side.' Then he unzips his jacket, roysh, we're talking his red-and-blue Armani sailing jacket here, and underneath it he's got his old Castlerock jersey on and he just looks me up and down and goes, 'The Emperor has won,' and he walks off.

I can see, like, Fionn and JP and Oisinn, all my so-called mates, over the other side of the pitch and they're, like, giving me filthies, and we're talking total filthies here.

Out on the pitch, roysh, all the old goys are there, all my old mates off the S, we're talking Eunan, Jonathon, Brad, Evan, Terry, Newer, Gicker, and I try to shut it out of my mind as the game storts. And I manage to do it pretty well, roysh, getting seven out of my eight kicks in the first half-an-hour and putting in what I have to say is an amazing tackle on Simon when he's, like, pretty much clean through for a certain try.

At half-time we're, like, 21-13 up, but the Castlerock goys stort to tackle me really hord in the second-half, there's total focking hatred there, and I sort of, like, go off my game a bit, miss a couple of, like, pretty easy kicks and suddenly Castlerock stort to get on top of us. Simon's having a focking stormer.

So to cut a long story short, roysh, two minutes to go and it's, like, 33-27 for them and we pretty much need a seven-pointer to win it. We're pressing, pressing, pressing in the last few minutes and suddenly the ball breaks to me, roysh, and I get over for a try roysh under the post and there's all this, like, booing roysh the way around the ground. All the goys on our team are coming up to me congratulating me, roysh, but also reminding me how important the conversion is, as if I need reminding. This is to win it.

As I'm walking back to take it, roysh, Christian runs onto the field, comes roysh up to me and goes, 'I know there's good in you. I've felt it,' and a couple of stewards come on and drag him away.

The kick is a piece of piss. I blow hord, take three steps backwards and three to the left, run my hand through my hair, blow hord again. I look over at Simon and Eunan, who have their hands on the crests of their jersey, we're talking tears in their focking eyes here. I look at Christian, roysh, who's got his eyes closed, like he's praying, probably trying to use the focking Force or something. I look at them all and think about all the great times we've had together and I think about how much I love those goys, without wanting to sound gay, like, or anything.

I run my hand through my hair and, like, blow hord again.

Then I send the kick high and wide and in the direction of the corner flag.

✳✳✳

Aoife says that Graham, some dickhead she knows from Annabel's, is SO good-looking that every girl in her year wants to be with him, but Sorcha says he is SUCH a Chandler when it comes to commitment, and I am already beginning to regret meeting the birds for lunch and my eyes, roysh, they keep, like, wandering over to where Erika is sitting with this really bored expression on her face, like she basically hates everyone at the table, no, everyone in the world.

I get out my phone, roysh, and text her and it's, like, **WAN 2 TLK?** and a couple of seconds later her phone beeps and she, like, reads the message and tells me, in front of everyone, that I'm a sad bastard. I can feel Sorcha staring at me, roysh, so I try to change the subject by asking Aoife how her brother's getting on with Clontorf, but before she can answer this waitress comes over and tells Emer that people aren't allowed to eat their own, like, food on the premises.

Emer just goes, '*Hello?* It's *only* a bag of popcorn,' and the waitress is like, 'It doesn't matter. House rules,' and Emer puts the bag away really slowly, roysh, while giving the waitress a total filthy and the waitress goes again, 'I'm sorry, it's house rules,' but Emer doesn't answer, just carries on staring her out of it.

The conversation suddenly moves on to some bird called Allison with two Ls, who's, like, second year Tourism in LSB and is, like, SO thin, according to Emer, and Aoife goes, 'OH! MY! GOD! did you see the dress she wore to Melissa Berry's 21st?' and Sorcha asks her what it was like and Aoife says it was a Chanel. Emer says that Allison is thinking of going to Australia for the year and so, apparently, are Caoimhe Kennedy, who I'm pretty sure I was with at the Traffic Light Ball, and Elaine Anders, who I've never focking heard of. Aoife tells Sorcha she should go to

Australia for the year herself and Sorcha tells Aoife she SO should go as well.

Emer was in Lillies on Saturday night, but there was, like, no one really in there, unless of course you call Amanda Byram and the lead singer from OTT someone, which she doesn't. Sorcha goes, 'OH MY GOD! I forgot to tell you, Claire is thinking of entering the Bray Festival Queen competition,' and Erika all of a sudden perks up and she goes, 'Oh, your little friend, the one who thinks coleslaw is cosmopolitan?' Everyone's looking for somewhere else to look. Erika goes, 'Yes, that would be SO her alroysh,' then she gets up, roysh, picks up her bags, we're talking Carl Scarpa, Morgan and Nue Blue Eriu, and just, like, walks out of the place, leaving her lunch on the table and her Marlboro Lights.

Aoife says that girl has SUCH an attitude problem and Sorcha tells her not to worry, she's sure Ross won't mind paying for her Caesar wrap, seeing as he's SO fond of her, and, to be honest, I've no problem with that at all. Emer says the new series of 'Ally McBeal' is SO not as good as the last one.

✸✸✸

The traffic on the Stillorgan dualler is a mare, and we are talking total here. I open the glove comportment, roysh, to get out my Eminem CD and it's, like, gone. So I ring the house, roysh, and the old man picks up the phone and he can tell from my voice that I'm seriously pissed off about something and he goes, 'I take it you've read it then?' Of course I'm like, '*What* are you focking talking about?' but he goes, 'To think I almost invited that man over here for New Year. I suppose he's never been a friend of schools rugby. We knew that.' I go, 'I don't even want to know what you are bullshitting on about. Just put the old dear on.'

So he gets her, roysh, and I'm like, 'Answer me one question and do *not* bullshit me. What have you done with my Eminem CD?' and she goes, 'I took it back to the shop, Ross. It was disgusting, some of the things he was singing about. It was eff this and you're an effing that, mother this and mother the other.' I'm like, 'It's none of your *focking* business what I listen to,' and she goes, 'You left it in the CD player in the kitchen, Ross. I thought it was my Celine Dion album. Delma was here for coffee.' And she's there giving it, 'I'm not the only one who brought it back, by the way. The young lady in the shop told me it's the most returned record they've ever sold. I would worry about the influence that that kind of thing might have on you, Ross.'

I'm like, 'Bitch, I'm a kill you,' and I hang up, roysh, and punch the *focking* dashboard and and and … FOCK*!*

And to cap it all the traffic is actually getting focking worse, and how many focking gears does that cor in front of me have? I turn on the radio, roysh, but – again – I can't get a decent song, it's all Christina Aguilera and Ronan focking Keating and I'm flicking from channel to channel, but it's like, 'normal lending criteria and terms and conditions apply', and 'regular savings and higher returns with personal investment plans', and 'help bridge the recruitment gap by skilling up your existing workforce'. 'And the slip light is out of action on the main streesh in

Bray and there's bad flooding around Baker's Coyner and electrical cables are dain on the Belgord Raid and there's the usual delays on all routes out of the city, including the Naas Raid, the Navan Raid and the South Circular Raid ...'

✳✳✳

Me, Christian and Oisinn, roysh, we're bored off our tits in the bor, so we head over to the Orts block, roysh, see if Fionn's around. Turns out he's got no lectures this afternoon but – get this, roysh – he's actually gone to a philosophy lecture, the dude's not even doing the course, roysh, but you know who is? Exactly. That focking kipper from Galway. He's giving her a rattle, no doubt about it. Me and the goy, roysh, we're curious, so we head into the lecture hall ourselves, sit down the back and OH! MY! GOD! I have never seen so many amazing-looking birds in my life. They're actually better looking than the birds on our course, which is saying something, roysh. I remember Fionn telling me before that all the, like, bimbos who do Orts always choose either philosophy or psychology because they think they pass for, like, depth, but I seriously didn't think there'd be this many crackers.

I turn around to Christian to tell him that if I could have a fourth shot at the Leaving, maybe aim for points this time rather than just trying to pass the thing, I'd try to end up in here. I go to tell Oisinn the same thing, roysh, but he's already talking to this bird beside him, Elinor I think her name is, I know her to see from Club Shoot Your Goo, looks a little bit like Maria Grazia Cucinotta, and I hear her asking Oisinn if he heard that Kelly is thinking of going to Australia for the year, and I wonder whether she's talking about Kelly who was in the Institute with us last year – tall bird, amazing bod, always has, like, sunglasses in her hair. Then I hear Oisinn asking her if she's wearing *Fifth Avenue* by Elizabeth Arden and it looks like he's clicked.

I still can't see Fionn. I'm looking around for him, roysh, and the lecturer's blabbing away, all I can basically hear is blah blah blah, but then I suddenly cop the fact, roysh, that everyone's looking at me and the lecturer's going, 'Well?' Of course I don't know what the story is here. I'm like, 'Sorry, what was the question again?' and he goes, 'I didn't ask you a question. I asked you to expound, for the rest of the class, if you'd be so kind, your understanding of the term metaphysics.'

Of course, I should tell the goy to go fock himself, roysh, but obviously I don't want to look stupid in front of the class, so I do what I always did at Castlerock, which is close my eyes, look as though I'm really in pain and keep going, 'Oh my God, I so know this. It's on the tip of my tongue,' but the focker lets me carry on doing this for, like, ten minutes before he finally throws the question to someone else.

He asks this bloke, roysh – he's a total howiya – and the goy goes, 'Well, metaphysics is one of de foyiv branches of philosophy. Dee udders are logic, ethics, aesthetics and epistemology. De term was coined by complete accident. It's de title of a buke written by Aristotle after he completed wurk on his *Physics,* and dis was sort of put at dee end of dat body of wurk. Now dat particular buke, *Physics*, dealt wit what you'd call dee observable world and its laws, whereas metaphysics deals wit de principles, meanings and structures dat underlie all observable reality. It's de investigation, by means of pew-er spekelation, of the nature of being, de cause, substance and de purpose of everyting.'

Of course I'm nodding through all of this, cracking on that that's what I was going to say. The lecturer goy's like, 'So metaphysics might ask, what?' and this cream cracker goes, 'What are space and toyim? What is an actual ting and how is it diffordent from an idea? Are humans free to decide der own fate? Is der a God dat's put everyting in motion?' The lecturer goes, 'And because the answers to such questions cannot be arrived at by observation, experience, or experiment ...' and the skanger goes, '... dee must be products of de reasoning moyind.'

Everyone's impressed, you can basically tell. I turn around to this bird behind me – the image of Asia Argento – and I go, 'Bit obvious when you're given time to answer,' then I turn around to Christian and I go, 'They're letting skobies into UCD now? When the fock did this happen?' and Christian shakes his head and I go, 'Let's get on the Internet, check out the website. There must be something in the terms and conditions about this.'

Then up the front, roysh, we suddenly hear all this, like, sniggering and there's these four Nure goys we know – they're sound even though they're, like, Gick – and they're sitting behind this bird in a pink Hobo top. Anyway, they've slipped something into her hood, a photograph or something. Of course we find out later, roysh, that the goys had gone on a knacker holiday, we're talking a real 'Ibiza Uncovered' job, after the Leaving, roysh, and the picture was of Kenny's dick, which the rest of the goys took when he was locked. So this little item ends up in this bird's hood, roysh, and of course she's the last one in the whole focking lecture hall to cop it, but when she finally realises there's something going on, she reaches back, pulls the picture out, jumps up and goes, '*Oh my God! Oh my God! Oh my God!*' and pegs it out of the place, basically in total shock.

Then it's, like, high-fives all round.

✳✳✳

To whom it may concern,

Many thanks for your recent letter and the small piece of masonry, which, a cursory inspection would suggest, is indeed a feather from one of *Eros*'s wings. Thanks also for the kind offer to cut your ransom demand by some fifty per cent.

Unfortunately, we still do not have the finance available to get involved with this project and this will remain the case until we contact you again. However, the summer is approaching and I am confident you will find casual work that will help alleviate whatever financial difficulties you are currently experiencing.

Apologies for the delay in replying, incidentally. I was off on paternity leave for four weeks. My wife gave birth to our third recently, a boy. He weighed eleven pounds at birth. Mother and baby are both well.

Love to *Eros*, if you'll pardon the Classics Department in-

[signature: Francis Hird]

Francis Hird,
Classics Department, UCD

***

I'm on the 46A, roysh, *trying* to have a conversation with Fionn, when all of a sudden we're going through Stillorgan, roysh, and all these knobs from Coláiste Iosagáin get on and stort, like, talking in Irish, or that's what Fionn said it was anyway. It's, like, SO head-wrecking. I'm there, 'What the *fock* are they trying to say?' and Fionn goes, 'They're talking about the teachers' strike,' and if that's the case I can't understand why they look so focking miserable. They actually seem disappointed that the Leaving might not be going ahead, the sad bastards.

I'm just wishing there was a focking lecturers' strike. I am SO going to have to repeat at this stage it's not funny, which is why I'm going out on the lash tonight, to try to forget about it. I'm telling Fionn that I'm SO not cancelling the States, roysh, I'm going on a J1er one way or the other and I'm not coming back to sit repeats, no *focking* way, I'll probably end up repeating the whole year instead, maybe actually going to a few lectures next year.

I'm trying to get my head around all of this, roysh, but all around me it's all, *Tá me, tá me, conas atá tú*, blah blah blah, and I turn around to these two knobs behind me and I go, 'There's no focking Leaving Cert this year. Get over it,' and one of them, roysh, she goes, 'Sorry, would you mind your own business, please?' And quick as a flash, roysh, I turn around and go, 'Only if you get a life,' which I'm pretty happy with. I'm like, 'Talking in that stupid focking language on the bus. School's over. *Hello?*'

I turn around, roysh, expecting Fionn to, like, back me up, but instead he's chatting away to these other two birds in front of us, telling them that it's the students he feels sorry for and that he's thinking of applying to become an exam supervisor and the birds think this is 'SO cool', and the goy thinks he's a stud.

I don't know which of the two he's trying to be with, roysh, but I can't watch and I decide to get off in, like, Donnybrook and see are any of the goys in Kiely's. As I'm heading down the stairs, roysh, I can hear him arranging to meet the girls in some bor in town after the Institute. The focker hasn't even noticed I've gone.

✳✳✳

Sophie phones me up, bawling her eyes out, roysh, telling me she failed philosophy and her parents are going to go ballistic and OH! MY! GOD! her old man is SO not going to give her the money to go skiing now, and it's all because of that complete dickhead of a lecturer who set *such* a hord paper, everyone said so, even Wendy, whoever the fock she is, and he was *such* an orsehole to her when she went to him to try to get her grade changed. And I can just picture her going in to see him in a little titty-top, trying to sweet-talk the goy. She tells me she SO needs someone to talk to and can I call over, roysh, and I'm pretty much certain I'm going to get my bit here, so I go, 'Is the bear a Catholic?'

I'm actually on the way back from Christian's gaff, roysh, and I'm pretty much home, but I turn the cor around and head for Glenageary. *Oh* my God, she goes, it wasn't like she was looking for a 2.1, or even a 2.2, all she wanted was a scabby pass and he was too much of a focking orsehole to give her that and – OH! MY! GOD! – now her points have, like, *totally* gone out the window because she's eaten, like, three bars of Dairy Milk, which is eighteen points in itself and that's all she's supposed to have in an entire, like, day and that's not even counting the Weight Watchers' lasagne, we're talking the beef one, not the vegetarian, which is, like, five-and-a-half, the four pieces of Ryvita, which is, like, two, and the bowl of Fruit and Fibre, which is, like, one-and-a-half, or five-and-a-half if you have it with full milk, which she did.

She goes, OH! MY! GOD! It was bad enough failing without going into that *dickhead* and making a complete tit of herself. She tells me she asked the goy what he would suggest she do, roysh, and he told her to, like, set her sights lower, maybe get a job with FM104 or one of the other radio stations, driving one of those big four-wheel drives around town. He said he was sure that a girl with her talent would be snapped up quickly.

I give her the old Ross O'Carroll-Kelly Hug, one hand stroking her hair, sort of, like, consoling her, and the other hand on her orse. Not blowing my own trumpet or anything, but I don't think I need to spell out what happened next.

CHAPTER SIX
'Ross has, like, SUCH commitment problems.'
Discuss.

'Ross, I cannot believe you're wearing a polo-neck in this weather. And a *black* polo-neck at that.' The old dear says this to me at the dinner table, roysh, and I'm just there, you know, yeah *what*ever, but the stupid bitch won't let it go, roysh, it's like she *knows* the focking reason I'm wearing it and she's trying to, like, embarrass the shit out of me. She's giving it, 'The hottest day of the year and you decide to wear something like that. In the middle of May. Charles, say something to Ross, will you?' The old man is just, like, staring at the back page of the *Sunday Indo*, going, 'Kerrigan … what's he *after?*'

The old dear goes, 'Put away the paper, Darling. Come on, it's salmon-en-croute,' and she kisses him on the forehead and I go, 'You two stort that lovey-dovey shit again and I'm getting my own gaff. You make me want to vom, you know that?' She totally ignores this, goes, 'Come on, Charles. Don't let that man upset you,' then turns to me and she's like, 'and Ross, why don't you go upstairs and change into a T-shirt. I've ironed your

Ralph-what-do-you-call-it. Much more appropriate for a day like today. Get some colour into you,' and I'm just there, 'Will you just shut the *fock* up going on about it. You are SUCH a knob, do you know that?'

I get up from the table and, like, storm out of the house and I get into the cor and check out my neck in the rear-view. There's only two types of people who wear polo-necks – one, total knobs, and two, anyone unlucky enough to have a big dirty Denis on their neck.

This Monday-night-in-Peg's thing basically has to stop. I should have seen it coming, of course, but I was completely off my face, bank-holiday weekend, roysh, why not? Originally went out for a few scoops, ended up, like, knocking back beers until, whatever, maybe two in the morning, and what with one thing and another I ended up being with Auveen, this total babe who's, like, second year Orts, roysh, and a little bit like Piper Perabo, except with, like, braces on her teeth.

Anyway, roysh, the goys – well, Fionn mostly – he calls her The Hound of the Baskervilles because when she's, like, shit-faced, roysh, she basically storts, like, sucking the neck off you. Of course, Monday night, I'm too off my face to fight her off, so I wake up this morning, roysh, in Christian's gaff – Ailesbury Road, focking amazing pad – and I am absolutely reeking of, like, toothpaste. Christian comes into the room, roysh, and I'm like, 'What the fock is that smell?' Of course, he goes, 'You must rest. You've had a busy day,' and I'm like, 'Will you quit it with that *Star Wars* bullshit. Why am I smelling of toothpaste?' and he's, like, all offended.

He goes, 'I put it on your neck last night. To try to get rid of the ...' and the whole night suddenly comes rushing back to me. Of course, it had to happen on the one weekend of the year when the sun is, like, splitting the trees, and I am focking burning up in the cor as I head for Kiely's and, by the sounds of it, roysh, the weather's going to hold for, like, half the focking summer. Some knob on the radio says there's a heatwave on the way because, I don't know, Fungie the Dolphin is wearing shades and a focking sombrero.

All I can say is that I'm glad I'm heading to the States in June, by which time the thing will probably be yellow, or some focking colour. I pork the cor around the corner, roysh, take fifty notes out of the old Drinklink and hit the battle-cruiser, feeling really, like, self-conscious and wondering whether the focking thing is visible. I get a pint in and head over to the goys. Zoey and Aoife are sitting with them and they're, like, locked in conversation, which is sort of, like, unusual because those two usually hate each other's guts.

Aoife asks Zoey why she didn't go out last night and Zoey says she did, roysh, and Aoife goes, 'Oh my God, how come you're looking so well then?' and Zoey says it's Radiant Touch and Aoife goes, '*Oh my God*, YSL,' and Zoey nods and says, OH MY GOD, it is *such* a life-saver.

Judging from his body language, JP is going to try to be with her, roysh, while Oisinn is definitely going to chance his orm with Aoife. JP asks Zoey whether she was in Reynards last night and she says no, she was in Lillies, and Aoife asks whether Bono and Matt Damon really were in there and she says no, that was only a rumour, and that the only famous people in there were two newsreaders off TV3 and the Carter Twins. Then she says she's going to the toilet, roysh, and when she's gone Aoife says, 'OH! MY! GOD! Not meaning to be, like, a bitch or anything, but Zoey looks like *shit*.'

When Zoey comes back from the toilet, roysh, she looks at me and goes, 'Oh my God, Ross, what the *fock* are you wearing?' and everyone looks at me, roysh – we're talking Fionn, JP, Simon, everyone – and I'm wondering whether they know what happened, whether Christian has, like, told them. I presume he hasn't and I just go, 'It's a polo-neck. What's the big deal?' and Aoife goes, 'You do look a bit of a knob in it, Ross.' I tell her that polo-necks are in and Zoey thinks for a minute, roysh, and goes, '*Oh my God*, they are. I read that in *Marie Claire*. They're the new, em, shirts, I think.'

I can see Simon sort of, like, sniggering, roysh, and also JP, who I think was actually in Peg's last night, can't remember, but I'm pretty sure now he knows the story, and basically all of a sudden, roysh, he tells me that I look like the goy off the Milk Tray ad and everyone storts breaking their shites laughing.

And then Fionn, roysh, he goes, 'And all because the lady loves ... Ross's neck.' And Fionn high-fives JP, and JP high-fives Christian, and Simon high-fives ... Let's just say that everyone high-fived everyone else.

Focking dickheads.

✳✳✳

Amanda, roysh, this bird who, I have to say, has the total hots for me – a friend of Eanna's sister – I saw her this morning at the bus stop in, like, Stillorgan, waiting for the 46A, so I pull over, roysh, ask her does she want a lift into college and she's like, '*Oh* my God, you are SUCH a dorling,' and I'm there, 'Hey, it's a pleasure to have such a beautiful girl in my car,' playing it totally cool like Huggy Bear.

We're getting on really well, roysh. She tells me all about this huge row she's just had with her old pair because her old man – a complete tosser apparently – is refusing to pay her cor insurance, and then about some friend of hers who's on the permanent guest list in Reynards. Anyway, to cut a long story short, roysh, we get to UCD and she says she so has to, like, buy me lunch later to say thank you for the lift and for listening to her problems, basically giving it loads, TOTALLY gagging for me, so I arrange to meet her in the Orts block, roysh, at, like, half-twelve.

She's in first year, we're talking Philosophy and, like, Linguistics, which is what she had that morning. I know because I basically just hung around waiting for her, roysh, but then I got bored so I ended up going into her lecture. She's sitting in the back row, roysh, with a couple of her mates, one of them I recognise from Knackery Doo, the old Club d'Amour, and she sort of, like, mouths the word 'Hi!' to me and I scooch up beside her.

The lecturer, roysh, he is SO boring it's unbelievable. He's like, 'In English, a double negative is a positive. In some languages, including Russian, the inverse is also the case, but there is no incidence in the English language where a double positive forms a negative.' I'm like, 'Yeah, roysh!' And everyone breaks their shites laughing, and I didn't even realise I'd, like, said it so loud, and I look at Amanda and her head is turned the other way and I can hear her going, '*Oh my God, oh my God, oh my God*, I am SO embarrassed.'

❋❋❋

I'm in my room, roysh, listening to a few sounds, bit of Eminem, bit of the Snoopster, when I'm suddenly, like, thirsty and I hit the kitchen for glass of Coke. When I get there, roysh, I'm just like, *What* are these two focking weirdoes up to now? The old man's standing outside the laundry room, roysh, holding the door shut and the old dear's standing behind him with the wok and she's holding it up in the air, roysh, as if she's getting ready to, like, whack someone over the head with it. I just ignore the two of them and open the fridge. The old man's shouting through the door, giving it, 'The guards are on their way. They'll put a stop to your fun and games, with a capital S, you mark my words.' The old dear goes, 'We're taxpayers,' and the old man looks at her over his shoulder and he's like, 'That's not *technically* true, Darling.' The old dear goes, 'And don't you touch my underwear in there. Unless you want another ten years on your sentence, you monster.'

Of course, the curiosity is storting to, like, get to me at this stage, roysh, so I go, 'What the fock are you two on?' The old man's like, 'Ross, you *are* home. Didn't you hear your mother screaming?' I'm there, 'Considering I was listening to music in my focking room, no, I didn't. What were you screaming about, you stupid wagon? Another halting site planned for Foxrock?' The old man goes, 'Would it were that simple, Ross. No, we've got an intruder. Your mother caught him in the laundry. In the *laundry*, if you please.'

I go, 'If there *is* an intruder, and the Feds are on their way, why isn't he trying to get out of there?' The old pair look at each other, roysh, and the old man's like, 'There's a point, Darling. How hard did you hit him with that thing?' She goes, 'Pretty hard. He was naked, Charles. Kept waving his ... thing at me. Oh the thoughts of it.' The old man goes, 'It'll be a bloody nuisance if he's dead. The police'll probably try to blame *us*. You saw that chap in England. Killed those four yobbos who were trying to steal his lawnmower and suddenly *he's* the one in the wrong.' She's like, 'What are you saying, Charles?' and he goes, 'There's all kinds of loopholes in the law to protect these people, Fionnuala. We're going to have to dispose of the body.' The old dear storts crying, roysh – the stupid focking sap – and the old man goes, 'Hennessy knows people who can take care of it.'

I'm bored listening to this crap, roysh, so I just push the old man out of the way and shoulder-charge the door and it, like, flings open, roysh, and what do I see – I should have focking guessed – *Eros* lying facedown on the floor with a big focking chunk, about the size of a wok, taken out of the back of his head. I break my balls laughing, roysh, while the old man leans up against the wall and goes, 'Thank heavens. Thank heavens for that.'

I stand the statue up again and ask Dick-features if he has any Pollyfilla, but he goes, 'What's that blasted thing doing here, Ross?' I'm there, 'If you must know, I stole it from the Classics Museum. Me and Oisinn are trying to extort a grand out of

UCD.' The old man goes, 'I say, what fun.' The next thing, roysh, the doorbell rings and, of course, it's the Feds, so I have to, like, stick the thing in the cupboard under the stairs.

The old pair go to the door and I can hear the old man giving it, 'Sorry, chaps. False alarm,' and the Feds saying something about wasting Garda time and the old man going, 'Well, I presume that's what they want me to pay my taxes for,' and he slams the door. And the old dear, roysh, she goes, 'Gosh, Charles, you sounded just like Spencer Tracy then.' The old man's like, 'I did?' and she's there, 'Yes. In *Bad Day at Black Rock*. Let's go upstairs, Darling.' I'm there, 'Hey, cut that shit out. You two doing it? The focking thought of it makes me wanna borf.'

The statue has got to go. I phone the goys and tell them.

✷✷✷

Still no word from, like, Sorcha.

✷✷✷

The old man's solicitor recommended that he reach a settlement with the Revenue Commissioners, roysh, so he's heading out to Portmarnock to discuss it with him over an early-morning round of golf. Anyway, roysh, he asks me to drive him, obviously planning to have a few scoops, and I tell him it's no problem at all, even though it sticks in my throat to be nice to the focker, but I'm heading off to the States in a few weeks and I'm gonna need seven or eight hundred notes to bring with me.

So there we are, driving along, roysh, and the old man's boring the ears off me, giving it, 'Hennessy wants me to settle for a hundred thousand pounds, Ross. Or a Rezoning, as he calls it. You know how he likes to joke about this tribunal nonsense,' and I'm seriously fighting the urge to call him a wanker and tell him to shut the fock up. Being up at, like, seven o'clock on a Saturday morning is bad enough without having to listen to his bullshit.

So anyway, roysh, basically what happens is that I end up breaking a red light at the bottom of, like, Stradbrook Road and suddenly, roysh, this old dear in a red Subaru Signet comes around the corner and, like, ploughs into the side of me. It's a good job I'm driving the old man's Volvo and not my Golf GTI because this thing has side-impact bors, it's like a focking tank, and even after the crash there's fock-all wrong with it. Which is more than can be said for the other cor, which is, like, pretty badly damaged and shit. The second it happens, roysh, the old man goes, 'Leave the talking to me, Ross. The first line here is all-important.'

The two of us get out and walk up to the driver's side of the other cor, roysh, and the bird winds down the window and straight away the old man goes, 'Is your neck alright?' and the woman, roysh, she's a total AJH, she goes, 'Me neck's grand.' The old man turns around to me and goes, 'You heard that, Ross. Nothing wrong with her neck. Little trick Hennessy taught me. Cuts off any possible spurious claim for whiplash at source,' and then he, like, whispers, 'Don't get me wrong, I've nothing against working-class people. Quote unquote. Hit one of them in your car, though, and one visit to their solicitor later, they're wearing a surgical collar and trying to sting you for fifty grand.'

The old man goes to the creamer, 'Well, let's be thankful there's no real damage done here. We'll bid you *adieu,*' and he goes to walk off. Of course the slapper's like, 'No damage? What about me car?' and she gets out. *Holy fock!* Leggings are SO focking unattractive. Why *do* poor people have to wear them? She's pointing to the front of the cor – a Subaru Signet, for fock's sake – and she storts getting a bit smart then, roysh, going, 'Someone's going to have to pay for this,' then basically accuses me of breaking a red light, which I totally deny, even though it's true.

The old man, you have to admire him even though he's a total knob, he goes, 'Am I to take it from your tone that you intend to claim from my insurance company for this accident?' and the woman's like, 'Course we bleedin' do.'

I go, 'Easier than holding us up with a syringe, I suppose,' and she's like, 'What d'ye mean by dat?'

Never mentioned it before, roysh, but she's got her daughter sitting in the cor beside her and she's an even bigger knick-knack than her old dear, and of course she decides to get involved herself then. She, like, rips open the cor door and storts giving me loads – ice blue denim mini and black tights, very focking tasteful – saying we better hand over our inshoorice details or there'll be moorder, fookin moorder. She says there'll be even wooorse if she misses her floy t'Englind, so there will.

I'm just there giving it, 'Fock off back to Knackeragua,' but the old man turns around to me and goes, 'Let me handle this, Kicker. I haven't kept my insurance premium so low for so many years without knowing a trick or six.'

He turns around to the daughter, roysh – rings all over her

fingers, looks like she's focking mugged Doctor Dre – and he asks her what time her flight is at, and she says that she's supposed to be checkin' in at half bleedin' seven, so she is. The old man looks at his watch and he goes, 'It's already a quarter past seven, you do know that, don't you?' and the daughter goes, 'So bleedin' wha'?' The old man – he's loving this, roysh – he's like, 'What I'm saying is that you're late for your flight. And you were obviously in too much of a hurry to watch the road in front of you.'

And she just loses the plot then, telling the old man he's this and that, then actually saying the crash happened because I was on my mobile. Basically, roysh, I wasn't on my mobile when I crashed the light, but I *was* checking my messages to see if Sorcha had replied to my text, though I wasn't going to admit that, not with the old man running circles around them.

He goes, 'I'm not saying that you were speeding to try to make the flight. That's just how a judge might look at it.' She hasn't a focking clue what to say then, the daughter. The mother, roysh, she goes, 'A judge?' and the old man goes, 'But of course. If you think you're sending my premium soaring through the roof for this bucket of bolts, you can think again.'

He goes, 'You're no stranger to the court system, I'd wager. Spot of shoplifting, perhaps. Handling stolen credit cards, that type of thing. Off to England then, were we?' Mummy skanger goes, '*She* is. She's off to see her fella,' and daughter skanger goes, 'Tell dem nuttin', Ma.'

The old man goes, 'Bit of a send-off last night then?' and the mother, roysh, she shrugs her shoulders and goes, 'The local,'

CLARKE.

real defensive, like, and she's there, 'Have ye a problem wit dat?' obviously not realising that the old man's going to blow her out of the water in a minute. He goes, 'Had a few drinks, did we? A few pints of this *lager*, perchance?' She goes, 'I know what yer getting at. I only had tree glasses,' but the old man's like, 'Did you know you could still actually be over the limit?'

The daughter, roysh, she jumps back in then, giving it, 'Are you sayin' me ma's locked?' and he goes, 'I'm not in any position to judge that. I'm going to call the Gardaí. They can breathalyse her.'

He storts, like, punching the number into his phone, roysh, then he stops and goes, 'There is another alternative, of course. You could get back in your little banger there and be on your way.'

Who knows what the Feds have on these two, roysh, because they only think about it for, like, ten seconds, roysh, then they fock off, calling me and the old man every name under the sun as they get back into their little shit-bucket and fock off.

The old man asks me whether I think he should still call the cops, roysh, maybe report them for leaving the scene of an accident, just so they don't have any second thoughts about claiming. It's tempting, roysh, but in the end I tell him not to bother.

***

I would SO love to know what Sorcha's game is. She hasn't returned any of my texts for the past, like, two weeks, roysh, then she sends me one today and it's like, **drnk 2moro queens @ 8**. She is SO focking with my head at the moment.

***

Sorcha gives me this look, roysh, we're talking total disgust here, and she goes, 'Spare me the character dissection,' and I go, 'I only asked what you thought of my baseball cap,' and she goes, 'Can we *please* change the subject?'

I nod at the borman, roysh, and he takes this as a signal that we want the same again and the lounge girl brings over a pint of Ken and a Diet Coke. I'm there, 'It's really nice to see you, Sorcha,' and she goes, 'We're friends. When Dawson and Joey broke up, that didn't stop them having their movie nights, did it?' and I'm like, 'Course not,' even though I haven't a focking clue what she's talking about.

She tells me she's, like, so chilled out these days and it's SO because of the music she's been listening to. She tells me she had Tchaikovsky's 'Scene from Swan Lake' on in the cor on the way in and Bizet's 'Au Fond Du Temple Saint', and even though the third CD takes a lot of getting used to, she's really storted getting into Strauss, Holst, Prokofiev and Copland. I tell her I've been mostly listening to Eminem, the new U2 album and a bit of Oasis, and she tells me my taste is SO up my orse it's unbeliev-able, and she offers to lend me her *Saving Private Ryan* soundtrack, which she says is SO easy to listen to and SUCH a good way to get into classical music, especially 'Hymn To The Fallen', 'Wade's Death' and 'Omaha Beach', and I'm there going, 'Cool.'

She stubs out a Marlboro Light, lights up another. I'm there trying to think of a way to bring up Australia, roysh, to ask her not to go. She goes, 'You heard about Sophie's exams then?' and I'm like, 'Yeah, she was a bit freaked.' She goes, 'She said you called over to her that night. Said you were very nice to her,' and I'm like, 'Em, yeah.' She goes there, 'How nice, Ross?' And quick as a flash, roysh, I'm there, 'What do you care?' and she storts breaking her shite laughing and goes, 'Don't flatter yourself, Ross. Do *not* flatter yourself.'

She takes off her scrunchy, slips it onto her wrist, shakes her hair free and then smoothes it back into a low ponytail again, puts it back in the scrunchy and then pulls five or six, like, strands of hair loose again. I go, 'So you're still heading to Australia?' and she's like, 'In two weeks.' I'm there, 'With what's-his-face?' and she goes, 'Cillian. You know his name's Cillian.' I go, 'What's he like, this goy?' and Sorcha goes, '*Amazing*. He works for PriceWaterhouse Coopers,' and I'm like, 'Just want to make sure he's treating you properly, that's all,' and Sorcha's there, 'For as long as we've known each other, Ross, you've treated me like shit. Why do you all of a sudden care?' There's no answer to that. I'm there, 'I don't suppose–' and she goes, 'I'd cancel my plans if you asked me? No, Ross. I wouldn't.'

Sorcha changes the subject, asks me if I heard about Sadbh and Macker and I tell her no, and she says they broke up, which is, like, *such* a pity, she goes, because they looked SO cute together, even though they SO weren't suited, and I can't work out whether Sadbh and Macker are real people, or, like, television characters, it's so hord to tell with Sorcha, but I agree with her because when we're getting on like this she is just SO easy to talk to.

I ask her whether she wants another drink and she says it's

her round and when she comes back from the bor she asks me how Christian is. I tell her his old man's moved out and she goes, 'Mum said he's living in Dalkey, in the aportment they own.' I'm like, 'Christian won't go and see him,' and she goes, 'That is SO unfair on his dad. From what I hear, his mum wasn't exactly blameless,' and I'm like, 'What is that supposed to mean?' maybe a bit too defensive. Sorcha goes, 'I'm just *saying*, Ross, that it takes two people to make a relationship and two to break one.'

When I think about Christian, it makes me sad. I'd love to have a big, deep conversation with the dude, but I find it, like, hord to talk to goys about shit like that when I'm sober, roysh, and whenever I'm locked Christian is always twice as bad as me and pretty much impossible to talk to. I've thought about sending him maybe, like, a text message, sort of like, **R U OK?** but it just doesn't, like, seem enough or something. I'm there, 'The States will take his mind off it, I think.'

She tells me he's SO lucky to have a friend like me and it's nice to hear, even if it is total bullshit. I tell her she's looking well and she tells me that's the third time I've said that tonight.

✳✳✳

The old dear asks me whether it was me who broke her John Rocha signature votive, roysh, and I'm like, '*Oh my God,* you are SUCH an orsehole. I cannot wait to get out of this country.'

✳✳✳

I was never so loaded in all my life, roysh, as I was when me and Oisinn muscled in on the fake ID racket in UCD. The whole of, like, first year was heading to the States for the summer, roysh, and they all needed fake driving licences and shit to get served over there. Of course we end up totally up to our tits in work so it was, like, no surprise to me that I didn't make it into any of my summer exams, although it was to the Dean of our course, who is SO trying to get me focked out of college it's unbelievable. I'm like, 'Hey, had things to do. People to see,' and he goes, 'I think you need to sit down and re-evaluate whether you're serious about a career in Sports Management or not,' and I'm just there, 'Get real, will you?'

I basically didn't give a fock, roysh, because I knew I was going to have to repeat anyway and suddenly I've got, like, eight hundred bills in my pocket and it's, like, money for old rope. A couple of knobs from Ag. Science were actually doing it first, roysh, but Oisinn goes up to them in the bor – they were, like, playing Killer – and he goes, 'You the goys dealing in the fake IDs?' Oisinn had picked up a focking pool cue at this stage, roysh, and the goys are like, gicking themselves, giving it, 'What do you mean, fake IDs?'

Oisinn goes, 'Maybe I'm not making myself clear enough. What I'm asking you is whether they're your flyers I saw stuck up in the Orts block? Outside Theatre L?' You can see, roysh, that these goys are totally bricking themselves, and we're talking TOTALLY. One of them goes, 'Yeah … em, they're ours,' and Oisinn's there, 'Well, what I'm telling you goys now is that there's a couple of new faces on the scene.' He points over at me and I'm, like, trying to look really hord, even though there's no need really because Oisinn is such a big bastard he could handle all of them on his own if he had to.

He goes, 'Time to take early retirement, boys. Enjoyed it while it lasted though, haven't you?' I turn around, roysh – and I have to say I pretty much surprise myself with this one – I go, 'Unless you want to face … involuntary liquidation.'

So basically that's it, roysh. We put the word around the Orts block that we're the men to see for all your fake ID requirements, then spend most of March and April in the bor, playing pool, knocking back beers and taking orders from people.

And fock, I've never been so popular in my whole life. Everyone *loved* us. The babes would come in, roysh, and we'd be giving it loads, looking at their passport photographs and going, 'You look too well in this picture to put it on a passport,' and, 'You must do modelling, do you?'

We're talking The Palace, Annabel's, Mono, I have never seen so much action in my life and, like, not being big-headed or anything, but that's really focking saying something. We'd get bored snogging one bird, roysh, and the next one was already queuing up behind her.

The goys loved us too, and I don't mean in a gay way. We were, like, celebrities. I'm walking through the library, or I'm heading down to 911 for the rolls and total strangers are coming up to me and high-fiving me, telling me they're getting the shekels together and they'll be in touch.

And I'm like, 'Yeah, *what*ever.'

Me and Oisinn, for six weeks we're, like, totally Kool and the Gang. And it wasn't only respect, roysh, there was a bit of fear thrown in as well. Every time Oisinn would hand over an order, he'd go, 'You breathe our names to the NYPD and you're fish food. *Capisce?*'

Sometimes, for a laugh, roysh, we'd print the words, *Póg mo thóin*, in, like, really official-looking writing on the fake driving licences, roysh. *Póg mo thóin* is actually Irish for All Cops Are Bastards, which basically completely rips the piss out of them without them actually knowing. Everyone loved that little touch. They were like, 'OH! MY! GOD!'

The work was a piece of piss. Oisinn, who knows a bit about computers, he downloads this thing off the internet, roysh, said it was a template for a driving licence, and he gives it to me on, like, a disk. So I go home, roysh, get onto the old man's computer, add in the customer's name, date of birth and all that shit, print it out, Pritt Stick the photograph onto it, then take them down to Keeva, this bird I know who works in the local video shop and she, like, laminates the thing.

We didn't cut her in on any of the profits. Oisinn said it was to protect her, roysh – he really gets off on that whole gangster thing – but the real reason was that she didn't want any money. Not being vain here, roysh, but the girl did it for love. She's been mad into me for years, ever since transition year actually when we both did our work experience in her old man's architect's firm. She's actually pretty alroysh lookswise, a little bit like Jennifer Love Hewitt, from a distance.

So for six weeks, roysh, me and Oisinn, well, we have it all. We're talking money. We're talking babes. We're talking fame. But all good things have to come to an end. As Christian always says, there's always a bigger fish. So this day, roysh, we're sitting in the bor, knocking back a few beers with this goy from second year Law, who we brought on the lash for being our five-hundredth customer, when all of a sudden these five Chinese goys come in and say they want a word with us.

Oisinn plays it totally Kool and the Gang, roysh, telling me he'll handle this on his own, then following the goys over to a table in the corner and talking for, like, five or ten minutes. Then the Chinese goys fock off.

Oisinn comes back over, roysh, takes a long swig out of his bottle of Probably and goes, 'We're folding the business, Ross,' and of course I'm like, 'Who were those goys? And why did they all have their little fingers missing?' He goes, 'Why do you think, Ross?' and I go, '*Oh* my God, they're not from Newtownmountkennedy, are they?' He shakes his head and goes, 'We're not talking genetics here, Ross. Those goys are Triads.' I'm like, 'Triads! *Fock!* He gets three more beers in and goes, 'You don't fock with those goys.'

I'm there, 'Good while it lasted though, wasn't it?' and he just, like, stares off into space. Eventually he goes, 'Involuntary liquidation. I liked that. Have to hand it to you, Ross, you're a stylish bastard.'

✳✳✳

I meet Chloë in the Frascati Shopping Centre, roysh, and I ask her if she's going to Sorcha's going-away and she says OH! MY! GOD! she is, she SO is. She asks me whether I went out at the weekend and I tell her I was in Annabel's and she goes, *Oh my God*, she was in The George and she had the most amazing time, and she went with Julian and Kevin, two friends of hers who, she says, are *actually* gay, but they're, like, really, really good friends of hers, and that's the thing about gay goys, they're, like, so easy to talk to and she says that even though she's not, like, gay herself, roysh, going to The George is *such* a good night out if you're a girl, because you're not, like, getting constantly hassled by goys all night, and I'm thinking, You should be so focking lucky.

***

Sorcha has her going-away porty, roysh, and – typical of the Lalors – it's a big, fock-off, black-tie affair in Killiney Golf Club, we're talking free bor, the whole lot. Anyway, roysh, I only found out the night before that my old pair were, like, invited as well and of course I went ballistic. I'm there going, How the fock am I going to score with the old man and the old dear in the same room? I'm like, 'You're not *actually* thinking of going, are you?' and the old dear's there, 'Mr and Mrs Lalor want us there. They're friends of ours, Ross,' and then she's like, 'I hope you've bought Sorcha something nice,' and I go, 'What I bought Sorcha is my business,' which basically means I bought her fock-all, because I totally forgot, what with me going to the States in a couple of weeks and having to go to the embassy to sort out my visa and shit.

So I head out to Stillorgan that afternoon, roysh, and I end up getting her a fake Burberry bag in Dunnes, which is a bit scabby I know, but I only have, like, ten bills to spend, and I don't want to break into my America money.

That night I meet the goys in the Druid's Chair for a few scoops beforehand, roysh, and then we head down to the golf club, and there's Sorcha's old pair at the door of the function room, roysh, welcoming everyone as they arrive, and Sorcha's sister, Afric, or Orpha, or whatever the fock name she has, she's collecting all the presents and making a list of who gave what, which will no doubt be discussed in detail at the Lalor breakfast table tomorrow morning.

I'm, like, standing in the queue behind this bird, Becky, roysh, who's, like, second year Commerce in UCD, a little bit like Jaime Pressly when she's wearing her contacts, and she's says she's, like, SO bursting to go to the toilet, roysh, and she asks me to mind her place in the queue for her and her present. A big fock-off present it is as well. So she goes off looking for the jacks, roysh, and I'm standing there with this little scabby present from me and this, like, massive one from Becky, and all of a sudden I'm at, like, the top of the queue and Becky still isn't back, so I switch the two cords, put her one with my present and my one with hers.

Sorcha's old dear air-kisses me, roysh, and looks over her shoulder to some friend of hers, maybe from the ladies' golf club, and goes, 'This is Ross. He was on the Castlerock team that won the cup,' and Sorcha's old man shakes my hand, real, like, formal and shit, and then Afric – I think that's her name – kisses me on the cheek and storts giving me the serious eyes, obviously jealous that her sister's getting all the attention tonight and deciding that being with me again would be the best way to piss her off. I hand her Becky's present, roysh, and I go, 'This is from me,' and she's there, '*Oh* my God, what is it?' and obviously I haven't a focking bog, but I go, 'Something special,' and she's like, 'Full of surprises, aren't you, Ross?'

And she looks at the other present, roysh, the wrapping paper all ripped and just, like, turns her nose up at it. The goys were, like, focking the thing around on the way down from the Druid's Chair, practicing their line-outs with it and shit. I'm like, 'That one's from Becky. I think she was too embarrassed to give it to you herself.' Afric says she doesn't blame her and, as I go to head inside, she puts her hand on my orse and tells me I so have to promise to dance with her later.

I get inside, roysh, and even though it's, like, totally jammers, who's the only person in the room I can see? Sorcha. I can't take my eyes off her. She looks in-*focking*-credible. She's wearing this little black dress, roysh, which I heard Emer say is a copy of the one that Jennifer Lopez wore to the Grammies and, I have to say, I've never seen her looking so well. Every goy in the place is, like, hanging out of her, but she comes over to me, roysh, and she air-kisses me and *oh my God* she smells amazing, *Issey* focking *Miyake*.

She goes, 'I didn't know if you were going to come ...' and I'm like, 'You look amazing,' and she goes, '... I'm glad you did.' I look into her eyes, roysh, and I'm like, 'Did you hear I might be playing for Blackrock next year?' and she turns away and goes, 'Don't, Ross.' I'm there, 'Jim Leyden invited me down to Stradbrook. Check out the facilities.' She's like, 'You're wasting your time. I'm going out with somebody. I don't want any trouble.'

Off she storms, roysh, and 'Stuck In A Moment' comes on and Oisinn comes over and grabs me in a headlock and goes, 'She is *gagging* for you tonight, Ross,' and I'm like, 'Told her I'm not interested, but she just can't seem to get her head around it.' Fionn goes, 'Would anyone with any information on the where-abouts of Ross's self-respect please contact Gardaí at Shankill,' and I just give him, like, daggers.

So we're there for the night, roysh, knocking back the pints, and about eleven o'clock Zoey and Sophie come around telling us all to go and 'get food' because there's, like, loads of it there and we can't let it go to waste, which, as Fionn says, is a bit rich coming from Calista Flockhart and Geri focking Halliwell. But we join the nosebag queue anyway, roysh, and who's standing roysh in front of me only the old man and he's chatting away to some total knob about, I don't know, the federal reserve, what-ever the fock that is. He sees me and goes, 'Ross, have you met Cillian? He's with PriceWaterhouse,' and the goy – a knob in a suit – goes to shake my hand, roysh, but I just look him up and down and go, 'Wow, Sorcha's done *real* well for herself,' and I turn around and join in a conversation with JP and Oisinn, who are talking about Formula One.

I'm heading back to where I was sitting with my food, roysh, and I pass the old dear and she's engrossed in conversation with Sorcha's old dear about Stella McCartney and some place in Greystones that is, like, the only shop in Ireland that sells her stuff, and they see me as I'm trying to squeeze past and the old dear goes, 'Ross, did you meet Cillian? Sorcha's new boyfriend. An absolute darling. He's with PWC,' and I tell her she's a sad bitch.

It's, like, an hour later, roysh, and I look over the far side of the bor and the old man is still there talking to the goy, and I feel like going over and asking him whether he still considers me his son at all. Christian is basically off his face. He keeps reminding me that we've been best friends since we were, like, five years old, roysh, and that I'm a great goy and that's not the drink talking, and I'm the best focking friend any focker could hope for, and even though I turned to the Dark Side for a little while, he always knew, blah blah blah.

I knock back the vodka and Red Bull that JP bought me and then this bird, Gemma, who's, like, repeating in Bruce, passes by looking pretty amazing, and I can see what the goys mean when they say she looks like Ali Landry, and all of a sudden I look up and Sorcha is, like, standing next to me again. She goes, 'She's seeing someone, Ross,' and I'm like, 'Gemma? I wasn't actually–' She's there, 'I'm only kidding. She broke up with Ronan ages ago. Do stay away from her, though, and I'm telling you that as a friend. The girl has a serious attitude problem.'

I look over, roysh, and now Fionn and JP are talking to this knob of a boyfriend of hers, and I'm wondering do I have any loyal friends left. Sorcha goes, 'How was the Florida salad? Mum made it. It's, like, a secret family recipe.' I go, 'Sorcha, you didn't come over here to ask me about Florida salad,' pretty confident at this stage that deep down she wants to be with me as much as I want to be with her. That dress …

She's there, 'You're right, Ross. I came over because I wanted to say sorry to you,' and I'm like, 'It's cool.' She goes, 'You don't even know what I'm saying sorry for yet. I misjudged you, Ross. I've just opened your present.' I'm like, 'Okaaaay. Go on,' obviously not knowing what the fock I gave her. She goes, 'Those suitcases are SO expensive, Ross,' and I'm like, 'Just a little token of my affection,' and she goes, '*Little? Hello?* They're Louis Vuitton.'

I'm like, 'Forget about it. By the way, what did Becky get you?' and Sorcha goes, 'Do *not* even talk to me about that girl. Anyway, Ross, the reason I was so happy about your present is that you seem to have accepted what's happening,' and I'm like, 'Happening?' She goes, 'Me and my boyfriend? Going away for the year? That's why you bought me the case.' I'm like, 'Yeah, of course. When, em … when are you going?' She's there, 'The day after tomorrow. Though this is going to have to be goodbye, Ross. I have *such* a lot of packing to do,' and she kisses me on the cheek, roysh, and she tells me she is SO going to miss me.

Fionn and JP arrive back over and stort going on about Cillian and how sound he is and how much money he's earning and how he has an offer to play for Mary's when he comes back. Christian throws his orm around my shoulder and asks me whether I know how long it is since we've been best friends, and I can feel tears in my eyes. And JP looks at me, roysh, and he asks me if I'm crying and I say of course I'm not focking crying, it's the dry ice getting in my eyes, and he goes, 'What dry ice?'

✳✳✳

The radio's going, 'If you're paying your home insurance to your mortgage company you could be paying too much,' and all of a sudden this complete orsehole in a red Corsa, roysh, he pulls out roysh in front of me, no indicator, nothing, and I have to hit the brakes and drop down to something like third gear or whatever, roysh, and I am going to be SO late because 'there's focking raidworks in operation on the Rock Raid and the saithbaind carriageway of the M50 between Scholarstown Raid and the Balrothery Interchange is still claised, causing severe delays on all approaches to the Spawell randabite,' and I'm wondering when the *fock* they're actually going to sort out the roads in this country, and all of a sudden we're stopped at lights, roysh, and I get out to have a focking word with the total penis in the red Corsa, and he sees me coming and, like, winds down his window and he goes, 'I'm really sorry about that,' and I'm like, 'If you don't know how to drive, you should have a focking L-plate on your cor, orsehole.'

✳✳✳

Emer goes OH! MY! GOD! she cannot *believe* that Rachel slept with Ross again, especially after Monica warned her off, the girl is SUCH a bitch it's unbelievable, and Fionn throws his eyes up to heaven and asks whether anyone's, like, going to the bor. Emer says that if anyone is, would they get her, like, a pint of Budweiser and Sophie shoots her this filthy, roysh, and Emer goes, 'You are *not* going to make me feel guilty about having a pint,' and, of course, Sophie's there, 'I'm just wondering what happened to your diet, that's all. You had a latte this morning,' and Emer's giving it, 'So?' Sophie's like, 'So ... that's, like, eight points or something. *And* a packet of peanut M&Ms.' Emer's like, 'You are SO not going to make me feel guilty about having a pint,' but when JP brings it over, roysh, she hordly even touches it.

Fionn, roysh, he stands up and goes, 'Look at this, everyone,' and he grabs the waistband of his chinos and, like, pulls it out and there's enough room to fit Sophie *and* Emer in there. Sophie goes, 'OH! MY! GOD! that is, like, SO unfair. You eat like a pig,' and Emer's basically like, 'How come your trousers are falling off you?' and Fionn's like, 'I just moved up from a 34" to a 38",' and he, like, cracks his shite laughing, roysh, and high-fives Christian and JP and then goes to high-five me, and when I don't respond, Fionn goes, 'Anyone with any information on the whereabouts of Ross's life, please contact Gardaí at Harcourt Terrace.'

JP goes, 'Yeah, what gives, goy? You're very quiet,' and I'm like, 'I'm cool. Leave it.' Then he goes, 'Hey, let me run something past you guys. Your reactions are requested. Why don't I call the old man, tell him that Hook, Lyon and Sinker is going to have to function without my considerable presence tomorrow, and the lot of us can go on the serious lash tonight. You goys are going to the States the day after tomorrow. Last chance.' Everyone nods, roysh, and Christian goes, 'I knew I should have put a toilet roll in the fridge.'

JP looks under the table, roysh, to see are any of us wearing, like, runners, then he says he thinks he could get us all into Lillies, he knows one of the bouncers, and Emer says OH! MY! GOD! we will never guess who was in there last Saturday night, we're talking that goy off 'Don't Feed The Gondolas', and Emer goes, 'And don't forget Niamh Kavanagh.'

Erika, who's in a snot as usual, says she's not going anywhere if Beibhinn is going to be there and Emer asks what her problem with Beibhinn is and Erika says it's because she's an orsehole and because of that stupid skanger accent she puts on. She goes, 'That whole knacker-*chic* thing is, like, SO sixth year.'

I'm having a mare of a night, and I really can't bear any more of this shit, so I tell the goys I'm hitting the bor, roysh, but I don't, I actually just fock off home.

Sorcha has been gone for, like, ten days and I never thought I'd miss her so much. I spend the rest of the night at home, basically going through old stuff, looking for the Mount Anville scorf she gave me one of the first nights I was with her. We'd beaten Clongowes in the cup, roysh, and her and all her friends came over to me after the game. It's like it was yesterday. We were all like, 'Here they come, goys. Mounties, looking for their men,' but she seemed so, like, sincere, if that's the roysh word. She goes, 'Congrats, you'd a great game,' and of course I'm like, 'Thanks,' playing it totally Kool and the Gang. She goes, 'Did you hear I got onto the Irish debating team?' and I'm like, 'Yeah,' even though I didn't.

I go looking for the Valentine cord she sent me last year, telling me she would always love me no matter what, but I can't find it, though I do find the menu from her debs, the one that she wrote on saying she'd never met a more amazing person than me before and if there was, like, one goy she'd like to spend the rest of her life with, then it would be, like, me. It's funny, roysh, I don't actually remember ripping it in half, but I must have at some stage because it's in, like, two pieces.

I check the time, roysh, and it's still only seven o'clock. I decide to drive out as far as the Merrion Centre. It's, like, Thursday evening, we're talking late-night shopping. As I pull into the cor pork, I'm thinking about the morning she went away, when I called up to her and made a complete tit of myself asking her not to go and she just, like, put her head in her hands and went, 'Ross, I cannot deal with the soap-operatic implications of what you're saying right now.'

I get out of the cor and go into the shopping centre. Don't know why, roysh, it's not like I'm going to see her or anything, but I walk by her old dear's boutique and have a sly look in. Her old dear's not in there either, just some other bird who works for her.

I wander around, not knowing what the fock I'm doing here, maybe it's just to feel close to her. I go into the chemists, roysh, head down the back to the perfume counter and pick up a bottle of *Issey Miyake*. I spray some on the palm of my hand and stort, like, sniffing it, roysh, and the woman behind the counter goes, 'Can I help you, Sir?' and of course I just blank her.

I spray some on my other hand, roysh, and it's weird. So many memories suddenly come flooding back and the bird in charge of the perfume suddenly comes out from behind the counter, roysh, and goes, 'Excuse me, Sir, do you know that that's ladies' perfume you have there?' and I'm like, 'No shit, Sherlock,' in no mood for this bullshit at all, but then she tells me to leave the shop or she'll, like, call security. Of course I'm there, 'I'm going nowhere,' but then this big fock-off security goy comes in, so I basically stort heading towards the door, and he tells me he never wants to see me hanging around the shopping centre again.

I really can't wait to get out of this country.

I mosey back downstairs to the cor pork and I think about texting Sorcha. But of course it's too late for that.

✳✳✳

I turn off the engine and check the time and it's, like, four o'clock in the morning. I ask Oisinn whether he's planning to talk all night and he goes, 'I'm having a conversation here,' then turns back to Christian and goes, 'Not a bad question, Christian. I would say Padme Amidala would be a Nina Ricci kind of bird. Probably something like *L'Air du Temps*.' Christian goes, 'Explain that to me,' and Oisinn's there, 'It's a floral, spicy fragrance that emanates a mysterious power of seduction. Hauntingly sensuous,' and Christian nods his head really, like, slowly and he goes, 'Like Her Highness herself.'

I go, 'Is that it, goys? Or is there any more of this shit?' and Oisinn's there, 'Hey, Ross, take a chill pill. You're lucky we agreed to come at all,' and I go, 'Sorry. Just a bit stressed, that's all.' Christian goes, 'I still don't see why we've got to fock the thing off Dún Laoghaire pier. Can't you just stick it back in the Classics Deportment when nobody's looking?' I pull the balaclava down over my face and go, 'Too risky. And anyway ...' and Oisinn straight away goes, 'Now don't stort with all that focking juju nonsense again,' and I'm like, 'I'm telling you, Oisinn, that thing has put a spell on my old pair. It's making me vom. It's put a spell on me as well. It's like I'm focking jinxed or something.'

We get out of the cor, roysh, I open the boot and the three of us look in. I pull back the blanket and *Eros* is there, smiling up at me. I'm sure that thing had a sad face when I robbed it. I go, 'It's brought me nothing but bad luck, goys. Look at Erika. Six

190

months ago, I'd have been in like Flynn there. But she doesn't want to know me. Explain that.' Oisinn goes, 'Maybe she thinks you're a penis,' and I stare at him, roysh, give him total daggers, and he goes, 'Might come as a shock to you, I know, but not every bird in the world wants to sleep with Ross O'Carroll-Kelly.'

I go, 'Are you two benders just gonna stand there, or are we gonna get rid of this focker and split?' Oisinn grabs one end and me and Christian grab the other. Oisinn goes, 'Seriously, though, Ross. You heard what Fionn said. Eros is the Fertility God. If anything, he's going to *help* you get your rock and roll.' I go, 'That's another reason to get rid of it then. The old pair don't need any more focking encouragement, and I'm certainly not splitting my trust fund with some mistake of a focking brother or sister. This thing weighs a focking tonne. Probably should have porked closer to the end of the pier.'

Christian says that Padme wasn't born a Royal, roysh, she was in fact the daughter of common parents from the mountain village of Theed and she never forgot her roots, fair focks to her, she used to take off her make-up and dress down to roam around her old village anonymously, see how the other half lived. I go, 'Cool,' because Oisinn's roysh, they're doing me a favour by being here.

We get the thing halfway down the West Pier and I tell the goys we've gone far enough. Oisinn goes, 'Well, let's get rid of it now before someone sees us,' and the three of us grab it, roysh, and – one, two, three – fock it over the edge and – *gloop* – it sinks roysh to the bottom of the sea.

And that's when I stort to feel weird, not weird in a bad way, roysh, just weird in a weird way. Strange things stort happening. The thing is, roysh, suddenly I couldn't give two focks about Erika, but I can't stop thinking about Sorcha. I get this amazing urge to, like, ring her, but then I remember that it's after four and she won't, like, thank me for it.

But I can't stop thinking about her. How she's a ringer for Gail Porter when she's got her hair down. How her mouth goes all, like, pouty when she's trying to be angry with me. How she never, ever orders dessert but always ends up eating pretty much all of mine. How she pays seven lids a week to Concern by direct debit to sponsor some focking African kid she's never gonna meet. The girl is amazing. And now she's ten thousand focking miles away in Australia, with some knob called Cillian. And she might never come back.

I sit down on this little concrete pillar thing, roysh, and I send her a text and it's like, **DRNK 2MORO NITE?** and I sit there for, like, ten minutes, staring out to sea and just, like, thinking about her. She tried to dye her hair once when we were about sixteen, roysh, and it ended up going orange. She used to work at weekends in some focking animal sanctuary, cleaning the shit out of the kennels, and when I found out she wasn't getting paid, I went, 'What a waste of time.' She used to have a Winnie the Pooh hot-water bottle.

I sit there for ages. It's, like, agony waiting for her to text me back and in the end she doesn't. Then I remember the goys. I walk back to the cor. Oisinn is outside, chatting to some bird by the sounds of it. He's going, 'What are you wearing? No, no. Let me guess. Something totally modern. Totally original. You might almost say a fragrance for the new millennium,' then he sniffs the air and goes, 'I can smell that blend of spicy, floral and Oriental notes from here. Hmmm, hmmm. *Ultraviolet*. Paco Rabanne's finest ever fragrance, in my humble opinion.'

I get into the cor and I look at Christian in the rear-view. I go, 'So focking clear to me now. Christian, I'm in love with Sorcha,' but he doesn't say anything. Oisinn gets into the passenger seat. He goes, 'Don't know why, just felt the urge to ring that bird I was with in Annabels last Friday. Emma Halvey.' I go, 'She was–' and he's there, 'Bet-down, I know. That's how I like them.'

Christian goes, 'Your old man's solicitor, Ross,' and I'm there, 'Hennessy? What about him?' He's like, 'What was that blonde bird's name we met the night of his fiftieth?' I'm like, 'Lauren, wasn't it?' and he goes, 'Lauren,' and he sits back in his chair and goes, 'Lauren,' again and sort of, like, stares off into space.

I stort the engine and I go, 'Something weird has happened here tonight, goys,' and no one contradicts me.

✳✳✳

YoU WErE WarNEd

not to FocK

wiTh us

eros is SleePing

WITH THE fIsHeS

CHAPTER SEVEN
'Ross so can't hold his drink.'
Discuss.

I'm standing at the check-in desk when my mobile rings and I'm like, 'Y'ello?' And who is it, surprise sur-focking-prise, only Knob Head himself. He goes, 'Hey, Kicker, where are you?' and I'm like, 'The airport.' He goes, 'You never said goodbye,' and I'm like, 'Get focking over it, will you?'

***

Our landlord in the States, roysh, turns out to be a goy called Peasey Pee, which isn't actually his real name, he's called Peasey Pee because basically he does a lot of drugs and PCP just happens to be the drug he does most. I've been told, roysh, on pretty good authority, that it's, like, an animal tranquilliser, but that means fock-all to Peasey, who snorts, like, thirty or forty lines of the shit a day. He's always offering it to us as well, but the goy looks totally wasted – Fionn goes, 'Think Iggy Pop with a coat-hanger in his mouth' – so he's not exactly a good advertisement for the shit.

But Peasey's actually sound, roysh, and we're pretty much talking *totally* here, because without him we would be so up Shit

Creek it's not funny. We basically arrived in Ocean City, Maryland, with, like, no jobs, nowhere to live, nothing. We had enough money to stay in, like, a hotel for the first few nights – we're talking the Howard Johnson, roysh – but the money soon runs out, especially when you're, like, drinking for Ireland, as we've been. After four or five nights in the hotel, roysh, we check our bills using the old television remote and *Holy Fock!* you should *see* how much we owe for our mini-bars alone. Mine's, like, five hundred and seventy lids. Fionn's is, like, four hundred and eighty. Oisinn's is, like, six hundred and nine. And Christian's is, like, over a thousand. So there's no other alternative, of course, but to peg it without paying.

So there we are, roysh, wandering around Ocean Highway with nowhere to live, place probably crawling with Feds looking for us, and all of a sudden we stumble on this, like, agency, which basically finds accommodation for students. We go in, roysh, tell the dude behind the counter we're Irish lads, just over, like, looking for work for the summer, blah blah blah, and we need somewhere to live. He tells us, roysh, that pretty much all of the accommodation in the town is already gone, that we've left it very late to be, like, arranging anything and I go, 'No shit, Sherlock.'

He goes, 'Are you going to be working while you're here?' and I'm like, 'Eh, you could say that, yeah,' and I just, like, break my shite laughing in the goy's face and Oisinn, Fionn and Christian, roysh, they're, like, cracking their shites laughing as well and they both high-five me, but when we turn around we notice that the goy hasn't got the joke – Americans have basically got no sense of humour – and he's in a bit of a snot now. He tells us that our only hope is this goy, Peasey Pee, who can usually be found down on the beach, flying his kite, and then he's like, 'Next, please.'

At first, me and the goys thought that this whole flying-his-kite thing was, like, slang for something, but we actually end up finding the dude down on the beach trying to control this big fock-off kite in the wind. He's about fifty, roysh, we're talking grey hair down to his shoulders, a big mad pointy nose and these crazy focking eyes which keep, like, darting all over the place. Fionn goes, 'The goy looks like a photo-fit,' which he actually does, roysh. I just march straight up to him and I go, 'We need somewhere to stay.' He doesn't answer me, roysh, just nods his head and carries on looking up at the kite. Fionn steps forward then and he's like, 'We can pay you four hundred dollars a month. We're talking each.'

And the goy, roysh, he looks at us for the first time, his crazy grey hair blowing in the wind, and goes, 'What kind of fricking shakedown merchants are you?' and it's like he's going to deck us, so I turn to Fionn and I go, 'Leave the negotiations to me, my man,' and I'm like, 'We'll pay you five hundred dollars a month each. No more.' He stares at me, no, it's more *through* me, and goes, 'I want three hundred and fifty dollars a month off each of you. No more, you leprechaun focks,' basically haggling himself out of six hundred bucks a month.

And ever since then, it's been more of the same, the dude's, like, the dream landlord. Doesn't give a shit, roysh, that the basement where me, Fionn, Oisinn and Christian sleep is knee-deep in beer cans, condoms and dirty clothes and that it smells like the focking chimpanzee cage at the zoo. We basically only see him, like, a couple of times a week, when he comes in to hide drugs in our cistern and then focks off again, and whatever you say to him, roysh, whether you're telling him that there's a letter for him, or you've accidentally put your foot through an-other window, he always does exactly the same thing, laughs really loud, shakes his head and goes, 'You goddamn Irish.'

✱✱✱

We all end up getting jobs in this local steamhouse, roysh, peeling prawns and crabs, and life is basically a laugh, except that the whole social side of things is, like, totally hectic, the old buck-a-beer nights really bringing out the pig in me and the rest of the goys. We've calculated, roysh, that we've been on the lash for, like, seven days running, roysh, basically spending every penny we earn on booze, so we decide this one night, roysh, that we're going to, like, crash, recharge the old batteries, whatever, because we are seriously in danger of getting the sack if we're caught falling asleep at work again, and we're talking TOTALLY here.

So there we are, roysh, sitting in, being very good, watching the wrestling, when all of a sudden Christian – who went out for a packet of Oreos four focking hours earlier – comes back to the gaff, off his focking tits, and tells us he's won two hundred bills playing Kino, this, like, lottery game they have down in Pickles. Of course me, Oisinn and Fionn crack on that we're really pissed off with the goy, roysh, and we tell him his tea's out in the kitchen if he wants to lash it in the microwave, and we just, like, carry on watching telly. Scotty Too Hotty is lashing Stone Cold Steve Austin out of it. I turn around to Mad Mal from Monaghan, this Belvo boarder who lives upstairs, and tell him this SO has to be rigged, and he says I'm deluded and he reminds me that Stone Cold never had what you would term 'great technical ability' and was always overrated as a wrestler, principally due to his ubiquity as the WWF's number one poster-boy.

Fionn, in the corner, roysh, he goes, 'Style is no substitute for substance, Ross,' the smug bastard and he pushes his glasses up on his nose and, like, out of the corner of my eye, roysh, I can see Christian still standing in the doorway, all upset because he thinks we're, like, in a snot with him. He goes, 'I was on my way to get the biscuits and one drink just turned into another, you know what it's like. Come on, I've brought you back a present,' and I notice that he's got a shitload of drink in a bag, we're talking Stinger Lager, we're talking twenty-four cans for six bucks or something, we're talking total piss here, but fock it, it gets you shit-faced eventually.

So anyway, roysh, to cut a long story short, the four of us and the three Belvo heads who're sharing the house, we all end up tucking into the cans while we're watching the wrestling, and what happens? Half-an-hour later and the beer's all gone and

Christian's there going, 'Come on, young Skywalker. Let's go to the battle-cruiser,' and I'm like, 'Christian, I am SO not going out tonight,' but, of course, ten minutes later, roysh, just as Stone Cold is talking us through his amazing comeback against Scotty Too Hotty, we're out the focking door to Ipanema, this club where we spend the whole night knocking back bottles for, like, a dollar a pop.

The Belvo goys – we're talking this Mad Mal dude, Codpiece and The Yeti – they're sound, even if they did go to a crap school, and we get a bit of a debate going about the time we lashed them out of it in the senior cup and whether the penalty try we were awarded in the last minute was, like, fair or not. Then we move onto, like, birds we all know and birds we've been with, with me dominating the conversation, of course, and all of a sudden Oisinn has that funny look in his eye. The nose is, like, twitching and Fionn's playing along, going, 'What is it, boy? You smell something?' like he's a dog or some shit. Oisinn's giving it, 'A fragrance that explores the essence of (*sniff, sniff*) honeysuckle, gardenia and (*sniff, sniff*) ylang ylang. Blended with notes of vanilla, (*sniff, sniff*) nutmeg and, unless I'm very much mistaken, sandalwood. It can only be ...'

He suddenly, like, whips around on his stool and goes to this bird sitting behind him, he goes, 'An ode to the eternal woman,' and of course the bird – American, twenty-four or twenty-five, looks a little bit like Kate Groombridge – she's a bit, like, taken aback and she goes, 'I beg your pardon,' and Oisinn's there, 'You're wearing *Organza*. By Givenchy,' and the bird smiles and looks really impressed and Oisinn goes, 'I apologise. I'm a sucker for its velvety and mythical seduction,' the smarmy focker, and he turns around to face her and the goy is in. He is so in. Fifteen minutes later they leave together and we're all there going, He got over that Emma Halvey pretty quickly.

No such luck for the rest of us. By the end of the night we're too locked off our faces to even think about scoring, no golden goals tonight, we're totally horrendufied, and we end up getting kicked out of the place when Codpiece and The Yeti get up on the tables and stort singing the Belvo song.

We decide to head back to Pickles then, roysh, but we can't get in because one of the goys on the door cops that Codpiece's ID is fake, and as we're walking off, roysh, basically telling the bouncers what a bunch of dickheads they are, I look at Codpiece's driving licence and it's a real, like, Fisher Price effort, and I'm going, 'This is a piece of shit. It's so obviously a fake,' and he goes, 'You focking sold it to me,' and what could I say to that? I go, 'Come on, let's get a tray of the old National Bohemian and hit the Laundromat,' which is what we basically do.

I'm totally in the horrors at this stage, roysh, and I'm there giving it, 'This whole buck-a-beer-night thing is bang out of order. I've a good mind to sue that place,' and Fionn's going, 'It's socially irresponsible to sell drink so cheaply,' always has to try and sound more intelligent than me. But he's even more locked than I am, so to get him back for being such a focking Know-Everything-Glasses-Wearing-Tit, I convince him to climb into one of the spin-driers and have a crack at

Codpiece's long-standing record of forty-two rotations. Never in a million years would he do this sober, but Fionn's a useless drinker and you can pretty much persuade him to do anything when he's shit-faced.

I take off his glasses, roysh, and he goes, 'Someone phone Norris McWhirter,' whoever the fock he is, 'I've a line for his next book,' and he curls up inside the thing and I slam the door, roysh, and The Yeti, who is a big, hairy bastard, as you've probably guessed, he drops, like, four quarters in the slot and the things storts spinning. Fionn ends up lasting what I tell him is a very brave thirty-four rotations – a Castlerock record – before he boots the door open, slides out onto the floor and borfs his ring up all over the place and Codpiece's Dubes. He's going, 'I've laid down a morker.'

I hand him back his glasses and we head off, and all of a sudden we realise that it's, like, bright outside. Ocean City is, like, waking up and we're all sobering up and suddenly everyone has gone really quiet, remembering what a shitty job peeling shellfish is when you've got a hangover, roysh, and you've had no sleep and you've got that skanky smell in your nostrils all day with your dodgy New Delhi. Coming home at that time of the morning, it's a straight choice between heading back to the gaff for an hour's kip or hitting the nearest 7-Eleven for a cup of black coffee and a packet of Max-Alerts, these pills that the long-distance lorry drivers take when they've got to drive, like, coast to coast.

I am seriously hanging, roysh, my head is thumping, I feel like I'm going to focking vom any minute and Christian has his orm around my shoulder and he's telling me he doesn't know why Vader ever bothered with Bossk, he was more of a slave-trader than a bounty hunter and was only ever good for catching Wookies and even at that the three-fingered Trandos-han was in the halpenny place compared to Chenlambec, and I tell him that even though he's my best friend, I need him to shut the fock up roysh now.

I get a coffee and wash down a couple of pills, roysh, then borf my ring up in some random doorway. Then the four of us – we're talking me, Christian, Fionn and Oisinn – we just trudge on with our heads down, none of us saying anything, in the direction of the steamhouse.

✳✳✳

I'm moseying down the boardwalk, roysh, eating a Payday, checking out the scenario, amazing-looking birds wearing half-nothing, we're taking big nids everywhere you look, when all of a sudden, roysh, I cop this bird who's looking straight at me and, like, smiling at me. She's working in this gaff, roysh, making fudge, using this mad shovel thing to turn over these big fock-off slabs of the stuff on this, like, hob. I give her this little wave, which is a bit gay, roysh, but she doesn't seem to mind, just goes, 'Hey there. You from outta town?' She looks like Sofia Vergara except with even bigger bazookas, if you can imagine that. Of course I'm playing it cool like Fonzie. I'm there, 'Yeah, I'm from Ireland. Just having a look around. And I like what I see.'

She goes, 'I'm Candice.' I thought Candice was an STD. I go, 'I'm Ross O'Carroll-Kelly. You from round here?' She goes, 'No, I'm a stoodent. I'm from Jacksonville, Florida. Just came here for the summer to, like, work. You working too?' Of course I didn't want to tell her about the steamhouse, because, let's face it, how un-focking-sexy is shellfish? I'm there, 'Yeah, I'm a dolphin trainer.' Birds *love* dolphins. She goes, 'No shit?' and I'm there, 'Yeah, seriously, I train dolphins. For, like, shows and shit.' She goes, 'That is, like, SO cool.' It's funny, the American accent's just like the Irish one.

I go, 'So what do you get up to at the weekend, Candida?' She goes, 'Well, me and the girls mostly play, like, volleyball down at the beach. Have a couple of beers and, like, hang out and stuff. Hey, you wanna come along this weekend?' I'm like, 'Saturday good?' She goes, 'Sure, Saturday's swell. Bring your buddies. We're dying to meet new people.' I'm there thinking, I bet you are. I go, 'See you Saturday then,' and she goes, 'Sure,' and I'm like, 'Later.'

I have to say, roysh, after that I'm pretty much on top of the world, too cool for school, and I decide to hit the Drinklink, see did Penis Head put that two grand he promised me in my credit cord account. Turns out he did, luckily for him, and I take out two hundred bills, roysh, thinking about maybe going out on the lash later to, like, celebrate.

The next thing, roysh, I'm suddenly getting this whiff, we're talking piss and B.O. and I turn around and there's this, like, goy standing beside me, roysh, looks like a tramp, or vagrant as they call them over here. He tries to shove this, like, book in my hand, roysh, and he goes, 'Have you heard God's news?' I'm there, 'I don't believe in God. I'm a Catholic.' He goes, 'A Catholic? Well, you evah thought of changing ya religion?' I'm like – and I'm pleased with this – I go, 'You ever thought of changing your deodorant?' The goy doesn't know what to say to that. He's like, 'I ... em ...' I'm there, 'You don't have *all* the answers then, do you? Try this one out. You believe in God. You look like a tramp, you smell of piss and you sleep, I presume, under the boardwalk here. I don't believe in God. On Saturday I've been invited to play beach volleyball with a bunch of supermodels. I suggest you have a word with that God of yours.'

I give the bum a buck and fock off.

✳✳✳

Coming to the States is, like, *such* a culture shock. 'Judge Judy' is actually on in the mornings over here. Fock-all about that in the USIT brochure.

✳✳✳

When we arrived in Ocean City, roysh, I think I mentioned we went on the total lash for the first few days. Anyway, I got up the first Saturday afternoon, roysh, totally hanging, and we're talking TOTALLY here, and somehow managed to write, like, two letters. One was to JP, who I feel a bit sorry for, being stuck at home working for his old man, though he's raking it in so fock him. The other letter was to the old dear, which sounds sort of gay, I know, but the thing is, roysh, I thought that if I let her know straight away that I was, like, settled in and whatever, she'd leave me the fock alone for the rest of the summer and I wouldn't end up hearing from either her or Dick-features again until I needed money sent over.

So the letter, roysh, it was just like:

> Greetings. Having a great time in Ocean City, which is on the east coast of the States. I've had a good look around the place, checked out some of the local history and stuff and found it really interesting. Christian, Fionn and Oisinn are really into it as well. We've been to about twenty museums so far. It really is a beautiful place, much quieter than Martha's Vineyard and Montauk apparently, which suits me because I'm planning to really knuckle down and work hard this summer because, to be honest with you, I'd like to come back with at least a few hundred bills in September. If I'm going to repeat first year, it's not fair that I ask you to pay for it.
>
> Speaking of money, I was wondering was there any chance you could send me some. Not much. Only like four hundred or something, because the rent is due and I've actually been so busy that I haven't even had time to ring Dad's friend about that job. Oh, hey, that's four hundred lids, not dollars. Anyway, I have to go now. We're off to see, I don't know, a castle this afternoon.
> Later, Ross.

About, like, four days later, roysh, I get this e-mail from JP, roysh, and it's like, 'What the fock are you on? What castle? Not fair to ask me to pay your way through college. You guys must be doing some serious drugs over there. Lucky fockers,' which is when I realised, roysh, that I'd actually put the two letters in the wrong focking envelopes and the old dear ended up getting JP's letter, which was like:

Yo, you are missing the best focking crack ever over here. You should have seen the state of us last night. Oh my God, three nights on the total rip and I can hordly re-member a thing. Couldn't stand. Couldn't even talk, for fock's sake. I arrived here with the eight hundred bills that the old man gave me and I actually haven't got a focking cent left to my name. Spent the lot in the first three nights. Most of it actually on the first night. The beer is amazing. Total rocket fuel. Milwaukee's Best or, as we call it, The Beast. Twelve pints and I was totally shit-faced and ended up in some focking illegal gambling joint with the goys, lost about four hundred notes on the blackjack table, then got thrown out by the bouncers for singing 'Castlerock Über Alles', giving it LOADS, roysh, really letting Ocean City know we'd arrived.

Ended up hitting this nightclub then to drown our sor-rows. Off our focking faces. We're talking totally here. Met these two birds, Barbara and Jenna with a J. They were as shit-faced as we were. They were like, 'So, what do you guys do for a living?' and I'm giving it, 'Christian's an actor, Fionn's a geek and Oisinn's a bouncy castle,' and they're like, 'And you?' and I'm there, 'I'm a Navy Seal. I never talk about it, though. What about yourselves?' And Jenna with a J goes, 'We're the President's daughters,' and we all broke our shites laughing.

Got focking nowhere, of course. Ended up pulling this bird, I don't know if you'd call her a hooker, but the deal seemed to be that I basically bought her drink and fags all night and she came back to the gaff with me for a rattle, no questions asked, no names exchanged, a bit like some of the birds from UCD I suppose.

Anyway, the important thing is I christened the old bed. I was telling the goys I'm joining Shaggers Anonymous. That doesn't mean I'm giving up looking for my bit. Just means I'm doing it under a false name. Must avoid Klingons at all costs. It's a short enough summer and there's a lot of birds out there who need pleasing.

Anyway, must go. I'm about to get pissed again and hopefully laid. There's a lot of beer out there as well and it's not going to drink itself. Rock rules, Ross.

And fock it, the old pair will have a knicker-fit when they read it. I'm not answering the phone and I've told the goys that, if they ring, roysh, I'm not in. They probably won't even send me the money now, wait'll you see.

✳✳✳

I know how to play beach volleyball. I was focking glued to it during the Olympics. Cecile Rigaux. Natalie Cook. Danja

Musch. All those birds rolling around in the sand. Hugging each other. What's the point of the men's event, though? Must be for benders. Anyway, roysh, what I'm saying is I know the ins and outs of the game, though I crack on to Candice that I don't, so she's there with her hands on my shoulders, showing me where to stand and the only thing I'm worried about, roysh, is if she looks down and cops the old Cyclops standing sentry. She's going, 'Okay, guys. This game is, like, *rul* easy,' which it probably is if you could concentrate on the focking ball.

Candice's mates look like they've stepped out of the best wet dream you've ever had. Her best mate, roysh, she says her name is Heather, but there's no focking way, it's Caprice Bourret, I'm telling you. Hello, Liv Tyler. Oh, Leeann Tweeden, nice to meet you. They're all, like, tanned and fit-looking, roysh, and we're a pretty sorry sight by comparison, apart from yours truly, of course. Oisinn really shouldn't take his top off. He's got bigger baps than anyone here and he'll give the birds a complex. Fionn, well he was too hungover this morning to get his contacts in and he's, like, blind as a bat of course, so he had to wear his glasses, and what with them and his skinny white body he looks like what he is: Woody Allen in a pair of Speedos. So Christian is my only competition, which basically says it all.

I can see all the birds checking me and I'm flexing the old pecs to give them a thrill. Leeann Tweeden actually turns to me and goes, 'You work out a lot, huh?' and I'm there, 'Be a sin to be given a bod like this and not look after it,' playing it Kool and the Gang, and I cop the four birds whispering away to each other, roysh, obviously trying to decide which one of them was going to try to be with me.

The mistake me and the goys made, roysh, was having a few scoops at lunchtime. We popped into the New Yorker bor for a few straighteners, then filled this big fock-off Eskie with bottles of the Beast before hitting the beach. The birds say they don't want any booze, roysh, that's how, like, serious they are about the game, but we're, like, half-trousered by the time it storts.

Whoosh! Candice serves an ace. *Whoop!* Then another. *Phissh!* What the *fock*! We don't even get a chance to move. After fifteen minutes of this, I call a time-out and we go into a huddle. I turn to Oisinn and I'm like, 'Sorry, are we the same goys who were the backbone of the Castlerock senior cup-winning team of 1999? Are we a bunch of wusses?' Oisinn goes, 'It's no good, Ross. I'm looking at them when I should be looking at the ball. I tell myself not to but ...' I turn to Christian and I'm like, 'You could have returned that last serve. You hit it straight into the net.' He's there, 'Sorry, young Skywalker. Watching them hugging and kissing each other every time they get a point, I can't get enough of it.' Fionn goes, 'Ross is roysh, goys. Let's show these admittedly attractive birds what we're made of. We're Rock, remember?' and we burst into this chorus of, 'You can't knock the Rock!'

But basically, they could. Ten more minutes it took. It was, like, one ace after another and we're left there, pretty much in a crumpled heap on the ground, roysh, and the birds haven't even broken a sweat, they're cracking their holes laughing and then they tell us that they all play for, like, the University of Flor-ida, which explains a thing or two.

We sit around talking for a couple of hours, roysh, getting to know the birds, scoping their racks when they're not looking and making pretty light work of what's left in the Eskie. Then the birds announce that they have to, like, mosey and Candice turns around to me when no one else is listening and goes, 'You wanna ride?' and of course I'm like, 'What?' thinking, There's no way it could be this easy. She goes, 'You guys wanna ride some-where?' and I'm like, 'How about my place?' and she goes, 'That's great, Ross. You wanna give me directions?' I go, 'Are you sure about this? We've only just, like, met,' and she goes, 'Shees, it's only a ride. No big deal,' and I'm like, 'I SO love American women. Happy days.'

I go and tell the goys, roysh, that we're in and they're all giv-ing it, 'What a ledge,' and, 'You the man, Ross,' and I'm there, 'Come on, we're meeting them in the cor pork.'

Candice's cor is this big, fock-off soft-top, a beast of a thing, red with white leather seats. All eight of us fit in it, even though it's a bit of a squeeze for the lucky bastards in the back. I'm in the front passenger seat, wondering whether Candice is on the Jack and Jill and listening to Brucie belting out, '*Born* in the USA, I was *born* in the USA,' when all of a sudden, roysh, don't know whether it's the heat, or the running around, or too much booze – but I actually feel sick. I'm there, 'Candice, em, I'm really sorry about this, but I think I'm gonna borf.' She goes, 'Shit, Ross, you coulda mentioned that before we got on the freeway. Can ya hold it?' I'm there, 'No, but don't panic, I'll lean out of the cor and do it. The G-force will take it away from the cor.'

And just as she's going, 'No, wait!' roysh, I lean out and – *weeeuuuggghhh! WEEEUUUGGGHHH!* – stort throwing my ring up. And of course the G-force doesn't bring it away from the cor, it throws it back into the cor and it's like – SPLAT! – all over everyone on the backseat and everyone screams, roysh, and I turn around to, like, say sorry and shit, but then my stomach just opens up and it's, like – *weeeuuUGGGHHH! WEEEUUUUUGGH!* – and it's like – SPLAT!SPLAT!SPLAT! – everyone in the back getting showered with, like, the gallon of beer I drank and the four shots of Wild Turkey and the pastrami-and-mozzarella panini I ate and the bottle of blackcurrant Sunny D. And the birds are all screaming, roysh, and the car swerves in the road and the goys are telling me they're going to focking kill me and eventually Candice pulls off the freeway and we come to a stop and everyone's just, like, silent. I turn around and I look at the goys and the three birds in the back and they're all in, like, shock, roysh, and their faces are all, like, streaked with purple vom, with little bits of, like, half-digested meat and cheese and, if I'm not mistaken, coleslaw dripping from their hair and their faces and I'm thinking, How the fock did I fit that lot in my stomach in the first place?

Candice, roysh, you can tell she's trying to control herself, she's staring straight ahead and doing these, like, breathing exercises, but it's no good, she just goes, '*Out!*' and I'm there, 'Me included?' She goes, *'I'M TALKIN' TO YOU!* I'm like, 'Sor-ee!' and I get out of the cor and so do the goys. The birds take off and leave us there on the side of the road. None of the goys says anything. They're still in shock. I go, 'Let's see can we thumb a lift back to the gaff. We'll be lucky, though. Look at the state of you three.'

***

Z ... Y ... X ... We're talking W ... V ... U ... Oh yeah, you can forget pretty much every bit of advice they give to students going to the States for the summer, roysh, the only thing you really need to know is how to say the alphabet backwards, that and how to walk in a straight line with your finger on your nose. If the cops stop you with a few scoops on you, roysh, and they know you're, like, Irish and shit, they are SO going to bust you unless you can show you're not, like, totally wrecked.

Oisinn is the undisputed master at – what does he call it? – feigning sobriety, and we're actually talking *total* here. I've seen that goy knock back fifteen pints of the Beast, roysh, and then do the whole ZYX thing while walking on a white line in the middle of Ocean Highway, we're talking *with* a full pint on his head. All these cors flying by either side of him, beeping and shit. Doesn't spill a drop. The goy's a legend.

Anyway, roysh, the other night, we're in the gaff and he's teaching me the whole alphabet thing – backwards, I know it forwards – and suddenly I hear this voice giving it, 'Will you two fags shut the *fock* up and go to sleep,' and it's, like, Gavin, who I should explain is a Gerard's boy, The Yeti's cousin and a total knob who arrived the day before yesterday.

He's actually bulling, roysh, because I ended up scoring his bird – or should I say *ex*-bird – Ciara, in Pickles the other night. *Oh my God*, what a *total* focking honey, we're talking the image of Katherine Heigl here. But I suppose I should stort at the beginning.

I go to work yesterday. Miracle of focking miracles, I've been here for three weeks and I'm actually still employed, though only just. Anyway, I'm wrecked as usual, roysh, not having slept for, like, three nights because it's still, like, Porty Central at our gaff and the bod is storting to build up a bit of a tolerance to the old Max-Alerts.

So there I am, roysh, standing over this big smelly barrel of, like, crabs and shit, having the crack with a few of the Haitians who work with me, and one of them – Papa Doc, they call the goy – he goes, 'You no look so good, Ireesh. You whiter than white,' which is when I tell him about the keg porties we've been having, we're talking five of the focking things in the last, like, seven days and the old pace is, like, storting to get to me. He just goes, 'I give you something for that,' and he brings me down to the steamroom, roysh, where he's got, like, twenty-four cans of the Beast stashed away. He goes, 'I believe to you Ireesh this is called hair of dogs?'

Happy days. So there's me and Papa Doc, eleven o'clock in the morning, roysh, in the steamroom, knocking back a couple of quiet, social beers and the next thing, roysh, he pulls out the biggest focking reefer this side of, I don't know, whatever the capital of Haiti is. I have to say, roysh, I've never been into, like, drugs and shit, too serious about my rugby, but this stuff was focking amazing. Had, like, three puffs of the thing and the next thing I know I'm waking up in the middle of the floor and who's standing over me, roysh, only the boss, we're talking Fatty Dunston himself, a complete dickhead, and he's there giving it, 'You focking Irish. This is the last year I employ any of you drunken focks,' and he tells me I'm out of here, which is American for sacked, roysh, and I don't know where I am at this stage and I look up at the clock and it's, like, nearly five o'clock.

Papa Doc comes over, roysh, and he goes, 'Sorry, Ireesh. Thought I let you sleep. You tired, man. You tired,' and I'm there, 'Thanks very much. Now I'm basically unemployed as well.' He goes, 'Don't worry. Fatty sack me many, many time. You come back tomorrow, he give you your job back, man,' and I'm there, 'How can you be so sure?' and he stares off into space for, like, twenty seconds, and just when I think he's going to say something really, like, deep, he goes, 'Who else gonna work in this shithole for six bucks an hour?' which is actually a good point.

I'll probably end up having to spend a week as the Trash Monkey, which is the job everyone hates, roysh, going through all the rubbish bags to make sure no knives and forks have been thrown out. The job is usually, like, rostered between about ten of us, but anyone caught acting the dick always gets given it.

But anyway, roysh, the upshot of all this was that I obviously decided to go on the lash for the night, so me and Christian headed for Hooters, roysh, and the Belvo goys, Mad Mal, Cod-piece, The Yeti, are already in there with a few heads they know, and this orsewipe, Gavin, who has just got off the plane and is totally trousered. He keeps going, 'I can hold my drink. It's the jetlag,' and we're all there, '*What*ever.'

This goy is a major pain in the orse with drink on him, and he corners me at one stage, roysh, and storts telling me all about his ex and how he's only really out tonight because he heard she was going to be there and how he loves her, even though he blew it by being with her best friend Jemma at the Muckross pre-debs, and she still hasn't forgiven him for it, even though that was, like, last year, but he's convinced she still has strong feelings for him, which is why he ended up coming to Ocean City for the summer, even though most of his mates were actually going to Toronto, but he wanted to be close to her because he thinks there's still a chance that blah blah blah.

I'm there going, *Hello?* Get me *out* of here. And then he storts focking crying, roysh, going, 'My head is SO wrecked, I focked up my exams and everything.' I think he's first year Commerce, UCD. He's giving it, 'I've got to go back to Ireland to sit the re-peats and just the thought that she might be with someone else while I'm away is, like, killing me.'

And while he's saying all this, roysh, I'm not really listening, I'm looking over his shoulder at this bird who is giving me loads, we're talking serious mince-pies here. I have to say, not being big-headed or anything, but I actually look really well at the moment, I always do with a tan.

Gavin's going, 'Will you look after her when I'm away?' and I'm telling him yeah, he can trust me, wondering when he's going to fock off and leave me alone so I can chat up this bird. Eventually, roysh, after crying into my ear for, like, twenty minutes, he goes up to the bor to get a round in, pint of Ken for me and fock-knows-what for him, probably a Baileys what with him being such a focking woman and everything.

So I'm about to go over and introduce myself to this bird, roysh, but she actually comes over and storts chatting to me, and the first thing I notice is that she's actually Irish. She goes, 'Are you a Yankees fan?' and I'm like, 'Sorry?' and she's there, 'Your baseball cap. Are you a Yankees fan?' I'm like, 'Oh that. No, I just liked the cap. I'm not into American football at all. I'm more rugby,' and she goes, 'American *football?* OH MY GOD! *Hello?* I thought they were, like, a basketball team. I am SO dumb,' and I'm like, 'I don't think you're dumb. In fact, I think you're really intelligent. And beautiful,' which is total bullshit because I know her ten focking seconds.

But she sort of, like, blushes when I say that, roysh, and then she goes, 'How do you know Gavin?' which is when I cop it, roysh – this is the bird that the dickhead's spent the last three hours crying into my ear about, and looking at her, roysh, I can understand why. She's Jayne Middlemiss with short hair.

I'm there, 'I actually don't know the dude. We're just living in the same house,' and she goes, 'The goy is like a limpet.' I'm like, 'I didn't know you were actually Irish until I storted talking to you,' and she's there, 'Oh? Where did you think I was from?' and I don't have a focking clue what to say next, roysh, what country would, like, sound good – I'm useless at geography – so I just give it, 'Who cares where you're from, as long as you're here now,' and she must think this is good, roysh, because the next thing I know she's making a move on me and I have to say, roysh, she's an amazing kisser, and I can understand why this Gavin goy is trying to get back in there.

I think I can also understand why he storts going totally ballistic when he arrives back from the bor with the drinks, roysh, and catches me and her wearing the face off each other. All of a sudden I open my eyes and he's standing in front of us, screaming the place down and we're talking TOTALLY here. He's there going, 'I trusted you, Ross. And this is how you repay me?' and he's about to throw a pint over me, roysh, when Oisinn arrives over, grabs him in a headlock and drags him out of the place, and Christian follows them outside going, 'Be mindful, Gavin. Strong is the Dark Side. Seduce you it can.'

Ciara tells me that Gavin SO needed to see her with someone else. I'm like, 'Oh, thanks very much,' and she goes, 'I didn't mean it like that,' and she smiles and goes, 'I'm SO glad it was you.'

I ask her for her number, and she gives it to me.

✳✳✳

The old man rings up when I'm out at work, roysh, and he leaves this message on the answering-machine. This is, like, word-for-word what he said, roysh. Now you tell me whether you think he's losing the focking plot. It's like, 'Hi, Ross. Pick up if you're in ... pick up if you're in ... pick up if you're in ... If not, well, I was just ringing to find out how you are, tell you we got your, em ... letter.'

I'm like, 'Fock.'

He goes, 'By the sounds of it, you're, eh ... having a good time. Just, you know ... be careful. Em, that's what your mother wanted me to say. Condoms and so forth. Oh, I posted you some money. And em ... That's it really. No other news. Just boring old work stuff really. Bit of trouble in the office at the moment. With the staff. Nothing for you to be worrying about, though, Ross.'

As focking *if*.

He's like, 'Don't, em ... don't be fretting about your old man, I can cope with these things. You keep on ... em ... you know, enjoying yourself. Okay, I'm not Bill Gates. Not by any stretch of the imagination. But I know how to run my business. That's one thing I do know, Ross. And if I left it to some of the inverted-commas experts who work for me, where would the company be today? Nowhere. That's where. With a capital N. Give these people a screen-break and the next thing you know they want a bloody crèche on every floor of the building.

'Do you remember that management seminar I went to last year, Ross, where you are, in the States? It was New York, I went with Hennessy. It was 'Say Pretty Please and Watch Your Profits Soar'. What a bloody waste of money that turned out to be.

Hennessy and his little fads. Five thousand pounds I paid to hear some so-called authority on employer/employee relations talking about the connection between morale and productivity levels. Rubbish. And I did give it a chance, Ross. Your mother will vouch for that. I stopped referring to the people who work for me as employees and started to call them stakeholders. Quote unquote. But you see the problem was that they thought this new name actually entitled them to something, the grabby so-and-sos ...

'I personally had to sack four of these so-called stakeholders when they started campaigning for an extension to the half-hour lunch break, which has been the standard here for years, Ross. Years! Only takes one or two bad apples, of course.

'Anyway, the whole office is up in arms at the moment. Up in arms, if you don't mind, because I had the coffee machine removed. Now I don't want to go into the whos, whys and hows of the whole affair, but the word has gone around the office that I did this to save the £60 a month that it was costing me to lease the machine, which is rubbish, Ross. Rubbish. With a capital R.

'Let's not go into the wherefores and the whatnots of the situation, but let's just say that this all started a couple of weeks ago at Heathrow of all places, where I found a fantastic book in the management section called *Are You Being Taken For a Mug?* I've got it here in front of me. It's all about caffeine and the detrimental effect it has on the performance of a workforce. Quote unquote.

'Now, I know what you're thinking and it did cross my mind, too. Surely caffeine *improves* productivity, acting as it does to increase alertness, enhance sensory perception, overcome fatigue and improve endurance and motor functions. Nice theory, Kicker. But – and I have to emphasise the but here, Ross – the chap who wrote the book, he points out that caffeine is an addictive drug, which has a sedative effect when it's taken in excess. You try operating a company and maintaining profit margins when you've got 400 people on the payroll doped up to their eyeballs on fresh ground medium roast by mid-morning, oh you'd know all about it then, by God you would.

'Didn't need to finish reading, Ross, my mind was made up. Did you know that coffee can cause panic attacks? Panic attacks! I mean we all know about heart disease and peptic ulcers, but panic attacks? And what was the other one, oh yes, insomnia, that was the one that really got to me, because this chap who wrote the book – I'm going to write him a letter, the man has changed my life – he claims that these things account for between eight and twelve percent of all cases of absenteeism. This is America mind you, but I'm sure the figures here are ...

'Oh wait, that was the other thing I was going to mention, he says that the average American worker spends, what was it, ah yes, I've got it here in front of me – I marked a lot of the more interesting points with post-its and had Susan type them up for me – here it is, the average American worker spends 114 minutes of every eight-hour day standing around chatting to other employees at the coffee machine or water cooler. And what he's saying is that this quote-unquote downtime costs American industry approximately $177 billion every year.

'Now even when you factor in whatever benefits there are from the stimulant effect that caffeine has on the central nervous system of your average worker – we're talking increased attentiveness, reduction in fatigue, etcetera, etcetera, you're still talking about $98 billion. Then factor into the equation the health problems caused by caffeine addiction and caffeine-related absenteeism and you're talking about losses in the region of $121 billion per year. Not my words, Ross. The words of Mark Finnerty, author of *Are You Being Taken For a Mug?*

'Now I'm not suggesting that I've lost anything like that amount of money, but if Maureen and Deirdre want to sit around for half the day talking about their husbands' vasectomies and the traffic on the Lucan bypass, then they can bloody well do it at their own expense, not mine, thank you very much indeed.

'The machine has been gone for the best part of a week now and I hear you, Ross, I hear you, you're wondering what the net effect of it has been, well I'm coming to that now. Must admit, productivity *is* down – marginally! – though I'm putting this down to the deliberate go-slow that the staff have organised in a fit of pique and which I'm sure will end when the next round of redundancies and wage reviews are announced just before the summer holidays.

'This Finnerty chap who wrote the book – I must ask Susan to get an address or telephone number for him – he says that an initial dip in output is normal, due to the 'cold turkey' effect that the withdrawal of any drug will have. The symptoms, according to the book, are lethargy, headaches and depression, but all are temporary and normal service will resume within four to six weeks.

'My next dilemma, of course, is what to do about the heat in the office. The same chap has written another book that I'm trying to get my hands on about how an overly comfortable working environment can induce feelings of contentment and sluggishness in workers, with a resultant fall-off in efficiency. Says in the blurb I read that cold workplaces tend to keep workers focused and more attentive, which is only common sense when you think about it

'Think I'll wait until the brouhaha over the coffee machine dies down before I start turning down the thermostat, bit by bit, every day, while carefully monitoring its effects.

'Anyway, I'm sure you've better things to be doing than listening to your old dad whittering on. A phone call would be nice, though. Your mother would love to hear from you. In fact, em, we both would, em ... me and your mother. We'll be in tonight if you want to, em ... you know, call us. Don't worry about the time difference, it's fine. So, em, talk to you soon.'

The thing is, roysh, I don't even know how he got the focking number. I certainly didn't give it to him.

✳✳✳

Christian has totally forgotten about this Lauren bird he was in love with before we came away, roysh, and has the hots for this

Chinese bird who works at 7-Eleven, we're talking the one on Ocean Highway here. Pretty much every night he goes in there on his way home from work for, like, M&Ms, or Peppermint Patties, or whatever we're having for dinner, and storts, like, chatting her up, giving it loads with the old, 'I feel a disturbance in the Force which I've not felt for a long time,' and even though most birds think he's a complete and utter weirdo, roysh, this one thinks he's, like, the funniest goy she's ever met. Or she did. Until two weekends ago, roysh, when he decides to go into the shop totally shit-faced, with a traffic cone on his head and his schlong in his hand, and ask her to the Film Ball next year. Her old dear went totally ballistic, focked a price-gun at him. It was really, really funny at the time, roysh, but of course we're all, like, borred from the shop now, and considering it's the only gaff around here that sells the old Max-Alerts, that's a problem, a *major* problem, as in how the fock are we going to porty *and* work?

Christian's answer, roysh, when I put this question to him the next morning was, 'Don't centre on your anxieties, Obi Wan. Keep your concentration here and now, where it belongs,' which is obviously a lot of focking help.

In the end, roysh, me, Fionn, Oisinn and Mad Mal from Monaghan, we sit down to discuss it, roysh, and between the four of us we decide the only answer is to, like, break into the shop and steal enough tablets to keep us going for the rest of the summer. We'll, like, climb up onto the roof, roysh, smash the skylight, and one of us will be winched down into the shop on a rope. At first, roysh, when Oisinn suggests it, we're all like, *Hello?* but as the night wears on, and we *are* drinking seriously fast, it becomes the best idea that any of us has ever heard.

At, like, three o'clock in the morning, roysh, Peasey Pee calls around to hide more shit in our cistern and we ask him if he has any rope, and he just, like, shakes his head, chuckles to himself and goes, 'You crazy, cattle-rustling Irish,' and a few minutes later he comes back with a huge length of rope, which is, like, four inches thick.

So there we are, roysh, half-three in the morning and we're all wearing our black 501s and our All Blacks' jerseys with the collars turned up, and we're climbing up on the roof of the shop. We're tiptoeing around on the slates, and I'm just about to ask how we're actually going to smash the skylight, roysh – did anyone bring, like, a hammer or anything? – when all of a sudden Oisinn marches straight over and puts one of his size-four-teens straight through the focking thing – *CRASH!* – and we're all waiting for the alorm to go off and the Feds to arrive and, like, throw us in the slammer.

But the alorm doesn't go off and when we're finished telling Oisinn what a complete focking dickhead he is, we lash the rope around Mad Mal's waist, make sure it's secure, and then stort lowering him down through the broken skylight into the shop. The goy's quite small, roysh, but he weighs a focking tonne and it takes the four of us to hold his weight.

And everything's going very smoothly, roysh, until the second he hits the floor and then the alorm – which we'd presumed mustn't have been working – suddenly goes off, though fair play to the goy, roysh, he doesn't panic, just uses the map that I drew him to find the roysh shelf, then he storts throwing packets of pills up through the skylight to us and we stort stuffing them into our pockets.

Oisinn reckoned beforehand that, if the alorm went off, we had, like, two hundred seconds to do the job before the cops arrived, though he said this wasn't based on any *actual* reconnaissance work he'd done on local police response times, but rather the way it always was in the movies. So Mad Mal's down there, like, three minutes, roysh, and we're all, like, telling him to hurry the fock up, but he goes, 'Wait, I just want to grab a few magazines,' and we're there, 'What the fock do you want magazines for?' and he looks up through the skylight at us, roysh, his face all blacked up with shoe polish, which he's obviously taken from one of the shelves, and he goes, 'For the long, lonely nights.'

Oisinn goes, 'Good one, Mal, see have they got *Hustler*,' but of course we should have known better. When we pull the little focker back up – it takes a good five minutes because we, like, drop him twice – he's got, like, three WWF magazines, all the same as well.

Anyway, roysh, we manage to get back to the house before the Feds are on the scene, and we empty all the tablets into a big bowl on the kitchen table and, like, burn all the packets in the garden. So that's grand, roysh. Had a couple more cans, ended up going to bed at five, set the alorm clock for seven to get up for work.

We've only been asleep for, like, half-an-hour, roysh, when there's all this, like, hammering on the door, and I look out the window and there's, like, a cop cor outside, and I'm there, *Fock*, it's a bust, goys!'

I wake up all the others, roysh, and we're all standing there in the sitting room, *totally* bricking it, and the banging's getting more and more, like, impatient, and it's obvious that someone's trying to boot the focking door down. We manage to convince Christian to go and answer it, roysh. We're there, 'Just play it cool like Huggy Bear,' so he goes and opens the door, and he's still totally jarred at this stage, roysh, so what does he say? At the top of his voice, he goes, 'WE'VE GOT FOCKING RIGHTS! YOU CAN'T SEARCH THIS PLACE WITHOUT A WARRANT!'

We hear this, roysh, and we decide there there's nothing else we can do except eat the evidence and suddenly we're all there, like, shovelling the pills into us. We must swallow, like, twenty or thirty each, roysh, when all of a sudden we hear the goy at the door go, 'How many times do I have to tell you, I'm not a fricking cop. I'm a friend of Peasey.'

Turns out he's, like, telling the truth. The goy says his name is Starsky, so-called because of his love of, like, cop cors. The one porked outside he stole from the cor pork of a bank in Salisbury, 'the chicken capital of the world' he kept calling it. He said he needed shit, roysh, and he asked whether Peasey had left anything for him, and when we said no, he goes, 'Always the fricking same, that goddamn long-hair,' and he focks off.

Of course we're all in the horrors now, having just, like, over-dosed on Max-Alerts, and we are talking TOTALLY here. Four nights later, roysh, we're all still totally hyper, you know that feeling when you're, like, focking wrecked but you still can't sleep a wink?

The following weekend, roysh, we still haven't come down, so the whole lot of us decide to head for the hospital, we're talk-ing the casualty deportment here, because it's getting, like, majorly scary by this stage. So we get a Jo down there, roysh, me, Fionn, Oisinn and Mal – fifteen dollars it cost us – and we burst into the place and I grab one of the doctors and I go, 'We've taken about thirty Max-Alerts each and we haven't slept for days.'

And he looks at me, roysh – this is no bullshit – and he goes, 'Sorry, we're not looking for ward staff at the moment.'

CHAPTER EIGHT
'Ross is, like, SUCH a no-good loser.'
Discuss.

I've made a bit of a habit, roysh, of trying to get home from work in the evenings before the rest of the goys, just so I can get to the answering-machine first, make sure Dick-features hasn't left any more of his stupid messages, because the slaggings are pretty bad at this stage. Here's the one he left this afternoon:

'Hey, Kicker, guess what … Oh, by the way, pick up if you're in … hello? Hello? Pick up if you're in, Ross … Oh, never mind. Promised I'd keep you abreast of developments *vis-à-vis* the withdrawal of the coffee machine and any improvements or otherwise in productivity pertaining therefrom. Nothing to report, I'm afraid to say, Ross, or rather, nothing positive. What I can tell you is that in a fit of what I can only describe as pique, with a capital P as well, Maureen – lippy little madam from accounts – went out yesterday and bought a kettle and four large drums of Nescafé Gold Blend. They were sitting there, Ross, on the draining-board in the canteen, brazen as you like, when I passed by there on Tuesday morning. Gold Blend, thank you very much indeed.

'All the girls from accounts were in there too, sitting around and sipping their coffees without a by-your-leave, wittering away among themselves, house prices in Shankill and Deirdre's going-away party. I'm paying for all of this, of course. And you know me, Ross, I'm not what you would call a quote-unquote vindictive man, but I don't mind telling you I headed straight for the petty-cash tin to see if these drums of coffee had been purchased from company funds. Gross misconduct. Instant dismissal. Capital I. But of course, Maureen's much too clever for that. Don't mind admitting the resolve was tested, Ross. The resolve was tested.

'Went home and couldn't sleep. Had a couple of brandies but they only gave me heartburn. Your mother tried to help, of course. She's a rock, your mother. Just give them their machine back and be done with it, was her advice. Just trying to be helpful, of course, but that'd be a climbdown I told her. They see one sign of weakness in me and we'll have that minimum wage nonsense all over again. Wouldn't be a climbdown, she said. You don't have to say anything. Just put it back and say it was being repaired.

'And then she said something that got me thinking. It got me thinking too much if the truth be told. She said, "Charles, I'm sure it takes longer to make a cup of this – what did you call it? – instant coffee, than it does to make a cup of the real thing." And that was me awake for the night. Couldn't get this blasted conundrum out of my head. Which takes longer to make: instant or machine coffee? Couldn't let it go. I had to know.

'By the way, Ross, if you're in pick up, it's unfair to leave me talking into a, em … where was I? Oh yes, which is quicker? Well, I remembered that a few months earlier I had chanced upon a couple of girls from the marketing department lounging around in the canteen, middle of the morning, drinking coffee without a care in the world. So I asked them what they thought they were up to. "Screen-break," they said. Screen-break, quote-unquote. So I asked Susan to launch a bit of an investigation, you know how she likes all that cloak-and-dagger stuff, to find out how long it actually takes to make a cup of coffee – using the machine, you understand.

'So, my curiosity having been pricked by your mother's earlier statement, I remembered that I had a copy of Susan's report in the study. Sleep was out of the question at that stage, so I went and ferreted the thing out. Made for very interesting reading. *Very* interesting. She estimated the time it took to brew the coffee first thing in the morning at eight minutes. Each cup made thereafter took approximately thirty-six seconds, adding five seconds for milk and seven seconds for each sachet of sugar used.

'So, armed with this information, I decided to head straight for the office. My pulse was racing, Ross, I don't mind admitting that to you. It was racing. I looked at the clock. It was four in the morning. The traffic wouldn't be bad for another half-an-hour yet. Made town in good time, parking the car on Stephen's Green, then letting myself in. Headed for the kitchen. Looked around. No one else in. Checked my watch. Waited for the second hand to reach twelve, then filled the kettle. Switched it on. And then as coolly as you like – or as coolly as my shaking hands would permit – I started to make a cup of this instant stuff, just as I'd seen it done once. Tried to remember the process as best I could. One-and-a-half teaspoons of coffee. A drop of milk. Two sachets of sugar. Add the hot water. Stir it until the granules dissolve.

'Well! Instant coffee, my eye. Took almost *twice* as long to make as the proper stuff. I went back home then, considering my findings in the car on the way, though in the end I decided to sleep on it and, well, it was such a stressful night I was out as soon as my head hit the pillow anyway.

'Still didn't know what to do when I went back in the next morning. Then when I got back into the office, who was there only these two scruffy-looking chaps with long hair, absolutely stinking they were, wearing sandals and God knows whatever else, hanging around the reception area.

'"Don't worry," I told Una, our telephone girl, "I'll handle this," and I turned to them and I said, just like this, I said: "There are bloody good support services out there for people like you. You'll not be getting a penny from me. Now leave before I call the Gardaí." You'll never guess what happened next, Ross. "You don't understand," one of them said. "We're from SIPTU. We're here for a meeting."

'Well, you could have knocked me down with a feather. SIPTU, if you don't mind. Maureen had only dragged one of these wretched trade unions into the whole sorry business.

And, well, that's what's really bothering me, Ross. Don't want those people hanging around. Could spell trouble and spell it with a capital T. There's been a lot of changes in employment legislation in recent years that I haven't really kept abreast of.

'Rang up Hennessy, see could he do anything about it, but he's keeping his head down. The word out at Portmarnock is that he's gone to the States. Not surprised with the hard time he's been getting at that tribunal. Happy with yourself now, Mister Cooper?

'But I think I might have bitten off more than I can chew with this union business. But don't you come rushing home, Ross. No charging off to the airport at a hundred miles an hour. No, I'll fight this battle myself. The gloves are off. I'm not giving in to the unions. Oh, no. Give them back their blasted machine and it'll be breast-feeding stations and gluten-free bread for the world and his mother next. Better go and think through my next move. Oh, by the way, ring your mother, will you? You know she worries.'

***

We get shit-faced in Hooters one night, roysh, and me and Christian take a cab, we're talking forty miles out of town, to go to this, like, lap-dancing club. And what a waste of focking money. The bird takes fifty bucks off you, tells you not to touch her and keeps asking you if you've got a credit cord. I turn to Christian and I go, 'This is a bit too much like having a focking girlfriend.'

***

Fionn and Oisinn, roysh, they end up quitting the steamhouse, without even telling me and Christian, the sly fockers, and they get jobs at, like, Ocean Pines Golf Club, porking cors and shit. They're actually amazing jobs as well, the bastards, the tips are supposed to be pretty amazing, though the uniforms are a bit skangery, we're talking grey Farah slacks, purple jacket and a black pointed cap. One of the Belvo goys told them they looked like two gay usherettes heading out for the night, and Oisinn basically decked the goy.

Anyway, roysh, we're in the gaff this day, we're talking me and Christian, both on a day off, both totally broke, and I mean TOTALLY, sitting in watching 'Judge Judy', knocking back the last of the cans, when all of a sudden this, like, envelope drops through the door and it's, like, a letter from Dick-features himself, full of the usual bullshit, roysh. It's like, 'Did you manage to see any of the Lions games over there?' and 'Hope you're working hard and putting a bit of money aside for college next year,' and I'm about to burn the focking thing, roysh, when all of a sudden – OH! MY! GOD! – there's, like, a cheque in the envelope and I *cannot* believe how much it's for, we're talking five hundred focking bills here, and I'm so happy I could nearly sit down and actually finish reading his stupid letter. I said nearly.

The old man is a dickhead and everything, roysh, but the money comes bang on time because we've been basically living on Cheerios (stale) and Raisin Bran (disgusting), we're talking breakfast, dinner and tea here. So me and Christian, roysh, we sit down and talk over how we should, like, spend the shekels.

Should we head down to Foodrite and stock up on provisions, or should we go on the complete lash? Should we pay off the electricity bill before they discover that Oisinn has put, like, a magnet inside the meter, or should we go on the complete lash?

We go and get changed. Christian decides we need something pretty strong to get the ball rolling, roysh, so he disappears under the stairs and comes back out with a bottle of the old Mad Dog 20/20, which he said he was keeping for a special occasion. We knock it back, roysh, do a couple of lines of this new shit that Peasey got from his Detroit connection, hit the bank, cash the chicken's neck and then mosey on down to Hooters.

The place is fairly packed, I have to say, for four o'clock in the afternoon and we're already pretty buckled by the time we get there. It's actually an amazing bor – we're talking Bap City, Arkansas here – and the waitresses are, like, practically naked and they flirt their orses off with you.

I get chatting to this bird, roysh, this American bird, who I thought looked like Jenny McCarthy, until I got up close and realised she was more like focking Mick McCarthy, but I was actually getting on alroysh with her, I could tell she was seriously interested in me and, of course, I'm there giving her the old chat-up lines – 'Let's not do what happened here today an injustice by pretending there's not an attraction between us' – basically giving it loads, but then she asks me what I'm doing for the summer, roysh, and I'd usually make something up just to impress her, but I'm too shit-faced to think of anything, so I tell her

I'm slaving away in the steamhouse and she immediately loses interest. She goes, 'I *thought* you were in IT or something,' and walks away, giving me this filthy look.

I fock off and look for Christian. It takes me, like, half-an-hour to find him, roysh, and when I do he's sitting up at the bor with Sophie and Chloë, as in Sophie and Chloë from home. They're in Montauk for the summer, but I had heard a rumour they were coming down here for a holiday. The last thing we want, though, is a couple of Klingons from home cramping our style for a couple of weeks. We've both scored both of them back home, loads of times as well, and there's, I don't know, a billion other birds in the States who we haven't been with. I'm over the other side of the bor, roysh, trying to get Christian's attention without the birds seeing me, but he's telling Sophie that the big mistake Grand Moff Tarkin made in the Battle of Yavin was deploying so many TIE fighters, whose surgical strike potential against ground and deep-space targets was rendered irrelevant by their basic lack of speed and poor manoeuvrability and that if Tarkin was half the military strategist that the Emperor thought he was, he'd have used more TIE interceptors, which you girls will, of course, recognise from their distinctive dagger-shaped solar panels. The birds are just looking at him blankly, going, 'Cool.'

I can't get the focker's attention so I have to go over, roysh, and Sophie and Chloë both go, 'OH! MY! GOD!' seven or eight times and air-kiss me and then they go, 'OH! MY! GOD!' a few more times. And even though I'm cracking on to be happy to see them as well, I'm pretty pissed off here, roysh, because I'm going to have to get them a drink. I slap a twenty and my fake ID on the bor, roysh, and get them in – two bottles of Ken for me and Christian and vodka and Diet 7-ups for the birds – and Sophie storts bitching about some girl who was on the organising committee for the Foxrock pre-debs with her and used to be so nice but has *such* an attitude problem these days and it's all since she got the jeep.

Chloë takes a Marlboro Light out of the box and she goes, 'Tell me about it. Her phone went off once in the middle of German. Me and Ultan were both like, duuhhh,' and Sophie goes, 'I know, it's like, ahhhh,' and Chloë goes, 'Oh, TOTALLY.' Of course I'm looking at Christian and eyeing the door, but he doesn't cop it, he asks Chloë who Ultan is and she goes, '*Oh* my God, he is SUCH a good friend of mine. He's actually gay,' and I don't know why I say this, roysh, probably because she's bugging the shit out of me at this stage, I go, 'What the *fock* has that got to do with anything?' and Chloë stops, like, fumbling around in her jacket for her lighter and she goes, 'Sorry, does that make you uncomfortable, Ross, talking about people who are gay?' and I'm there, 'No, I just don't see what him being gay has to do with the story. It's like if you said, you know, "He's a really good friend of mine. He's actually got red hair." I mean, what does it have to do with the story? That's all I'm saying.' Chloë stares at me for ages, roysh, not saying anything, then she goes, '*Oh* my God, you are SO homophobic,' and she finally finds her lighter in the pocket of her jacket.

Christian gets a round of drinks in then and Sophie asks me whether I've heard from Sorcha and she's basically being a bitch to me. I'm there, 'Why would I have heard from her?' and she goes, 'We all got postcrods from her. She's having an amazing time. Cillian's trying to get her to do the bridge climb,' and Chloë goes, 'Oh yeah, and they went out for dinner in Dorling Harbour. She said it was SO romantic,' and I'm there going, 'Do I *look* as though I give a shit?' and the two of them just, like, smile at each other, all delighted with themselves.

Anyway, roysh, four or five pints later, the old beer goggles are on and basically Sophie and Chloë are the best-looking birds we've ever seen in our lives, and it's pretty obvious that Christian's going to end up being with Sophie and I'm going to end up scoring Chloë, who, I think I mentioned earlier, actually looks a bit like Heidi Klum. Especially after what I've drunk.

So ten o'clock, roysh, Christian offers the birds a lift back to their hotel and I pull him aside and I'm like, 'We can't focking drive in this state and – *Hello?* – we don't have a cor.' He goes, 'No, but we know where we can get one,' and he tells the birds we'll be back in a minute, roysh, and we ended up catching a cab up to Ocean Pines Golf Club, bang on time as it happens because Fionn is about to pork this big, fock-off, eight-litre Viper.

This cor, roysh, is an animal and we're talking TOTALLY here. I walk up to Fionn and I'm there, 'We're taking this beast for a little joyride,' and Fionn's like, 'No *focking* way, man,' and I look at him and I go, 'You either let us take this, or I break every pane of glass in your face.' He goes, 'There is no *focking* way you are driving this cor out of here, Ross,' but then I offer him a little persuader, roysh – we're talking a hundred bucks here – and he says alroysh, we can go for a spin, roysh, but only if *he's* doing the driving. I'm there, 'Hey, Kool plus guests.'

So the next thing, roysh, we've picked the birds up and after they've, like, air-kissed Fionn for, like, twenty minutes – 'OH! MY! GOD! How oooor you?' – we're pegging it down Ocean Highway, burning the orse out of the thing, me and Buddy Holly in the front, Christian and the two birds in the back, heading back to their hotel for a night of passion, knowing we're guaranteed our bit. We'll get Fionn to drop us off, then tell him to fock off.

But then all of a sudden, roysh, we hear this, like, siren and the Feds are behind us, telling us through this, like, megaphone to pull over and, of course, Fionn is shitting it because he knows he's going to end up, like, losing his job over this. For about ten seconds, roysh, he actually considers trying to outrun them, but then Sophie says something about Rodney King, and at first I think she's asking me to put on a CD, but Fionn goes, 'Shit, you're roysh,' and pulls into the hord shoulder.

Sophie goes, 'OH! MY! GOD! If I get deported my parents are SO going to go majorly ballistic.' Two cops get out. We are totally cacking it. One of them walks up to the driver's window, roysh, while the other one storts looking the cor over. The cop's like, 'Do you know what speed you were doing?' and Fionn goes, 'I'm going to guess here and say forty.' The cop goes, 'Are you Irish?' and Fionn's there, 'Yeeaahhh,' like this is a good thing, but the cop goes, 'So was my fawtha, so I know goddamn blarney when I hear it. You were going ninety-frickin'-five miles an hour. In a forty zone.' He goes, 'Now, let me see your identification.'

And Christian, roysh, he leans forward and waves his hand in the cop's face and goes, 'You don't need to see his identification.' I'm thinking, We're going to end up in focking Sing Sing here. The cop goes, 'What?' Christian waves his hand again and goes, 'These aren't the droids you're looking for.' The cop goes, 'You, out of the cor. *Now!* but Christian goes, 'Move along.' The cop reefs open the door, roysh, and he's about to drag Christian out. The birds are, like, screaming their heads off, but then the next thing, the cop, he gets this, like, message on the radio, roysh, and it's like, 'Armed robbery in progress on Hudson and Atlantic. All units proceed,' and him and the other cop, they don't say anything else to us, they just go, 'Hoooly shit!' and peg it back to their cor, and they're gone. Christian's there, 'They must have been Tridarians.'

Fionn tells us that that is it, that is SO it, he's bringing the cor back to the golf club roysh now and he doesn't give a *fock* how we get back to the hotel with the birds and, not wanting to piss him off any more than he already is, I tell him it's alroysh, if he drops us off at his work, we'll phone a cab from reception.

We turn off into the golf club, roysh, which is up this big long driveway. Sophie's telling Chloë that dieting and exercise won't get rid of cellulite on their own and that Kylie – I presume she means Minogue – swears by dry skin-brushing, hot water with lemon in it and salt baths, and Chloë says she knows, but she also SO has to stop drinking water with her meals because it just, like, bloats the food in your stomach and Sophie goes, 'I know, it's like, aaahhhh.'

Oisinn is standing in front of the clubhouse, looking pretty focked-off. He's there, 'Fock it, goys, the dude who owns the cor, he came back for it, his wife's gone into focking labour. Kept telling me to fetch his goddamn cor fast. I tried to stall him, but he knew something was up. I told him it was stolen. He's gone to see the focking manager.' Fionn goes, 'We are SO fired.'

But Oisinn, roysh, he goes, 'Well ... maybe not. I've an idea,' and of course Fionn goes, 'Shoot.' Oisinn's like, 'We'll just tell the manager that the goy's a drug trafficker. And we were just trying to buy some time until the Feds arrived.' Doesn't sound very convincing to me. Fionn goes, 'He's never going to buy that.'

But Oisinn, roysh, fair focks to him, he pulls out this massive bag of, like, green powder, roysh – it looks suspiciously like the stuff that Peasey had stashed in our cistern – and he opens up the dash and throws it in and then goes, 'OH! MY! GOD! look what I found when I went to look for a cloth to wipe the inside of the windscreen ... goys, call 911.'

✳✳✳

When we arrived here first, roysh, there were, like, eight goys staying in our gaff, but of course as the summer wears on, roysh, more and more stort arriving, goys who came over after sitting the repeats, friends of friends who were focked out of other gaffs for portying too hord, blah blah blah. Suddenly, roysh, we ended up with, like fifteen goys in the gaff, or sixteen if you count Blair, which we never really do because he's always so out of it, we're talking a total pisshead here. Out of the four weeks he's been here, roysh, I'd say he's spent, like, three of them lying unconscious on the floor of the kitchen, which is how he got the nickname Lino Blair.

Come home from work the other night anyway, stinking of fish as per usual, and I go to grab a beer, but the goy's lying on the floor in front of the fridge and I can't get the door open without whacking it off his head. So I open the door, roysh, whacking it off his head, and he doesn't even wake up, no movement out of him at all. But, roysh, the second he hears the ring-pull going, he's like, 'Ross, you stole my place on the Leinster Schools team two years ago. You steal one of my cans and I'm beating the shit out of you,' and I'm basically there, 'Chill out, Clongowes boy. This is my beer I'm drinking,' and he's so lucky he's lying on the ground because if he wasn't, I'd deck the focker.

Anyway, roysh, I'm far too busy for his shit because I've got this bird, Jenni with an i, coming round, second year B&L in UCD, chambermaiding in some focking hotel or other for the summer, we're talking pure quality here, a little bit like Jessica Alba except better looking, if that's possible. She's also doing waitressing three nights a week in Secrets, roysh, which is where me and the goys first saw her and, of course, they're all totally bulling that I was the one who actually ended up getting in there.

Went out for a drink with her the night before last, roysh, then made the mistake of inviting her round to the gaff tonight to grab a bite to eat, listen to some sounds, totally forgetting that our gaff is a complete shithole, we're talking empty beer cans, used johnnies, cigarette butts and squashed mince-pies strewn all over the shop and a big pool of beer, we're talking an inch thick here, covering the whole floor of the kitchen. But of course by the time I remembered this I'd already asked her round, roysh, and it was far too late to try to clean the gaff up.

I decide to go for the old damage limitation instead, roysh. I end up borrowing a brush from work and I sweep most of the, like, debris, out of the sitting room, my plan being to try to contain her to just the one room while hoping against hope that she doesn't notice the smell. Of course, the first thing she says when I open the door and show her in is, 'Oh my God, *what* is that smell?' and – quick thinking, roysh – I go, 'Oh, it's just something I was cooking,' and she looks at me sort of, like, searchingly, if that's the roysh word, probably wondering whether I'm some kind of Jeffrey Dahmer freak.

She storts to relax, though, when I lash on the old *Pretty Woman* tape, me slyly fast-forwarding it to the end of 'Real Wild Child' and then, halfway through 'Fallen', giving her the old, 'I've never felt so close to anyone in my life,' bullshit as we both try to get comfortable on the futon. She says OH! MY! GOD! that song is, like, SO one of her favourite songs of all time, but

progress is slow, roysh, and by the end of 'Show Me Your Soul', we're still far from naked.

Basically, it turns out, roysh, that she has a boyfriend back home, some knob called Ryan, who's, like, second year Social Science in UCD and who, she tells me, is working in Cape Cod for the summer, as if I actually *give* a shit. She ends up boring the ear off me for, like, half the night about this dickhead, it's like, 'Oooh, he's *such* a good sailor, even I feel safe on the water with him and I can't swim,' and it's, 'Oooh, he's SO romantic, you should have seen what he did for my eighteenth,' which is when I cop it, roysh, she's actually trying to convince herself that she's *not* going to do the dirt on him, but at the same time the bird wants me bad. The head's saying No, but the body's saying Go.

So there I am, roysh, basically changing my approach all of a sudden, going, 'What's he doing in Cape Cod, this Richard tosser?' and she goes, 'You mean Ryan? He's working. His best friend's uncle owns, like, a country club.' I raise my eyebrows and I go, 'And *you're* in Ocean City?' She's there, 'We just decided to take a break from each other. For, like, the summer. We're going to New York afterwards for a holiday. *Oh my God*, I am SO looking forward to seeing him again.'

I'm like, 'And do you think *he's* being faithful?' and she goes, 'Of course he is,' though she doesn't sound, like, convinced. She changes the subject, storts asking me about my exes, some of whom she actually knows. Then we stort having this whole discussion about, like, relationships and love and shit. And that's when I decide to make my move. It's like rugby. You see a space and you exploit it. I'm like, 'Do you love Richard?' and she's there, 'Ryan?' and I'm like, 'Yeah, whatever,' and she hums and haws for ages, roysh, blabbing on about how you can never really know whether someone is, like, the roysh person for you, and how she SO knows that now, especially after what happened with Andrew – whoever the fock he is – and at the end of all this babbling, roysh, she goes, 'I suppose I do love him, but I'm not *in* love with him, if you know what I mean.'

I know what she means alroysh. We're talking green light for go here and it comes not a minute too soon, because at this stage, roysh, the futon is seriously storting to hurt my orse, and I remember that Fionn told me that 'futon' is actually the Japanese word for torture, which might be bullshit because he's always, like, taking the piss out of me for being, like, thick. I just go, 'All I know, Joanne,' – I actually call her Joanne and she doesn't cop it! – 'all I know is, if you were *my* girlfriend, I wouldn't want to be away from you all summer. I wouldn't want to be away from you for five minutes,' and the next thing I know, roysh, she's pulling my baseball cap off and we're playing tonsil hockey, *totally* wearing the face off each other, roysh, when all of a sudden she jumps up and says she has to use the bathroom. Of course, I know what this is all about. Ten minutes of, like, agonising in front of the mirror, trying to decide whether this Ryan dickhead's doing the dirt as well and whether she'd be a fool to pass up this opportunity to be with yours truly. Only one answer to that, of course.

I nip into Oisinn's room, roysh, to see has he any of the old love zeppelins left, and he's in bed watching SVU. He goes, 'Can you two keep it down out there. You're making me borf,' and I go, 'That girl is SO gagging for me,' and he's there, 'Sounds like an edge-of-the-bed virgin to me. Twenty bucks says she just wants to talk tonight.' I'm like, 'Quit the shit, Oisinn. I need johnnies.' He goes, 'We don't have any. We used them all last week. At the keg porty? The water fights?' and I'm like, 'Shit, yeah. Hey, some porty wasn't it? Fock, but what the fock am I going to do?' He's like, 'You'll just have to get off at Sydney Parade, my man,' and I'm like, 'No *focking* way,' but all of a sudden, roysh, Christian, who I presumed was asleep, he goes, 'There's a six-pack in my grey Diesel jeans, Skywalker. They're hanging on the back of the chair,' and I'm like, 'Thank you SO much, Christian. Thank you SO focking much.'

To cut a long story short, roysh, I'm heading back into the hall when suddenly I hear all this, like, screaming and shit, and the next thing Jenni with an i comes pegging it out of the bathroom and she's having a major knicker-fit – and we're talking MAJOR – bawling her eyes out, the whole lot. I'm like, 'Calm down, calm down. What's wrong?' and she goes, 'The bath, OH! MY! GOD! it's, it's, it's dis*gusti*ng.' I'm like, 'It's only Mad Mal's home-brew. Didn't have a container big enough for it so he just made it in the bath.'

But she's not listening, roysh, she's there, 'I'm going. Get me a cab. Now.' She's *totally* losing the plot and I just want to basically get the hysterical bitch out of the gaff at this stage. Of course we can't make outgoing calls, roysh, so I have to grab Fionn's mobile to ring the local cab firm. She calms down a bit, but still doesn't say a word to me while we're waiting for the Jo to arrive.

I know enough not to bother asking if I can see her again. As I'm seeing her out, she goes, 'Well, this was certainly a night to remember,' and she gets into the back of the cab, winds down the window and she's like, '*Oh* my God, just to think, I was actually going to let you be the first.'

I head back inside, open all the condoms and leave the silver wrappers on the floor beside the futon, basically for the goys to see in the morning, though I know that makes me a sad bastard. Then I go into the jacks to flush the unused johnnies down the pan, roysh, and I'm still wondering why she reacted the way she did, and that's when I look down to my roysh and see this big fock-off rat swimming around in Mal's home-brew. And that's basically when I decided that we seriously needed to clean up the gaff.

✲✲✲

The phone rings, roysh, and I'm actually in the middle of having a shave, but no one else is bothering to answer the thing, and of course I'm cacking it in case it's Dick-features again, so I have to peg it to it before it switches onto answer-machine and half the house hears what a total knob he is. So I answer it, roysh, and I'm like, 'Y'ello?' and I hear the voice on the end of the line and – oh, *fock it* – it's, like, Christian's old man.

I go, 'How are you?' and of course he's there, 'You don't care how I am. Put Christian on the line.' I'm like, 'Look, I just wanted to explain–' and he's there, 'I have nothing to say to you. Go and get my son.' I go, 'He's, em, not in,' and he's there, 'Do you want me to ring your parents with my news instead?' and I'm there, 'I'll go and get him.'

I put the receiver down on the table, roysh, and head down to the basement. Christian's lying on his bed with his Walkman on and it's 'Stuck In A Moment', I can hear it, and when he sees me he takes off his headphones and goes, 'Hello there, young Skywalker,' and I tell him that his old man's on the phone. I'm, like, totally crapping it. I'm just surprised he can't, like, hear it in my voice.

He just goes, 'I'm not in,' and I'm like, 'I think I might have already told him you were here,' and he goes, 'Well just tell him I don't want to *focking* speak to him then.' I'm like, 'Okay, man. Take a chill pill,' and I go back upstairs to the hall, roysh, and pick up the phone and I go, 'Em, he says he doesn't want to talk to you.'

His old man doesn't answer for ages, roysh, and eventually I go, 'You're not going to tell him about–' but suddenly the line goes dead.

✳✳✳

Me and Christian, roysh, there was no way we were going to carry on working in the steamhouse after Fionn and Oisinn left, so we jacked it in, roysh, and basically ended up getting jobs in Ascelpis Healthcare, this, like, pharmaceutical factory, roysh, we're talking, like, twenty bills an hour for doing basically fock-all, just letting them use us as sort of, like, guinea pigs to test out all these vaccines they're developing for malaria and shit. The goys said we were off our whacks, but they were bulling because they know we're going to be earning serious sponds. There's really fock-all to worry about, although we did have to sign this, like, waiver, basically saying that if we suddenly grow, I don't know, horns and a focking beak, we've no comeback against the company. But it's only, like, malaria tablets, so me and Christian are there, 'Twenty bucks an hour? Where do we sign?'

We spotted the ad in the *Ocean City Advertiser*. It was like:

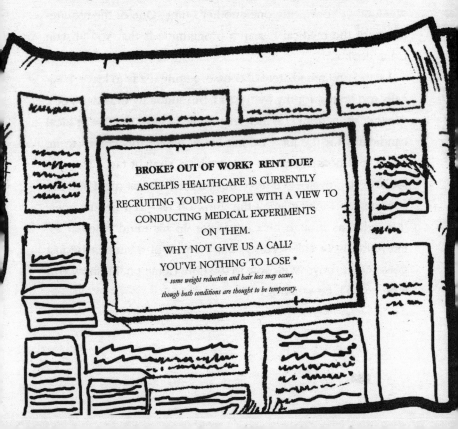

BROKE? OUT OF WORK? RENT DUE?
ASCELPIS HEALTHCARE IS CURRENTLY
RECRUITING YOUNG PEOPLE WITH A VIEW TO
CONDUCTING MEDICAL EXPERIMENTS
ON THEM.
WHY NOT GIVE US A CALL?
YOU'VE NOTHING TO LOSE *

* some weight reduction and hair loss may occur,
though both conditions are thought to be temporary.

Fionn's giving it the usual routine, calling us Frankenstein's monsters, trying to get up my nose. But fock him, we phone the freephone number anyway and the next thing we know, roysh, the two of us are sitting in this goy's office, we're talking the Head of Research. The first thing he asks us is, 'Do you guys drink?' and of course me and Christian look at each other and we're thinking, Happy Days, and Christian goes, 'Pint of Ken, if it's going.' And the goy, something McPhee his name was, big fat bastard with a red face and Bobby Charlton combover, he looks a bit embarrassed, roysh, and he's like, 'Em, I'm just taking your personal details. I'm not asking whether you want ... Look, I'll level with you guys and you can decide right now whether we're wasting one another's time. One of the requirements of the medical research programme is that you abstain from alcohol.'

I stand up immediately of course, getting ready to leave, basically too honest for my own good, but suddenly Christian goes, 'Neither of us drinks. Which makes me believe that we're ideal candidates for the job.' I don't know where this comes from, roysh, but he manages to say it with a straight face. The goy looks at us, roysh – we were out on the lash last night and I'm sure he can focking smell the drink off us – but he just goes, 'Alriiiight,' as though he can't make up his mind whether to, like, hire us or call security, but then all of a sudden he just goes, 'Okay, boys. Welcome to the firm. Come on, I'll show you where you'll be working.'

So there we are, roysh, wandering down all these corridors and he's telling us all this shite about how long the company has been established, the products they make, blah blah blah, and I turn around and go, 'Give us the lowdown on these malaria pills we're going to be checking out for you,' and the goy suddenly stops walking, roysh, and he goes, 'Excuse me?' I'm like, 'We were told on the phone that it was malaria pills?' And the goy goes, 'It is. But we don't talk about products that haven't yet been passed by the FDA. That's ground rule number one. It's best that you know nothing about these pills. In fact, it'd be better all round if you forgot my name. And what I look like.'

He brings us into this, like, lounge area and Christian pulls me to one side and goes, 'Suddenly, I have a baaaad feeling about this.' I go, 'So do I, Christian, but we need the shekels.' He goes, 'There must be another way.' This goy McPhee, roysh, he hears us whispering and he goes, 'Problem?' and I'm like, 'Just give us a minute to talk,' and he sort of, like, makes himself scarce.

I turn around to Christian and I'm like, 'What did you have for dinner yesterday?' and he looks away from me and goes, 'You know what I had for dinner yesterday.' I'm there, 'Just *focking* tell me. What did you have?' and he's like, 'A bowl of Cinnamon Grahams. The same as the night before.' I'm like, 'And the night before that. Well tonight, Christian, you're having a change. There's no milk left. So it's Cinnamon Grahams with water. That's until the Cinnamon Grahams run out. And then ...'

He just nods his head, like he's resigned to it. I go, 'Look, we'll get this fat focker to sub us a hundred bucks each out of our wages. Think what that'll mean. A hot meal tonight. Think about it. We won't have to hide under the stairs again when Peasey comes around for the rent. We can sort out that misunderstanding with AT&T. Make outgoing calls again. Just think of it. You could maybe ring that Lauren bird back home.' He goes, 'I haven't stopped thinking about her for the last week. Do you think I could?' and I'm there, 'Of course. Although she might not want to know you when she sees you've storted growing hair on the palms of your hands.' We both crack our holes laughing.

The bossman comes back. He's like, 'All sorted out, boys?' and we're like, 'Yeah,' and he brings us into this other room, roysh, this, like, adult playroom, with a big fock-off television and DVD player, computer games, the whole lot. And food. Tables and tables of nosebag. I'm like, 'This is where we're going to be, like, *working?*' and the goy goes, 'Sure. There's nothing to the job, like I told you. You take a couple of pills in the morning. We hook you up to a heart monitor and you spend the rest of the day in here, watching the television, playing computer games, whatever you want. End of the day, we take a blood and urine test from you and then you go home. Look, I'll leave you guys to get acquainted with the place.'

He focks off, roysh, and me and Christian just look at each other and break our holes laughing. I go, 'A hundred and sixty bucks a day to watch 'Jenny Jones' and play *Grand Theft Auto II*. We've struck gold, dude.

And about half-an-hour later, roysh, this McPhee dude comes back into the room and he goes, 'I have your waivers here for you to sign. Oh and tuck into the food. Eat as much as you can. I didn't mention it before, but we pay an extra forty bucks for any stool samples you can give us.'

Christian goes, 'And we shall provide. We SHALL provide.'

✱✱✱

MTV's on, roysh, but no one's really watching it, we're all just spacing, focked after the weekend, when all of a sudden Peasey comes in and asks what happened to the bag of green shit that was in the attic. He goes, 'You guys snort that stuff?' looking me and Fionn up and down, like he's looking for side-effects or some shit. I'm like, 'We never touched it,' and I'm giving Oisinn daggers, roysh, basically telling him to make up something fast because it was him who took it. But then, all of a sudden, roysh, I notice that the front door's off its hinges – another keg porty at the weekend, don't ask – and quick as a flash I go, 'The place was, em … raided. The Feds.'

Peasey throws his hands up, roysh, and he's like, 'Hooooly shit,' and I'm like, 'You probably noticed the door on your way in.' He doesn't seem to mind about the door, just goes, 'You tell 'em anything?' and I'm there, 'No.' He goes, 'You mention my name?' I don't even know the mad bastard's name. I'm like, 'Course I didn't.' He goes, 'And they took the shit with them?' Fionn goes, 'They didn't charge us or anything. They just said they had to take the stuff away for analysis,' and he pushes his glasses up on his nose, like the nerd that he is.

Peasey sort of, like, nods, roysh, really slowly, as though he's trying to, like, take this in. Then he goes, 'Don't worry, guys. You're safe. Ain't no scientist even heard of that shit yet.' Then he's like, 'They, em, mention anything about that robbery on Hudson and Atlantic? Jewellery store?'

My blood just runs cold. I look at Fionn. He was the one who said the photo-fit on 'America's Most Wanted' last night was him. Fionn goes, 'No ... em ... they don't seem to be on to you,' and Peasey's like, 'Let's keep it that way. Now I'm going down the beach. Fly my kite. Still got these goddamn headaches. Could be meningitis. But that doesn't explain the goddamn voices.'

On his way out, he bumps into Christian, roysh, and he puts on this, like, leprechaun voice and he goes, 'Top o' da morning, to ya,' even though it's, like, midnight.

✱✱✱

Me and the goys are in Hooters, roysh, two o'clock on a Saturday afternoon, slowly getting shit-faced, watching the ice hockey on the television in the corner of the bor, when I hear this laugh that, like, sends a serious shiver down my spine. It couldn't possibly be ... No, it couldn't, so I carry on chatting to the goys. Christian says that another of his toenails has fallen out, which makes four, and I go, 'There's no proof that it's the drugs,' and Fionn goes, 'It'll be a beak and webbed feet next,' the shit-stirring focker.

Then I hear the laugh again. It can't be. *It focking is!* Sat over the far side of the bor, cigar clamped between his teeth, a bird either side of him, hookers by the looks of them, is ... Hennessy. Oisinn cops him at the same time as me. He goes, 'Isn't that your old man's solicitor?' and I'm there, 'Unless he's got a focking double.' He hasn't. He twigs me and goes, 'Hey, young Ross. How the hell are you?' I'm like, 'What the *fock* are you doing here? My old man sent you to spy on me, didn't he?'

He staggers over to the other side of the bor where we're sitting, totally off his tits he is, and he goes, 'Ssshhh! Ssshhh! My name's Edward. Edward Horlock. And I'm in real estate. Got it?' I'm there, 'What are you focking talking about, orsehole?' and he offers to buy us all a drink. Wanker or not, none of us is gonna turn that down. He goes, 'Skipped out of Ireland a week ago, chaps. Suppose you could call me a fugitive.' I'm there, 'Why?' He goes, 'They're trying to put me in prison for something I didn't do.' Fionn goes, 'Yeah, pay your taxes. My old man told me, it was on 'Primetime'.'

Hennessy goes, 'Oh, let's not worry about the what-nots and the who-nots. Let's – what is it you young people say? – party on,' and he shouts over to the birds, 'Ladies, come and meet the chaps. A splendid bunch.' The birds come around. None of your gap-toothed, Bulgarian lap-dancers these two, roysh, these are, like, high-class prossies, probably five hundred bucks a night and *way* out of our league. One of them – a blondey one, real innocent-looking in a, like, Britney Spears kind of way – she turns around to me and goes, 'So, how do you know Edward?' and for a second I'm totally thrown and then I remember she's talking about Hennessy and I go, 'He used to be my dealer,' totally ripping the piss. She goes, 'Coke?' and I'm like, 'Every*thing*,' and suddenly, roysh, she obviously gets the smell of serious money off the dude because she storts, like, rubbing the back of his neck and playing with the little bit of hair he has left over his ears.

The bird behind the bor goes, 'You boys want more drinks?' and Hennessy goes, 'Oh good Lord, yes. Same again. Keep them coming. Tonight's on me.' The other hooker, roysh, a black one, not *that* unlike Beyoncé Knowles, she says why don't her and the first hooker – Sugar, she said her name was – go and score some coke, 'like last night,' and Hennessy goes, 'Okay, but don't let me get up on that balcony again,' and he peels about four hundred dollars off a wad of bills, hands it to them and slaps both of their orses on the way out. He lorries another brandy into him, then goes, 'Decided to go to America to lie low for a bit. I remembered your father telling me you were in a place called Ocean City, so I thought, why not? Place sounds as good as any.'

Free drink or not, roysh, the goys are getting pretty focking bored with the twat at this stage and we're about to, like, make our excuses and leave when all of a sudden he goes, 'You know what those fools think I'm worth?' I drain off the last of my pint and I'm there, 'Who?' He's like, 'The cops back in Ireland. They've put a reward out for me. Ten measly grand. Surely I'm worth more than that. I mean, who'd turn me in for that kind of money?' I look at the goys in the mirror behind the bor and I'm thinking, Well, there's four of us here would.

Oisinn's first up off his seat. He goes, 'Must go to the toilet.' I'm there, 'Yeah, I've got to go get cigarettes.' Hennessy's like, 'I didn't know you smoked, Ross.' Christian goes, 'I need some … em, air.' Fionn doesn't even bother his orse trying to think of something. The four of us are out of there and straight across the road where there's this, like, bank of payphones. We all get there at the same time, bang in 911 and then it's a matter of who's the lucky bastard who gets an answer first.

✳✳✳

I get home from work and there's, like, post for me and it's, like, a cord from Sorcha that the old pair have sent on. I stare at the front of it for ages, roysh. It's, like, the Sydney Opera House, I can see that, and loads of other, like, skyscrapers and shit and on the front it says, *City Skyline from Kirribilli*, and I head into my room and lie on the bed and read the back ten, maybe twenty times. She says she's basically having the time of her life, even though it's pretty cold over there because it's, like, winter at the moment. She's working in, like, *Golden Pages*, roysh, or whatever the equivalent of it is over there, basically taking ads over the phone. She's only going to be able to work there for, like, three months, roysh, unless they offer to sponsor her, which they probably won't, but she doesn't care because she SO wants to travel and see a bit of Australia, especially Cairns and the Gold Coast, which are supposed to be amazing, and Uluru and Darwin.

She says she might be doing the bridge climb next weekend, even though she's, like, really scared of heights and she says she wouldn't mind getting four or five bottles of Smirnoff Ice into her first, but they actually breathalyse you before they let you do it, and she says that Dorling Harbour is amazing, especially at night, but she was really disappointed with Bondi Beach, which is basically a dump and a bit of an Irish ghetto and that's the reason she's pretty much staying away from it.

I notice that she hasn't mentioned that penis she went with once and at the end, roysh, she says she really misses me and after her name she's put, like, three kisses. I hear the rest of the goys coming in from work, roysh, so I slip the cord into my back pocket. Oisinn says he's got something he thinks I should see, but I tell him I've got to go to Foodrite because we need, like, beers and shit.

Instead I head down to Cindy's, this diner down the road from our gaff, and I order coffee and sit there, in one of the, like, booths, reading the cord over and over again, then taking it line by line, trying to pick up, like, hidden meanings that may or may not have been there, then just studying her handwriting, trying to imagine what was going through her head when she said that she missed me, whether she put that on everyone's cord, or whether she really meant it in my case, and what she was thinking when she put those, like, three kisses on it.

I stort thinking about going home, which I'm dreading, for loads of different reasons. And, of course, for one in particular. Christian's old dear basically throws herself at me and I'm going to be the one who ends up taking the heat for her and Christian's old man breaking up. I focking know it. Explain that one to me. I'm wondering whether anyone at home knows. Christian's bound to find out, I know that. He can't stay not talking to his old man forever and his old man's not going to let his old dear be the one who comes out of this looking like the innocent porty. He'll definitely tell him.

But she basically threw herself at me. If Christian doesn't understand that, then he's no kind of best mate.

But I know that things would be so much simpler if I never went home. Maybe I could stay in Ocean City. Keep taking the tablets, although I've been really badly constipated the last couple of weeks and it's storting to worry me. I could stay here for a few more months, save up enough money to go to Australia myself and see how serious things are between Sorcha and this Cillian tosspot.

I take off my baseball cap and scratch my head and a huge clump of hair comes off in my hand. Might not be the tablets. Might be allergic to, I don't know, coffee. I just, like, drop it onto the floor under the table and read the cord again, and suddenly I hear Cindy, the owner, going, 'Stare at that any lawnga and the print's gonna come awf. You want more cawfee?'

I tell her no, roysh, best be going and I head back to the gaff. Oisinn, Christian and Fionn are sitting around the table in the kitchen, staring at this piece of paper. Oisinn goes, 'Ross, you *really* need to take a look at this.'

Straight away, of course, I'm thinking, It's a letter from Christian's old man, spelling the whole thing out, blow by blow, so I end up going, 'One thing you have to understand, Christian. I tried to fight her off, but she was gagging for me.'

He looks at me like I've got ten heads and he goes, 'Those drugs are *really* focking up your head, Padwan. I mean, I've lost some hair and I haven't had a shit in a week, but nothing as bad as you.'

I'm thinking, *Fock*, it must be something else. Oisinn goes, 'Have you been thinking much about Sorcha lately?' I'm like, 'Sorcha? No, she's made her bed.' Fionn goes, 'And someone else is in it,' and he straightens his glasses, which are going to be shoved up his orse in ten seconds flat. Oisinn goes, 'Come on, Ross, what's the *scéal*. It's confession time. For the last week I've had this unbelievable urge to ring Emma Halvey. And Christian says he's thinking about this Lauren bird again ...' Christian nods. I'm there, 'I wondered why we were getting through so much bog roll,' but no one laughs. Oisinn goes, 'Fionn was on the Internet at lunchtime,' – focking geek – 'and he found this. It was in *The Irish Times* last week.' He hands me the sheet of paper. Fionn goes, 'Do you want me to read it out for you?' but I ignore the focker.

'Two members of a local sub-aqua club
have recovered a stolen statue from the
sea in Dún Laoghaire. Gardaí have confirmed that the statue of *Eros*, the God
of Love in Greek Mythology, was stolen
from the Classics Department in UCD
some time ago. Gardaí kept news of the

robbery and a subsequent ransom demand
quiet in an attempt to flush the
thieves out. The statue was found on
the seabed, close to the West Pier, on
Saturday morning. Gardaí admit they
have no leads as yet, but have ruled out
paramilitary involvement. Eros was the
son of Aphrodite and was represented as
beautiful but irresponsible in his in-
fliction of passion.

'It's an absolute miracle to get the
statue back,' said Francis Hird, Head
of the Classics Department. 'We don't
know how, but they do say that love always finds a way.'

Fionn goes, 'Very good, Ross. You managed to read it without putting your finger under each word,' and I'm like, 'Shut up,
you geek.' Oisinn goes, 'Answer my question, Ross. Have you
been thinking about Sorcha?'

✳✳✳

There's another message from Orsewipe on the answering-
machine when I get home. It's like, 'Pick up if you're in, Ross.
It's a disaster. Pick up if you're in, Ross. Pick up if you're in. It's
your mother's car, Ross. The Micra. It's *failed* the NCT. Again, stay
where you are. There's nothing you could do even if you were
to come home. She's heartbroken, though, Ross. Heartbroken.
Capital H and everything.

'I told her of course that I'd buy her a new one, but no, if she couldn't have her Micra, she didn't want anything. Took to the bed for a few days. Now I'm not what you would call, inverted commas, anti the environment, Ross, you know that, but this whole car-test business is nothing more than a money-making scam by the government. Force people to buy new cars. Dress it up as an environmental concern, fuel emissions and so forth, and nobody dares to complain.

'Oh, I phoned up the so-called Department of the Environment on Monday morning, gave them a right earful. Asked to speak to the Minister, but ended up getting some bloody minion. As if the Government doesn't get enough money out of me already, I said. I employ over two hundred people. "It's the law," he said. *"But you made the bloody law,"* I told him. Hung up on me, he did.

'Such a pity Hennessy's out of commission. Not sure if you heard, but he's been arrested. In America, of all places, and not a million miles from you. They're talking about extraditing him back. Go on, Hennessy, give the bastards hell. A witch hunt, that's all this nonsense has ever been about.

'But ... oh yes ... the car test. Oh the day of the test was painful, Ross. Like a funeral. And it was in bloody Deansgrange as well, appropriately enough. An 8.30am appointment, quote-unquote. I won't bore you with the details, but we drove into the industrial estate, parked the car outside and this chap in green overalls came out, asked your mother for the keys. Of course getting them out of her hand was a job in itself, but eventually, using a few stern words, not to mention the car-jack, we managed to loosen her grip on them and then the chap drove the car into this garage affair and I helped your mother into the office, where they asked for our details and the logbook.

"When will you know?" your mother asked the lady behind the desk. "Forty-five minutes," the lady said. It was an hour at least. Your mother spent the whole time pacing up and down the floor, asking me every five minutes what I thought was keeping them. "They have a lot of checks to make," I told her. "Sit down. Read a magazine. Look, *VIP* have done an eighteen-page feature on 'At Home with IFA farm leader Tom Parlon."

'Well, the bad news was that the chap returned after what seemed like an eternity, all full of himself with his clipboard, and delivered the verdict. Wheel alignment, front axle – FAIL. Wheel alignment, rear axle – FAIL. Shock absorber, front axle – FAIL. Shock absorber, rear axle – FAIL. Brake test, front and rear axle – FAIL. Service brake performance – 40% and FAIL. Parking brake performance – 10% and FAIL. Exhaust emissions – FAIL. Right indicator, steering lock, tyre pressure, windscreen wipers – all defective, FAIL. Dip beam, full beam, fog lights – FAIL, FAIL, FAIL.

'It was too much for your mother, of course. She collapsed. And while the staff tried to resuscitate her, I got on the phone, called the bloody gangster we bought the car from in the first place. "Good morning," he says, without a care in the world. "I haven't got time for good-mornings," I told him. "I think you know why I'm phoning."

"Who is this?" he said, just out with it like that. I told him I'd a complaint to make about a car he sold me. "What's the matter with it?" he said. What's the matter with it, ladies and gentlemen. Well, I gave it to him. "Pretty much everything except the radio, according to the NCT people. And even that chewed one of my Phil Coulter cassettes."

"When did you buy the car?" he asked. "It was 1993," I said. "Sorry," he says, "did you say 1993?" "That is what I said, yes." "Well," he says, "it'd be out of warranty by now." I said, "Don't give me blasted warranty. You told me the car had one previous owner. An elderly lady, you said. Used it to go to the shops and back." He says, "Yes." I said, "Where were these bloody shops? *Kabul?*"

'Had to hang up on him in the end, Kicker. Could see I was getting nowhere, and anyway your mother was starting to come around at that point. I offered the car-test chap a couple of hundred pounds to, well, basically pass the car, but he got all offended, told me that was called bribery and that he was going to report me. Bloody tribunal culture has a lot to answer for. Are you listening to me Mister G Kerrigan Esquire, Middle Abbey Street, Dublin 1?'

I actually nod off for a few seconds, roysh, but then when I hear the next bit, I'm suddenly sitting up straight in the chair and my whole body goes cold.

He goes, 'There's also something your, em, mother wanted me to put to you, Ross. Em, it's delicate. Bit embarrassing. But there's a certain rumour going around about, well, Christian's mother and father, or, well, Christian's mother mostly. Oh, it's nothing of course, just rumours, I told her, I'm sure there's nothing in it. It's just that people are, em, people are saying that the reason they broke up, or one of the reasons they broke up – it's never really one thing that breaks up a marriage – the reason was that, well, you might have something to do with it, shall we say. You know the way people like to gossip, Ross. Especially at those coffee mornings your mother goes to. But maybe give her a call. Put her mind at rest.'

✱✱✱

I'm in the jacks in work, roysh, sitting in Trap Two having a shit, basically trying to get a few bills together for the weekend, when all of a sudden I hear the door open and then Christian's voice going, 'What are you doing, Luke, ones or twos?' He goes into Trap One and I hear him, like, undoing his belt and his trousers and sitting down. I presume he's talking to me. I go, 'Em, twos.' He goes, 'Panning for gold, huh?' and I'm there, 'Think I'm constipated again. Looks like I'm staying in this weekend.'

I can hear him opening a newspaper. After a couple of minutes of rustling, he goes, 'When he said they pay for stool samples, do they pay for each one, or is it based on, like, tonnage?' I'm there, 'He didn't say,' and he's like 'You'd think he would have, wouldn't you? Could save an embarrassing court case some way down the line.'

Christian goes back to reading his paper and I go back to reading the graffiti on the wall. There must have been, like, loads of Irish students working here before us because there's a couple of names I think I recognise and the rest is, like, bands, the usual shit, Therapy?, Marilyn Manson, U2, AC/DC, all that stuff, and then a couple of old jokes that I've seen loads of times before, Dyslexia rules KO, shit like that.

I think being away from home has really, like, helped the dude. I mean, yeah he's still a spacer, roysh, but he just seems a lot happier. I've been able to, like, *reach* him, if that doesn't sound too gay.

I still can't shit.

Christian goes, 'Home next week. You looking forward to it?' and I think about our friendship and how it's about to come to an end and I go, 'No. Wish I could make time stand still.'

But then I think to myself, *fock it*, I am SO not taking a hit for this one. His old dear, roysh, she threw herself at me. She was *gagging* for it. I can't help it if I've got the looks. What am I supposed to do – sit at home all day in a focking darkened room? She wanted me. And she had to have me. Couldn't control herself. I just took what was going. Like any goy would. Fed my needs. Use and abuse is the name of the game. If Christian doesn't understand that, then fock him. He can get himself a new best friend.

I go, 'You finished with the sports section?' and the next thing it comes flying over the wall between the two traps. I flick through it. It's full of focking American sport, which I hate.

I hear the door into the jacks opening again, roysh, and someone coming in. I hear footsteps and then they stop. I can see a shadow under the door. Whoever it is knocks on the door of Trap One. Christian goes, 'This one's taken. And I may be some time.'

Then I hear, 'Christian, we need to talk,' and I'd recognise that voice anywhere. And this, like, shiver runs up my spine. *Holy fock*! Not here. Not now.

Christian goes, '*Dad?*'

His old man's there, 'I had to come, Christian. Couldn't leave it a day longer.' Christian's like, 'What the *fock* are you doing here?' and the old man goes, 'There's things I have to say to you.' Christian's there, 'I told you already. I have nothing to say to you.' But his old man goes, 'I know you're upset at what's happened between your mother and me, but there's things you need to know.' I close my eyes and get ready for the worst. He goes, 'There's things you need to know. And some of them you're not going to like …'

And suddenly, I'm not constipated anymore.

DO YOU WANT MORE OF THE MAN? ...

I know you so do ...

Ross O'Carroll-Kelly, The Orange Mocha-Chip Frappuccino Years
(As told to Paul Howard)

So there I was, roysh, enjoying college life, college birds and, like, a major amount of socialising. Then, roysh, the old pair decide to mess everything up for me. And we're talking TO-TALLY here. Don't ask me what they were thinking. I hadn't, like, changed or treated them any differently, but the next thing I know, roysh, I'm out on the streets. Another focking day in paradise for me. If it hadn't been for Fionn's aportment in Killiney, the old man paying for my Golf GTI, JP's old man's job offer and all the goys wanting to buy me drink, it would have been, like, a complete mare. TOTALLY. But naturally roysh, you can never be sure what life plans to do to you next. At least, it came as a complete focking surprise to me.

Ross O'Carroll-Kelly, PS, I Scored the Bridesmaids (As told to Paul Howard)

So there I was, roysh, twenty-three years of age, still, like, gorgeous, living off my legend as a schools rugby player, scoring the birds, being the man, when all of a sudden, roysh, life becomes a total mare. I don't have a Betty Blue what's wrong, but I can't eat, can't sleep. I don't even want to do the old beast with two backs, which means a major problem, and we're talking big time here. Normally my head is so full of, like, thoughts, but now I'm down to just one: Sorcha. I'm playing it Kool and the Gang, but this is basically scary. I mean, I'm Ross O'Carroll-Kelly for fock's sake, I don't *do* love.